About the Authors

USA Today bestselling author **Naima Simone** writes romance with heart, humour, and heat. Her books have been featured in *The Washington Post* and *Entertainment Weekly*, and described as balancing 'crackling, electric love scenes with exquisitely rendered characters caught in emotional turmoil.' She is wife to Superman, and mum to the most awesome kids ever. They live in perfect, domestically challenged bliss in the southern US.

USA Today bestselling author **Jules Bennett** has penned more than fifty novels during her short career. She's married to her high school sweetheart, has two active girls, and is a former salon owner. Jules can be found on X (formerly Twitter), Facebook (Fan Page), and her website julesbennett.com. She holds competitions via these three outlets with each release and loves to hear from readers!

When Canadian **Dani Collins** found romance novels in high school, she wondered how one trained for such an awesome job. She wrote for over two decades without publishing, but remained inspired by the romance message that if you hang in there, you'll find a happy ending. In May of 2012, Mills & Boon bought her manuscript in a two-book deal. She's since published more than forty books with Mills & Boon and is definitely living happily ever after.

Sinfully Yours

Sinfully Yours:
The Enemy

NAIMA SIMONE

JULES BENNETT

DANI COLLINS

MILLS & BOON

First Published in Great Britain 2024
by Mills & Boon, an imprint of HarperCollins*Publishers* Ltd,
1 London Bridge Street, London, SE1 9GF

www.harpercollins.co.uk

HarperCollins*Publishers*
Macken House, 39/40 Mayor Street Upper,
Dublin 1, D01 C9W8, Ireland

Sinfully Yours: The Enemy © 2024 Harlequin Enterprises ULC.

Ruthless Pride © 2020 Harlequin Enterprises ULC
Hidden Ambition © 2020 Harlequin Enterprises ULC
Consequence of His Revenge © 2018 Dani Collins

Special thanks and acknowledgement are given to Naima Simone for her contribution to the *Dynasties: Seven Sins* series.
Special thanks and acknowledgement are given to Jules Bennett for her contribution to the *Dynasties: Seven Sins* series.

ISBN: 978-0-263-32302-3

This book contains FSC™ certified paper and other controlled sources to ensure responsible forest management.

For more information visit: www.harpercollins.co.uk/green

Printed and Bound in the UK using 100% Renewable Electricity at CPI Group (UK) Ltd, Croydon, CR0 4YY

RUTHLESS PRIDE

NAIMA SIMONE

To Gary. 143.

One

"*If your success was earned through hard work and honesty never apologize for it.*"

Joshua Lowell silently repeated the Frank Sonnenberg quote that had been a favorite of his father's. He pinched the bridge of his nose, a low, dark growl rumbling in the back of his throat. Too bad Vernon Lowell hadn't believed in the "practice what you preach" school of thought. According to that quote, his father had a ton of apologizing to do. Wherever he was—hell or a bungalow in some country without extradition policies.

Dropping his head, he refocused his attention to the spreadsheets displaying the previous month's profit-and-loss numbers for Black Crescent Hedge Fund's investment in stock of a telecommunication company. Compared with this time last year, the investment was doing very well. Their clients would earn more than a modest return, and Black Crescent would receive a substantial management and performance fee...

Unlike his father, Joshua had stuck to the more traditional investments such as stocks, bonds, commodities and real estate. Vernon had been a daredevil in business, which initially had made him one of the richest men in the tristate area of New York, New Jersey and Connecticut. That fearless and adventurous spirit had also increased the millions his very select clients had invested with him into high-yielding portfolios, and grew his boutique business into one of most successful in the area.

It'd also cost those select clients millions. It'd devastated them.

So no, while some might call Joshua's business decisions rigid and even too conservative, he refused to do anything different. Too many people's livelihoods and futures depended on him making those safe choices. He refused to be another Lowell who betrayed their trust. Who destroyed them.

He'd been the last man standing when Vernon Lowell disappeared—for both the company and his family. Because he'd left with not only his clients' money, but the majority of his family's, as well. So even though the last man sometimes wanted to yell and rage at the unfairness of it all, at the grief and shame that often pounded within him like a second heartbeat—at the death of his own dreams—one thing the last man *couldn't* do was slip up or falter.

He couldn't afford to. Literally.

"Josh, did you hear what I said? Of course you didn't." Haley Shaw, his executive assistant, snorted, answering her own question before he could respond. "Or you're just ignoring me, which you should know by now doesn't work. Whatever you're doing now can be put aside for just a few moments. This is important," she insisted, an edge invading her tone.

"Haley. Not now," he said without glancing up from his spreadsheet.

"Well, I'm sorry to interrupt," a brisk, husky but very feminine voice that carried zero hint of apology interjected, "but I'm afraid it's going to have to be now."

Two small hands with slender, unadorned fingers flattened on either side of his computer monitor. Surprised, all he could do for several long seconds was stare at those delicate hands. At the short, unpolished nails, the thin map of light blue veins under sun-kissed skin. Why did he have the odd but strong urge to place his mouth right on the joint where hand met wrist—and sip?

Hell. They were fucking hands.

The mental but mocking admonishment didn't stop him from traveling up the lengths of her arms clad in white sleeves to slim shoulders partially hidden by light brown and gold-streaked hair, past a graceful neck and slightly pointed but stubborn chin with its slight indent to a face that—*goddamn*.

Deliberately, he eased back in his office chair, careful to control all the muscles in his face. He forced himself to maintain the cold, aloof expression that he'd adopted and mastered fifteen years ago as a defense. But inside… inside, lust slammed into him like a hurricane intent on leveling every structure in its path. And right now he was the only thing remaining, and *Christ*, he was shaking right down to his foundation.

Thickly lashed silver eyes that gleamed with barely suppressed anger. Striking cheekbones that lent a bold strength to otherwise ethereal features. A gently sloped nose and a mouth that had him gripping the arms of his chair like they were the last lifeboat that kept him from drowning. Thing was, he wanted to leap from the safety of the raft and dive into that wide, full-lipped mouth. Teach it what

it was created for. Show it how it could give both of them
the filthiest of pleasures...

His heartbeat echoed its thundering rhythm in his cock,
pounding out a need that ricocheted through him.

Unsettled by his visceral reaction to this stranger—a
stranger who had barged into his corporate office unin-
vited—he narrowed his eyes on her, allowing the corners
of his mouth to curl in a derisive snarl.

Haley heaved a sigh. "Joshua, let me introduce you to
Sophie Armstrong," she said, a thick coat of resignation
painting her words.

"I don't know a Sophie Armstrong," he stated coldly
to his assistant, although he didn't remove his gaze from
the woman in front of him. Maybe some instinctual part
of him recognized that she was the biggest threat in the
room—a threat to his schedule, his carefully laid-out day...
his control.

"The name would be familiar if you bothered to answer
any one of my phone calls or emails." She snorted, cocking a dark eyebrow. "I've been trying to contact you, Mr.
Lowell, and you've ducked and dodged every attempt."

He frowned. Yes, he'd been busier than usual lately,
but he would've remembered if she'd reached out to him.
"I've never ducked or dodged anyone." Not even when he'd
desperately longed to. "Especially someone who doesn't
have enough manners or sense to not force herself into
a place of business where she wasn't invited or wanted
without an appointment. Now that you're here, you have
exactly thirty seconds—twenty-nine more seconds than
I would give anyone else—to explain what the hell you're
talking about."

Others would've—had—recoiled and backed down
from the hard, ice-cold fury in his voice. But Sophie Armstrong didn't even flinch. Instead, she met his glare with

one of her own. A quicksilver flash of surprise flickered within him. He wasn't arrogant, but he also acknowledged his appeal to the opposite sex. Understanding his money proved just as much of a lure as the appearance he'd inherited from his handsome father, he never lacked for female attention. Or sex.

But to this woman, he might as well be Quasimodo taking a break from his Notre Dame tower to hang out in the Black Crescent offices. Sophie Armstrong didn't bother to employ any advantage her beauty might press—not that it would. But she didn't know that.

No, unless antagonism passed for charm these days, she was confrontational and contemptuous.

And goddamn, if it wasn't hot.

She reached into the bag over her shoulder, withdrew a stack of papers and slapped the pile on his desk. "That's what I'm talking about. All the emails I've sent you. And I can pull out my phone and scroll through and play every voice mail—there are fifteen of them. All asking you to reply in a timely manner. Apparently, your idea of timely and mine don't coincide because I meant at least a couple of days and yours apparently runs along the line of seasons in Narnia."

The snort slipped from him before he could contain it. He shouldn't be amused. And he certainly shouldn't let her see it.

"You have five seconds left," he informed her, leaning forward and with a will that had been forged in the fires of desperation, humiliation and pride over a decade ago, he shifted his attention back to his screen. "I suggest you make the most of it."

A soft, feminine growl filled the air, and the reverberation of it rolled in his gut, clenching the muscles there so hard he nearly grunted in pain. With the wrenching came the dark but HD-clear image of her, head thrown back, all that hair sprawled across black sheets, beads of sweat dotting the slender column of her throat. And that same, rumbling growl vibrating from her. Only it sounded hungrier, needier...

Christ, he needed her out of his office.

"I'm assuming that king-of-the-manor-got-no-time-for-peasants thing intimidates other people, but I hate to break it to you. It does nothing for me." She crossed her arms over her chest, and if Jesus had come down at that moment and warned him against giving in to his baser needs, Joshua still wouldn't have been able to stop his gaze from dipping to the slightly less-than-a-handful but firm breasts that pushed against the plain white dress shirt. Guilt streaked through him, slick and dirty. He wasn't his father; he didn't ogle women or treat them like eye candy, there for his pleasure. Even women who made his dick hard but he didn't particularly like. "I'm telling you now—like I did in my last voice message and two emails—I'll be writing my story with or without you. But it would be a better one *with* you."

Story. What *story*?

A sense of foreboding wormed its way into his chest, hollowing it out. Making room for the churning unease.

"I repeat," he stated, the flat tone revealing none of the steadily encroaching panic that crept into his vision, that squeezed his rib cage like a steadily tightening vise. "What are you talking about?"

"The anniversary piece on the Black Crescent fiasco that I'm writing for the *Falling Brook Chronicle*. And unlike all of the articles written about that time period, I would like to include an interview with the company's current CEO."

Anger crystallized within him, hard and diamond

bright. And sharp enough to cut glass. The "get out" burned on his tongue, singeing him. But he extinguished the words before they could escape him, refusing to betray any emotion to this woman who sought to rip open the seams of the past, to expose old but unhealed wounds for public consumption. To relive the nightmare of his father emptying the family bank accounts as well as embezzling millions from his clients and disappearing, abandoning him, his mother and brothers to the wolves. The abrasive rub of judging eyes and not-so-hushed whispers. The smothering guilt that ten families were left devastated and destitute because of his father's actions. The agonizing pain from being deceived and abandoned by the man who'd raised him, who'd loved him and who he'd respected.

This woman had no clue about the pressure from the weight of that guilt, that responsibility. How they straddled his shoulders to the point of suffocation at times. How dealing had become second nature to him. There'd been no one to lean on when his father disappeared, when he'd taken on the responsibility of repaying the families so they wouldn't sue for the remaining money his father hadn't disappeared with. When his mother withdrew from the exclusive community of Falling Brook, New Jersey. When his twin brother, Jacob, fled to Europe to backpack his problems away, and his youngest brother, Oliver, dropped out of college and become the poster child for professional playboy, complete with a nasty cocaine habit.

Nothing in his Ivy League education—not even the economic courses he'd taken at his father's insistence—had prepared him for being alone, grieving and terrified with the fate of not just his family but ten others on his still-young shoulders. Of having to make the bitter decision of burying his own dreams so he could repair those of others.

He'd grown up fast. Too fast.

And damn if he needed an article written by an ambitious reporter—no matter if she possessed the face of a fairy queen and the body of a Victoria's Secret Angel—to drag him back to those desolate, black times when he'd breathed fear as much as he did air.

"No."

Joshua gave her credit—she didn't flinch at the flat, blunt answer.

Instead, she tilted her head to the side, that fall of thick caramel-and-sunlight hair sliding over her shoulder, and studied him as if he were a problem to solve. Or an opponent to wrestle and pin into submission.

"I can understand why you would initially be reluctant to speak with me—"

"Oh, you can?" he interrupted, trying but failing to keep the bite from his voice. Silently, he cursed himself for revealing even that much. The last fifteen years had taught him that he couldn't afford to betray the slightest weakness of character lest he be accused of being just like his father. Other people were allowed room for mistakes. He was not offered that courtesy. While others could trip up in private, his missteps were splashed across newspapers and online columns for fodder. Including *her* paper. "So you've had a—how did you so eloquently put it?—fiasco in your life and had every paper in the country report on it? Including the *Falling Brook Chronicle*? Which, if I remember correctly, was one of the harshest and most critical? Well, good," he continued, not granting her the opportunity to answer. "Since you have experienced it, you'll understand why I'm ending this conversation."

"I've read the past articles from the *Chronicle*, and you're right, they did cover it...punitively," she conceded. In the small pause that followed, the "can you blame them?" seemed to echo in the office. "But those reporters aren't me. You don't know me, but I graduated from Northwestern University with a BS and MS in journalism. While there, I worked with the Medill Justice Project that helped free an unjustly convicted man from a life sentence in prison. I've also won the Walter S. and Syrena M. Howell competition, was a recipient of the NJLA's journalism award and was a member of the journalistic team who won the Stuart and Beverly Awbrey Award last year, all well-respected awards. I don't intend to do a hatchet job on you or Black Crescent. As a matter of fact, I would like to write this article from a different angle—the artist submerged. From my research, I discovered you were once a very accomplished artist—"

"We're done," he ground out, rising to his feet, flattening his palms on the desk.

Hell, no. Pain, like crushed glass, scraped his throat and chest raw.

He hadn't been called an artist in fifteen long years. And hadn't picked up a camera or paintbrush in just as long. Once, his trademark had been oversize, mixed-media collages that provided cultural commentary on war and human rights. He'd poured his being into those pieces, falling into endless pockets of time where nothing had mattered but losing himself in photographs, oils and whatever elements captured what swirled inside him—metal, newspapers, books, even bits of clothing. But when his father had vanished, Joshua had put aside childish things. At least that was what Vernon had called Joshua's passion—a childish hobby.

It'd been like performing a lobotomy on his soul. But now, instead of channeling his anger, grief and pain into art, he suppressed it. And when that didn't work, he funneled it into making Black Crescent solvent and powerful again. Or took it out on a punching bag at the gym.

The whole shitfest with the hedge fund had left him
with precious little—the death of his art career, the erad-
ication of his relationships with his brothers, a ghost of a
mother, an overabundance of shame and a ruined family
company. But they'd been *his* choices.

All that had remained in the ashes after the firestorm
were the ragged tatters of his pride because he'd had the
strength, the character, to make those choices.

And now Sophie Armstrong sought to steal that dignity
away from him, too.

No. She couldn't have it.

"Mr. Lowell," she began again with a short shake of
her head.

But again, he cut her off. "I have a busy day, and you've
had more than the thirty seconds I allotted. We're through
talking. You need to go," he ordered, knowing his mother
would cringe at the lack of the manners she'd drilled into
him since birth. Not that he gave a damn. Not when this
woman stood here prying into an area of his life that wasn't
open for public consumption.

"Fine, I'll leave," she said, but nothing in the firm, almost combative tone said she'd conceded. She drew her
shoulders back, hiking her chin in the air. Though she
stood at least a foot shorter than him, she still managed to
peer down at him with a glint of battle in her silver eyes.
"You can try to erase the past, but certain things don't go
away no matter how hard you try to bury them. The truth
always finds a way of resurrecting itself."

"Especially if there are reporters always armed with
a shovel, ready to dig up anything that will sell papers,"
he drawled.

The curves of her full mouth flattened, and her eyes
went molten. He waited, his body stilling except for the

heavy thud of his heart against his rib cage. And the rush of hot anticipation in his veins.

It'd been years since anyone had challenged him. Not since he'd proved he was his father's son in business and, at times, in ruthlessness. But Sophie Armstrong... She must not have received the memo, because she glared at him, slashes of red painting her high cheekbones, as if even now, she longed to go for his throat. Was it perverse that part of him hoped she did? That he wanted that tight, petite, almost fragile body pressed to his larger frame with those delicate but capable-looking hands wrapped around his neck...exerting pressure even as he took her mouth as she attempted to take his breath?

Yeah, that might make him a little sick. And a hell of a lot dirty.

Still... He could picture it easily. Could feel the phantom tightening of her grip now. And he wanted it. Craved it.

But not enough to rip open old, barely scarred-over wounds so she could have a byline.

"Thank you for your time, Mr. Lowell," she finally said, and disappointment at her retreat surged through him.

God, what was wrong with him? He wanted—no, needed—her to drop this "artist submerged" bullshit and get the hell out of his office.

She whirled around on her boring nude heels and stalked across the room to his office door. Without a backward glance, she exited. He half expected her to slam it shut, but somehow the quiet, definite snick of the lock engaging seemed much more ominous.

Like a booming warning shot across his bow.

Two

"*The Black Crescent Scandal: Fifteen Years Later.*"

Joshua gripped the Monday issue of the *Falling Brook Chronicle* so tightly, it should've been torn down the middle. She'd done it. Sophie Armstrong had run with the story, placing his family's sordid and ugly history on the front page as fodder for an always scandal-hungry public.

He lifted his gaze to stare out the windshield of his Mercedes-Benz at the Black Crescent building. He knew every railing, every angle, every stone inch of the modern midcentury building built into a cliff. His father's aim had been for the headquarters of his hedge fund to stand out in the more traditional architecture of Falling Brook. And he'd succeeded. The building was as famous—or infamous—as its owner.

And his infamy had made page one of the local paper. Again.

Studying the imposing structure offered the briefest

of respites. Almost against his will, he returned his attention to the newspaper crinkling under his fists. He'd already read the article twice, but he scanned it again. It recounted his father's rise in the financial industry, his seemingly perfect life—marriage to Eve Evans-Janson, the pedigreed society daughter and darling whose connections further installed Vernon as a reigning king of Falling Brook; his three sons, who'd shown great promise with their Ivy League educations and fast-track career goals; the meteoric success of his business. And then his epic fall. Millions of dollars missing from the hedge fund's accounts. The death of Everett Reardon, his father's best friend and CFO of Black Crescent, who'd crashed his car while trying to elude capture. Vernon's disappearance.

The ten clients his father had stolen money from plunged into a nightmare of bankruptcy and destitution. The company's—Joshua's—agreement to pay back the families so they wouldn't file a lawsuit. How some of them still hadn't recovered from Vernon's selfish, unforgivable and criminal actions.

And then Joshua.

The artist turned CEO who had stepped into the vacant shoes of his father to save Black Crescent. Yes, it shared how he'd left his promising art career and turned the company around, saving it from ruin, but it also painted him as Vernon's puppet, coached and raised to take over for him since Joshua's birth. Which was bullshit. At one time, his path had been different. Had been his.

The article also cited that no one had heard from Vernon in a decade and a half, but despite rumors that he'd been killed in retribution for his crimes, there was also the long-held belief that his father was alive and well. And that his family was secretly in contact with him. That Vernon still pulled the strings, running Black Crescent from some remote location. Which was ridiculous. After his father initially vanished, his mother had hired a team of private detectives to locate him. Not to mention the FBI had searched for him, as well.

Fuck. He gritted his teeth against releasing the roar in his throat, but his head echoed with it. What did he have to do to redeem himself? What more did he have to sacrifice? He'd stayed, facing judgment, scorn and suspicion to rebuild the company, to restore even some of the money lost. He'd stayed, doing his best in the last fifteen years to repay those affected clients at least part of the fortune they'd lost to his father as promised. He'd stayed, enduring his brothers' ridicule and disdain for following in dear old Dad's footsteps. He'd stayed, caring for their mother, who'd become something of a recluse.

He'd stayed when all he'd wanted to do was quit and run away, too.

But he hadn't gallivanted off to Europe or found sweet oblivion in drugs and parties. Pride and loyalty had chained him there. Fatherless. Brotherless. Friendless.

And Sophie Armstrong dared insinuate he hadn't busted his ass all these years? That his father had done all the soul-destroying work.

His sharp bark of laughter rebounded against the interior of the vehicle. Its serrated edges scraped over his skin.

A part of him that could never utter the sacrilegious words aloud secretly hoped Vernon was dead. Just thinking it caused shame, thick and oily, to slide down his throat and smear his chest in a grimy coat. But it was true. He hoped his father no longer lived, because the alternative… God, the alternative—that he'd abandoned his family and emptied their bank accounts without the slightest shred of remorse and never looked back—sat in his gut, curdling it. If Vernon wasn't dead, then that would mean the man he'd loved and had once admired and respected had truly never existed. And with everything else Joshua had endured these past few years, that…that might be his breaking point.

His cell phone rang, and a swift glance at the screen revealed Oliver's number. On the heels of his past staring him in the face this morning, his chest tightened. He and his younger brother's relationship was…complicated. Oliver lived in Falling Brook, but he might as well be across the Hudson River or even farther away.

Once, they'd been close. But that had been before Joshua had stepped in to head Black Crescent in place of their father. He'd lost some respect in Jacob's and Oliver's eyes that day. And a part of Joshua mourned that loss. Mourned what had been.

Briefly closing his eyes, Joshua slid his thumb across the screen and lifted the phone to his ear.

"Hello."

"I'm assuming you've seen today's paper," his brother said in lieu of a greeting.

"Yes." Joshua stared across the parking lot, no longer seeing the building that had been the blessing and curse on his family. In front of him wavered an image of a perfect family. Of a lie. "I've seen it."

A sound between an angry growl and a heavy sigh reached him. "This shit again. Why can't people just let it die?" Oliver snapped.

"Because it makes for good copy apparently," Joshua drawled. "We'll ride this one out like we always do."

He uttered the assurance, and it tasted like bitter ashes on his tongue. He was tired of weathering storms. And more so of being the stalwart helm in it.

Oliver scoffed. "Right. Because that's what Lowells do." Joshua could easily picture his brother dragging his hand through his hair, a slight sneer twisting his mouth. "Do you know if Mom has seen the article?"

"I don't think so." Joshua shook his head as the stone of another burden settled on his shoulders. "I've sent Haley over to make sure the paper isn't delivered."

Thank God for Haley. She was more than his assistant. She was his taskmaster. Right-hand woman. And the bossy little sister he'd never had.

When the scandal around Black Crescent had broken fifteen years ago, and employees as well as friends had abandoned the company and the Lowell family, Haley—a college intern at the time—had remained. Even forgoing a salary to stay. Through the last decade and a half when Joshua had given up his own dreams and passion to step into the gaping, still-hemorrhaging hole his father had left, she'd been loyal. And invaluable. He couldn't have dragged Black Crescent from the brink of financial ruin and rebuilt it without her at his side.

The woman could be a pain in his ass, but she'd proved her loyalty hundreds of times over to his family. Because she was family.

"Since Mom doesn't leave the house too often, I'm not concerned with her mistakenly seeing it," Joshua continued.

Eve had become something of a hermit since her husband's crime and disappearance. Unfortunately, that option hadn't been available to Joshua.

"Good. I don't even want to imagine what this would do to her. Probably send her spiraling into a depression," Oliver said, and while Joshua and his brothers might not agree on much, this one thing they did—their mother's emotional health and protecting her. "I'll go by and see her this evening just to check in."

"That sounds good. Thanks," Joshua replied.

A snort echoed in Joshua's ear. "She's my mother, too. No need to thank me. Talk to you later."

The connection ended, and for a long second, Joshua continued to hold the phone to his ear before lowering it and picking up the newspaper again. He zeroed in on one line that had caught his attention before.

But is Joshua Lowell that different from his father? Appearances, as we know, are often deceiving. Who knows the secrets the Lowell family could still be hiding?

The sentences—no, not so thinly veiled accusations— leaped out at him. What the hell was that supposed to mean? Every skeleton in their closets had been bleached and hung out for everyone to view and tear apart. They didn't have secrets.

And where had she uncovered the photos included in the article? He scrutinized the black-and-white images. A few of his art pieces. His father as he remembered him with his mother on his arm. God, he hadn't seen her smile like that in years. Fifteen of them, to be exact. Him and Jake on their college graduation day, hugging Oliver between them. A family portrait taken at their annual Christmas party. The ones of him and Jake on campus. The snapshots of him painting in art class. The concentration and...joy darkening and lightening his face. He analyzed that image longer, hardly recognizing the young, *hopeful* man in the photo.

Well, Sophie had done her grave-robbing expedition well. He'd accused her of using her shovel to dig up old news. To acquire these photographs, she must've found a fucking backhoe.

Where had she gotten her information? She shouldn't have had access to those pictures, so who'd provided them to her?

There was only one way to find out.

Joshua tossed the paper to the passenger seat and pressed the ignition button to start the car.

He would go directly to the source.

"Great article, Sophie," Rob Jensen, the entertainment columnist, congratulated with a short rap on the wall of her cubicle.

"Thanks, Rob," she said, smiling. "I appreciate it."

"You did do an excellent job," Marie Coswell added when Rob strode away. She rolled in her desk chair to the edge of her cubicle, directly across from Sophie's. "But wow, woman," she tsk-tsked, shaking her head and sending the blunt edges of her red bob swinging against her jaw. "You didn't hold anything back. Aren't you even the least bit concerned the Lowells will retaliate? I mean, yes, their names were persona non grata around here for a while, but that was a long time ago. They have serious pull and power. Makes me real thankful that I'm over in fashion. No way in hell would I want to tangle with a Lowell, especially Joshua Lowell. Well, hold on. I take that back." She grinned, comically wriggling her perfectly arched eyebrows. "I'd love to tangle with that man—but nekkid."

Sophie laughed at her friend's outrageousness even as heat streamed up her chest and throat and poured into her face. Times like these, she cursed her father's Irish roots. Even her Italian heritage, inherited from her mother, couldn't combat the fair skin that emblazoned every emotion on her face. Good God. She was twenty-eight and blushing like a hormonal teenager.

"Holy shit. Are you blushing, Sophie? At what? The thought of Mr. Tall-Insanely-Rich-and-Hot-as-Hell?" Marie gave an exaggerated gasp. "Oh, you *so* are. All right, give. What happened when you stormed over to his office like it was the Alamo? Did you rip something else besides a strip off his hide? Like his clothes? What aren't you telling me?"

Sophie groaned, closing her eyes at her friend's exuberance and the *volume* of it. She loved the other woman, but she really should've been the gossip editor with her sheer adoration for it.

"Nothing happened. Clothes remained intact. The only thing stripped away was my pride." She winced, just remembering her ill-conceived decision to charge into Joshua Lowell's office and the ensuing confrontation.

That definitely hadn't been one of her finer moments. Thank goodness the front desk receptionist at the main level had been away from her desk. Otherwise security would've probably been called on her. Wouldn't Althea Granger, the editor in chief, have loved to receive that call about one of her investigative reporters needing to be bailed out for trespassing?

Why Joshua hadn't had her escorted out still nagged at her. Just as memories of the CEO did.

She shook her head, as if she could dislodge the question and the man from her mind with the gesture. As if it were that simple.

"Sophie." Althea Granger appeared next to her cubicle, as if her thoughts had conjured the older woman. With thick dark hair, smooth, unlined brown skin and beautiful features, she could've easily been mistaken for a retired model rather than the editor in chief of the exclusive bedroom community of Falling Brook's newspaper. But after stints in major papers across the country, she'd run the *Chronicle* with a steel hand, judicious eye and the political acumen of a seasoned senator for years. And she was Sophie's mentor and idol. "Could you join me in the conference room, please?"

"Absolutely." Sophie rose from her desk chair, ignoring Marie's concerned glance. Too bad she couldn't do the same for the kernel of trepidation that lodged between her ribs. Usually, if Althea wanted to speak with her, it was in her office. Not the more formal conference room.

Could this be about her article? No, it couldn't be. She instantly rejected the thought. Althea had personally read and approved the story before it'd run in this morning's paper. If she'd thought Sophie had gone too far, hadn't been professional or objective in her reporting, the other woman would've had no problem in calling her on it.

Then what could it…possibly…be… *Oh God.*

She almost jolted to a halt in the doorway of the room where most of their editorial meetings were held. Somehow, she managed not to grab on to the jamb to steady her suddenly precarious balance.

Joshua Lowell.

He stood at the head of the long, rectangular table, hands in the pockets of his perfectly tailored, probably ridiculously expensive navy blue suit, those unnervingly sharp and beautiful hazel eyes fixed on her.

How wrong that eyes so lovely—light brown with vivid brushes of emerald green—were wasted on such a hard, cold…gorgeous…face.

Okay. So, she hadn't fabricated how unjustly stunning the man was. It seemed unfair, really. Joshua Lowell, a millionaire, CEO, son of a powerful if notorious family, educated and sophisticated, and then God had deemed fit to top that sundae of privilege with a face and body that belonged pressed on an ancient coin or forever immortalized in marble for some art collector's pleasure.

She tried and failed not to stare at the angular face with its jut of cheekbones and stone-hewn jaw—the stark lines should've been severe, made him appear harsh. But the beauty of those eyes and the lushness of his too-sensual-for-her-comfort mouth with its fuller bottom lip softened the severity, making him a fascinating study of contrasts. Cruelty and tenderness. Coldness and warmth. Carnality and virtue.

Her gaze reluctantly drifted from his face to his broad shoulders, the wide chest that tapered to a narrow waist and hips. She couldn't see his thighs from her still-frozen position in the doorway, but her brain helpfully supplied how the muscular length of them had pressed against his slacks days ago. With his lean but powerful body, the man obviously worked out. Probably unleashed a lot of aggression there.

How else did he release emotion?

Stop it, she snapped at her wayward mind. *We don't care.*

Mentally rolling her eyes at herself, she forced her feet to move forward, carrying her farther into the room. Joshua Lowell might look like he flew down on winged feet from Mount Olympus, but he was still an arrogant ass. One who, most likely, was here either to try to get her fired or threaten a lawsuit. That ought to knock down his hot factor several notches.

Should.

"Sophie, please close the door behind you," Althea instructed. Once Sophie shut the door with a quiet click, the editor in chief nodded toward Joshua. "Mr. Lowell, I'd like to introduce you to Sophie Armstrong, the journalist of the article in today's edition."

Her pulse echoed in her ears as she waited, breath snagged in her throat, for Joshua to out her to her employer. But after a long moment, he only arched a dark blond eyebrow. His gaze didn't waver from her as he smoothly said, "Ms. Armstrong."

Relief flooded her, almost weakening her knees. Above

all things, Althea was a professional, and she wouldn't have appreciated finding out Sophie had met him before. No, correction. *How* she'd met him.

But suspicion immediately nipped at relief's heels. *Why* hadn't he told Althea the truth? What did he want? She didn't know him, but she doubted he did anything magnanimously without it benefiting him. And he owed nothing to her, the reporter who had just aired his family's dark past all over the front page.

"Ms. Granger, I would appreciate it if you gave Ms. Armstrong and me a moment alone, please." He'd added *please*, but it wasn't a request.

And Althea didn't take it as one, though she did turn to her and ask, "Sophie?"

No. The answer branded her tongue, but the last time she'd checked, she wasn't a coward. And since she'd crashed Black Crescent's proverbial gates, it would be the height of hypocrisy to claim fear of being alone with him now. Even if her heart thudded against her chest like a bass drum.

"It's fine," she said.

"Okay." She continued to peer at Sophie for several more seconds, and, apparently satisfied with Sophie's poker face, she nodded. "Fine, but, Mr. Lowell," she added, swinging her attention back to Joshua, "I'm going to trust the words *lawsuit* and *libel* won't be thrown around in my absence. If so, I fully advise and expect Sophie to end the conversation so I can introduce you to our legal department."

With a smile that belied she'd just threatened to sic lawyers on him, Althea exited the room, leaving her alone with Joshua. And a table that had provided adequate enough distance before seemed to shrink, leaving her no protection.

"I assume your editor doesn't know about your little excursion to my office," he stated, with that flat note she'd come to associate with him.

"No," she said. "But of course you already figured that out. Why didn't you tell her?"

"Because it doesn't serve me well to do so right now. And—" his voice deepened to a slightly ominous timbre that had trepidation and—*God*—whispers of excitement tripping down her spine "—if anyone is going to deliver trouble to your doorstep, Sophie Armstrong, it's going to be me."

That statement might not have contained *lawsuit* or *libel*, but it was still most definitely a threat.

"I assume you're here about the piece in the *Chronicle*." She switched the subject, not wanting to dwell on what kind of "trouble" he wanted to visit on her. "Why don't you just get to it?"

He studied her, his silence heavy but fairly vibrating with the tension that seemed to crackle beneath his stoic facade. And something—call it a reporter's instinct or a woman's sixth sense—assured her that it was indeed a facade. Which meant more lurked beneath the surface that he didn't want anyone to see, to know. Secrets. The journalist in her, definitely *not* the woman, wanted to ferret out those secrets. Hungered to expose them to the light.

"Yes, why don't we just 'get to it,'" he repeated, making her suggestion sound like something more wicked. "I want to know how you acquired the photographs in the article."

She crossed her arms over her chest and shook her head. "From my sources, and before you issue a demand wrapped up in a request, I can't reveal them."

"Can't," he pressed, "or won't?"

She shrugged a shoulder. "In this case, it's the same difference."

Another long beat where his unwavering, intense gaze

scrutinized her. "Do you know what you are, Ms. Armstrong?" he finally murmured.

"Let me guess. A bitch," she supplied, slipping a bored note into her voice. Wouldn't be the first time a man in his position had called her that name when she'd pressed too hard, questioned too much or just didn't go sit behind a desk or on a set and look pretty. Journalism, especially investigative journalism, wasn't for the weak of heart or the thin of skin. And that word seemed to be the go-to to describe a strong woman with an opinion, a spine and unwillingness to be silenced.

"No." A flash of disgust flickered across his face as if just hearing that word sickened him. Or maybe the thought of calling a woman that particular insult did... "Maybe you would prefer if I called you that. Because then you could justify my being here as sour grapes and damaged pride over a story. But I refuse to make it that easy for you. No, Ms. Armstrong, you are not a bitch," he continued, and the disdain that had appeared in his expression saturated his voice. "You are a vulture. A scavenger who picks at carrion until there's nothing left but the bleached, dry bones."

That shouldn't have hurt her. But, God, it did. It slashed across her chest to burrow deep beneath bone and marrow to the core of her that believed in fairness and truth. Never in her reporting had she gone out of the way to hurt someone. Which had been one reason why she'd gone to see Joshua in the first place. She'd wanted his side, to ensure the article hadn't been skewed.

Maybe it was a remnant from being the child of divorced parents. From that hyperawareness that ensured neither her mother nor her father feel like she loved one more than the other. That she didn't confide in, call or lavish attention on one without making sure she gave the other equal affection. That balance had been stressful as a child who'd felt torn between two warring parents. And now, as an adult, that careful balancing act had carried over into her job. She ensured she presented both sides of an issue. And for Joshua to attack that vulnerable center of her... It shook her. It *hurt* her.

"In your thirst for a juicy story and a byline, did you even once stop to consider the consequences? Did you pause to ask yourself how it would affect my family? My mother? She's had to deal with the fallout of someone else's actions for years. *Years*," he bit out, true anger melting the ice of his tone. Sunlight streamed through the windows behind him, hitting his dirty-blond hair and setting the gold strands aglow. Like an avenging angel. "She's suffered, and dredging up ancient history for the sake of salacious gossip will only inflict more harm. But, of course, you couldn't be bothered to take into account anyone or anything else but your own ambition."

"My own ambition?" she repeated, grinding the words out between clenched teeth. She lowered her arms and her fingers curled into fists at her thighs, as she almost trembled with the need to defend herself. To tell him that wasn't her at all. But screw that. She hadn't done a hatchet job; she'd simply done her job. Period. And she'd been fair. *Damn fair.* "You don't know the first thing about me, so don't shove your own biases on me. I understand that you might not be able to view the article objectively, but believe me, I showed admirable restraint. I could have included the complete, unvarnished truth about who and what you are. A truth I'm sure the 'hero'—" she sneered the word "—of Black Crescent wouldn't want to get out."

He didn't reply. Didn't react at all. His hazel gaze bored into her, and she refused to flinch under that poker face that reduced hers to an amateurish attempt.

"I have no idea what you're alluding to. I haven't done

anything wrong or that I need to be ashamed of. As much to the contrary as your story hinted at, I haven't been my father's puppet. I've done nothing but try to repair the damage he caused. That's all I've ever done."

Joshua probably wasn't aware of the strained note in his voice, the almost silent fervency that stretched from his words. Yes, she couldn't deny the truth of his statement. Even if the possibility existed that Vernon was pulling the strings all these years, it didn't negate the fact that Joshua had abandoned what had appeared to be a very promising art career to take over the family company. To head it and bear all the heat, enmity and distrust as well as the responsibility on his still-young shoulders. His twin, Jake, hadn't been seen in Falling Brook for fifteen years, and the younger brother, Oliver, had fallen into a destructive partying lifestyle. So everything had fallen to him, and Joshua had put aside his own dreams to take up the burden.

No matter how she felt about the man and his actions, she had to respect that sacrifice.

"Anything I've done, it was and is to protect and take care of my family. I have no shame in that," he said, and that air of arrogance, of utter lack of remorse just... Dammit, it just pissed her off.

"Now, that is rich coming from you," she drawled, propping a hip against the conference table.

His aloof expression remained, but he cocked his head to the side. "And what the hell do you mean by that?" he demanded, almost...pleasantly. But the glitter in his eyes belied the tone.

"Oh, I think you know... *Daddy.*"

He blinked, continuing to stare at her. And his lack of response, of reaction, only stirred the anger kindling in her chest.

"Really?" she snapped. "You're going to continue to

pretend to not know what I'm talking about?" She chuckled, the sound brittle, jaded and lacking humor. "You only protect and care for the family you decide to acknowledge. But," she chided, tapping a fingertip to the corner of her mouth, "I suppose that a four-year-old daughter would be extremely inconvenient for someone who lives on that high horse you're so afraid to tumble off of."

Joshua slowly leaned forward and, with a deliberate motion, flattened his palms on the table. "I don't know why you seem to believe that I have a child, but I don't. That's crazy," he said, narrowing his eyes on her.

She snorted. "Just because you might claim you don't— and you definitely act like you don't have a daughter— doesn't make it so."

He didn't reply, but that piercing gaze didn't leave her face. His tall, rangy body remained motionless, coiled as if pulled taut by an invisible string—a string that was seconds from snapping.

She frowned, stepping back from her indignation and, okay, yes, battered pride and feelings, to analyze him more closely. Confusion, and, *oh God*, whispers of uncertainty darkened his eyes.

Could it… *Could he really not know?*

"I—I…" She stopped. Inhaled. And started again. "I'm not making this claim casually or lightly. I have very good reason to believe that you do have a daughter."

"I don't know what your reasons are, and I don't care," he said with the barest hint of a rasp. "And if you knew anything about me beyond your so-called research, you would realize how ridiculous your accusation is. Because that's what you telling me I have a child I've neglected is, Ms. Armstrong. An ugly, unfounded and *untrue* accusation."

She should've flinched at his menacing growl, at the

blistering curse. She *should not* be electrified by it. Should
not be riveted and fascinated by the sign of heat and a loosening of his iron-clad control.

Should not be considering poking more at the bear, to
see if he would roar instead of growl. To see if he would…
pounce.

Ill-conceived and unwelcomed desire leaped and ca-
vorted in her veins like a naughty, giggling child. One
who didn't care one bit for the rules. She steeled her body
against the dark urge to draw nearer to him. Against the
almost irresistible need to discover if his body warmth
seeped through his suit and see if it would touch her. To
find out what scent his skin held. Something earthy and
raw, or would it be cool and refined? Fire or ice?

She cleared her throat and inched back, her hip bumping one of the chairs flanking the table. *Jesus, woman.
He's not the pied piper, and you aren't some glaze-eyed
mouse.* And besides, if she decided to follow any man
somewhere—which hell would have to fall into a deep
freeze and sell snow cones for extra income for that to
happen—it wouldn't be this icicle of a man who carried
more baggage than a Boeing 747.

"Listen, I received this information from a source—one
that I trust. And if you recall, I attempted to reach out numerous times to interview you for the article. If you had
bothered replying to any of my calls, voice mails or emails,
I would've addressed this with you. But the fact that you
refused only lent credence to my suspicions that you had
something to hide." She ignored the scoff he uttered and
spread her hands wide, palms up. "I know you doubt my
credibility, but I thoroughly researched your family to prepare for my article. And the truth is the rumor about an
illegitimate child surfaced several times."

"This source you trust," he countered, "would it be the same one who provided those pictures?"

She hesitated but, after a second, nodded. "Yes."

Of the people she'd interviewed, Zane Patterson had proved to be the most helpful…and rich in information. Rich, hell. He'd been a gold strike. And none of what he'd had to share had been flattering. But considering his family had been one of those directly affected by the Black Crescent scandal, Sophie couldn't blame him for his animosity and bitterness. He'd lost everything—his family's financial security, his home and then his family. His parents had divorced a year later. And he blamed it all on the Lowells. The man still harbored a lot of anger toward that family.

Still, just because he hated them didn't mean he hadn't been able to give her plenty of material. Zane had been a year younger than Oliver Lowell, so they'd run in the same circles in high school. Therefore, he'd had the means to supply her with the kind of info that hadn't been available with a Google search as fifteen years ago social media hadn't been as prevalent as it was today. Not only had Zane given her the photos Joshua seemed so fixated on, but he'd also been the first person to mention Joshua having a love child that he refused to acknowledge. But, like she'd assured Joshua, Zane hadn't been the only person to assert the same.

"Fine. Keep your secrets," Joshua said. He turned away from her, studying the just-awakening main street of Falling Brook. The newspaper's offices were located in one of the older brick buildings lining the street, tucked between a women's clothing boutique and a bookstore. As he stared out the window, the sun's rays caressing his sharply hewn profile, he was like a king surveying his realm.

And maybe he was. The insular bedroom community

with its two-thousand-strong population of surgeons,
CEOs, a few A-list actors and pro athletes had once looked
at Vernon Lowell as a ruler, and Joshua's father had gorged
on the admiration and reverence. By all appearances,
Joshua seemed to be a more benevolent king, but no one
could mistake the power, the air of authority and command that clung to him, as tailor-made to fit as his suits.

Part of her acknowledged she should be intimidated by
that level of influence. In this community where money not
just spoke, but screamed at the tops of its lungs, power of
the press was a buzz phrase. If he wanted, he could have
her fired. Blackballed, even.

So yes, she should be at least a little leery. But fear
didn't skip and dance over her skin, leaving pebbled flesh
in its wake. Exhilaration did. Being in this man's presence
agitated and animated her in a way only burgeoning new
stories did. And the why of it—she lurched away from digging deeper, scrabbling away from that particular crumbling, dangerous edge.

When he turned back and pinned her with that magnetic, intense gaze, she barely managed to trap her gasp.
The force of it was nearly physical. The inane image of
her holding her hands up, shielding herself from it, popped
in her head.

"You're right," he announced.

She blinked, taken aback. Replaying their conversation through her mind, she shook her head, still confused.
"About?"

"You offered me the opportunity to give my insight into
the story, and I didn't take it. But now I'm offering you a
chance no other reporter has been extended. Come spend
a day with me at the Black Crescent offices. I'll grant you
access to my world, and you can see and decide for yourself whether or not the rumors stated in your article are

true. Or you might just discover that I'm just a business-man trying to repair the past while making a way for the future." He arched an eyebrow. "Either way, it will be an exclusive."

It's a trap. The warning blared through her head. And if she had the intelligence God gave a gnat, she would decline. But she was aware enough to recognize that the woman whispered that caution. The reporter's blood hummed with anticipation at this unprecedented oppor-tunity. She could pen a part two to her piece, and maybe it and the first one could possibly be picked up by the *Associated Press*.

Plus you get to spend more time with Joshua Lowell. The sly whisper ghosted across her mind. Spend more time with the enigmatic, sexy man who kindled a need inside her that she resented. A need that, if she wasn't careful, could compromise her objectivity and her job.

And that she absolutely couldn't allow. Nothing could get in the way of her goals, of her independence. Her mother had shelved her dream of becoming an architect to marry her father. And years later, when her marriage ended, she'd had to start from scratch, dependent on the scant alimony her father had grudgingly provided, having to work low-paying jobs to make ends meet while attend-ing college part-time. It'd taken years of dedication and exhausting, backbreaking work, but she'd finally attained her dream job. But Sophie had learned a valuable lesson while witnessing her mother's struggle. She would never become a casualty of a relationship. And never would she prioritize a man above her own needs, giving him every-thing while he left her with just scraps to remind her of what she could've had but had thrown away.

She had to take only one look at Joshua Lowell, spend one minute in his company, take one glance in those lovely but shuttered eyes to know he could strip her of everything. And not look back.

If she allowed him to. Which she wouldn't.

"I accept your offer," she said, resolve strengthening her voice.

He dipped his head in acknowledgment. "I'll have my assistant contact you to set up an appointment."

With one last, long stare, he strode toward her, heading toward the conference room door. As he brushed past her, she ordered herself not to inhale. Not to find out—

Sandalwood and dark earth after a fresh spring rain. Earthy and raw, it is.

Dammit.

"Ms. Armstrong." She jerked her head in his direction and met the gaze of the ruthless businessman who had dragged a failing company back from the edge of the financial abyss. "Don't mistake this for an olive branch or a truce. When you wrote and published that article, you threatened the peace and well-being of my family, and I don't take that lightly or forget. Use this as a chance for another smear campaign, and I'll ensure you regret it."

Long after he left, his warning—and his scent—remained. No matter how hard she tried to eradicate both.

Three

Joshua pulled his car into the parking lot of his gym and stabbed the ignition button a little harder than necessary, shutting the engine off. Restless energy raced through him, and it jangled under his skin. He'd been this way since yesterday and his visit to the *Falling Brook Chronicle*'s offices. Since his confrontation with Sophie.

Tunneling his fingers through his hair, he gripped the short strands and ground his teeth together. Trapping the searing flood of curses that blistered his tongue. He'd gone there to question her about the photographs and her source for them. And he'd been slapped with a paternity accusation.

The *fuck*.

Even now icy fingers of shock continued to tickle his spine, chilling him. Trailing right behind it came the hot slam of helpless fury. He hated that sense of powerlessness, of—goddammit—self-doubt.

And he resented the hell out of Sophie for planting it there. For hauling him back to a time when he'd been drowning in fear, desperately swimming toward the surface to drag in a life-giving lungful of air. Despairing that he never would again.

Through the years, there'd been plenty of gossip about his family on top of the ugly truth about his father and his actions. It would be a lie to claim the whispers hadn't hurt him. That he didn't have scars from that tumultuous period. But he'd survived. He'd always had pride in the knowledge that he wasn't his father, that he didn't harm people out of selfishness and greed. He'd clung to that knowledge.

And in one conversation, Sophie had delivered a solid blow to that source of honor, causing zigzags to splinter through it like a cracked windshield.

Had he been a monk? Hell no. He enjoyed sex, but he still practiced caution. A man in his position and with his wealth had to. So he chose his partners carefully—women who understood he didn't want a relationship, just a temporary arrangement that provided pleasure for both of them—and ensured he used protection. Still, he understood that mistakes could happen. Nothing was infallible. But none of his ex-lovers had ever approached him about an unexpected pregnancy or a child. Because if they had, he would've never abandoned the woman or the baby. *Never.*

For Sophie to suggest—no, to accuse him of being able to neglect his own flesh and blood...

With a low growl, he shoved open his car door and stepped out, slamming it shut behind him. Seconds later, with his duffel bag in hand, he stalked toward the gym, ready to work off some of the anger and tension riding him like a relentless jockey on a punching bag.

An hour later, sweat poured from his face, shoulders and

chest in rivulets. Pleasurable weariness born of pushing his body to the limit sang in his muscles. Yanking off his boxing gloves, he picked up his bottle of water and gulped it while inhaling the scent of perspiration, bleach and the musk from bodies that had permanently seeped into the concrete floors and walls. This gym, located in the next town over from Falling Brook, wasn't one of those trendy establishments soccer moms and young CEOs patronized with stylish athletic wear and skin that glistened or, for God's sake, *dewed*.

Fighters grappled and trained in the boxing ring at the far side of the room. Huge tires leaned against a wall and a smattering of paint-flecked, scratched gym equipment hogged one corner while free weights claimed another. Grunts, the smack of rope hitting the concrete floor and rock music permeated the air. People didn't come to this to be seen, but to push their bodies, to beat them into submission or perfect working order.

So what the *fuck* was Sophie Armstrong doing here?

He scowled, studying the petite, frowning woman as she whipped the battle ropes up and down in a steady, furious pace. Even as the familiar anger and suspicion crowded into him at the sight of her in the gym he'd frequented for years—his sanctuary away from the office and home— he couldn't stop his gaze from following the slender but toned lines of her small frame that the purple sports bra and black leggings did nothing to hide. Without the conservative clothes that halted just shy of being plain, he had an unrestricted view of the high thrust of her smallish and utterly perfect breasts that slightly swelled over the rounded edge of her top. Though he ordered himself to look away, to stop visually devouring the enemy, he still lingered over the taut abdomen that gleamed with hard-fought-for sweat and the gently rounded hips and tight, sleekly muscled legs that seemed impossibly long for someone of her stature.

Like a sweaty elf princess who'd momentarily traded her gilded throne for a dusty battlefield. The silly, fanciful thought swept through his head before he could banish it. Thoughts like that belonged to the artist he used to be, not the sensible, pragmatic businessman he was now. Still... Watching her muscles flex, her abs tighten and those strong thighs brace her weight, he was impressed at the power in her tiny frame.

Impressed and hard as hell.

"Goddamn," he growled. Frolicking puppies. Spreadsheets with unbalanced columns.

His mother's shuttered face and devastated eyes when she read Sophie's article.

Yeah, that killed his erection fast.

And maybe it didn't snuff out the hot licks of lust in his gut, but it gave fury one hell of a foothold.

Clenching his jaw, he stalked across the gym toward the woman who had infiltrated his life and cracked open a door he'd hoped, fucking prayed, would remain locked, bolted and welded shut. Just as he reached Sophie, she gave the battle ropes one last flick, then dropped them to the floor with a thud.

"Stalking me, Ms. Armstrong?" he drawled, his fingers gripping his water bottle so tight, the plastic squeaked in protest.

He immediately loosened his hold. Damn, he'd learned long ago to never betray any weakness of emotion. People were like sharks scenting bloody chum in the water when they sensed a chink in his armor. But when in this woman's presence, his emotions seemed to leak through like a sieve. The impenetrable shield barricading him that had been forged in the fires of pain, loss and humiliation came away dented and scratched after an encounter with Sophie. And that presented as much of a threat, a danger to him as her insatiable need to prove that he was a deadbeat father and puppet to a master thief.

"Stalking you?" she scoffed, bending down to swipe her own bottle of water and a towel off the ground. With a strength that could be described only as Herculean, he didn't drop his gaze to the sweet, firm curve of her ass. He deserved a medal, an award, the key to the city for not giving in to the urge. "Need I remind you, it was you who showed up at my job yesterday, not the other way around. So I guess that makes us even in the showing-up-where-we're-not-wanted department."

"Oh, we're not even close to anything that resembles *even*, Sophie," he said, using her name for the first time aloud. And damn if it didn't taste good on his tongue. If he didn't sound as if he were stroking the two syllables like they were bare, damp flesh.

She didn't immediately reply, instead lifting the clear bottle to her mouth and sipping from it. His gaze dipped to that pursed, wicked mouth, and a primal throb set up in his blood, his dick. *Stand down*, he ordered his unruly flesh. His loose gray basketball shorts wouldn't conceal the effect she had on him. And no way in hell would he give her that to use against him.

"I hate to disappoint you and your dreams of narcissistic grandeur, but I've been a member of this gym for years." She swiped her towel over her throat and upper chest. "I've seen you here, but it's not my fault if you've never noticed me."

"That's bullshit," he snapped. "I would've noticed you."

The words echoed between them, the meaning in them pulsing like a thick, heavy heartbeat in the sudden silence that cocooned them. Her silver eyes flared wide before they flashed with...what? Surprise? Irritation? Desire. A liquid slide of lust prowled through him like a hungry—so goddamn hungry—beast.

The air simmered around them. How could no one else see it shimmer in waves from the concrete floor like steam from a sidewalk after a summer storm?

She was the first to break the visual connection, and when she ducked her head to pat her arms down, the loss of her eyes reverberated in his chest like a physical snapping of tautly strung wire. He fisted his fingers at his sides, refusing to rub the echo of soreness there.

"Do you want me to pull out my membership card to prove that I'm not some kind of stalker?" She tilted her head to the side. "I'm dedicated to my job, but I refuse to cross the line into creepy...or criminal."

He ground his teeth against the apology that shoved at his throat, but after a moment, he jerked his head down in an abrupt nod. "I'm sorry. I shouldn't have jumped to conclusions." And then because he couldn't resist, because it still gnawed at him when he shouldn't have cared what she—a reporter—thought of him or not, he added, "That predilection seems to be in the air."

She narrowed her eyes on him, and a tiny muscle ticked along her delicate but stubborn jaw. Why that sign of temper and forced control fascinated him, he opted not to dwell on. "And what is that supposed to mean?" she asked, the pleasant tone belied by the anger brewing in her eyes like gray storm clouds.

Moments earlier, he'd wondered if fury or desire had heated her gaze. Now he had his answer. Because he now faced her anger, now had confirmation that when she looked like she wanted to knee him in the balls the silver darkened to near black.

But when she looked like she just wanted to go to her knees for him, her eyes were molten, pure hot silver.

God help him, because, masochistic fool that he'd suddenly become, he craved them both.

He wanted her rage, her passion...wanted both to beat at him, heat his skin, touch him. Make him feel.

Mentally, he scrambled away from that, that *need*, like it'd reared up and flashed its fangs at him. The other man he'd been—the man who'd lost himself in passion, paint and life captured on film—had drowned in emotion. Willingly. Joyfully. And when it'd been snatched away—when that passion, that *life*—had been stolen from him by cold, brutal reality, he'd nearly crumbled under the loss, the darkness. Hunger, wanting something so desperately, led only to the pain of eventually losing it.

He'd survived that loss once. Even though it'd been like sawing off his own limbs. He might be an emotional amputee, but dammit, he'd endured. He'd saved his family, their reputation and their business. But he'd managed it by never allowing himself to need again.

And Sophie Armstrong, with her pixie face and warrior spirit, wouldn't undo all that he'd fought and silently screamed to build.

She must've interpreted his silence as an indictment, because her full mouth firmed into an aggravated line, and her shoulders slowly straightened, her posture militant and, yes, defensive. As she should be. "If it makes it easier to look at that pretty face in the mirror, then go ahead and throw verbal punches," she sneered. *Pretty face.* He didn't even pretend to take that for a compliment. Not that way her voice twisted around the words. "But I did the research, and the information I received was solid, and my sources were legitimate."

"Sources," he repeated, leaping on that clue. "So you had more than one?"

She didn't move, but she might as well as have slammed up an invisible door between them. "Yes," she replied after a long moment. "I didn't rely on gossip or groundless rumors."

"Your sources seem to believe they know a lot about not just my family, the inner workings of Black Crescent, but my personal life, as well," he said, drawing closer to her.

The seeds that their earlier conversation in the *Chronicle*'s conference room had planted started to sprout roots. Roots of suspicion and hated mistrust wound their way into his head, threading around his heart. He resented Sophie for planting those kernels of suspicion about the people who existed in his small inner circle. Small for a reason. Trial by fire had taught him he could trust a precious few, and only those precious few had access to his family, the details of his life. Could one of them be the "source" she referred to? As he'd done on the drive back to his office yesterday, he again ran through their faces: Haley, Jake, Oliver.

Haley, no. Never. She'd proved her loyalty hundreds of times over. But his brothers... Jesus, he wanted to dismiss any notion that they could've turned on him, but... He couldn't. They resented him, resented that he'd become their father, never appreciating the sacrifices he'd made so they could live free of the burden of Black Crescent and the dark shadow it cast. A shadow he constantly existed in but strove to, if not be free of, at least lighten.

"I want names, Sophie," he bit out, the dregs of fear, grief and anger at the possible identities of her sources swirling in his mind roughening his voice. He stepped closer until the scent of citrus, velvet, damp blooms and woman—*her*—filled his nostrils. Ignoring the lure of that sensual musk, he lowered his head, forcing her to meet his gaze. "If someone is digging into my life and giving information about me, then I deserve to know who they are." *Who I need to protect myself from.* "Every man has the right to confront their accusers."

She shook her head, her golden-brown ponytail brushing her bare shoulders. "No. The people who spoke to me did so on the assurance of confidentiality, and I won't betray that. And I absolutely refuse to expose them to the wrath of the Lowell family."

The wrath of the Lowell family? What kind of shit was that? "My wrath?" he murmured, edging closer. And closer still until one shift of his feet and their chests would press together. Their sweat-dampened skin would cling. His cock would find a home nestled against her taut stomach. "Do you still have your job? Have you found yourself and that paper you work for served with a defamation suit? If you went to any of the stores or restaurants around here, would you still be waited on or served? No, Sophie." He leaned down, so close his lips almost grazed her ear. So close, he caught the shiver that worked through her body as his breath hit her lobe. "If I wanted to wage war against someone who came after me, after mine, the first casualty would be you. And since you haven't been shunned or blackballed yet—because believe me, even with the stain on my last name, I have the power to do all I've mentioned—you haven't felt my wrath. Besides," he added, and this time he let his mouth brush the rim of her ear. Let himself get his first feel of her skin, her body even if it was just something as small as that. "I would never include others in the battle between us. This, sweetheart, is personal."

Air, quick and harsh, rushed from her lips, bathing his cheek, stirring the flames already stroking him from the inside out. God, he wanted to... Grinding his molars together so hard he should've tasted dust, he inched back, placing between them the space he'd so foolishly eliminated. As it was, he now fought the impulse to rub his thumb over the spot where his mouth had glanced her ear. Rub that sensation into his flesh as if it wasn't already branded there.

"Is that supposed to scare me? Should I file that under the threat category?" she shot back. And it would've been effective if it hadn't been uttered in a throaty whisper that rasped over his too-sensitive skin.

Damn her.

Damn him.

"No, Sophie. The last thing I want from you is fear." Let her translate that how she wanted. "But make no mistake, I intend to have those names from you. And that's not a threat, but a promise."

Not waiting for her response, he turned and strode away from her. But not for long. They had an appointment for a day together at his office. And he would see the vow he'd made come true.

Sophie would divulge the identities of her sources.

One way or another.

And as his blood hummed in his veins, still lit up like a torch from his interaction with her, it was the "another" that worried him.

Four

Back in the lion's den.

Sophie summoned a smile as she gave the first-floor receptionist of the Black Crescent building her name and waited while she called to verify her appointment. Turning, she stared at the large picture window, not really seeing the parking lot or the ring of towering trees beyond that shielded the property like an inner wall in a medieval fiefdom.

No, images of Joshua Lowell from when he'd cornered her at the gym yesterday flickered before her eyes. Flickered, hell. Paraded. Him, his lean but large and powerful body encased in a sweaty white T-shirt that clung to tendon and muscle, and loose gray knee-length basketball shorts. God, those shorts. If the shirt had her itching to climb those wide shoulders as if they were a scratching post and she was a cat in heat, then those shorts had her palm itching to slide beneath the damp waistband, skim

over his ridged abdomen and farther down to grasp the
long and thick length that she'd glimpsed the imprint of
under the nylon.

Joshua freaking Lowell had been hard. *For her.*

And he'd called her sweetheart.

She still couldn't wrap her mind around that. He hated
her. Okay, *hate* might be too strong a word, but he very
strongly disliked her. Okay, *disliked* might be too soft a
word.

Sighing, she shook her head, dispelling the mental picture, but could do nothing for the sensitive spot just under
her navel. The spot where his cock had pressed against
her as he'd whispered threats—forget *promises*, those had
definitely been *threats*—in her ear. Idiot that she was, she
should've been furious, or even a little intimidated, but no.

She'd just been turned the hell on.

And all she could think of was whether or not that sandalwood, earth and rain scent would transfer to her skin
if his naked, big body covered hers. Would she wear him
on her? Or would they create a new fragrance together—
one made of him, her and sex?

Stop this. Now. The silent but strident admonishment
rang inside her head, and she heeded it. She *had* to. In several very short minutes, she would once again face Joshua
on his turf. Only this time she wouldn't have the benefit
of surprise. He would have home-court advantage, so to
speak, prepared for her, her questions, her preconceived
perceptions of him. Joshua Lowell would be ready to battle. And as he'd warned her, he wouldn't lose.

She had to be focused and professional and, above all,
could not think of how that beautiful body would feel moving over her…in her.

Dammit!

"Ms. Armstrong, they're expecting you upstairs. If

you'll take the elevator to the second floor, Mr. Lowell's executive assistant, Haley Shaw, will be waiting for you." The woman gave her a polite but friendly smile as she gestured toward the bank of elevators that Sophie was all too familiar with. She'd covertly stole into them to barge into the Black Crescent offices to interview Joshua Lowell.

"Thank you," she murmured, and followed the receptionist's directions.

Moments later, she stepped out onto the executive floor and approached Haley Shaw's large circular desk. The pretty blonde stood in front of it, smiling up at a tall, handsome man with light brown hair and a presence that screamed confidence and an intensity he couldn't mask. It was that intensity that had Sophie frowning slightly as she approached the couple.

Though both of their voices contained a light note of flirtation, and Haley didn't appear uncomfortable, the man seemed to invade the other woman's personal space, dwarfing Haley's not-inconsiderable height. As a woman who'd often encountered inappropriate advances in the workplace, maybe Sophie was extra sensitive, but it didn't stop her from nearing them and stopping at the executive assistant's side, facing the man, whose smile widened to include her.

Yeah, she didn't trust that smile at all.

In her experience, people who grinned that wide and tried hard to appear affable were usually hiding something. Using overt friendliness and charm as a deflection.

Something whispered to her that this guy was no different.

"Good morning, Ms. Armstrong," Haley greeted Sophie, surprising her a little with the warmth emanating from the welcome. The last time Sophie had been here, she hadn't made such a good first impression. "Can I introduce you to Chase Hargrove?"

"Mr. Hargrove." Sophie nodded, and he extended his hand toward her.

"Ms. Armstrong. It's a pleasure to meet you." Giving her another of those too-amicable smiles, he switched his attention back to Haley. "I have to go. I'll talk to you later, Haley. Hopefully see you then, too, beautiful." With a wink and crooked grin that even Sophie had to admit had her wanting to fan herself, he turned and strode toward the elevators.

"Wow," Sophie muttered as soon as the doors slid closed behind him. "He's definitely...not shy." She shook her head, huffing out a laugh. "Were you okay with how strong he seemed to be coming on? If not, you should tell—" *Joshua* hovered on her tongue, but after a brief hesitation, she said, "Mr. Lowell."

She scoffed, waving a hand toward the direction Chase had disappeared. "He's harmless. Believe me, I can handle him." Pushing off the desk, she swept a hand toward the double doors that led to Joshua's office. "He's waiting for you. Did you need anything? Coffee, tea, water?"

"I'm fine, thanks." Sophie would die on the hill of denial before admitting it aloud, but her stomach twisted with nerves and wouldn't be able to handle anything on it.

Haley nodded, and when they approached the door, she gave it a swift knock, then opened it. "Joshua, Ms. Armstrong is here."

Sweat dotted Sophie's palms, and her heart rapped against her sternum, but she managed a smile of thanks and shored up her mental shields as she moved into the office. After his visit to the *Chronicle* and their impromptu meeting at the gym, she didn't even try to delude herself into believing she could prepare herself for coming face-to-face with him again and not be slammed with the intense presence that was Joshua Lowell.

So when he rose from behind his desk, exposing that tall, rangy body to her, she just let herself soak him in. Took in the short, dark blond hair that emphasized the clean but sharp facial features. Met the green-and-light-brown gaze that seemed determined to strip her of all her defenses. Traced the wide, soft-looking mouth with its too-tempting, full bottom lip. Wandered over the muscular strength and animal magnetism that his steel-gray suit accentuated rather than hid in a cloak of civility.

Maybe not resisting the magnetic pull of his utter sexiness but rather immersing herself in it would strengthen her immunity.

Like a freaking flu shot.

"Sophie," he said, rounding the desk with a confident and commanding stride that shouldn't have set her pulse pounding. But God, did it. "I'm glad you could make it."

She arched an eyebrow. "You doubted I would?"

He halted several feet from her. And it reminded her of how close he'd been in the gym. How his scent had engulfed her. How his lips had brushed her ear even as he whispered threats into it. No. Not threats. Promises, he'd assured her.

And how sick did it make her that a part of her wanted him to follow through on them?

Very. Any therapist worth her or his degree would rub their hands in glee at the thought of getting their hands on her.

"Not for a second," he murmured, that gaze skimming over her emerald sheath and nude pumps before returning to her face.

Her skin hummed from the visual contact, and she fought not to rub her palms up and down her bare arms.

She wouldn't give him the satisfaction of knowing he affected her.

"Well, thank you again for the opportunity to tour the inner sanctum of Black Crescent Hedge Fund." See? She could be professional around him. "I'm looking forward to this."

He nodded. "If you'll follow me…"

For the next several hours, Joshua granted her an exclusive peek behind the curtain. Not only did he introduce her to his employees and explain what they did, but he also revealed how he'd implemented safeguards and a checks-and-balances system so what'd occurred with his father didn't happen again. In other words, he'd willingly policed himself.

She discovered a side of the company she hadn't known existed. Over the years, Joshua had donated a mind-boggling amount of money and time to local and statewide programs that assisted domestic abuse victims, literacy and the foster-care system, including his assistant Haley Shaw's own nonprofit organization. But not only did he help his community, he also invested in his own employees' futures by helping put the staff and their families through college with scholarships and almost-zero-interest loans.

And then there were the reparations he'd made to the families affected by his father's crimes. Joshua had made good on that agreement to repay the stolen funds.

By the time she followed him back to his office that afternoon, she was convinced Black Crescent wasn't the coldhearted, corrupt organization portrayed in the news and even by some of her sources.

By her.

"What you've done here is remarkable," she said as he closed the office door behind them. She shook her head. "Especially in the last few years. But I've only heard of maybe two of your philanthropic efforts. Why haven't you shared with the public what you've shown me today? I think most people would be amazed and as impressed as I am with all that you do for the community on a local and even national level."

"If someone brags about what should be their privilege and right to do, I question not just their motivations but their hearts. Besides—" he slipped his hands into the front pockets of his pants and a faint smile quirked the corners of his mouth "—I've found that most people, particularly the press, have never been interested in reporting anything positive about my family or the company."

She tried not to wince. And didn't quite manage it. "Touché. But to be fair, my article didn't attack you, personally."

"Fair?" he repeated, sarcasm hardening his voice. "Forgive me if I've never associated *fair* with the media. And attack? No. But for an article that was supposed to be about the so-called anniversary of the Black Crescent incident, you invaded my personal life in a way that seemed intrusive and unnecessary."

Her chin snapped up and her shoulders back, offended. "Am I supposed to apologize for being good at my job? I can't control what my sources tell me or where my investigation carries me. I *won't* apologize for the truth. Ever." She narrowed her eyes on him. "If anything you should be thanking me for not including the truth about your illegitimate daughter in the article. I can't say the same would've happened if—"

"Don't say it again," he barked. No, growled. And the ominous rumble of it snapped off her words like a branch cracking from a tree. Thunder rolled across his face, shadowing his eyes and pulling the skin taut across his cheekbones. He took a step forward but drew up short the next instant. "I am. Not. My. Father," he snarled. And some-how, that low, dark statement stunned her more than if he'd yelled it at her. "I would never, ever turn my back on my family the way that bas—"

He broke off, but the rest of his sentence might as well as have been shouted in the room, it echoed so loud, mo-mentarily deafening her.

"The way your father did," she whispered, the words rasping her throat.

Joshua's face could've been carved from stone, but his eyes. God, his eyes damn near glowed with fury…and pain. Such deep, bright pain that the breath caught in her throat, and she ached with it. Ached for him.

She crossed her arms over her chest and turned away from him, eyes momentarily closing. Until this moment Vernon Lowell had been a story, a shadowy, almost urban legend–like figure who'd committed an infamous crime, then disappeared into thin air. But now, in his son's eyes, she saw him as a father—a father who had abandoned and hurt his son so deeply with his actions that even years later, that son suffered. Suffered in ways he hid so successfully that no one—least of all Sophie—had suspected.

That emotion—the intensity of it—couldn't be faked. So was Joshua telling the truth about the child? Did he re-ally not know of her existence? Not only did she rely on her investigative skills in her job, but her instincts. And they were screaming like a pissed-off banshee that maybe, just maybe, he didn't.

Pinching the bridge of her nose, she bowed her head. *I can't believe I'm doing this.* But her heart had made the decision seconds before her brain caught on. And she moved toward the laptop bag she'd left on the couch in the sitting area of his office before leaving for the tour of the company.

Moments later, she had her computer removed and booting up on the coffee table. Glancing up at a still stoic and silent Joshua, she waved him over. "I have something to show you, Joshua," she murmured, using his name for the first time. Something had shifted inside her with that glimpse into his eyes. Standing on formality seemed silly now.

After a brief hesitation, he strode over and lowered onto the cushion next to her. Resolutely attempting to ignore the heat that seemed to emanate from his big body, she focused on pulling up a password-protected file. In several clicks, a report filled the screen.

A DNA report.

He stiffened next to her, and his gaze jerked to her. Silence throbbed in the office, as loud as a heartbeat, as he stared at her. She met his penetrating study evenly, not betraying the wild pounding of her pulse in her ears or the sudden case of dryness that had assaulted her mouth. She couldn't swallow, couldn't move. Common sense railed that she was making a huge mistake, maybe even violating her ethics. But her sense of decency—her soul—insisted that if she could somehow make this right, she should. If she could ease the pain that he would probably deny even existed, she needed to. Whether that was by confirming his daughter's existence or even having a hand in reuniting them... She didn't know. But she had to try.

He turned to her laptop and, leaning forward, scrutinized the report. Taking in his name at the top and the mother's name, which was blacked out. Scanning the results that ended in one determination: Joshua Lowell was a match for a baby girl born four years ago.

Slowly, he straightened. Shock dulled his eyes, flattened the lush curves of his mouth. Only his fists, clenched so tight the knuckles bleached white, betrayed the hint of a stronger current of emotion that could be coursing through him.

Finally, he shifted his gaze to her. "Where did you get this?" he asked, his deep voice like churned-up gravel. It scraped over her skin, abrading her. "Who sent it to you?"

"I can't tell you that."

"Goddammit, Sophie," he snapped. "How can you show me this and then deny me the resources to determine whether it's true or not. Real or not?" he demanded, fury sparking his eyes.

"I can't, Joshua," she insisted. Shaking her head, she spread her hands wide, palms up, on her thighs. "I wish I could, but I *can't*. I will tell you this, though. I believe the report is authentic. My source… I've held the actual report in my hand. If it's faked, it's a fabulous forgery."

"Dammit." He surged off the couch and stalked across the floor to the floor-to-ceiling window that made up one of the walls of his office. Thrusting the fingers of both hands through his short hair, he uttered a soft "dammit" again, then pressed a fist to the glass and cupped the back of his neck with the other. "How would they even be able to run a DNA test? I've never been asked or consented to giving a sample." He whirled around, his sharp features drawn, taut. "This doesn't make sense. Someone is playing games. They have an endgame that I don't know about and can't figure out."

Sophie stood and ventured a couple of steps in his direction. But didn't travel farther than those steps. Those pinpricks of caution that she'd felt in his presence before now stabbed at her. Warning her to. Back. Off. To retreat and regroup. Because at some point, she'd become too vulnerable to him. Too open.

And that should have her snatching up her belongings and running for the door like he'd just sprouted fur and fangs. Because in her position, vulnerability was a liability. For her and her job. God, she'd already revealed some of her research to him. What next? Ignore a lead? Refuse a story?

End her career?

She'd seen it with her mother.

She'd *been* her mother.

Shame, glittering bright and filthy at the same time, slicked through her like an oil stain. One would think she'd learned her lesson. Because it'd been brutal, but a good one. But those were the best. Or at least, they should be.

Bumping into Laurence Danvers at a local campaign rally four years ago had been an accident, so she'd believed for a long time. She hadn't known then that he'd planned the meeting that had seemed serendipitous. Fated. And she'd fallen so hard for his handsome features, his wide smile, his charm…his lies. She'd allowed her heart to blind her to his true nature. So when he'd first suggested a different perspective on an article she was writing about the city council election candidates, she saw it as his helping her see a different angle. When he'd convinced her that reporting an indiscretion from a candidate's past would be inflammatory and unfair—even though that candidate was running on a family platform—she'd conceded because he was only looking out for her career and reputation as a reputable reporter.

And when he'd demanded that she resign rather than reveal this same candidate had been accused of sexual misconduct by several women, she almost conceded. Almost. Too many times during her relationship with Laurence, she'd ignored her intuition. But that time, she'd listened, done some digging and uncovered that he was a longtime family friend to the candidate whose rally they'd met at.

Meeting her, seducing her, making her fall in love… It'd all been so calculated in an effort to use her.

In mere months, she'd almost thrown aside her career, her dreams, her integrity for a man. As Laurence had walked out her apartment door for the final time, she vowed never to be that vulnerable, that *foolish* again.

And as she stared at Joshua, she could feel herself already climbing that slippery slope. One misstep, and it would be a long, painful slide down. Hell, she'd already shown him part of her research. She shuffled back and away from him, both physically and mentally. She had to approach Joshua and this element of her story as a journalist, not a woman who wanted to cradle that strong jaw and massage away the deep crease between his eyebrows. Or soothe the confusion, anger and pain in his eyes.

"Someone is setting me up," Joshua continued, dropping his gaze to his clenched fist. As if disturbed by the outward display of emotion, he stretched his fingers out, splaying them wide and lowering them to the side of his thigh. "Nothing else makes sense. No one has contacted me about possible paternity or approached me for money. Not even threatened blackmail. Logic says that if there was a woman out there with a child I fathered, she would reach out to me for child support."

Sophie couldn't argue with his assumption. Joshua Lowell wasn't only a beautiful man; he was obscenely wealthy and very well connected, even in spite of the scandal. He could more than afford to provide for a child. And a particular kind of woman would use the situation to her advantage and try for more than money. Like forcing a relationship, marriage. Through her research for her article, she'd discovered that from the moment his father disappeared, Joshua had become a choirboy—well, if choirboys had the bodies and faces of Greek gods and exuded sex like a pheromone. But no hint of impropriety had ever been connected to his name in the media. A person didn't need to have a psychology degree to determine the reason behind that. And a woman looking to permanently bind herself to a powerful and rich family would realize that bit of information, as well.

She tapped a finger against her bottom lip. "That is… curious. Especially since the child is four years old now." This was her cue to walk away. To pack up her things, thank him for the opportunity to see the inside of Black Crescent and leave. "I can't give up my sources. But…if you need or want the help, I'll assist in finding out what's going on. Or try to."

Damn.

So much for walking away.

Joshua stared at her for so long, his eyes shuttered, his stony expression indecipherable, that the rescission of her offer hopped on the tip of her tongue. But as she parted her lips, he asked, "Will what you find out end up in the *Chronicle*?"

She extinguished the bright flash of irritation and offense that flared in her chest. Part of her understood his caution and suspicion. But the other half… "I'm not offering my help as part of some tell-all article," she ground out.

God, he really didn't think too much of her.

Which was fair because she didn't trust him, either. From her experience, most men—especially those with something to lose—did everything in their power to protect themselves.

Several more taut seconds passed, but Joshua finally dipped his head in a short, abrupt nod. "I appreciate your offer, then. If there's even the slightest chance that I could be a father, then I owe it to myself—and that little girl— to find out."

A rush of warmth flooded her.

Those aren't the words of a deadbeat father.

Her subconscious taunted like the know-it-all it was.

But her experience with Laurence had hammered home the truth that nothing—or no one—was as it appeared on the surface. Especially someone who had so much to lose like Joshua did—reputation, money and the added burden of a child. Though he managed to keep his private life more contained than others in his position, she'd still gathered images of him and gossip about him with socialites, some A-list actresses and businesswomen.

No middle-class, student-debt-ridden peasants. In other words, no one like you.

Oh, shut it.

Awesome. Now she was arguing with herself. She really needed to get the hell out of this office. This building. This side of town. The more space between her and Joshua right now, the better. If not, she might do something really inane and unforgivable. Like hug him.

Suddenly wary of herself, she turned, retracing the few steps back to the coffee table and couch. Clearing her throat, she sank to the cushion and, tucking a rebellious strand of hair behind her ear, closed her laptop. "I'll start looking into it on my end tonight." With hurried movements, she slid the computer into her bag and stood. Fixing a smile on her lips, she lifted her head and met his impenetrable gaze again. God, the man could give the Sphinx lessons in stoicism. "Thank you for the tour today. I really appreciate it, and I learned more about Black Crescent that I didn't know. That I'm sure many people aren't aware of. If I have your permission, I'd like to share the information in a follow-up article."

"Why?"

She frowned, stilling midprocess of slipping the strap

of her bag over her shoulder. "Because the public deserves to know about your philanthropic programs and generosity to the community. I get your reason for staying mum on the subject, but—"

"No." He cut her off with a hard shake of his head. "When I invited you here I knew it was for a follow-up article. I meant why are you volunteering to help me?"

Because you looked so lost, and I want to bring home what will make you whole.

The explanation lodged in her throat, stuck. And she didn't try to free it. One, he wouldn't appreciate her reason. Wouldn't believe her. Two, she was disgusted with herself for thinking it. For thinking she could give him anything, much less peace and comfort.

Yes, Joshua Lowell had the whole brooding, tortured millionaire thing down pat. His cold mask of reserve had slipped enough times that she glimpsed the dark mass of emotions he concealed. She shivered, unable to restrain the telltale reaction. What would it be like to be on the receiving end of all that unleashed passion? Because she sensed that when or if he finally let it all loose… It would be a thing of wild, raw beauty to witness. Like a roiling, ominous thunderstorm threaded with lightning. And when those bolts struck the earth? Electricity, heat, smoke.

Her pulse thundered in her ears, and she couldn't tear her gaze away from him. She couldn't deny it; she hungered to be that rich, open earth electrified by him. But he would assuredly leave her scorched beyond recognition afterward. And while her body might crave that burning, her scarred heart feared it.

Inhaling a trembling breath past the constriction blocking her throat, she shrugged a shoulder, grabbing for nonchalance and praying she accomplished it. "Because I'm an investigative reporter, and that's what I do. Investigate."

Hiking her purse strap up, she again curved her lips into a polite smile that she—please, God—hoped didn't look as fake as it felt. "I need to head out so I can get back in the office to take care of a few things." Dear Lord, she was babbling and couldn't stop. "Thanks again, and I'll be in touch."

Crossing the room, she extended her hand toward him even though her mind screamed, *What the hell are you doing? Don't touch him!*

But her body had a mind of its own. And as his strong, elegant fingers—an artist's fingers—closed around hers, she cursed the voltage that sizzled from their clasped palms up her arm, down her chest and belly to crackle between her legs. If he dipped his eyes, he would catch the hardened tips of her breasts that were probably saluting him from beneath her dress. No more lace bras around this man. Definitely not enough coverage.

Every primal, self-protective instinct within her had her muscles locking in preparation to jerk her hand free. But pride overrode the need, and she met his hazel stare with a steady one of her own. To prove how she refused to let her body's obviously questionable taste rule her, she even squeezed his hand.

But when his nostrils slightly flared and his eyes darkened to an emerald-flecked amber... Oh no, she'd miscalculated. Flames licked at her flesh, and in that instant, she had a vivid premonition of how he would look in the throes of passion. Hooded, but glittering eyes, skin pulled taut over razor-sharp cheekbones, mouth pressed to a flat, almost severe line, and that big, wide-shouldered, powerful frame held rigidly still as he let her adjust to the blazing, overwhelming invasion of him planted deep and firmly inside her.

Pride be damned.

She yanked her hand out of his grip and refused to rub her still-tingling palm against her thigh.

"Why do I think you're lying to me?" he murmured, and after a few seconds of bewilderment, she realized he referred to her weak explanation about her offer of assistance. "What are you hiding, Sophie?"

"I think you're trying to uncover conspiracy theories where there are none," she replied, flippant. "I'm the reporter. That's my job, to be suspicious."

"Where you're concerned, my fail-safe is suspicion." He cocked his head to the side, studying her so closely she sympathized with those butterflies pinned to a corkboard. He wouldn't make her fidget, though. Or make her reveal any of her closely held thoughts regarding him. They were hers, and not his to use to his advantage.

"Then why are you willing to accept my help?" she asked, bristling.

"Maybe for once I'd like to know how it feels to have the press working with me instead of against me. And—" his voice dropped, and an unmistakable growl roughened the tone, causing her flesh to pebble "—I believe in keeping my friends close and my enemies closer. And you, Sophie Armstrong, I plan to be stuck to."

Another threat he would probably call a promise.

A promise that shouldn't have sent waves of molten heat echoing through her.

But it did. They swamped her, and dammit, she wanted to be taken under.

"Like stink on shit, you mean?" she shot back, pouring a bravado she was far from feeling into her tone.

He shifted forward until only scant inches separated them. Like in the gym, his body filled her vision and his warmth reached out for her, surrounding her along with his sandalwood and rain-dampened earth scent. She held her ground, not in the least intimidated as he invaded her personal space. No, not intimidated. She was throbbing. Hungry.

"Closer," he whispered, his breath feathering over her lips in a heavy but light-as-air caress.

Just in time, she caught herself before she tilted her head back, chasing that ephemeral touch.

Okay, screw pride and standing her ground.

Any wise general recognized the wisdom of retreating to fight another day.

And as she pivoted and escaped Joshua's office, she convinced herself she was being wise not running scared.

She almost accomplished the task.

Almost, but not quite.

Five

Joshua pulled open the door to The Java Hut, Falling Brook's upscale coffeehouse on Main Street. The air from the air conditioner greeted him like a lover, wrapping around him with chilled arms of welcome. It might be only May, but the temperature already crept toward the midseventies. And he silently bemoaned the loss of the cooler spring weather. While many people worshipped summer because of days spent on the beaches, lounging by the pool and less clothing, he loved the dynamic and vivid colors and crisp breezes of fall and the rain-scented air and reawakening of life that spring brought.

But no matter which season reigned, coffee remained a constant. And a must.

The fresh, dark aroma of brewing coffee filled the shop, and he inhaled it with unadulterated pleasure. At nine o'clock on a Saturday morning, he needed caffeine like an addict itching for his next hit. It was his one vice. And yes, he got how pathetic and boring that made him.

But considering his father's roaming eye, Jake's wanderlust and Oliver's taste for drugs, he couldn't afford to indulge any. The Lowell men had a proclivity toward addiction, and compared with his father's and brothers', coffee was the least harmful and the only one Joshua could afford.

He glanced down at his watch: 9:11 a.m. Another forty-nine minutes before his mother's doctor's appointment ended, and he had to return to the office and pick her up. Tension tightened his shoulders, and an ache bloomed between them. Deliberately, he inhaled, held the breath and, after ten seconds, released it. The monthly...dammit, not chore. Eve Evans-Janson could never be a chore. Responsibility. As the oldest son, she was his responsibility. But the monthly task of escorting his mother to her doctor always weighed him down like an albatross slung around his neck. Not because he didn't want to be bothered. Never that. He loved Eve, and she'd suffered just as much—if not more—than him and his brothers.

But each visit reminded him of how far she'd deteriorated from the vibrant socialite who'd raised him, loved him and had been his biggest supporter and fan when it'd come to his art. While Vernon hadn't understood and viewed his passion as a passing fancy, his mother had been so proud and celebrated along with him when he'd scored his own gallery show. She'd been his loudest cheerleader.

That woman had disappeared, fifteen years ago, replaced by a quiet, withdrawn recluse who only rarely ventured past the gates of the family's Georgian-style mansion. Her numerous friends had been abandoned and now the butler, maid and chef were her friends. She left the house only for doctor's appointments, the rare appearance at a charity function or the occasions he practically forced her out of the house to go to lunch or dinner with him. Vernon's betrayal had humiliated her. Especially since she'd initially defended him with unshakable faith. When he'd disappeared, she'd believed he might've been kidnapped—or worse. The victim of foul play. But never would he have cheated his clients and friends or stolen from his family and abandoned them to be the recipients of controversy, scorn and pain. Yet, as the days turned into weeks and then months, and the FBI's evidence piled up, Eve had to face the truth—her husband and their father was a criminal who'd bilked millions from those who'd placed their trust in him, then thrown those who'd loved and depended on him the most to the wolves. She'd never recovered.

And now...now he did what he could to ensure she didn't fade away behind the walls that were less her sanctuary and more her prison.

He clenched his fingers into a fist, then purposely relaxed them, exhaling as he did. Dammit, if he had his father here right now, each finger would be wrapped around his neck. Disgust twisted in his chest. If only what he felt toward his father was as simple as anger.

Stepping to the counter, he shoved everything from his mind and focused on ordering. Moments later, with his Americano in hand, he turned toward the entrance, but slammed to a halt.

A petite woman stood next to a table near the huge window, her back toward him, the ends of her unbound hair grazing the tank top–bared skin below her shoulders. The black top molded to the slim line of her back. Dark blue jeans clung to the gentle flare of her hips, the gorgeous tight ass that could be an eighth wonder of the world and legs that could grace a runway and climb the rocky, tough face of a mountain.

An achingly familiar itch tingled in his palms and hands. Familiar and painful. The need to hold a paintbrush. To capture the beauty and strength before him. To immortalize it. His medium had been mixed-media collages, but he'd also loved to paint. And right now he would use bold, rich colors to portray the golden tones of her skin, the power in that tiny body, the larger-than-life vibrancy of her personality, the thick softness of her hair.

That hair.

The thick golden-brown strands reminded him of a mare his father had doted on when Joshua had been a boy. Like raw umber with lighter strands of deep, burnished sunlight. His father had babied that horse, brushing her coat himself until it shined.

A yearning for a return to those idyllic times yawned so wide and deep, Joshua barely managed to restrain his free hand at his side so he wouldn't rub the knot that had formed just below his rib cage.

He could hate her alone for dragging that memory out of the abyss even as he fought against the need to burrow his hands in the wavy mass up to his wrists, fist it, tug on it… Bury his face in it. He already had personal knowledge of how far he would have to bend to inhale her citrus-and-flowers scent. As small as she was, he could completely surround her. Until he met Sophie Armstrong, tall, statuesque women had been his type. But now…now he got the lure of a petite woman he could cover with his bigger body. She triggered a primal, almost animalistic desire in him to take down and conquer her even as he did everything in his power to drown her in pleasure. Not that Sophie would take anything easily. No, he imagined she gave as good as she got in bed as much as she did out…

Molten heat swarmed through him at the thought of holding those slender, strong arms above her head, pressing his chest to her small, firm breasts, having those toned thighs clasping his waist as he drove inside her. She would be so tight, so perfect, damn near strangling his dick.

As if sensing his scrutiny, Sophie glanced over her shoulder and met his gaze. Surprise flickered over her face, her gray eyes widening slightly. He wanted them to do that when he first pushed into her sex. Hungered to see them darken like they did now as she slid a long glance down his body, and he swore he could feel that perusal as if her fingertips brushed over his collarbone, chest, abs, thighs…cock. Blood rushed to his flesh, thickening it behind the zipper of his pants. Hell yes, he wanted that touch on his bare skin, light then hard. Gentle then bruising. Yeah, he wanted this fairy of a woman to mark him.

A frigid blast of ice skated over his skin, digging farther to muscle and bone so he was chilled from the inside out.

Of all the women he could get hard over, Sophie Armstrong, reporter for the *Falling Brook Chronicle*, was the absolute last. Just this morning hadn't he witnessed the evidence of her recent rehashing of the scandal with his father in the creases on his mother's face and in the slump of her stooped shoulders? Haley might have managed to nab the paper before it was delivered to his mother's home, but Eve had overheard the maid and butler talking about it in hushed tones. And she'd demanded to see the paper. Reading that article had taken a toll on her.

So even with Sophie's offer to help him determine if the paternity accusation was true or not, he could never trust her. Could never believe that he wasn't just the means to another juicy story. Who knew what her follow-up article would contain? Why the fuck did he agree to it?

No. Sophie was a threat to his business, his family… to his sanity.

But he'd never been led around by his dick, and he wouldn't start a new trend now.

Still, as her lush mouth curled into a smile, he had to remind his body of that.

He tossed his still-full cup in the trash and crossed the room toward her, because no way in hell would he run from her. Or the need that strung his body so tight. It was a wonder he didn't snap in two at the slightest movement.

"Sophie," he greeted, for the first time thankful for the avaricious media and eyes that forced him to perfect a mask of indifference. He swept a glance over the laptop bag that hung near her hip. "Working?"

"Yes, but from home today. I'm a creature of habit, though. Every morning I stop in here for a coffee and their cinnamon-and-brown-sugar scones. Have you had them yet? They're God's way of saying He loves us."

She released a throaty hum that had his gut clenching. Hard. He wanted to hear it again even as he longed to trap the sound inside her...with his mouth.

Goddammit, he needed to get control. And quick.

"No, I can't say I've had the pleasure," he replied. "I'll take your word for it."

She arched a brow. "Oh, really? That would be a first between us."

"Sheathe your sword, Sophie," he said.

"So you finally admit that you need every bit of help you can muster when going up against me?" she challenged, amusement lighting her eyes like glittering stars.

"I never said I didn't. Only a fool would encounter you and not be battle ready with everything in his arsenal available to him."

She heaved an exaggerated sigh and splayed her fingers wide over her chest. "I do believe that's the nicest thing you've ever said to me."

His wry chuckle caught him by surprise. The last thing he'd ever expected to do with Sophie was laugh. A warning for caution blared in his ears. He couldn't afford to let down his guard, become too comfortable around her.

"What are you doing on this side of town? The coffee here is great, but I've had what you keep at your office and it's pretty good, too."

"I'm not headed to work this morning. I'm waiting for my mother. She has a doctor's appointment right down the street."

She frowned and laid a hand on his lower arm. "I'm sorry. Is she okay?"

For a moment the flare of heat emanating from her touch seared his voice, rendering it useless. She might as well have settled her palm over his dick the way he throbbed and ached.

Gritting his teeth, he ignored the lust coursing through him like a swollen river and said, "Yes. It's just a regular checkup."

"Oh, okay." Her frown deepened for a moment, and it seemed as if she was going to probe further, but in the next instant she skated a quick survey up and down his frame. "So you're not going to the office, but *this* is what you wear on a Saturday morning?"

He didn't bother glancing down to take in the white long-sleeved shirt and black slacks. "Problem?"

She snorted, a smirk flirting with the corners of her lips. "Oh no. No problem at all. I'm just wondering what you wear to bed. An Armani suit? Or maybe a tuxedo."

The humor fled from him, chased away by the desire flaring inside him by the mention of "bed." Hell, she'd reduced him to a fourteen-year-old boy who got hard with the switch of the wind. That didn't stop him from cocking his head to the side and murmuring, "You're wondering what I wear to bed, Sophie? All you have to do is ask."

Slashes of red tinted her cheekbones and her eyes turned to liquid silver. Neither of them spoke as the air hummed with tension, pulsed with an unacknowledged lust volleyed between them. God, he wanted her. Why her—a reporter who sought to paint him as a puppet for his deadbeat father? Would she screw him, then riffle through his drawers to find dirt she could use for the follow-up piece on him and his family?

Something deep inside him objected to that, argued that she wasn't that kind of woman, but this time logic ruled. He'd known too many people who would sooner use him than blink. As a Lowell, men and women looked at him and saw money, connections, information and sometimes a good fuck. But never the man. Never the son struggling to make good and be honorable where his father had failed.

Sophie blinked, the desire clearing from her gaze, and at the same time he edged back a step.

"Pass," she rasped, then, clearing her throat, turned back to her table and gathered up her empty coffee cup, paper plate and plastic fork. "Seriously, though, Joshua," she continued in a stronger voice, that hint of humor returning. "Jeans. Ever heard of them?"

"Sounds familiar," he drawled, following her toward the exit. She dropped her trash in the receptacle and pushed through the coffeehouse door. "What is this sudden fascination with my clothes?"

She laughed as they moved out onto the sidewalk, stepping aside as more customers entered the café. He ignored the curious glances shot their way. After fifteen years, he should be immune to them. But he'd never managed it. They still got under his skin.

"Not your clothes. I'm just curious if you ever relax. If you're ever not Joshua Lowell of the Falling Brook Lowells, CEO of Black Crescent Hedge Fund and just Josh. Does anyone call you that?"

"My brothers did. But it's been a long time," he murmured. *Just Josh.*

There was no such person. Once upon a time there'd been. Josh had been an artist on the precipice of a promising career. He'd been the older brother to Jake and Oliver, who'd been friends as well as brothers. Back before they'd looked on him with scorn and resentment for following in their father's tainted footsteps. Josh had been carefree, laughed often and pursued his passion.

His family and the company wouldn't survive if he reverted to Just Josh.

If he tasted the joy, the life-giving fire of art again, *he* might not survive.

So no, Joshua Lowell, savior and CEO of Black Crescent, was much safer.

Sophie studied him with narrowed eyes, then, slipping the strap of her laptop bag over her head so it crossed her torso, she grabbed his hand in hers and tugged him forward. The shock of her skin touching his reverberated through his body and stunned him long enough that he didn't resist her leading him down the sidewalk. He should pull away from her, cauterize the connection that bled fire into his veins...

He flipped their hands so he enfolded hers, so soft and delicate, in his.

Minutes later, she paused in front of Henrietta's Creamery, the town's only ice-cream shop. He stared at her, confused and more than a little taken aback.

"Ice cream?" he asked, not bothering to eliminate the skepticism from his voice. "At nine thirty in the morning?"

She shook her head and mockingly patted his arm with the hand he wasn't clasping. "See? This right here is what I mean. When is there ever an inappropriate time for ice cream? Joshua, that stick in your ass. Was it surgically implanted, or did it just grow there naturally?"

The bark of laughter abraded his throat, shocking him

as much as her teasing. No one would ever dare to say that to him. Hell, no one would dare to tease him. But this slip of a woman knew no boundaries or fear. From the first, she hadn't been cowed or intimidated by him. And God, it felt good.

"Naturally. And it required effort and a lot of pruning and nurturing," he deadpanned, causing a grin to spread wide over her face. Jesus, she was gorgeous.

"Well, I volunteer as tribute to help you remove it. Starting with an ice-cream cone for breakfast. C'mon." She didn't brook any disagreement but jerked on the door to the shop and entered, pulling him behind her.

After a brief but spirited debate over the best flavors, they walked out with two waffle cones topped with a double scoop of ice cream—salted caramel for him and butter pecan for her.

Him.

Joshua Lowell.

Walking down the sidewalk lining Main Street. Eating an ice-cream cone.

Jesus, how did he get here?

But as Sophie tipped her head back and smiled at him, the light of it reflecting in her beautiful gray eyes, he embraced the moment. Embraced, hell. Hoarded it. In less than half an hour, he would be returning to pick up his mother, and the mantle of responsibility that he'd prematurely donned would fall back around his shoulders. Weighing them down with a pressure that was at times suffocating. Pressing them down with an anger-rimmed sadness that he'd never been able to completely banish no matter how many times he'd told himself that they didn't need his father. That they were better off without him.

Yeah, he was going to embrace this moment and grab on to it selfishly. Because as Joshua Lowell, Vernon's son, he didn't have many. The cost for that kind of greed was too high. As his father's actions had taught him.

"Now, I don't want to say I told you so…" she said, an impish smile curving her lips. "Oh hell, who am I kidding? I *so* do want to say it. I told you so."

"I think you might have held that in for two minutes and twenty-eight seconds," he drawled. "Congratulations."

She twirled her hand in front of her, dipping slightly at the waist. "Thank you. I'll have you know my restraint was hard fought."

He snorted, swiping his tongue through the cold cream and barely managing to contain a moan. When was the last time he'd indulged like this? Years. It'd been years.

"I don't want to alarm you, but people are staring," Sophie informed him in a stage whisper. As if he hadn't already noticed. "One woman just almost rear-ended the car in front of her at the stoplight." She gave a mocking gasp, splaying the fingers not holding the ice-cream cone wide across her chest. "Whatever do you think it could be that they find so interesting?"

Joshua didn't answer, but some of the peace and joy filtered from his chest, replaced by a slick, grimy stain that was a murky mixture of guilt, anger and helplessness. The sludge tracked its way across his chest, down to his gut, where it churned. He deliberately relaxed his grip on the cone but couldn't prevent the clenching of his jaw. A hint of neon-red pain flared along the edge.

"It must be so tiring," Sophie murmured, all notes of teasing evaporated from her tone. He glanced down at her, and those gray eyes looked back at him, warm and velvet with a sympathy he never believed he'd glimpse. At least not for him.

"What must be tiring?" he ground out.

"Feeling like an animal in a zoo. Always being on display," she replied softly.

Her observation struck too deep...too on point. He hated it that she saw it. Hated more that he'd allowed her to.

"Being fodder for any newspaper or online gossip column," he lashed out with a biting coldness that was meant to burn.

She bent her head over her treat and licked a melting trail of ice cream. In spite of the anger knotting his gut, lust slid through him in a thick glide, flowing straight for his already pulsing flesh. He wanted that delicate pink tongue on him. Trailing over him like he was the most delicious thing she'd ever tasted. He hungered to hear her moans of pleasure in his ears, have it vibrate over his skin.

His control was soaked tissue paper when it came to this woman.

"I left the door wide-open on that one," she said long moments later, voice quiet. "I won't apologize for my job—it's an important one, and I love it. But I will say I'm sorry that it's contributed to making you feel as if you were a fish in a bowl. I can't imagine that kind of scrutiny is easy."

"But deserved, some would say." They continued to walk down the sidewalk in a silence taut with tension. Or more specifically, the roil of emotions tumbling inside him. Shoving against his sternum, his throat, seeking an escape. A release. "There are days I believe I deserve it. Give people their due. They need to watch me and make sure I'm not exhibiting signs of becoming Vernon Lowell. They have the right to that transparency. Even years later. Even though—"

Even though there were times he wanted to yell that he wasn't his father. That it wasn't him that had wronged them. It wasn't his fault.

But he couldn't. Because in the end, the sins of the father were visited upon the sons.

In their eyes, as the head of Black Crescent, as the only one available to direct their anger and mistrust at, it was his fault.

And he couldn't argue with them. Because deep inside, in that place that creaked open only in the darkest part of night when he had no energy left to keep it closed, he agreed with them.

Beside him, Sophie sighed and tunneled her fingers through her hair, dragging the strands away from her face and offering him an even more unencumbered view of her clean, elegant profile. A small frown wrinkled the smooth skin between her eyebrows.

"Deserve?" she mused almost to herself. She shook her head. "I don't agree with that. While I do believe in the truth and that people have the right to be aware of events that affect their welfare and lives, they aren't owed pieces of a person's security, peace or soul. Each of us should have the right to privacy, and we don't need anyone's permission to covet it or request it. And this is from a reporter." She lightly snorted, again shaking her head. Pausing, she took another swipe of the ice cream, and her tone became more thoughtful than irritated. "My parents divorced when I was almost thirteen, and it was… Well, *unpleasant* would be an understatement. The nasty arguing and name-calling had been bad enough. But they saw me as an ally to be wooed, a prize to be won in a contest. And they attempted this by competing in who could tell me the foulest, most humiliating things about the other. How my father cheated or how my mother had sent them to the poorhouse with her spending. So many things a child shouldn't be privy to, especially about her parents.

"But they twisted the truth about each other in this acrimonious and desperate need to make the other appear as horrible as possible. Never realizing how they were slowly picking me apart ugly word by ugly word. Because all I heard was how it was my fault they were divorcing. My father cheated. That just meant he was so unhappy at home with me for not doing better in school or being a pest at home that he went somewhere else to find happiness. Or if my mother spent too much money, it was on me because I asked for too much."

She inhaled a breath, and he caught the slight tightening of her hold on the cone. After several seconds, she released a trembling but self-deprecating chuckle.

"Sophie…"

But she interrupted him with a wave of her hand. "No, I know none of that is true. Now, anyway. But back then…" Her voice trailed off, but seconds later, she lifted a slim shoulder in a half shrug. "They made my teenage years hell, but I should thank them. Because of all that, plus the shuffling back and forth to different homes, never feeling truly rooted or secure, I made sure that I would be able to stand on my own two feet as an adult. That no one would ever have the power or ability to ever rip the rug out from under me again. They also directed me on the path to my career. They fueled my desire to filter facts from half-truths or fiction. And, when it was called for, to shield the innocent from it."

He digested that in silence. "Which is why you didn't print the rumors about me having a daughter in the article," he added.

She nodded, not looking at him. "Yes. I know what you think of me, Joshua, but I wouldn't deliberately smear someone's name or hurt them. Not without all the facts that can be backed up and confirmed beyond doubt. Am I perfect? No. But I try to be."

He licked the melting ice cream in his hand, warring within himself about how much he could share with Sophie. Why he *shouldn't* share. But after her baring some of her chaotic childhood, he owed her. Still...

"Off the record?" he murmured.

She jerked her gaze to him, and in the dove-gray depths he easily caught the surprise. And the flicker of irritation. As if annoyed that he'd ask. But as lovely as she was, as honest as she'd been with him, he couldn't forget who she was. *What* she was.

"Of course," she said, none of the contrasting emotions in her eyes reflected in her voice.

"Of course," he repeated softly, staring down at her. *What the hell are you doing?* he silently questioned his sanity, but then said, "I deserve their censure because of my life before my father decided to screw us all six ways to Sunday. Mine was charmed. I won't say perfect, because in hindsight, it wasn't. Nothing is. But for me, it was close. My brothers and I—we didn't have to want for anything. Not material, financial or emotional. Dad was always busy building Black Crescent into one of the foremost hedge funds, but Mom? She'd been there, attentive, supportive, loving. We weren't raised by an army of servants, even though we did have them. But Mom—and even Dad to an extent—had been involved. We attended one of the most exclusive and premier prep schools in the country and, later, Ivy League universities. I knew who I was and what I wanted to be. I never had doubts back then. I held the world in my palm and harbored no insecurities or fears that I could have it all."

"I always wondered about that," Sophie said, that intuitive and insightful gaze roaming his face. "If you faced any backlash or disapproval from your father for choosing art over the family business."

Why the hell am I talking about this? He never discussed his art or his career ambitions. A pit gaped in his chest, stretching and threatening to swallow him whole with the grief, disillusionment and sense of failure that poured out. Those dreams were dead and buried with a headstone to mark the grave.

Forcing the memories and the words past his tightening throat, he barely paused next to a garbage can and pitched his cone into it. He couldn't talk about this and even consider eating. Not with his gut forming a rebellion at just the unlocking of the past.

"From my mother, no. Like I said, she supported me from the very first. When I was a child, she enrolled me in art classes, encouraged me to continue even when my father scoffed at it or dismissed my interest as a passing fancy. But art was...my passion. My true friend, in ways. Growing up in Falling Brook, we had to be careful about image, about never forgetting we were Vernon Lowell's sons and Eve Evans-Janson's sons. There was a trade-off for the life of privilege we led, and that was perfection. But with art? I never had to be perfect. Or careful. I just had to be me. I didn't have to curtail my opinions to make sure I didn't offend anyone or reflect on my father. I could be unfailingly and unapologetically honest. I could trust it more than anything or anyone else."

A vise squeezed his chest so hard, so tight, his ribs screamed for relief. Just talking about that part of him he'd willingly—but without choice—amputated brought ghostly echoes of the joy, the freedom he'd once experienced every time he took a picture, picked up a piece of metal, lifted a paintbrush...

He shook them off, shoving them in the vault of his past and locking the door. If he were going to discuss that part of him, of his life, he had to separate himself from the emotion behind it. Besides, that was who he'd been. That man had ceased to exist the moment his father had gone on the lam, leaving his family and ten others broke and broken.

"But to answer your question, there wasn't any strife. More so because I believe Dad thought I would indulge in art, get it out of my system and then come work for Black Crescent. Even when I scored my first gallery show the summer after I graduated from college, Dad was pleased for me, but he also told me I had a choice to make and he hoped I chose wisely. 'Wisely' being coming into the business with him."

Had his father known even then that he would be going on the run? Had he already planned his escape plan? Because only two months after that conversation, he'd disappeared.

"While researching the article, I always thought that was amazing. Do you know how many artists are capable of getting their own gallery shows so soon in their careers? But then again, I saw pictures of your work. God, you were phenomenal," she breathed.

The unadulterated awe in her voice snagged on something inside him, jerking and tugging as if trying to bring that ephemeral and elusive "thing" to the surface to be acknowledged and analyzed. He shrank from it. Not in the least bit ready to do that.

He never would be.

"Can I ask you something? And disclaimer—it's going to be intrusive," she said, dumping her cone into a nearby trash can before slipping a sidelong glance at him. When he dipped his chin in agreement, she murmured, "How could you step away from it? I'm just thinking of how I would feel if I suddenly lost my career. Or if I couldn't do it anymore. And not just reporting, but my purpose. Empty. And lost. How could you give it up so easily?"

"Easily?" His harsh burst of laughter scraped his throat raw. "There was nothing easy about it, Sophie. I had a choice to make. Family or a career in art." Leave, move to New York to escape the judgment and condemnation and pursue his passion, or stay and save his family and the business. Try to repair what his father had torn apart. Even when Jake had done just that, Josh had stayed. And there'd been nothing simple or easy about that decision. "In the end my father had been right. I would have to choose, and I did. Not that it'd been much of one. I couldn't abandon my family."

Not like him remained unspoken but deafening in the silence that followed his words.

"I'm sorry," she whispered.

He slipped his tightly curled fists into the pockets of his slacks. "For what?" he rasped.

"For assuming it'd been an easy decision. That you had to make it in the first place."

He drew to an abrupt halt, absently thankful they'd made it to the parking lot at the far end of Main where his car waited. Thankful no one loitered in the area, and that for once, they were away from prying eyes.

No one—no *fucking* one—had ever said that to him. Had ever thought to consider the cost of his sacrifice, the effect of it on him. And no one had ever thanked him or sympathized that he'd given up the best part of him to take care of family. A family in which two of its members resented him for making that choice.

Alone. Here, in this parking lot, partially insulated from the public that had judged him so harshly, the remnants of the past clinging to him like skeletal fingers, he could admit that for fifteen years, he'd been so damn alone.

That choice had cost him the closeness he'd once shared with his brothers. It'd stolen the plugged-in mother from his youth. The so-called friends he'd believed he had. Most of all, it'd left him bereft of his dreams and—how had she described it?—empty.

Yes. Empty.

But in this space, in this fleeting moment, he didn't. With this woman, with her silken skin, molten eyes and temptress mouth, he felt...seen. And it sent heat rushing through him like air caught in a wind tunnel—loud, powerful and threatening to rip him apart. He edged his feet apart, slightly widening his stance as if bracing himself against the overwhelming longing to touch, to hold, to *connect*.

He lifted his hand to brush his fingertips over her delicate jaw, waiting, no, expecting, her to wrench away from him to avoid his caress.

She didn't. Sophie stood still, her headed tilted back, gaze centered on him. She didn't flinch from him. Didn't question what the hell he was doing. No, those sweet lips parted on a soft gasp that went straight to his dick, grazing it.

Locking down a groan behind clenched teeth, he shifted closer, turning slightly to shield her from any curious spectators. A thick cocoon of desire might be enfolding them, but it didn't erase the fact that they stood off Main Street. But where minutes ago that would've prevented him from lowering his head over hers, moving nearer still until his chest pressed against hers and his thighs cradled the slim length of hers, more than ever, he was aware of the disparity in their heights and frames. His body nearly covered her, and the top of her head just barely skimmed his chin. The surge of lust sweeping through his veins, lighting them like an SOS flare, competed with the urge to protect. The impulse to conquer warred with the need to shelter. But instead of being torn in two by the opposing instincts, they melded, mating. Assuring him he could do both. That, by God, he *should* do both.

His fingers continued to explore her jaw, her cheek, the thinner skin over her temple, the slope of her nose in spite of the lust baying in his head like howling dogs. He followed the graceful arches of her eyebrows before traveling back down to trace the upper curve of her mouth, linger in the shallow dip in the middle. Then, he moved to that plumper bottom lip, savoring the soft give of it under his fingertips. He didn't offer just his thumb the treat of it. All his fingertips got in on the pleasure of the caress.

Her breath hitched, and again he fought back a moan at the gentle gust of air against his suddenly overly sensitive skin. Words crowded at the back of his throat.

Tell me I can have this temptation of a mouth that has woken me up, hard and hurting, for days now.

Will you let me fuck this mouth, Sophie? Will you let me defile it so you can taste the dirtiness of my kiss for days? Weeks?

But he didn't utter them. Instinct warned him that breaking this lust-drenched and pulsing silence with any sound would rip this opportunity away from him. Shatter the cords that held them here in this moment—cords that shimmered with heat but were as fragile as glass.

He'd hungered for this chance for too long. Battled himself over it too hard to abdicate it.

So, instead, he planted his thumb in the middle of the bottom curve, pressed until the tip of his finger grazed the edges of her teeth. When she didn't draw away from him but tilted her head forward to lean into the pressure, he shuddered.

And when she parted those beautiful lips and flicked her tongue over his flesh, he had his answer.

Not bothering to trap his groan in this time, he dipped

NAIMA SIMONE   87

his head and took her. Releasing the greedy sound into
her mouth, replacing his thumb with the slick glide of his
tongue.

God, the taste of her.

Sweet like the butter-pecan ice cream she'd been eating. Sultry like air thick and perfumed after a spring rain.
Heady like a shot of whiskey. Deliciously wicked. Like sex.

With hands going rough with greed, he burrowed one
into her hair, fisting the strands and tugging. Tugging until
her mouth was right where he wanted it...needed it. Her
swallowed her small whimper, giving her a growl in return as she opened wider for him. Granting him entrance
to her. To heaven.

He thrust between those beautiful lips, tangling his
tongue with hers, dancing, dueling. Because Sophie wasn't
a passive participant. Just as she challenged him in his office, in a newspaper conference room or a gym, she gave
as good as she got here, as well. She sucked and licked,
stroking into his mouth to demand and take.

His grip on her hair and hip tightened, dragging her
closer, impossibly closer. His hips punched forward,
grounding his erection against the softness of her belly.
Fire ripped a scorching path up his spine, then back down
to his dick. Jesus, she was about to set him off like a teenager copping his first feel behind the gym bleachers. Cocking his head, he delved deeper, a desperate hunger for more
digging into him. One nip of her lips, one sample of her
taste, and he was hooked, ravenous for more.

"Josh," she breathed against his damp lips. Hearing
the abbreviated version of his name had his flesh hardening further, had him aching. And he couldn't not reward her—hell, thank her—with another drugging kiss
and roll of his hips.

The ring of a phone shattered the thick haze of lust that enclosed them.

He lifted his head, the air in his lungs ragged and harsh. She stared up at him, those storm-gray eyes clouded with the same desire coursing through him like electrified currents. Her swollen mouth, wet from his tongue, glistened, and he'd lowered his head, submitting to the sensual beckoning of them when the peal of the phone jangled again.

Dammit.

Disentangling his hands from her hair and releasing the sweet curve of her hip, he stepped back, reaching in his pocket for his silent cell phone. At the same time, Sophie retrieved hers from the front pocket of her bag. Tapping the screen, she held the cell to her ear.

"Hi, Althea," she said, her gaze meeting his for a second before she turned away. Althea Granger, the editor in chief of the *Falling Brook Chronicle*. Her boss. "Yes, that's not a problem. Has anyone else picked up the story yet?"

A frigid deluge of water crashed over him in a wave.

For moments, he'd felt young again. Free again. He'd allowed himself to forget who Sophie was. Who he was. But reality had a way of slapping the hell out of a person and reminding him that life wasn't hand-holding and ice-cream cones or kissing a beautiful woman. It was hard, sometimes grueling work, disappointment and constantly brushing off scraped knees and bruised hands to get up and face it again.

He could still taste the unique and addictive flavor of her on his lips, his tongue. But he couldn't let Sophie Armstrong in. And her being a reporter was just one reason. A very good reason to keep his distance from her, but not the only one.

When Vernon had left, he'd broken his ability to trust. And his brothers had trampled on the pieces on their way out of Falling Brook. Even his mother had abandoned him. Not physically, but definitely emotionally. When he loved people, when he let them in, they left. They eventually abandoned him.

They eventually devastated him.

No, he couldn't trust Sophie. Leaving himself vulnerable again came at too high a price. And he had nothing left to pay it with.

"Okay, I'll head to the office now. See you in a few." Sophie ended the call and faced him again. "Sorry about that." She cleared her throat, twin flags of pink staining the slants of her cheekbones. Left over from their kiss— if that was what that clash of mouths, tongues and teeth could be labeled—or from the phone call. "I need to go into work for a few hours."

"I heard," he said, deliberately infusing a sheet of ice into his voice. As if just seconds ago it hadn't been razed to hell by lust. He glanced down at his watch. "That's fine. I have to leave, too." While he'd been taking her mouth, time had raced by, and he was due to pick up his mother in five minutes. But the errand was just a handy excuse to put distance between him and Sophie. Because in spite of his resolve and the reminder of why he couldn't become involved with her, he still had to threaten himself with self-harm to avoid staring at her mouth like a marauding beast. "Have a good weekend, Sophie."

Not waiting on her reply, he pivoted on his heel and strode back in the direction they'd come. And if that cloak of loneliness settled across his shoulders again, well, it was preferable to pain.

Preferable to betrayal.

And Sophie smacked of both.

Six

Sophie wove a path among the many businessmen, socialites, philanthropists and even a handful of celebrities crowded into the Ronald O. Perelman Rotunda of the Guggenheim Museum in Manhattan. The annual Tender Shoots Art Gala brought all the tristate area's glitterati out in support of the New York–based arts program.

Taking a sip of her cocktail, she dipped her head in a shallow nod at a woman whose diamond necklace and ruby-red strapless gown could probably pay off the entirety of Sophie's student loans. She held her head up, meeting the assessing gaze of every person she had eye contact with. Or maybe it just felt assessing to her. As if they were attempting to peer beneath the expertly applied makeup and strapless, glittery, floor-length dress that she'd needed a crowbar and a prayer to squeeze into in order to determine if she belonged.

Well, at an invite-only event that required fifteen thousand a plate fee plus a hefty donation for entrance, she didn't belong. She'd grown up in Falling Brook, one of the most exclusive, wealthiest communities along the Eastern Seaboard, but her family had been among the few middle-class residents who either owned businesses in town or worked for Falling Brook Prep, the independent K–twelve school. The kind of excess and luxury represented in the grand, open space surrounded by the spiral-ramped architecture capped by a gorgeous skylight exceeded her imagination and bank account. Thank God, Althea's partner was a stylist who had let Sophie borrow a designer gown for the night. And didn't that just increase the surreal feeling of Cinderella attending the ball before her carriage turned back into a pumkin that had filled her since stepping onto the curb outside the famous museum?

If not for Althea receiving an invitation because of the paper's piece about the event, the organization and the underprivileged youth it benefited, Sophie would be home, catching up on season two of *The Handmaid's Tale*. But since it'd been Sophie's article that had garnered the invite, Althea had convinced her to accept and attend. She should be grateful and flattered. But while she had no problem reporting on the country's wealthy elite, she drew a line at socializing with them. It reminded her too much of a time in her life when she'd been blinded by their world and the man she'd once loved who'd belonged to it.

Too bad she hadn't remembered not to cross that line that morning with Joshua Lowell.

A convoluted mixture of embarrassment, self-directed anger and a relentless, aching need jumbled and twisted deep inside her. Just thinking of how he'd cupped her jaw, gently caressed her face and then claimed her mouth had her shouting obscenity-laced reprimands at herself...even as she pressed her thighs together to fruitlessly attempt to stifle the throbbing ache in her sex. And all that led to her embarrassment. The man had sexed her mouth, then walked away from her without a backward glance. As if that devastation of a kiss hadn't affected him at all. If not for the insistent, commanding grind of his thick erection against her belly, she would've believed he hadn't been.

But no matter that he'd moaned into her mouth and had granted her a clear premonition of what it would be like to be controlled and branded by that big, wide-shoul-dered body, he *had* transformed from the approachable, almost vulnerable man who'd strolled down Main Street with her, licking ice cream in a way that had her sex ready to throw itself at his feet, to an iceberg who'd dismissed her as if their connection had been of no consequence. As if *she* were of no consequence. And hell, maybe to him, she wasn't.

Staring down into the glass, she didn't see the pale gold champagne but his shuttered expression and flat stare as she'd ended her phone call. A shiver ran through her, as if the ice that had entered that measured inspection skated over her exposed skin now. She didn't believe in deluding herself; she acknowledged that it'd been Althea's call that had changed him. He'd no doubt suddenly been reminded of what they were to one another. She was the woman who had dragged the darkest, most scandalous parts of his his-tory back out, dusted them off and planted them on the front page of the newspaper for public consumption. Again.

Half of her was surprised he hadn't asked her if that kiss was off the record. Despite her best efforts, her lips twisted into a slight sneer. As if she'd treat him to an ice-cream cone just to butter him up for a scoop—no pun in-tended. Screw it. That pun was totally intended.

Smothering a sigh, she lifted her fluted glass to her lips

and sipped. At least this gala provided one purpose. Distract her from thoughts of—

Joshua.

Her gaze locked with a beautiful and all too familiar pair of hazel eyes. Lust gut-punched her like a prizefighter with a penchant for ear biting. If not for her locked knees and sheer grit not to humiliate herself in the four-inch stilettos, the blow would've knocked her on her ass. Beneath the bandage-style bodice of her dress, her nipples drew into taut, pebbled points begging for just a whisper of a caress from those long, blunt-tipped fingers. Pinpricks of electricity rippled up and down her exposed spine, sizzling in the base of her spine. And her feminine flesh... She stifled a needy and shameful moan. Her flesh swelled, damp and sensitive from just a hooded glance from those green-and-gold and way too perceptive eyes.

Good God, had she conjured him with her own wayward thoughts?

"Ms. Armstrong?" a low, cultured voice called her name, and Sophie yanked her scrutiny away from Joshua. A tall, powerfully built and handsome man stood next to her. Black hair waved back from a high forehead, emphasizing a face with strong facial features, a full, sensual mouth and intense blue eyes. He smiled, flashing perfect white teeth. "You are Sophie Armstrong, correct?" he asked, extending a large hand toward her.

"Yes," she replied, accepting the hand. He squeezed it lightly before releasing it. "I'm sorry, do we know one another?"

"No, we haven't officially met. But I've followed your career these past few years from Chicago to the *Falling Brook Chronicle*. I'm a fan of your journalistic style. Most recently, I enjoyed the pieces you wrote on the Tender Shoots Arts Council as well as the one on the Black Crescent scandal. Considering the topic and the many times it's been reported on, I thought you wrote an objective, well-researched article. Especially about Joshua Lowell and his former art career. I don't think many people remember the accomplished artist he was and the potential career he once had."

Accomplished artist he is.

The words burned on her tongue. No one with the kind of talent she'd seen in his work or whose voice contained the passion his had while describing what art had meant to him could turn off the God-given gift he'd been blessed with. Joshua might be the CEO of his father's company, but now more than ever after this morning's conversation with him, she was convinced the artist who'd created such awe-inspiring, magnificent pieces of art still existed beneath those expensive, perfectly tailored suits.

"Thank you. I appreciate the compliment, Mr...." She trailed off. The man still hadn't given her his name.

A half smile quirked one corner of his mouth. "Christopher Harrison. I'm one of the organizers of the gala and on the board of trustees for the Tender Shoots Arts Council."

"Mr. Harrison." She nodded. "It's a pleasure to meet you."

"Christopher, please. The pleasure is mine." He crooked an arm and held it out to her. "Can I escort you into dinner? I believe we're sitting at the same table."

A little bemused, she settled her hand in the bend of his elbow. "I'm sitting at your table?" she repeated, unable to keep out the edge of incredulity.

He chuckled. "I confess to using my position with the organization to finagle a favor and moving your seat." He shrugged, but nothing about him said *repentant*. "It's one of the perks of the job."

"Do I need to be worried about why you want my company at your table?" she mused, part of her amused, but the other part wary. Years ago, another sophisticated, handsome man had approached her at a function. And his motives had been anything but pure. Too bad that by the time she'd figured that out, he'd nearly devastated her heart and her integrity. Old suspicions died hard.

Speaking of suspicions...

The charged tingle dancing across the nape of her neck informed her where Joshua stood. And she directed her glance in that direction. Immediately, his hazel gaze snared hers. Burning into hers. For a second, it released her to flicker to the man guiding her through the throng of people. Even across the distance, she caught the firming of his full lips, the darkening of his eyes. And when he returned his narrowed scrutiny to her, the fire in them seared over her exposed skin.

She sucked in a breath, jerking her head forward. Because she needed to pay attention to where her feet and the man next to her were taking her.

Not because she could no longer stand meeting that slightly ominous stare that had heat spiking in her body like she'd transformed into a thermometer.

At least that was what she told herself. As she settled at one of the tables closest to the dais erected at the far end of the rotunda, she continued to remind herself of that. And even as the electrified crackle hummed under her skin, she refused to allow her attention to slip toward the table to her right. Joshua Lowell was just a man. Yes, a beautiful, imposing man who wore a tuxedo as if it'd been created with the sole purpose of adorning that tall, powerful body. A complicated man who was like a puzzle missing several pieces. Pieces she wanted to hunt down and fit into the empty spaces so she could determine who he really was. The arrogant, commanding CEO with the icy reserve? Or the passionate artist who revealed tantalizing glimpses of vulnerability and kissed like he could consume a woman whole and make her beg him to take more?

He's a man who wants revenge because of the story you wrote on him and his family. A man who denies the existence of his child and is using you to control if you reveal it or not.

Or maybe one who just desperately sought to discover if he truly had a daughter that he'd known nothing about?

Jesus, she was arguing with herself. It was official. Joshua—or this unwarranted and dangerous fascination with him—was driving her nuts.

That same fascination had her casting a glance to the neighboring table. She was a masochist. There was no other explanation. And yet, she found herself once more helplessly ensnared by a copper-and-emerald stare as she'd been in the reception area.

Flayed. That was what that intense, gorgeous and entirely too-perceptive scrutiny did to her. Leave her flayed, open and exposed. Did he see the dueling emotions he stirred in her—the desire for distance, to borrow some of that renowned aloofness, and the desire to feel the intimidating thick length of him again. Not against her stomach this time, but inside her. Stretching her. Marking her.

The woman next to Joshua, a stunning redhead in a black sequined dress that screamed couture, leaned into him, whispering in his ear. He turned to her, releasing Sophie from their visual showdown.

A shaft of…something hot and ugly pierced her chest. She couldn't identify it. *Wouldn't* identify it. Because it wasn't jealousy. The woman, with the onyx jewels dripping from her ears and encircling her neck, belonged to his world. They were perfect for each other.

"Do you know Joshua?" Christopher's question yanked

NAIMA SIMONE   97

her from the rabbit hole that she'd been in the process of
tumbling down. She met his curious gaze. Saw when it
flickered toward the other table and Joshua and returned
to her. "Are you two acquainted?"

"God, no," she denied with a small deprecating chuckle.
Not a lie, exactly. She doubted anyone really *knew* Joshua
Lowell. And something whispered that he preferred it that
way. "I just wrote an article on one of the darkest periods in
his and his family's lives. I'm sure he's not a fan of mine."

"Hmm." Christopher studied her, and she refused to
fidget beneath that assessing regard. "I can understand
that, I guess. Although, like I mentioned earlier, all things
considered, it was a fair piece." He lifted a glass of wine
and sipped from it, continuing to study her over the rim.
"He's one of our major contributors to the nonprofit. Not
surprising, really, with his own background in art."

Yes, she could see that. He might not create pieces anymore but imagining him pouring financial support into
the lives of underprivileged youth so they might have the
advantages of following the path he'd walked away from
wasn't hard.

Still… She glanced over at one of the walls where numerous canvases, pen-and-ink drawings and framed photographs hung. The oversize, mixed-media collages that
used to be Joshua's trademark would seamlessly fit in here.
Did he ever wish they were? Did he ever dream of walking into this famed museum and seeing his pieces adorning these off-white walls?

Did it cause him pain to attend a gala celebrating art
knowing he couldn't have this? Knowing others were doing
what he'd been created to do?

She forced herself not to look at Joshua this time. Afraid
she would see what she wanted to instead of who he really
was. Maya Angelou had said, "When someone shows you

who they are, believe them the first time." That day she'd barged into his office, he'd shown her the ruthless, dismissive and cold businessman. She needed to remember that, brand that image into her mind so when she started to visualize more—a sensitive, burdened man who grieved all that he'd lost—she'd shut that down.

And if that didn't work, remember Laurence Danvers. Remember how she'd spectacularly crashed and burned by almost choosing a man over her career, over her ethics. She'd paid for those errors in judgment, for her willing blindness.

Never again, though.

Returning her attention to Christopher, she finished dinner with a smile and surprisingly entertaining conversation. Charismatic and funny, he effortlessly charmed her, and when the dishes were cleared and the guests headed back toward the reception area for dancing and more cocktails, she accepted his invitation to join him out on the dance floor.

Tilting her head back, she smiled up at him. "Not that I doubt you could enjoy my company, but, call it a reporter's intuition, I just have the sense you didn't seek me out because of my smile. Or this dress. As gorgeous as it may be."

He grinned, his fingers tightening around her fingers. "It is that, but not as beautiful as the woman wearing it." When she arched an eyebrow, he tipped his head back, laughing. And drawing the attention of the couples swaying to the jazz music along with them. "Your reputation for a no-nonsense investigative journalist is well earned, Sophie Armstrong. I did have an ulterior motive when I approached you this evening."

"I'm waiting."

"Our nonprofit is always seeking out new ways to bring in donations and media coverage that will result in even more donations. Funding and philanthropic gifts are this organization's lifeblood," he said, the humor evaporating from his voice and the intensity that had radiated from him since their initial meeting intensified. "I read your article on the Lowell family and Black Crescent. But my particular interest in the piece was the attention placed on Joshua Lowell. The artist submerged, if I remember correctly. It started me thinking. What if the artist reemerged? Returned to the world where he once stood on the cusp of a promising career? Can you imagine the stir and the money that would bring to Tender Shoots?"

Against her will, excitement kindled in her chest. Yes, she could imagine this. All too easily. Maybe not if she hadn't walked along a sidewalk with him and caught the embers of a deliberately banked passion in his eyes, in his words. But Christopher was correct on all accounts. Joshua returning to the art world would be huge—for both the nonprofit and him.

"I agree it would benefit all involved," she replied vaguely. "But what does it have to do with me?"

"I have an admission to make, Sophie," he said, and unlike his playful confession earlier about the seating arrangements, this one caused an unsettling dip in her stomach. "After the article in the *Falling Brook Chronicle*, I researched you. I believe you, more than anyone, can appreciate the need to protect my sources, but despite telling me earlier that you didn't know him, I discovered you were spotted in Joshua Lowell's company several times."

She remained silent, not confirming or denying. But her heart thundered against her rib cage. Though there'd been nothing untoward or illicit about their meetings— *don't even* think *about the kiss!*—just the perception of conflict of interest could be detrimental to her reputation and career. Her original instinct to be wary around Christopher deepened, and she schooled her features into a polite but distant mask.

"I can guess what you're assuming, Sophie, and you're wrong," he murmured, voice gentling. "I don't intend to accuse you of anything or use my information against you or him."

"Then what are your intentions?" she demanded.

"I need your help in convincing him to consider a showing next year. Just because of who he is—the CEO of Black Crescent Hedge Fund—but also because of how he walked away from what critics had predicted to be an important art career."

Before he finished speaking, Sophie was already shaking her head. "I don't know why you'd think I possess the influence to convince Joshua Lowell to do anything, but—"

"Because I've seen how he hasn't been able to tear his gaze off you all evening. And how you've pretended not to notice—when you haven't been staring back at him," he interrupted. "Tell me I'm wrong."

Her pulse was a deafening beat in her ears, in her blood. "You're wrong," she rasped. And hated that her voice held the consistency of fresh-out-the-package sandpaper. "We barely know each other. And even if we were…more acquainted, Joshua Lowell has buried that side of himself. And it would take much more than a few words from me to resurrect it." *But what if there was a chance for him to discover his passion again?* She waved the hand that'd been resting on Christopher's shoulder. To dismiss his request or her own thoughts? Both applied. And anyway, it wasn't her business. Joshua wasn't her business. "I'm sorry, Christopher. I've enjoyed your company tonight, but your efforts on me were wasted. What you're looking for is a miracle, and unfortunately, I'm not in that market."

NAIMA SIMONE
101

A sardonic smile curved a corner of his mouth, although his gaze on her remained sharp. Too sharp. "Okay, Sophie. But, if you please, just think about what I'm asking. And if one day you do find yourself in the position to carry influence with him, I and my organization would appreciate it if you would broach the possibility of a show with him. It would help so many students and could very well affect lives."

"Really?" she drawled. "The change-lives card? You're pulling out the big guns."

He chuckled, squeezing her fingers. "I'm nothing if not persistent and shameless."

Thankfully, he dropped the subject. But after their dance ended and she strolled off the crowded floor, a weariness crept over her. She was ready to call it an evening and moved across the room, removing her cell from her purse to place a call to the car service that had picked her up and dropped her off here hours ago. Accepting her thin wrap from the coat check minutes later, she stepped out into the warm May evening. Sounds and scents of the City That Never Sleeps echoed around her—honks, voices carried in the night, exhaust from the passing traffic and the frenetic energy that popped and crackled in the air. There'd been a time when she'd believed her future lay in New York or a busy city like it. But Falling Brook, with its slower pace and smaller population, was home, and she wouldn't want to live anywhere else.

"Leaving so early?"

She shivered as the deep, dark timbre of the voice that held a hint of gravel rolled over her. Vibrated within her. Tightening the wrap around her shoulders, she glanced at Joshua. Several inches separated them, but the distance meant nothing with that stare blazing down at her. Lighting her up. Pebbling her nipples. Wetting the insides of her thighs. Another tremble worked its way through her, and those narrowed eyes didn't miss her reaction.

"Are you cold?" he asked, already slipping out of his tuxedo jacket. The relief coursing through her that he'd misperceived the source of that shiver stripped her of her voice. But Joshua didn't need her answer. He shifted closer and draped the garment over her shoulders. Immediately, his delicious sandalwood-and-rain scent enveloped her, surrounded her as effectively as if it were his arms warming her instead of his jacket.

"Thank you," she finally said, mentally wincing at the hoarseness of her tone.

He nodded. A valet approached them, and Joshua handed him a slip of paper. After the young man strode away, Joshua returned his regard to her, sliding his hands into his pants pockets. "You're ending the evening before it's over?" he rumbled. "Did Christopher Harrison say or do something to make you uncomfortable enough to leave?"

"No," she said, adding a sharp head shake for emphasis. "He was fine. I'm just...tired. And I have a forty-five-minute ride ahead of me. So I'm getting a head start."

"You're driving?"

"Althea arranged a car service for me."

He didn't reply, but the full, sensual curves of his mouth tightened at the corners. He'd had a similar reaction to her editor in chief's name earlier today. As if he resented the sound of it.

"What are you doing out here?" she asked, glancing over her shoulder in the direction of the museum. "From what I saw, you seemed to be having a good time."

And by "good time" she meant the statuesque, gorgeous redhead he'd been seated next to at dinner. The ear whisperer. When she'd left the reception area for the coat check, Sophie had been unable to not take note of Joshua. And he'd stood on the rim of the dance floor, the other woman plastered to his side closer than ninety-nine was to a hundred. God, she sounded bitchy to her own self.

"Were you watching me, Sophie?" he murmured, that dark-as-sin voice dipping lower, stroking her skin in a smoky caress.

"Were you watching me, Joshua?" she volleyed back, just as quietly.

They stared at one another, the challenge they'd lobbied between them vibrating. The air thickened, taut with the tension emanating from their bodies.

"Come home with me."

The request edged with demand struck her in the chest. She locked her knees, but that only prevented her from falling onto her ass. It didn't prevent her mentally wheeling and sprawling in shock. She blinked up at him, felt her eyes widening, and her lips parted on a gasp she couldn't contain.

"What?" she breathed.

"Come home with me," he repeated in that slightly impatient tone that hummed with notes of frustration, anger and even surprise. But not directed at her. Through her rapidly ebbing surprise, she suspected all that emotion was aimed at himself. "I'll take you back to Falling Brook, but come home with me first. We need a place where we can talk openly...privately."

"About what?" she questioned, her heart racing for and nestling in her throat.

"About business that is just between us," he replied, purposefully vague, she suspected. Here, in front of the Guggenheim and anyone walking the Manhattan streets, he wouldn't be more specific than that.

She studied him, her grip tight on her sequined clutch.

Alone with Joshua. For possibly hours. Her mind—and common sense—balked. Absolutely not. The last time they'd been together, within feet of Main Street, he'd shown her the real purpose of her mouth. To mate with his. What would happen without the chance of prying eyes catching them? Without the constraints of being in public? He would probably be able to maintain his intimidating control, but her? She wouldn't advise any Vegas high rollers place bets on her. This man was proving to be her weakness, the chink in her professional and personal armor, and getting close enough to let him chip away more was lunacy.

Yet... She stared into his eyes. And almost glanced away from the coolness there. But at the last second, she looked deeper. And caught the shadows of need, of...loneliness. Both echoed within her, and something inside her reacted to them. Reached for them. For him.

Instinctively, she stepped back and away from him. To protect herself. But not from him. Herself. It'd been this same longing to soothe, to please, to be loved that had led her down the wrong path before. With Laurence, she'd been blind. But now, her eyes were wide-open to who and what Joshua was. And if she traveled this road, she would have only herself to blame for the catastrophic results to her career, her integrity, her heart. And God, she harbored zero doubts he would decimate her heart, leaving not even ashes behind.

"Come with me, Sophie," he murmured, holding out a hand to her as the valet pulled to the curb in a sleek black sports car that even her limited knowledge identified as an Aston Martin.

She stared at that palm with fascination, yearning and trepidation. Yes, she wanted him—what was the point in lying about the plain, bald-faced truth? But her body didn't rule her. Not anymore. If he intended to discuss her help on the paternity issue, they definitely couldn't do it out here on the sidewalk where anyone could overhear. And, her inner reporter chimed in, if he went off the record with her before, maybe he would agree to going back on and be willing to let her get that interview he'd denied her for the original story. Her deadline for the follow-up article was fast approaching.

And maybe she was just trying to justify her reasons for unwisely accepting his invite.

"Okay," she said quietly, slipping her hand over his and locking down the shiver that wanted to ripple through her as his fingers wrapped around hers. "But just for a couple of hours."

He nodded, his intense perusal scanning her face, then dipping down her body before returning to her eyes. Without a word, he escorted her to his waiting car. Within moments, she was tucked against the sinfully luxurious leather seat with Joshua behind the wheel. When he pulled away from the curb and merged with the moderate traffic, she couldn't help but admire the expert manner in how he handled the vehicle. A begrudging but warm throb settled just under her navel. If the man wielded such control over this four-thousand-pound rocket, how much would he exert in other places? Or... What would he look like if he loosened the reins on it?

Not my business, she informed herself with a mental sneer. Turning her attention to her phone, she called the car service back and canceled her ride. Then she settled back against the seat for the forty-five-minute ride back to Falling Brook. Other than asking her if the air was too cold and if she was comfortable, they barely uttered a word. But it didn't matter. The screaming tension crowded into the car with them did most of the speaking.

By the time he guided the car into the underground parking lot of a tall brick apartment building, she practically vibrated with the strain of fighting the desire coiled so tight within her and pretending as if he didn't affect her. Business. This was about the article. About their side investigation. She could keep it professional, because that was who she was.

Pep talk delivered, she didn't wait for him to round the car and open the door, but pushed it open herself and exited. He wouldn't open doors for his colleagues at Black Crescent, so he shouldn't for her, either.

Coward. You just don't want him any closer than necessary.

She flipped her inner know-it-all the finger.

And if she stiffened but didn't shift away from the broad hand he settled at the small of her back, well... She just didn't want to be rude.

Joshua led her to an elevator, and soon they were alighting from it into a huge apartment that could've fit her whole childhood home inside. She couldn't trap the gasp that escaped from her. Just as the charity event had exposed her to another level of wealth and luxury, so did his place.

Gleaming and pristine floor-to-ceiling windows that offered an unhindered and gorgeous view of Falling Brook and beyond. A king surveying his kingdom. The impression whispered through her head, and she had to agree. Shaking her head, she moved farther into the foyer, taking in the rest of his space. An open floor plan that allowed each room to flow seamlessly into the next. A sunken living room, freestanding fireplace, dining room with a table large enough to fit a large family with no trouble, a large kitchen with a floating island, beautiful oak cabinets and what appeared to be stainless steel, state-of-the-art appliances. Because why not? Although, something told her he most likely used the double-door refrigerator for takeout instead of cooking with the wide six-burner stove and oven.

Beyond her stretched a dim but deep hallway, and just off the living room stretched a railless staircase to an upper level. Expensive-looking but comfortable furniture filled the vast space, but there was something missing.

Art.

No paintings decorating the cream-colored, freestanding walls. No sculptures that people often staged on tables or in the wide foyer. Not even a knickknack on an end table. The absence glared at her, and she glanced sharply at Joshua, who remained standing next to her, watching her survey his private sanctuary.

"Let me take this for you." He settled his hands on her shoulders and his jacket that she still wore. Though it was undoubtedly made of the finest wool, it should've disintegrated under the heat from his palms. Grinding her teeth against the inappropriate response, she nodded. "Would you like a drink?" he asked, opening a door behind them and hanging up the jacket and her wrap.

"Sure." She headed toward the living room, where a large and fully stocked bar stood next to the dark fireplace.

"What would you—" His phone rang, cutting him off. He removed it from his pants pocket and glanced at the screen. "I need to take this. Help yourself, and I'll be right back." Pivoting, he headed toward the hallway, pressing the cell to his ear. "Joshua Lowell."

She stared after him for several moments as he disappeared into a room, shutting it quietly behind him. Only then did she move into the living room, releasing a heavy sigh.

A scotch sounded really good right about now.

Before long, she had a finger of the amber alcohol in a squat tumbler, and she raised it to her mouth for a slow, small sip. She hummed in appreciation at the full-bodied, smooth taste as it burned a path over her tongue and down her throat, settling a ball of warmth in her chest.

"Wow, that's good," she muttered, taking and savoring another mouthful.

Grasping the glass between her hands, she headed toward one of the windows and the magnificent and tranquil view. But there was a scattering of papers on the low chrome-and-glass table in front of the couch. How hadn't she noticed it before? The haphazard pile contrasted so sharply with the pristine order of everything else in the room. Hell, the apartment.

Unable to resist the lure it presented, she approached the table. Guilt crept inside her. Joshua hadn't invited her here to snoop. Yet, she still peered down at the papers.

A printout of names and notes written beside each in his heavy scrawl. Women's names. Now, even if God himself came down and admonished her for breaking the eleventh commandment—thou shall not poke thy nose into thy neighbor's business—she still wouldn't have been able not to look.

She recognized some of the names. A high-powered attorney who lived there in Falling Brook. A society darling known for her parties and benevolent efforts. A B-list actress one blockbuster away from catapulting onto the A-list. And about three other names she didn't recognize. But each one had dates typed next to them. Then a handwritten note about whether Joshua had called, made contact and the result.

No baby.

Child but two years old. Not the right age.

Has a little boy. Same age, wrong sex.

Her grip on the glass of scotch tightened until her fingers twinged in protest. Joshua hadn't been idle. This list bore that out. A list that apparently included the names of women he'd been intimate with in the last four years, if the earliest date was an indication. She wrestled down the hot flare of dark and unpleasant emotion that flashed to life in her chest and twisted her belly. Six women wasn't a lot, but damn, she resented each one because they'd experienced the passion he'd very briefly unleashed on her. With grim effort, she refocused on the paper in front of her. Joshua had clearly been working on finding the woman who was supposed to have birthed his child.

Shock and a softer, far more precarious emotion stirred behind her breastbone, melting into her veins like warm butter. Lifting her free hand, she rubbed the heel of her palm over her heart. Since her offer to Joshua on Wednesday to help research more about the DNA report, she'd done some digging. But she kept hitting dead ends.

She wouldn't stop investigating but… Could the DNA results have been mistaken? Either that or Joshua's outrage at her accusation of being an absentee father had been genuine, and he really didn't know he had a child out there. He hadn't left these papers out for her benefit, because he couldn't have predicted they would meet tonight. Briefly closing her eyes, she ran his past reactions in her head like a movie reel. The pain, anger and, yes, grief. Viewed in a different, more objective lens, she had only one conclusion.

She believed him.

"Snooping, Sophie?"

Body jerking in surprise, she tugged her scrutiny from the table to meet Joshua's hooded gaze. So absorbed in what she'd discovered, she hadn't heard him enter the room. But he stood several feet away, head cocked to the side, studying her with an impenetrable expression. Didn't matter, though. The anger emanated from him, sending the guilt in her belly into a tighter, faster tailspin.

"Yes," she admitted quietly. If her honesty startled him, he didn't reveal it. That shuttered mask didn't alter. "I'm sorry. I shouldn't have invaded your privacy."

He didn't reply, his eyes narrowing further. Finally, he closed the short distance between them. But he didn't approach her but headed to the bar and fixed a drink. Turning to face her moments later with a tumbler in hand, he continued to study her, slowly sipping.

"Go ahead and ask," he said, his tone as dark and smooth as the alcohol in his hand. "Don't hold back. Isn't that—" he waved the glass in the direction of the table and papers "—what you're here for?"

"Yes," she replied. It was the reason. At least the least complicated and safer reason. And the only one she wanted to admit to. "From your notes, I'm assuming you didn't find a woman with a child or if she did have one, not a child who was the correct age or gender."

He shook his head, tipping his drink up for another swallow. "No. None of them are behind the email you received or the DNA report. I'm not any closer to finding out the truth about whether or not I have a daughter."

"Is this list…complete?" She hated to ask—part of her didn't want to know the answer. No. More specifically, didn't want to know if there were more names. Not when a kernel of resentment and envy lodged just under her breastbone. But the question needed to be posed.

Joshua stared at her for several seconds before tipping his head back and loosing a hard and loud crack of laughter. But no hilarity laced the jagged edges of it.

"You're asking if I have more pages with a longer list of names hidden somewhere?" he drawled.

"Six women. Four years." She shrugged. And fought

back the hot blast of embarrassment from staining her cheeks. "It does seem a little on the thin side."

"When you're a man in my position, you can't afford to be reckless with women. Especially when your father was a whore." He chuckled. "Come now, Sophie," he mocked. "You didn't come across that bit of information in all of your research?" Oh yes, she had. But her poker face must've been woefully inadequate because he arched a dark brow and downed the rest of the alcohol in his glass in one gulp. Setting the glass on the bar behind him, he cocked his head to the side, a razor-sharp half smile tilting the corner of his mouth. "Of course you did," he murmured. "Well, don't leave me in suspense. Tell me what you dug up on Vernon Lowell's propensity for adultery."

"Joshua," she whispered, her mind, her traitorous heart rebelling at engaging in this.

Not for his father's sake? No, Vernon had been the whore his son had called him. She didn't want to go there for Joshua's sake. Because underneath that taunting, I-don't-give-a-damn tone, his pain echoed like a distant fog-horn warning of upcoming danger.

"Don't stop now." The smile sharpened. "Do tell."

Inhaling a breath, she held it. Then slowly released it. He wasn't going to let this go. For some reason, he appeared in a masochistic mood, and was using her as his weapon of choice.

"Vernon was known to have a…" She hesitated, searching those gold-flecked hazel eyes. "Roving eye," she finished. Lamely.

"He fucked anything in a skirt." The bald, flat statement crashed between them like shattered glass. "That is what you were so diplomatically trying to say, correct? He was an unfaithful bastard who betrayed his marriage vows on a regular basis and didn't care if his wife found out. And she did find out. My mother always knew when he found a new mistress. And we—Jake, Oliver and I—all knew because they weren't quiet about arguing over it."

Surprise rippled through her. Vernon had married up when he'd wed his wife. Eve Evans-Janson had been a society daughter with a pedigree that dated past colonial times. Her connections had opened many doors for him. Most people would consider her rather plain in the beauty department, but Sophie had always thought her loveliness exceeded mere looks. From pictures and her own memories, she remembered the other woman carrying herself like a queen. Dignified. Proud. So why would a woman like her accept a husband who cheated so openly without care for her feelings?

"Why would she—"

"Put up with a man who not only couldn't, but wouldn't, keep it in his pants?" he finished in a derisive drawl. "Simple. Comfort. Money. Even though my father did whatever he wanted and refused to give her the one thing she desperately wanted—a daughter—she stayed with him because divorce was embarrassing. Reputation and the image of a perfect marriage and family were vital to her. So she looked the other way in public and cried and raged in private. And... Despite all his selfishness, she loved him. Desperately."

Sadness coiled around her heart and squeezed hard. She should be outraged on his mother's behalf—even angry with her for settling. For not demanding more for herself, for her children. But... Hadn't she been Eve at one time? Hadn't she loved a man so completely she'd been willing to ignore her instincts, look the other way, almost ignore her ethics? The only difference between her and Joshua's mother was she finally walked away and refused to lose her independence to another man again.

Another of those serrated barks of laughter echoed in the room, and Joshua raked a hand through his hair, disheveling the thick blond strands.

"God, why in the hell am I telling you this?" he snarled, turning away from her and stalking across the floor to the window.

The "of all people" didn't need to be said. It bounced off the glass walls, deafening in its silence.

She tried not to flinch. Tried not to allow the hurt to filter through. Tried...and failed.

"I'm not your enemy," she said to his wide back.

His shoulders tensed, but he didn't face her. "And I'm sorry if I implied that you were like your father. I didn't intend to." How to explain it'd just shocked her that such a virile, intense man who oozed power and sexuality had been intimate with only six women in four years? Hell, that didn't even average out to two a year. But given his history, the depths of which she hadn't known until this moment, she understood.

Sighing, she traced his steps and paused beside him, staring out over the beautiful view of Falling Brook at night. Houses, large and small, sprinkled among the trees and interconnecting map of streets, glittering like fairy lights. From this height, the town appeared almost magical. Serene. Made it seem as if they were hundreds of miles away instead of just several floors up.

"What do you see when you look out there?" she asked softly.

Tension and a cauldron of emotion continued to emanate from him, but when he replied, it was just as quietly. "A reminder."

"Of what?" It required everything in her not to glance at him, but to keep her gaze trained on the vista stretched out before them.

"Of why I do this." *Do what? What's* this? The questions bombarded her mind, but she forcibly held her tongue. And her patience was rewarded. "Why I continue to run a company I didn't ask for in the first place. Live this life that was my father's and not my own. For the last fifteen years, I've given it and Black Crescent everything—my dedication, my time, my loyalty, my goddamn soul. And in return? In return, I have a shade of a mother who I am powerless to help. My brothers don't speak to me because they hate who I've become a reflection of. My father is still MIA, and I have no idea whether he is dead or alive. And no matter how hard I work, how many hours I put in, how much money I bring in to repay those robbed and devastated by my father, it's never enough. I'll always be looked at with suspicion, judged for having the same blood in my veins as a criminal."

Her palms itched to touch him. To slide between him and the glass, smooth her hands up his hard chest and strong neck to cup his jaw between them. To, in some way, assume the pain that he wouldn't allow himself to show. But she caught herself, nonetheless. The sheer magnetism of this man dominated any room he stood in. Yet... How could anyone, after spending time with him, not see the emotions that roiled beneath that austere surface like water just under a boil?

"There's this gaping hole in my life," he continued in that gravel-and-midnight-silk voice. "And it doesn't matter what I do, I can't fill it. I don't know *how* to fill it." He shook his head, and he scoffed. "And the funniest, most pathetic part? When you first told me I might have a daughter, a part of me was thrilled. Because it meant that my life hadn't been a waste. That I had a purpose other than rebuilding the legacy my father nearly destroyed. That

I would be more than Vernon Lowell's son. I would be someone's father."

"You're not your father," she contradicted him, taken aback at her own vehemence. Even more so at the knell of truth that bloomed in her chest...deeper. Somewhere between the meeting where he agreed to take her help and finding that list of names, she came to believe him about not knowing he had a child out there. Or even if the child from the DNA report was his. She released a trembling breath, spreading her hand over her suddenly tumbling stomach. "You're not Vernon," she repeated, stronger, firmer.

And maybe he heard the belief in her voice. Because he finally looked at her, his green-and-gold eyes burning down into her. Straight through her.

"You're sure about that?" he ground out. But before she could answer, he turned fully toward her, his palm flattening on the glass above her head. "You were the one who accused me of denying my illegitimate child's existence. Of carrying on and not caring that I had fathered a baby and left it out there somewhere for her and her mother to cope on their own."

Yes, she had. Regret eddied inside her, and she briefly closed her eyes against the oily, slick slide of it. Her article had dragged the scandal out of the past, buffed it up and placed it out all shiny and new for people to feast on again. She had a direct hand in him standing here, surrounded by a darkness that seemed ravenous and ready to swallow him whole.

Her fault. So at least, she owed him the truth. Her truth. Even if he could give two shits about it.

"It's true," she murmured, tipping her head back and meeting his piercing gaze. "I did believe that. But that was before I knew you—"

"You don't know me," he growled.

"That's where you're wrong," she objected, shifting into his space. Surprise flared in his eyes, flecks of gold brightening. But then his lids lowered, gaze becoming hooded and hiding his thoughts. His reaction. But it didn't stop her from claiming another inch. If she took a deep breath, her breasts would brush the wide, solid wall of his chest. The tips of her shoes nudged his, and his scent, so earthy, so virile, so delicious, enveloped her, and she battled the pull of it. For now. "You might be several things—ruthless, proud, arrogant, rude and at times so cold I'm afraid you'll leave burn marks on my skin—but you aren't a deadbeat father. You would never force a child to suffer what you have. Much less one who belonged to you."

He didn't move; his chest didn't even rise and fall on ragged breaths. Like hers did.

"So you're wrong," she said, surrendering to her earlier need and reaching for him. His hand shot out, quick as a snake, and encircled her wrist, his grip firm but not bruising. The dominance of his hold throbbed low in her belly. Her heart thudded against her sternum, but not in fear. Excitement. Need. They both streamed through her, one a sizzling current, the other fierce and liquid hot.

Testing him—pushing him—she lifted her other hand, cupping his face and half expecting him to evade her. But he didn't. He remained still, rigid. Yet, he let her hand mold to the blade of his jaw and the hollow of his cheek. The bristle of his five o'clock shadow abraded her skin, and she logged it as another sensory memory to hoard and savor.

"I know you better than anyone else. More than the people who only see what you permit them to. More than the brothers who left you to fix what was so broken. More than the women you've allowed to touch your body." She traced the curve of his bottom lip with her fingertips. "Does that scare you, Josh?"

She deliberately used the shortened version of his name, increasing the charged intimacy snapping between them like a loose live wire.

With a low rumble, he cuffed her other hand, trapping it against his mouth. His teeth sank into the fleshy heel of her palm, and her groan rolled out of her, unbidden and unrestrained. The flick of his tongue against the same flesh, as if soothing it of the tiny sting, drew another moan from her, this one softer...hungrier.

"No, you don't scare me, Sophie," he said, nipping again at her. "Because that would mean you had the power to hurt me. And I don't trust you enough to give you that power." Tugging on her wrist, he eliminated the negligent amount of space separating them, and she shivered as her breasts crushed his chest, her thighs pressed against his. His erection nestled against her belly. Whatever air remained in her lungs evaporated into vapor at the evidence of his arousal. For her. All for her. "But I want you. As much of a goddamn idiot it makes me, I want to fuck you until your voice is raw from screaming my name. Until you come around me, squeezing me so hard that my dick is bruised. Until my body aches from giving both of us what we need."

Oh. God. Each erotic word stuck her like tiny blows, her sex clenching over and over. Begging for the carnal image he drew. Pleading to be filled, taken, branded. She trembled, harder this time, thankful for the hard body and grips on her hands that held her up.

But doubts and threads of fear wound their way through the fiercely pounding desire. If she were smart, if she'd truly learned from the past, she would halt this...this thing with Joshua before it went any further. At the very least, she could be in danger of losing her job for a serious conflict of interest if anyone found out about this. But not even her career trumped the very real terror of being that woman she'd been with Laurence. Her love for him had turned her into someone she hadn't known, dependent on his approval, his affection, his attention. She'd almost lost everything over him—her career, her future, herself.

She wasn't in love with Joshua, though. The lust turning her into this clawing, biting sexual creature demanding to be satisfied was unprecedented, but that was physical. Chemical. Not emotional.

As long as she kept her fickle, hardheaded heart out of this, she could give her body what it craved and protect herself.

"One night," she said, almost wincing at the note of desperation in her voice. And how he, again, went still, that multihued stare boring into her. But neither made her rescind the condition. "One night," she repeated. "No strings. No expectations. Just two people beating back their demons together."

God, why had she said that last part? It revealed too much.

And Joshua didn't ignore it. Releasing her wrists, he cupped the nape of her neck with one hand and cradled her hip with the other. Holding her. Steadying her. And because it would be only for the night, she allowed herself to lean into his strength. To depend on it.

"You have demons, Sophie?" he murmured, his gaze roaming her face as if already searching out the answer for himself rather than trust her to give an honest answer to him.

Smart man.

"Don't we all?" she countered, and it would've been flippant if not for the rasp betraying the power of hers.

"I'll exorcise them," he growled, pulling her impossibly closer. "We'll exorcise them together."

His mouth crushed hers.

On a whimper, she willingly, eagerly parted her lips for the sweet and wild invasion of his tongue. Impatiently twisted hers around his, dueling, parrying, meeting him thrust for thrust, stroke for stroke. With her hands free, she fisted the lapels of his tuxedo jacket, not caring that she was wrinkling the clothes that no doubt had cost thousands. Nothing mattered except the taste of him, the power of him, the raw passion he whipped to a frenzy in her.

Greedy for more, she rose to her tiptoes, the stilettos she still wore aiding in the endeavor. She opened wider for him, silently demanding he take more, give her more. The hand on her nape shifted upward, tunneling through her hair, twisting, tugging. Tiny pinpricks danced across her scalp, and every one of them echoed in a path down her spine, settling in the small of her back. Restless, she slid her hands up his chest, over his shoulders and into his shorter hair. Clutching the strands, she held him to her, drowning in this kiss that should be either illegalized or memorialized.

Joshua tore his mouth from hers, trailing a scorching path over her chin and down her throat, licking and sucking. She slicked the tip of her tongue over her kiss-swollen lips, savoring the flavor of him on her. Teeth scraped over her collarbone, and she tipped her head to the side, granting him easier access. Her lashes fluttered, lowering, and she basked in each gloriously wicked sensation.

And yet, it wasn't enough.

An urgent need to touch bare skin—his bare skin— riding her, she released him to dive her hands beneath his tuxedo jacket and shove it over his shoulders and down his arms. He straightened, staring down at her from beneath a hooded gaze, letting her strip him. Unable to meet it, she dipped her head, focusing on loosening the buttons down the front of his dress shirt. And as she revealed inch after inch of taut golden skin, all traces of awkwardness vanished. She sighed, fingers slightly shaking, anticipation soaring through her. When she pushed the last button through its corresponding hole, she placed her palms on his corrugated abs, her sigh transforming into a dark, low moan at first contact of skin to skin.

Jesus, did the man harbor a furnace in his big body? Heat simmered underneath her hands, skating up her arms, over her chest and tightening her nipples beneath her dress before flowing farther south to culminate between her wet, trembling thighs. She squeezed them together and shuddered as it only increased the aching emptiness. The desperate need.

"You're so beautiful," she breathed, stroking up his chest and under the open sides of the shirt, slowly peeling it, too, from his body so it tumbled to the floor with his jacket. "Like a work of art."

She stiffened as soon as the words tumbled from her lips and jerked her gaze from his magnificent form to his face. But if her slip caused him any pain, he didn't show it. Or maybe, in this place where they were baring the bodies and just a little bit of themselves, the thought of his former passion didn't bother him.

Or maybe she was assigning more importance, more intimacy to this night of sex than it warranted.

Regardless, he deserved to be admired. To be worshipped. Smooth, tight skin stretched across wide shoulders and chest and down over a flat, ridged stomach. Brown hair dusted across his pecs and narrowed to a silken line that bisected the ladder of abs. Twin grooves lined both hips, disappearing beneath the waistband of his pants. Heeding the call and invitation of that delineated arrow, she followed the lines with her fingertips, dipping beneath the band…

"Slow down," Joshua ordered in a sharp voice that carried a bit of a snap. He emphasized the command by grabbing her wrists and, turning her with his body, pressed her back against the window. Transferring both of her wrists to one hand, he lifted her arms above her head, caging them against the cool glass, as well. It didn't stop her from twisting in his grip, arching toward him. Rolling her hips over the prominent thickness tenting the front of his slacks. "Dammit, Sophie," he growled.

Then, with a jerk that left her breathless, he yanked down her dress, exposing her breasts to the air, his glittering gaze and, *oh God*, his mouth.

She cried out, her knees close to collapsing as he sucked so hard on her, the pull of it resonated high and deep in her sex. Could she orgasm just from this? Before Joshua, she would've scoffed at the idea of it, but with his tongue curling around her nipple, flicking it, drawing on it—she was a convert. Especially with her feminine flesh spasming, her hips bucking, seeking to grind that same flesh over him…

"Josh," she pleaded, tugging against his hold. "Please. Let me touch you." Yes, she was begging. And didn't care.

He loosened his grip, and she immediately took advantage, clutching his shoulders, digging her nails into the dense muscle. His grunt of pleasure fueled her on, and she raked a path down his back, then surrendered to the need to just…hold him.

Wrapping an arm around his shoulders and the other around his head, she embraced him, savoring the heat of him, the power of him even as he continued to sensually torment her flesh. Tipping her head back against the glass, she released another cry when he switched breasts, treating it to the same attention as its twin. Big, clever fingers plucked at and pinched the damp tip his lips didn't surround. He was driving her crazy. And damn if she wasn't enjoying the trip.

"No, don't stop." The plea escaped her along with a whimper when he dragged his mouth from her breasts down her stomach. She burrowed her fingers through his hair, cradling his head, attempting to pull him back.

"Not done, sweetheart," he murmured, straightening to swing her up in his arms. Once more rendering her lungs incapable of taking in air with both the show of strength and the softly spoken endearment.

They didn't go far. Just across the room to the dark freestanding fireplace. He lowered her back to the floor and, in seconds, had her side zipper down, the dress gone, and leaving her clothed in a skimpy black thong and silver heels. Her toes curled inside her shoes. For several long, charged moments, he stared down at her, his eyes more brown than green. Lust burned in them, throwing more kindling on the same fire razing her to the ground.

"Why do you hide this gorgeous body under those clothes," he ground out, his fingers flexing next to his thighs. "But if I'd known those conservative shirts covered these perfect breasts and lovely nipples... Or had a clue those knee-length skirts slid over these sweet little curves—" he slid a hand over her hip "—and legs created for squeezing a man's hips tight... Or how pretty and wet you would be—" he cupped her, and she swallowed a small scream at the possessive touch "—I would've had you up on my desk the first day you walked into my office, pretty much telling me to go screw myself. Did you know I wanted you then, Sophie? That I was picturing you laid out on top of my files and spreadsheets, your thighs wide, letting me pound inside you until everyone on the other side of that door knew that I was taking you, owning every scream and cry? Owning you?"

Shock rippled through her. At his explicit words and that he'd wanted her as far back as when she'd charged into his office. A tenderness that had no place between them tried to infiltrate the lust, but she battled it back. Self-preservation. She had to keep this about the sex.

Joshua didn't give her an opportunity to respond—if she'd been able to anyway—because he knelt between her legs. After whisking off her shoes, he stroked his hands up her calves, over her knees and palmed her inner thighs. Her breath, loud in her own ears, soughed in and out of her chest as she waited for him to graze the swollen, damp flesh covered by black lace. Air whispered over her but did nothing to cool the heat building inside her, stoked by his words and caresses.

His fingertips danced over her, and with a mewl that would probably embarrass her later, she rocked into the too-light but too-much touch. Sensitive and so deprived, her sex clenched hard, sending a spasm through her. She was ready to beg, to write a freaking formal entreaty, if he would only give her what her body literally wept for when he tugged aside the soaked panel of her panties and plunged a thick, long finger inside her.

She screamed.

And shattered. The release swept through her, over her, the pinched quality of it bordering on pain. It was good. So good. But still not enough. Even as the final waves of orgasm ebbed, the need returned, brewing underneath the blissed-out lethargy.

With a snarl curling his lips, Joshua yanked her panties down her useless legs and spread her wide for him. He dived into her, his mouth covering her still-quivering flesh, his tongue curling around the pulsing button of nerves cresting her mound. He growled against her, the sound vibrating against her, shoving her closer to sensory overload. He lapped at her, sucked, feasted on her in a way that should've been lewd, but instead was hot as hell.

"Josh." His name burst from her, a half shout, half whimper. Pleasure ratcheted from simmering to full-out conflagration. Her fingers drove into his hair, gripping his head, holding him to her. Pushing him away.

Too much.

Oh God, not enough.

He had to stop.

She'd kill him if he dared to stop.

If her mind was conflicted, her body knew what it wanted. What it craved. Her hips bucked and rolled under his mouth, urging him on. Demanding he give her everything he had. And as her lower back tightened and tingled in that telltale sign of impending orgasm, she gasped. Never, as in *never*, had she come more than once. She didn't think it possible for her. But the jerking of her hips, the shaking of her limbs, belied that belief, proving that she just needed the right partner to bring her to the brink of pleasure—and surpass it.

No. Not the right partner.

Joshua.

Another scream built in her throat, scratching its way up when he pulled away. Leaving her aching, throbbing, *hurting* on the edge of release.

"What?" she rasped. "Please." The two words were all she could manage, lust and an aborted orgasm confusing her.

Above her, Joshua surged to his feet. He snatched his wallet from his pants and tossed it on the floor next to her shoulder. In seconds, he wrenched his pants, shoes and socks from his big body, leaving him standing extraordinarily, unbearably beautiful before her. Joshua clothed in suits and tuxedos was gorgeous. Naked, stripped of all signs of civility, was...devastating.

As if drawn to him by an invisible thread, she sat up, rising to her knees, settling her palms on lean, powerfully muscled thighs that flexed under her palms. She sighed, sliding them up the defined columns...reaching for the thick, heavy, long length of him.

"No." His long fingers caught her hand before she could touch him. He knelt between her legs again, pressing her palm to his mouth and placing a searing openmouthed kiss there. "If I let you get your hand on me, this would be over quick. And, sweetheart, when I come, I plan to do it buried balls deep inside you, not on these pretty fingers."

He leaned over her, grabbing his wallet and removing a square foil packet. Quickly, he ripped it open and sheathed himself, then, *thank God*, he was over her, his erection nudging her entrance. Slowly pressing into her. Stretching her. Burning her.

Branding her.

Pain and pleasure mixed in a wicked, confusing blend that sent quakes rippling through her.

"Shh," Joshua crooned, brushing a kiss over her cheekbone, temple and, finally, lips. "Easy, sweetheart. You can take me. All of me." Until his reassurances, she hadn't been aware of the whimpers spilling from her or the restless shifting to get closer, to back away... She didn't know. The pressure of his possession... It filled her almost to overflowing. It overwhelmed her.

For a stark second, panic seized her. In this moment, she felt owned. Not just herself anymore. With him planted so deep inside her, she didn't belong to herself—she belonged to him. To them.

"Look at me, Sophie," he murmured, the soft tone carrying an underlying vein of steel. She couldn't help but obey and opened her eyes to meet his. Golden flames burned in a nearly dark brown field, scorching her. "Do you have any idea how you feel to me? So wet, tight like the most brutal fist but utterly fucking perfect surrounding me, squeezing me. Holding me. It's the sweetest hell. I might be covering you... I might be so goddamn deep I don't know if I can find my way out... But you have the control here. The power. So what are you going to do with me, Sophie? What are you going to do with us?"

His corded arms bracketed her head, and he held his large frame suspended above her, a very fine tremor running through him and belying the gentleness of his voice. And his words. God, they seeped into her, heating her, relaxing her tense muscles, dulling the edges of pain until only the pleasure of his dominance, his possession remained.

She released her grip on his upper arms and, sliding her hands up and over his shoulders, wound her arms around his neck, pulling him down for a slow, raw kiss.

"I'm going to take you. I'm going to wreck us," she whispered against his lips.

Hunger, dark and fierce, flashed in his gaze, but also delight flared bright and quick. Claiming control of the kiss, he pulled free from her body, then sank back inside, dragging a soft cry from her. Lifting her legs, she wrapped them around his waist, and he hissed, surging deeper. Filling her more. Thrust for thrust, she met him, taking him just as she promised. Wrecking them with each roll of her hips, each wet, voracious kiss, each scratch of her nails and whispered demand for "more, harder."

Carnal. Wild. Hot.

Joshua rode her hard, granting her no mercy. He buried himself inside her over and over, setting off sizzling currents with each drag of his cock through her channel. She cried out with the intensity of the pleasure, from the onslaught of it. Twisting and writhing beneath him, she chased the orgasm that loomed so close.

"Josh," she pleaded, desperate, greedy.

"Give it to me, Sophie," he ground out. "Come for me."

He palmed one of her thighs, spreading her wider, lifting her into his thrusting body. Sliding the other hand down between her breasts, he didn't stop until he circled the nerve-packed nub nestled between her folds. Thrust. Circle. Thrust. Circle.

The scream ripped from her throat as she exploded. For a moment, she fought against the release, afraid of the sheer ferocity and wildness of it. But it swelled stronger, swamping her, threatening to break her. Then reshape her into someone she was afraid she'd no longer recognize.

Closing her eyes, she surrendered.

Seven

Joshua stared at his computer monitor, but just like the previous hour, the report from his chief financial officer remained a blurred jumble of numbers.

"Dammit." Disgusted, he threw his pen down on his desk and shot to his feet. His chair rolled back, bumping against the bookcase behind it.

He scrubbed a hand down his face, then wrapped it around the back of his neck. Massaging the tense muscles there, he strode to the floor-to-ceiling window and stared out. Usually, the sight of the parking lot full of his employees' cars sent a surge of satisfaction spiraling through him. There'd been a time after he'd taken over Black Crescent when the lot had been almost empty. Only he, Haley and a few other loyal staff members had remained when the company fell apart. Those days had been…grim. Though he'd kept up a stalwart front for everyone, he'd been terrified. Of failing to rebuild the company and paying back the families his father had devastated. Of letting down those few who'd still believed in and trusted him when his father hadn't given them a reason to.

Of proving those who'd condemned him with "like father, like son" right.

His father. It always came back to him.

But it wasn't Vernon who had him distracted and unable to concentrate this Monday morning. How easy it would be to place the blame on him instead of *her*.

Sophie.

As if just the thought of her name jammed open a door he'd padlocked shut, images from Saturday night rushed through his head, a ceaseless stream of erotic snapshots.

Sophie, hips rolling and bucking to meet his devouring mouth as he held her thighs spread wide for him.

Sophie, twisting and undulating beneath him, voice cracking as she begged him to possess her harder.

Sophie, body arched tight, beautiful breasts pointed toward the ceiling, eyes glazed with pleasure as she came so hard it required every bit of his tattered control to prevent immediately following her.

Sophie, curled up against his side, her head resting on his shoulder, her soft, even breath caressing his damp skin. Her small, delicate hand splayed wide on his chest.

If the mental flashes of her uninhibited passion had his body hardening and arousal clenching his gut, then it was the memory of her cuddled into his body, sleeping so trustingly, that had a vise grip squeezing his heart.

And that grip unnerved him.

One night. No strings. That had been their agreement. The reasons for it—for him, at least—hadn't changed come the morning when they dressed in silence and he drove her home.

She was a reporter who had just done a story on him

and his family. How he'd let his guard down Saturday
night and confessed his unhappiness about his life and
the jacked-up state of his family even before the scandal
still astonished him. That—his penchant to reveal things
he'd never told another soul—was her superpower. And
his downfall. He'd basically handed her information for
her follow-up on him, and if she did write it, he had no
one to blame but himself.

What was it about this woman that made him so vulnerable? That had him ignoring every self-protective instinct?

He couldn't do that again. Couldn't afford to. Couldn't
afford to open Black Crescent up to any more controversy
and couldn't afford to let her in. To open his heart.

Everyone he'd ever loved had abandoned him. His father with going on the lam. His mother by mentally leaving him. His brothers by withdrawing from him, then icing
him out of their lives.

No, if she hadn't set the limits on their one night of
the hottest sex he'd ever had or believed possible, then he
would've.

"Joshua, I've been buzzing you," Haley announced from
behind him. He pivoted sharply, bemused. He'd been so
deep in thought he hadn't heard the phone intercom or his
assistant enter his office. "Where were you just now?"

He shook his head, slicing a hand through the air to
wave away her question. "Just going over my eleven o'clock
appointment with Clark Reynolds from Venture Investments. What'd you need?"

Haley tilted her head, studying him through a narrowed
gaze. She didn't outright accuse him of lying, but the speculation in her hazel eyes did. "Nice try. But deflection
has never worked with me. Are you sure you weren't just
mooning over Sophie Armstrong?"

He snorted, striding back toward his desk. "I've never mooned a day in my life."

"I know. And that's your problem."

"My problem?" He sank into his chair. "I wasn't aware I had one. Well, other than a bossy executive assistant who doesn't know when to let stuff go."

"Oh, you have one," she drawled, folding into the armchair across from his desk. Leaning forward, her dark blond eyebrows drew together in a frown. "When was the last time your life didn't revolve around this company, the employees or paying back the families affected by the scandal?"

"Haley," Joshua said, stiffening. "I don't—"

"I know you don't want to talk about it. You never do," she cut him off. "That's another problem. You might be the savior of Black Crescent, Josh, but that's not all you are. You deserve more. You deserve to have time to yourself, take a vacation. Leave this place at a decent hour. Have a private life. Yes, you've had relationships in the past, but when was the last time you just let yourself fall for someone? Let them interfere with your carefully regimented schedule and order? Let them make your life messy with laughter and love? I know the answer to all those questions. Never."

Joshua clenched his jaw, trapping the heated words that threatened to burst free. He didn't want to hurt her feelings. Haley might be his assistant, but she was also family. Like his younger sister. But this topic was off-limits. "Haley, I don't want to hurt your feelings. But this is—"

"None of my business, I know. But this—" she stood and set down the tablet she held on the desk, sliding it toward him "—makes it everyone's business."

He stared at her for several moments before dropping

his gaze to the screen. His irritation evaporated, dissolved by shock.

Pictures from Saturday night's art gala. Some depicted him and other partygoers, including the redhead he'd been seated next to at dinner, who'd propositioned him with a nightcap after the event. Those images didn't ensnare his attention or had his heart pounding like an anvil against his chest. Didn't have desire flaming bright and hot inside him.

The photograph of Sophie, so beautiful in the silver strapless gown that had molded to her slim figure and highlighted every curve, and him standing outside the museum had him battling back the surge of lust brewing low in his stomach.

Unlike with the redhead, he'd lost the polite but aloof mask he usually donned at those occasions. Though a small distance separated them, he stared down at her with an intensity—a hunger—that was anything but polite. And Sophie, head tipped back, exhibited a vulnerability that he immediately hated the photographer for capturing.

He tore his gaze away from the image and scanned the caption underneath.

Black Crescent Hedge Fund CEO Joshua Lowell and mystery guest...or date? Could it be the famous—or infamous—businessman is finally settling down?

Flicking a glance to the top of the page, he glimpsed the name of the site. And fisted his fingers next to the tablet. A notorious gossip website that focused on dishing dirty on high society. If he had a dollar for every time his or his family's names had been mentioned in this column, he'd have been able to compensate the bankrupted families years ago, and with interest.

Dammit. Had Sophie seen this? Possibly not. She might be a reporter, but she was also an investigative journalist. Not some gossipmonger.

"What's going on between you and Sophie Armstrong?" Haley asked softly.

He jerked his head up, having momentarily forgotten she stood across from him. "Nothing. She happened to attend the same gala as I did, and we were leaving at the same time. She wasn't my date."

"The columnist mentioned you two left together. That she got into your car," Haley persisted.

Dammit. Anger pulled hard and tight inside him. Fucking media. "I gave her a ride home since we were both headed back to Falling Brook. End of story." If the end of the story included his driving into Sophie's sweet body on a rug that he wouldn't ever be able to walk by again without seeing her coming apart on it.

Haley silently studied him again, her scrutiny too seeing, too knowing. "Neither of your faces say 'casual acquaintance' or 'friendly ride home.'" Before he could snarl a reply, she continued, voice soft, "And I'm glad."

He frowned, taken aback. "You're glad my privacy was invaded and I'm now a topic of speculation and gossip? Again."

Haley straightened, a flicker of emotion rippling across her face. But before he could decipher it, she arched an eyebrow, her eyes direct and unwavering. "No, I'm positively delighted that someone has managed to get through that thick layer of 'back the hell off' that you've wrapped yourself in these past fifteen years. I'm happy that you've found someone that you would let down your guard long enough to be captured by some random photographer. Because whether or not you want to admit it—or are ready to admit it—she *is* important to you. Now I'm just praying that you don't mess it up by pushing her away."

She turned away and strode across his office and left,

closing the door behind her with a quick snick. But her warning reverberated in the room like a report of a gunshot.

I'm just praying that you don't mess it up by pushing her away.

Mess it up? Push her away?

He'd have to let her in first.

And that wasn't happening. Ever.

Eight

What the hell am I doing here?

The question ricocheted off Joshua's skull as he sat in the back seat of his Lincoln town car outside Sophie's apartment building. Showing up here after the photo of them on the gossip site didn't rank among his smartest decisions. If anyone saw him here, it would only feed the fires of speculation. But he'd tried to call her to see if she'd seen it and give her a heads-up if she hadn't. Either she hadn't seen his phone call or she'd refused to answer, because he hadn't been able to reach her.

Logic argued that he leave it alone—leave her alone. But the thought of her being blindsided... Well, here he was sitting outside her home like some kind of goddamn stalker. Growling a curse, he shoved open the back door.

"John, I'll give you a call when I'm finished here," he instructed his driver.

The younger man behind the wheel nodded. "Yes, sir."

Closing the door shut, he stalked across the street and up to the two-story brick building with its neat side lawns and sidewalk bordered by honeysuckle. Just as he approached the door, a couple with a small child pushed through the entrance.

"Oops, sorry 'bout that," the man apologized with a grin. "This one's a little anxious to hit the park."

"No, no, it's fine," Joshua said, stepping out of the way and catching the door before it could close.

But his gaze remained ensnared by the little girl who couldn't have been older than four years old. The same age the child Sophie accused him of having was supposed to be. A sudden longing jerked hard in his chest, catching him by surprise. Years ago, when the world had been his to conquer, he'd wanted what this husband and father had—family.

Now? Now, a wife, a child... They just meant a person had more to lose.

Shaking his head, he moved into the large lobby, letting the door close behind him. An elevator ride later, he stood in front of Sophie's apartment. Before he could again question the wisdom of being here, he knocked. And waited. And knocked again.

Hell. He glanced down at his watch: 6:48 p.m. She should've been home by now, but then again, Sophie had the same work ethic as he did. It was one of the things he admired about her despite her choice of career. So she very well could still be at the office.

He had turned and taken a step away from her door when it opened.

"Sophie," he greeted, running his gaze from the brown-and-gold wavy strands that fell over the shoulders of a purple slouchy T-shirt that hung off one shoulder, down the black leggings to her bare feet with pink-painted toes.

Dragging his perusal back up, he couldn't look at her—not those slender, toned thighs, high, firm breasts or lovely dove-gray eyes—without thinking of how she'd looked, naked and damp from sweat, under him.

"Joshua, what are you doing here?" Joshua, not Josh, as she'd called him for most of those hot, dark hours they'd spent together.

Part of him wanted to demand she call him the shortened version again. And in that sex-drenched, husky voice. Instead, he slid his hands in his pants pockets and kept a careful distance between them.

"I needed to talk with you about something. I'm sorry for dropping by unannounced, but you weren't answering your phone today."

"Yes." She thrust a hand through her hair, drawing the strands away from her face. "I saw the missed calls. I intended to call you back but just got really busy."

He cocked his head. "You make a shitty liar, Sophie."

She dropped her arm, heaving a sigh. "What are you doing here, Joshua?" she repeated.

"I need to talk to you. And not out here in the hallway."

"I—" Indecision flicked in her eyes, her full lips flattening. Finally, after a brief hesitation, she nodded and stepped back. "Fine. Only for a minute, though. I'm working."

Suspicion flared quick and hot in his chest. Was she writing the follow-up article on him? On what he'd revealed to her? He hadn't stipulated that Saturday night had been off the record. Would she…?

He snuffed the thoughts out as he entered her apartment and closed the door behind him. But the embers of doubt… He couldn't extinguish them. How messed up was it that he harbored reservations about her trustworthiness, but he still wanted her with a hunger that gave him stomach pains?

"Can I get you something? I was about to fix a cup of coffee. But I have wine or a bottle of water," Sophie said.

The reluctance in her offer had a corner of his mouth quirking into a humorless half smile. Good manners probably had her extending the courtesy instead of truly wanting him to stick around and enjoy a drink.

So he accepted.

"Coffee is fine."

Again, her lips tightened, but she headed to the kitchen that was separated from the living room by a breakfast bar. Taking the opportunity, he surveyed the apartment. Though on the small side, the living room with its overstuffed couches, wood coffee and end tables and big arched windows appeared cozy rather than cramped. Lived in. Compared with his condo, her place was a home, not a place to just crash instead of the office sofa.

The room flowed into a space that could've been a dining area but Sophie had jammed with filled-to-overflowing bookcases, a tiny love seat and lamps. A reading nook. Easily he could imagine her curled up on those cushions, book in hand.

He tore his gaze away, returning it to her as she finished up the second coffee in the one-cup brewer. Though irritation practically vibrated off her petite frame, her movements were fluid, graceful.

"What are you working on?" he asked, needing to remind himself of who she was. What she did. What she was capable of.

"The follow-up article from my visit to Black Crescent. I need to have it in by the end of the week."

There it was. The reminder. Ice trickled through his veins. Yes, he'd invited her into the inner sanctum of his company and revealed the programs that were close to his heart, but now, tiny pinpricks of doubts stabbed at him over that decision.

"What?" Sophie propped a hip against the counter and crossed her arms over her chest. "Having second thoughts? *You* asked *me* to Black Crescent, remember? This time I didn't force my way in," she drawled.

"I don't need any help remembering…anything," he said, and yes, it made him an asshole to feel hot satisfaction well in him as slashes of red painted her high cheekbones. But he didn't care. Not when she couldn't hide the gleam of arousal in her eyes before abruptly turning back to the counter and the coffee cups.

"Do you take sugar or cream?" she rasped. And the sound of the slightly hoarse tone…

He barely stopped himself from stalking across the space separating them and pressing his chest to her ramrod-straight spine. From notching his hard dick just above the tempting curve of her perfect ass.

"Black," he ground out.

Seconds later, she handed him the mug with Shouldn't You Be Writing? emblazoned along the side along with a picture of a shirtless Thor and his hammer. He would've assumed the choice in cup was by accident if a smirk didn't ride the corner of her mouth.

"Cute," he drawled.

"It's one of my favorites. Nothing but the best for you," she purred, strolling past him with her own plain black mug back into the living room, where her laptop sat propped on the coffee table in front of the couch. "Not that I don't doubt my coffee is wonderful, but what are you really doing here, Joshua?"

The pointed question shoved away any vestiges of humor, and he took a sip of the steaming-hot, fragrant brew before replying. "Pictures of us together from the art gala were posted online in a society gossip column. I didn't know if you were aware. But in case you weren't, I wanted to give you a heads-up. Although you weren't named, the columnist included some speculation about our relationship to one another."

She huffed out a dry laugh. "Oh yes, I already know about it. Althea called me into her office today and asked if anything was going on between us. She's worried about the conflict of interest for the paper if the reporter of the story on Black Crescent is involved with the CEO."

"What did you tell her?"

"I told her no, of course."

"So you lied," Joshua drawled.

If he hadn't been watching her so closely, he might've missed the slight tremble in her hand as she set her mug on the coffee table. But he didn't. And he had to battle back the urge to cross the floor, take that hand, lift it and still the shivering with his mouth.

"It wasn't a lie. There isn't anything between us. Saturday was one night. One time. That was our deal."

"And if I want to renegotiate the deal?" he murmured.

The same shock that widened her eyes reverberated through him. Where had that come from? Asking for another night—another taste of her lips, another chance to drive into that sweet little body—hadn't been his intention when he'd pulled up outside her building. *Warn her, get out.* That had been the plan. But lust had overridden common sense and hijacked his mouth. But he couldn't exist within four feet of her and not crave her. Not want a repeat of the night that was branded into his memory with startling and unnerving clarity. Maybe he just needed to convince himself that his brain had exaggerated the pleasure he experienced. That nothing could be that good in reality.

And maybe he was just seeking an excuse to get her under him again.

He still didn't trust her. Didn't 100 percent believe that she wasn't using him for another story. But none of that stopped his dick from throbbing like a toothache—insistent, hurting and needing relief.

"Joshua..." She shook her head, ducking her head as she pinched the bridge of her nose. "I don't think—"

"Look at me, Sophie," he ordered, setting his cup on the breakfast bar behind him. He moved farther into the living room, not stopping until only inches separated them. She lifted her gaze to his, and her obedience in this when she refused to give it to him anywhere else had excitement and arousal plowing through him. "Look at me and tell me that you're not already feeling my hands on you. Tell me your nipples aren't already hardening, begging for my fingers, my tongue. Tell me you're not already hot and wet for me, desperate to have me stretching you again, filling you." He grasped her chin between his thumb and forefinger, tilting her head farther back. "You can tell me all of that, Sophie, and I'll walk out of here."

Her moist, warm breath broke on her parted lips, echoing in the room. For several long moments, she stared up at him with those molten silver eyes, her slender body swaying toward his, as if seeking his warmth, his possession.

A shudder worked through her, and, lowering her lashes, she stepped back, breaking his hold on her.

Rubbing her hands up and down her arms, she turned away from him. *Give me those eyes. Look at me*, battered his tongue, needing to get out. But he clenched his teeth, trapping the command. Pride imprisoned what sounded too damn close to a plea.

"Is it so easy for you?" she whispered.

He frowned, shifting forward, reclaiming a little of the

distance she'd inserted. It was an unconscious movement, as if his body couldn't stand not feeling her warmth or being wrapped in her scent.

"Is what easy for me?" he pressed.

"This." Pivoting to face him again, she waved a hand between them. "You don't trust me," she said flatly.

"No," he replied, just as blunt. "I don't."

Hurt spasmed across her face, but in the next instant her expression hardened into a cool mask that somehow appeared so wrong on her. Like an ill-fitting dress.

"Then why would you want to be with someone you believe would possibly sell you out for a story?" she scoffed, but a thin line of anger edged the question.

"A relationship with you and fucking are two different things," he said, voice hard, matter-of-fact. "And if that's what you're looking for from me, then we can end this now. I don't do long-term commitments. I'm not the man who can give you the happy home with a perfect, smiling family and well-behaved dog. But I am the man who can make you come so hard it hurts. Yes, Sophie. I'll make it hurt in the very best way," he murmured, lust gripping him so hard, so tight, he could barely draw in a breath. "I don't need to trust you for that."

Her thick fringe of lashes lowered, and her hooded silver gaze razed his skin. Red stained her cheeks and that lush mouth appeared even plumper, bitable. The aloof coldness had evaporated from her expression, leaving this one behind. And he recognized it. This face, stamped with arousal, had haunted his every waking and sleeping hour since Saturday night.

Yet, he couldn't deny glimpsing the flicker of pain beneath the lust.

Before his mind could check him, he took a step to-

ward her to…what? Ease it? Order her to tell him how to
make it disappear?

She shot a hand up, palm out, and he halted.

Thank God.

"I have my own stipulations. I don't have your trust,
fine. But I will have your fidelity. While we're doing…this
arrangement, you don't sleep with anyone else. Just me."

"Of course," he growled. "And the same with you. I'm
the only man inside you."

"Of course," she said, throwing his words back at him
with a snap. "And at any time either of us wants out, it's
over." He nodded, but she continued, "One last thing. This
stays here. No one else knows. Anyone finding out could
cost me my job. I might be losing some of my pride entering into this with you, but I refuse to lose my career."

She murmured the last part of that almost to herself,
and he scowled. What the hell did that mean? Before he
could demand an explanation, though, she stuck out her
hand toward him, the fingertips nudging his chest.

"Deal?" she asked.

He stared down at it, anger and wild, raw need crowding into him. Pride? Being with him stripped her of pride?
What else could he strip her of?

Grasping her wrist, he tugged her hand up to his mouth.
And licked the center of her palm, swirling his tongue over
the soft flesh. Her gasp reverberated around them, and she
tried to curl her fingers into her palm, but he stayed the
motion with his other hand, holding her spread wide for
him. He flicked a wet caress in between each finger before
sinking his teeth into the heel of her palm.

A shudder racked her body, followed by a throaty moan
that had his dick twitching.

"Joshua," she whimpered.

"Josh," he corrected, voice harsh, roughened by the hunger that gnawed at him like a voracious beast. "Say it." He trailed a finger down the elegant line of her throat, tracing the shallow dip in the middle of her collarbone.

"Josh," she whispered, and her swift capitulation was a stroke over his thick, pulsing flesh. And a caress to his pounding heart. She moved forward until her thighs bumped his and her breasts plumped against his chest. He fought to lock down the urge that howled at him to take her down to the floor and claim. Rising to the tips of her bare toes, she brought her mouth a breath away. He slid his tongue out, brushing that temptation of a full bottom lip. "Josh," she repeated, softer, huskier.

In answer, in reward, he took her mouth.

Releasing her hand, he cradled her jaw, pressing his thumb on her chin and tugging down to open her more to him. She tilted her head, complying. Breathing a snarl into her, he thrust his tongue past her lips, rubbing and twisting, coaxing her to play with him. Not that she needed any persuading. She met him, danced with him. Dared him. Nails digging into his shoulders through his suit jacket, she coiled her tongue with his, sucking hard, and the pull arrowed straight to his dick.

A savage, almost animalist burst of lust exploded within him, and he bent his knees to cup her ass in both hands and straightened, hauling her up his body. Her legs wound around his waist, her arms around his neck, settling her sex right over his erection. *Goddamn.* He clenched his molars together, reaching for his rapidly dwindling control. Still, nothing could stop him from punching his hips forward and stroking her up and down his dick. Her thin yoga pants and his slacks might as well as have been created of air. Her folds slipped over him, shooting electric pulses down his spine.

"Bedroom?" he ground out.

"Down the hall," she rasped. "Last door on the right."

In the small apartment, it didn't take long to find her room. With long, impatient strides, he entered and headed straight for the bed. Carefully, he lowered her to the floor, sliding his hands up over her hips, the indents of her waist, the sides of her breasts until he held her face in his hands. Tipping her head back, he stared into her eyes. And though desire rode him like a jockey hell-bent on leather, he paused, seeking any flicker of hesitation, of second thoughts.

"I need to hear you say it, Sophie," he said, his voice seeming to boom in the tense quiet of the bedroom. "Say you want this. You want me to touch you. You want me inside you."

He waited. And he would continue to wait. Because a part of him—the stubborn part that grief, pain and betrayal hadn't managed to amputate—*had* to hear her utter those words. Craved it like a drowning man seeking that life-giving gulp of air.

"I want this. I want you," she whispered, threading her fingers through his hair and pulling his head down until their noses bumped and her lips grazed his. "I want you to touch me. Want you so deep inside me I'll feel you tomorrow. Will you give it to me, Josh?"

He didn't answer her. At least not with words. But with his mouth, his tongue, his hands? God, yes. He dug his fingers into her hips, jerking her closer so she would have no doubts of her effect on him. Unable to help himself, he ground his cock into the softness of her belly, even as he devoured her mouth. And she held nothing back from him. Not her response, not her sexy little whimpers and cries. Had a woman ever fully let herself be so uninhibited, so vulnerable with him before?

No.

And he'd never been that way with another woman.

But with Sophie? Regardless of his claims of not trusting her, he couldn't throw up his protective shields with her. Not in this.

Here, they could be fully honest with each other. Naked in more than the baring of bodies.

Naked. As soon as the word entered his head, the longing, the greed in him intensified until it became a chant in his head.

Tearing his mouth from hers, he fisted the bottom of her T-shirt and yanked it over her head. And *oh God.* "All that time you were offering me coffee and arguing with me, you didn't have a bra on?" he snarled, palming her pretty, firm breasts and thumbing the pink nipples. Already tight, they pebbled further, and Jesus himself couldn't have stopped him from dipping his head and having a taste. And when she tugged on his hair, her groan accompanying the pricks across his scalp, he indulged himself and sucked her into his mouth, lashing the tip. Pulling free, he rubbed his lips across the beaded flesh. "If I'd known you were bare underneath that top, you would've been against the wall with my mouth on you as soon as I closed that door."

He grazed her with his teeth, wringing another cry from her. It became his mission to drag them from her, to earn a shudder from her slender frame. His mission and his pleasure.

While he switched from one breast to the other, Sophie removed his jacket, pushing it off his shoulders and arms, casting it to the floor. His shirt followed. Her nails raked down his bare back, trailing fire in their wake, and it was his turn to shiver.

Releasing her with a soft pop, he straightened, shifting forward and moving her backward until the backs of her knees hit the edge of the mattress. But at the last second, she twisted and, grabbing his upper arms, turned him. They switched positions, and she pressed her palms to his chest, her touch like live coals on his skin.

"My turn," she said, eyes so bright he swept a thumb underneath one. Then brushed his lips over the same spot. "Can't distract me," she breathed, and pushed.

He sank to the bed, his palms slapping down beside his thighs. She didn't hesitate, but knelt in front of him, and his thighs automatically spread, making room for her. His breath hitched in his lungs, and his body froze. Anticipation, lust and excitement hurtled through him, and he could only stare down at this beautiful, sensual creature as she fumbled with his thin leather belt and the closure to his pants.

The metallic grind of the zipper ricocheted through the room, deafening in his ears. She pushed the edges apart, exposing his black boxer briefs. Together, they studied the almost obscene bulge of his thick, long erection. Was she remembering the same thing as he? How he fit inside that too-tight and too-perfect sex? How he'd had to work his way inside her, claiming her bit by bit as she softened around him, strangling his dick even as she embraced it?

Because, God, he remembered. Remembered and wanted it so bad he'd become one huge walking ache.

Finally, when she snagged the waistband, his paralysis broke. He covered her hand with his, squeezing.

"You don't have to do this, sweetheart," he rumbled, offering her an out. Even though the thought of her tongue sliding down his column nearly had him coming without one touch.

"I know I don't *have* to," she said, lifting her gaze from his cloth-covered dick to meet his. "I *want* to."

Then she was gripping him. Stroking him.

Pleasure so sharp it danced on the edge of pain seized

him, and, head thrown back, palms flattened on the mattress, he strained against it.

Nothing, *fucking nothing*, had ever felt as good as this woman's hand on his cock.

Oh damn.

He stood corrected. Hot, wet warmth bathed the head, followed by gentle swipes of a tongue. His head jacked forward, *needing* to take in the sight of Sophie with her mouth full of his flesh.

Locking his muscles, he fought down the ball of fire coalescing and swirling at the base of his spine and lower. God, he was going to come. Right down her throat from just the swipe of her tongue. He closed his eyes but, seconds later, snapped them open, unable to not look. To stare. To behold this picture of knee-shaking carnality and brand it on his brain.

Lashes lowered, color painted her sharp cheekbones and one of those hungry whimpers escaped her as she swallowed him down, tongue rubbing, mouth sucking. Her fist pumped the bottom half of his pounding column, and her damp lips bumped her fingers each time she bobbed over him. Up and down, she tortured him, loving him, making him her slave.

Because right now he would do anything for her if she. Just. Didn't. Stop.

"Sweetheart," he growled, and the endearment was churned-up gravel in his throat. "You're trying to break me with your greedy little mouth. And I'm going to let you do it. I'm going to let you take me apart."

His words seemed to galvanize her, to fuel her passion. Tunneling both hands in her hair and tangling them in the thick strands, he didn't try to control her, just allowed himself to be swept along in the ride.

She took him deeper and deeper until the tip of him nudged the back of her throat.

She let him slip into that narrow passage, swallowed around him.

She elicited shudder after shudder, curse after curse from him.

And when the telltale sizzle snapped and popped down his spine, legs to the soles of his feet and then back up to the base of his dick, he didn't hold back. Didn't pull her off him.

He gave her everything. Every last bit of him.

Chest heaving, he waited for the dark edges crowding his vision to retreat. Only then did he loosen his grasp on Sophie's head and suck in a much-needed breath into his screaming lungs. That orgasm should've destroyed him, laid him out. Instead, it fed the desire that still flowed through him like an open pipe.

He clutched her shoulders and, surging to his feet, dragged her up with him. In seconds, he had her naked on the bed and under him. He attacked her mouth, voracious. The taste of him on her tongue only inflamed him more. Snarling against her lips, he nipped the full bottom one, then treated her chin and throat to the same erotic bites.

Once more he feasted on her breasts, licking, lapping and tweaking until she writhed beneath him, those kitten mewls spilling from her. God, he loved them. Hoarded them in his head so he could replay them later when he was alone in his bed.

He shook his head, dislodging the thoughts and the sharp stab of loneliness they lugged along with them. Skimming his lips down the center of her chest, he paused to flick his tongue in the bowl of her navel, then continued until he reached his goal.

Inhaling, he trapped the musky sweet-and-tart scent

of her. He jerked awake last night with this scent teasing him, tormenting him. Unable to resist the lure, he dipped his head and dived into her sex. One hand splayed wide on her lower belly to hold her down, he palmed her inner thigh with the other, granting him easy access to the flesh that he couldn't get enough of. Her scream danced around his ears as he slid his tongue through her swollen, soaked folds, circling the bud of nerves at the top of her mound. Over and over he returned to gorge on her like the delicious, addictive feast she was.

Her thighs clamped around his head, and her fingers dug into his hair, grasping tight, and he didn't let up. Not until he pushed her right to the edge of release—and over it.

And as she still shook and gasped on the waves of pleasure, he shoved from the bed and stripped. Removing his wallet and then a condom from the billfold, he tossed his pants to the floor and climbed back onto the mattress, crawling over her. Quickly, he sheathed his rock-hard flesh in the protection, then maneuvered her until she straddled his hips. His erection surged up between them, and he swore he could feel her labored gusts of breath on the tip.

"Ride me, sweetheart," he grated, cupping her hip and fisting his dick. "Take me."

Her eyes found his, and, without breaking their visual mating, she rose over him. Then sank down on him.

He was the first to break their locked gazes. Closing his, he released a hiss as she enveloped him, slowly accepting him. Both hands gripped her hips, steadying her. She fell forward, her palms slapping his pecs. Head bent, she pulsed up and down his flesh, taking more and more of him until, finally, she was seated on top of him. And he was so deep inside her, he had to, once more, battle back the rising of his orgasm.

"Sophie," he growled, bucking his hips as if he could screw just a little bit more of himself inside her, when there was nothing left of him to give. "So tight. So wet. So damn hot. I didn't—" He cut himself off before he could utter the rest of the too-revealing sentence. He hadn't imagined how perfect she took him. How she undid him. "You good, sweetheart?" he asked, flexing again, unable to help himself.

"Yes," she breathed, crushing a kiss to his lips. "God, *yes.*"

"Take me, then," he ordered. "Take us both."

Lifting off him until only the head of his dick remained, she hovered for only a second before slamming back down on him.

Moments ago, he'd thought nothing had felt as good as Sophie's mouth on him. So wrong. Watching her rise and fall above him, face saturated with lust… Having her lush, muscular core sucking at him, fluttering around him— nothing could compare to this.

Jackknifing off the bed, he sat up, burrowed his fingers in her hair and captured her mouth, swallowing each sob, each whine. Wrapping her arms around his shoulders and head, she rode him, jerking on him, hips swiveling like the most carnal of dances. She wrenched her mouth from his, tipping her head back on her shoulders, lost in the pleasure she chased. The pleasure bearing down on him like a freight train with greased wheels.

Not without her, though. He wouldn't go without her.

Reaching between them, he slid his fingers down her quivering belly to the small, swollen bundle of nerves cresting her sex. One stroke. Two. Three, and he pressed down hard.

Her core clamped down hard on him like a vise grip, feminine muscles milking him. Grabbing her hips, he held her aloft as he thrust up into her, granting her every measure of the release that shook her like a leaf in a passion-whipped storm. Only after her screams ebbed to muted whimpers did he let go, hurtling into the dark, shattering abyss of release.

As he fell, slender arms encircled him.

And he held on.

Nine

Sophie rested her head on Joshua's chest, his steady heartbeat a reassuring thud under her ear. She should move. Should order him to leave since the sex was over, and her senses had winked back online. But her limbs, weighted down by postorgasmic lethargy and wrapped around his torso and thigh, wouldn't obey. Besides, when he'd left the bed to get rid of the condom, he'd returned with a warm, wet bath cloth to clean her. After that tender and thoughtful consideration, it would be rude of her to kick him out.

Okay, and that sounded weak even to her own ears.

She might as well just admit it; she wanted him here in her bed. His weight next to hers. His heartbeat echoing in her ear.

So dangerous. She was entering such treacherous, risky territory.

Saturday night, she'd been so certain that she would be able to contain the passion between them to one night. That she could walk away unscathed.

God, she'd been so arrogant.

He'd left her singed to her soul. And days later, she still felt the burn. So much that when he'd shown up on her doorstep, she'd tried to convince herself again that she could separate physical from emotional. That she didn't need his trust. Didn't need anything but another release that left her feeling like a postapocalyptic refugee.

Closing her eyes, she tried to block out the direction of her wayward thoughts, but that only caused a livestream of how she'd spent the last hour with Joshua. Of their own volition, her fingertips brushed her lips. And she shivered, experiencing again the fierceness of his possession.

He was the first man she'd gone down on. Had he been able to tell? No other had stirred the need to share that intimacy, to make herself so vulnerable. To give so much—her mouth, her throat…her control.

But Joshua wasn't just any man.

Somehow, he'd sneaked beneath her carefully constructed armor and touched more than her body. He'd infiltrated her heart.

Terror barreled through her as she admitted the truth to herself.

And this time, when she squeezed her eyes shut, it wasn't the erotic reel that played over the backs of her lids. It was her, alone, curled up on her couch, hurting. Her, staring at her computer screen staring at an image of Joshua with another woman on his arm. Her, crushed and lost, gazing at her apartment door, willing a knock to sound. For him to be standing on the other side.

Pain cascaded through her in a crimson shower. Pain and fear.

He'd warned her about not wanting a relationship. Straight up told her he didn't want to be in one with her or any woman. But especially not her. He might not have voiced that, but the words had been there, ringing in the room. Not a woman who might betray him or use him for a story. He would never be able to disassociate her from her job. So once more, she faced the decision—love or her career.

Well, she would be faced with that decision if he wanted her for more than sex.

Which he didn't.

But the fear went deeper than his rejection. It reached down to the core of her that dreaded becoming dependent on a man for her happiness, her security. Because when he left, where would she be?

A shell.

"That's the second sigh in as many minutes," Joshua said, his voice rumbling under her ear. He traced a meandering trail up and down her arm, and she savored his touch. Committed this relaxed version of him to memory. "What're you thinking about?"

Of how I'm foolishly falling for you even though I know you will shatter me.

"Actually, I was thinking about you." Not exactly a lie. But sharing the truth wasn't an option.

Tension invaded his body, and she hated it. "What about me?" he asked, the same stiffness coating his question.

Heaving a sigh—her third—she sat up, her hip pressed to his, drawing her knees to her chest and wrapping her arms around them. "While I was working on my follow-up article, it struck me again how much you do for those who are in your employ and this community. All without any expectation of credit or acknowledgment. It's so admirable, and if I could put all of that in bold, font size eighteen, I would. People should know that you're not just a CEO consumed with making money. You're not just another businessman with the 'rich getting richer' mentality. You actually care about people and their welfare and their success."

Joshua rose, resting his back against her headboard, the sheet he'd pulled over them pooling around his lean waist. "I don't do it for accolades or recognition, Sophie. None of that is important to me."

"Isn't it?" she whispered. His hazel gaze sharpened, narrowing on her. Though her heart lodged in the base of her throat, she pushed on. "You might not do it for public consumption, but I suspect personal acknowledgment drives you even more."

A frown creased his forehead, and anger, as well as another unidentifiable emotion, flashed in his eyes. "You have no idea what you're talking about," he snapped.

She should let it go. He obviously didn't appreciate her playing armchair therapist. Especially not from the woman he was just fucking. But she couldn't. Joshua might not want her outside this bedroom, but God, he deserved so much more than this half life he lived. He was too good a man, had sacrificed so much for family and those who had been devastated by the Black Crescent scandal. And if no one else cared enough to tell him so, to let him off the hook he'd leaped on himself, then she would.

"Maybe not. But I know what I've seen. And as I told you before, I know you." Lowering her legs, she curled them under her hips and fully faced him. "Every time you set up a new program assisting those less fortunate than you... Every time you donate to a worthy cause... Every time you make another payment in reparation to the families bankrupted by your father's actions, you attempt to erase a black mark you believe mars your name. A black mark that you didn't put there and isn't yours anyway."

"Sophie, stop," he growled, throwing the sheet back and swinging his legs over the side of the bed.

But she shot her hand out, grabbing his wrist. He could've easily shaken her grip free, but he didn't. Maybe he didn't want to hurt her, and she had no problem taking shameless advantage of that display of thoughtfulness.

She rose to her knees and crossed the small space of the bed until she knelt at his side. Tentatively, she reached for him, her hand hovering above his shoulder. Not willing to back down now, she gently touched him. He didn't jerk away, but he remained stiff, unyielding. A slash of pain lacerated her heart, but she refused to back down.

Not when his happiness could be the casualty.

"You've lived in your father's toxic shadow all these years. When do you come out of it?" she asked softly. "When do you get the chance to live in the sun in your own light?"

"That sounds like a pretty fairy tale, but there is no coming out of it for me. Not as long as my last name is Lowell."

"But what if there is? You have nothing left to prove— you've rebuilt what Vernon almost destroyed. You've repaired your family's reputation with your hard work, dedication and loyalty. You've reimbursed the families your father stole from. What more can you give? Your life…your soul?"

He scoffed, but she didn't let him accuse her of being dramatic, which she was certain had been his next comment. Before he could reply, she slid off the bed and scooped up her discarded shirt from the floor with a "Be right back. Don't move."

By the time she returned moments later with a black binder in her arms, she half expected him to be already dressed and ready to leave her apartment. He had pulled his pants on, but they remained unbuttoned, and he sat in the same place she'd left him.

Relief flooded her, even as fear trickled underneath. Would she be revealing too much when she handed him the binder? Would he see what she so desperately tried to keep hidden?

Inhaling a breath, she crossed the few feet separating them and perched on the mattress next to him. "Here," she whispered, handing him the thick folder.

He glanced at her, his gaze steady and unwavering on her face. Searching. Though everything in her demanded she protect herself from that too-knowing, too-perceptive stare, she met it.

"What is it?" he asked, voice low, intense.

"Look," she instructed instead of answering. "Please."

After another long second, he finally nodded and accepted the binder. Her heart slammed against her rib cage like a wild thing, reverberating in her head and deafening her to everything but the incessant pounding.

Slowly, he flipped the top open.

And froze.

Afraid to lift her gaze to his face—afraid of what she'd glimpse there—she, too, studied the image of one of his mixed-media collages. This one reflected the tragedies of war. With haunting photographs, pieces of metal that appeared to be machinery, newspaper and paint, he'd created a powerful work that, even though it was a black-and-white copy, thrust into her chest and seized every organ. She *felt* when she looked at his art. Anger, grief, fear but also hope and joy. Jesus, how could one man create such raw, wild beauty? How could he walk away from it? Had it been like cauterizing a part of himself? She couldn't imagine…

Silent, Joshua flipped to the next page. A black-and-white copy of a piece commentating on homelessness. Another page. A work celebrating women, their struggle, their suffering, their strength, their beauty. Page after page of his art that both criticized and celebrated the human condition.

When he reached the last copy, he sat there, unmoving, peering down at it, unblinking.

"Why?" he rasped, the first word he'd spoken in the last ten minutes as he perused his past and what had once been his future.

She didn't pretend to misunderstand his question. "When I was researching you and your family for the first article, I came across several stories about you as an artist. From your college and local newspapers as well as several art columns. They carried pictures of your art. And they were so... *Good* is such an inadequate choice. They were visceral. And to think you, Joshua Lowell, had created them..." She shrugged a shoulder. "I guess it became kind of an obsession. I hunted down any image of your work I could find. Finding out about this man who could drag this from his soul and share it with the world? I needed to talk to him, to discover how he'd become a CEO instead of an artist. And that's why I wanted the article to include that side of you. Because I was struggling with reconciling the two."

"That man doesn't exist anymore," Joshua stated flatly. "You're searching for a ghost. He was buried fifteen years ago."

"I don't believe that," she countered. He glanced sharply at her, but she didn't tone down her vehemence. "You might have tried, but he trickles through when you help others follow their own dreams about art. When you support them and give your time and money toward them. If you'd truly put that man aside, he wouldn't help others who need him. That passion to educate people about this world may not have been exhibited in artwork these past years, but you still reveal it in your actions."

He shook his head, and despite the grim line of his full mouth, a tenderness entered his gaze. "You see what and who you want to, Sophie."

"No, I see you. This." She smoothed a hand over the image of his artwork. "This is you. A visionary. An activist and change agent in your own way. An *artist*." She tilted her head, studied his face. "What if your life doesn't end with Black Crescent? What if, after all these years, it's your time to live your own life, the one you left behind for family? A family that you owe nothing to but love and loyalty. You once said you couldn't abandon your family. But then you abandoned yourself. What's the worst that could happen if you followed your own delayed dreams, your own passions? Your mother will be okay and taken care of. And your brothers? If they choose to cut you out of their lives, then that's their problem and issues, not yours. Now's your time. And you never know. Maybe if given no other chance but to step up and assume the mantle of responsibility that you've worn for so long, your brothers might surprise you and do it."

She hesitated. Did she tell him all of it? In for a penny and all that... Inhaling a deep breath, she held it, then exhaled. And leaped.

"I didn't tell you before now, but Christopher Harrison with the Tender Shoots nonprofit approached me about you at the gala. He read my article, saw the pictures of your art included in it. He wants to offer you your own show in Manhattan, at the Guggenheim. Not only to bring in money for the organization, but he would be excited about seeing you reemerge as the artist you were. Are."

For a moment—a quick, heart-stopping moment—a light glittered in his eyes. A light that could've been hope or joy. But then, in the very next, his hazel eyes dimmed. And disappointment squeezed her chest, her heart. He

glanced away from her, staring at the far wall as if it revealed precious answers.

"That's not possible, and I'm not interested. You have no clue how it is to live under the weight of society's expectations," he murmured. His fingers curled into a fist atop the binder. But deliberately, he stretched them out, splaying them across the page—covering the image of his art. "You don't understand the burden of always knowing someone's waiting for you to misstep to prove that bad blood will out. It doesn't matter whether I continue to run Black Crescent or pick up a camera or paintbrush again. I can't escape, because I can't evade who I am. Joshua Lowell, Vernon Lowell's son."

She swallowed the silent sob of frustration, anger and grief. Grief for the man who believed he was forever tainted by the actions of his father. Who believed the only road available to him was the one he trod—even if it led to a future that wasn't his.

"Maybe not," she murmured, cupping his cheek and turning his face toward her. "But maybe I can help you bear the burden. Just a little."

Leaning forward, she brushed her lips across his, then covered his mouth with hers. His groan vibrated between them, before he turned, letting the binder fall to the floor, and hauled her up the bed. He took control of the kiss, crawling over her, finding his place between her thighs.

And as he consumed them both with his burning passion, she wept inside for him.

For the both of them.

Ten

"Josh, I'm heading home now," Haley announced from the doorway of his office. "Do you need anything before I leave?"

Joshua looked up from his computer. "No, I'm good."

Nodding, she stepped back, then paused, tilting her head to the side. "Everything okay with you?"

He leaned back in his chair, frowning. Other than a busy schedule and meetings all day, he was fine. He also had plans to meet Sophie at her apartment, so he was actually more than fine. But that, he kept to himself. "Yes, why do you ask?"

"You seem, I don't know—" her hazel eyes narrowed on him "—relaxed this past week. Something up I should know about?"

He snorted. "No, Haley. I'm good, like I said."

"Okay, if you say so."

"I say so."

"Well, not saying I don't believe you, but whatever—or

whoever—has turned you into the Zen version of Joshua Lowell, give them—or her—my thanks." With an impish smile and arched eyebrow, she stepped back and shut the door behind her before he could reply.

"Brat," he muttered, but after a moment, chuckled. Yes, she was definitely the annoying younger sister he never asked for. But he didn't know what he'd do without her, either.

Glancing at the clock at the bottom of his monitor, he nodded. Six ten. Finishing a review of the report his CFO had sent him would take only about fifteen more minutes, twenty tops. Then he could head out.

When was the last time he'd looked forward to leaving his office that had become his second—hell, first—home? Not until Sophie. A lot of things in his life could be separated into two eras. Before the Scandal and, now, After Sophie.

God, when had she become that significant in his life?

The answer blazed bright and sure. From the moment she barged into his office, demanding and so beautiful.

From the release of the article, to her revelation about his supposed child, to her ice-thawing passion and kindness... She'd changed his world.

She'd changed him.

A kernel of fear rooted inside him, and try as he might, he couldn't dislodge it. It'd been there since Monday night after she'd shocked him with the binder full of his previous artwork, and damn near taken him out with her body and the abandoned pleasure she'd offered him.

No one had ever taken the time to look further than the persona he presented. No one had bothered. Except for Sophie. She'd challenged him, as she'd been doing since their first meeting. Daring him to grab ahold of the dreams, the future he'd aborted when his father had disappeared. For a moment, he'd glimpsed what he could have, who he could be through her eyes. And the joy that had spread through him like the brightest and warmest of lights had been stunning. And terrifying.

Stunning because he hadn't felt such happiness in years—fifteen to be exact.

And terrified because he wanted it so badly. His old life back. The opportunity to work in his passion again. The possibility of his own show.

Sophie.

But he couldn't have any of them.

None of them were meant for him.

All he could do was be satisfied with the here and now, because it, too, would eventually end. Sophie would eventually leave him when she became discontented with what he could offer her. What he couldn't give her.

But he knew that going in. Everything ended. Everyone left.

Shaking his head, he frowned, refocusing on the work he had left to finish. But then a notification for an email popped up on the bottom of his screen.

The frown deepened, as did an unnerving sense of dread.

He hesitated, his cursor hovering over the notice. Dammit, what was he doing? It could be anyone. His clients and some of his employees worked longer hours than him. The message could be from any one of them.

Clenching his jaw, he resolutely clicked on the notification.

Anonymous.

Just like the name on the message that had arrived in his inbox yesterday.

Congratulations, Papa! Your daughter can't wait to meet you!

He'd passed it off as some kind of joke. Since no one had contacted him about a possible child, and Sophie hadn't found anything more concrete yet, he'd assumed the DNA test had been a mistake. Or a way to just mess with him by inserting his name at the top. Wouldn't he know, somehow *feel*, if he had a child out there? Though it'd thrown him, he'd ignored the email yesterday...and hadn't told Sophie about it.

But now, he stared at another email from the same person. Disquiet settled over him like a suffocating weight. Trepidation churned in his gut, and his grip on his mouse tightened until the casing squeaked a threatening crack.

He didn't want to open it.

So he did.

Don't know why you're denying it. I paid good money to make sure you'd get the proof.

The words blurred, jumbled together, then leaped into startling clarity. They glared up at him, almost blinding him. Tearing his gaze from the message, he pushed from his chair and stalked across the room, thrusting his fingers through his hair. But he couldn't escape the image branded into his head.

I paid good money to make sure you'd get the proof.

There was only one person who'd brought an illegitimate child to his attention.

One person who'd provided him with the so-called proof.

Sophie.

Anger rolled through him like an ominous storm cloud spiked with bolts of lightning. Hot, heavy, sizzling.

He'd been so stupid. So goddamn blind.

What had been her endgame? Send him on this wild-goose chase, pretend to help him just to get close and what? Write a story on the whole journey? Paint him as some deadbeat? Or a pathetic father on the search for a child who wasn't his? That maybe didn't even exist?

Pain tried to course through him, but he blocked it. Allowed the fury to capsize it.

Fury was better. It razed everything to the ground. Including the fact that he'd started to trust this woman, and he'd been betrayed.

Again.

Sophie stepped off the elevator onto the second floor of the Black Crescent building. Anticipation danced a quick step inside her, and she smiled. Joshua would be surprised to see her there, since they'd planned to meet at her apartment later. But she couldn't wait. She'd finished the follow-up article and wanted to give him the first look at it before Althea saw it Friday morning.

God, this trod so close to her experience with Laurence. She'd made the mistake of granting him the opportunity to read her articles first. But unlike her ex, Joshua wouldn't use this as a chance to sabotage the story or have her change it to fit his needs or agenda. One, Joshua didn't have an agenda. But two, and most important, he wasn't Laurence.

Nerves trotted in her belly, but they didn't trump the happiness spilling through her veins. This week had revealed even more of the man she'd fallen so hard for.

Yes, she could admit it to herself.

She loved Joshua Lowell.

And no, he hadn't rescinded his "no relationships" condition, but he felt more for her than someone to warm his—

or her—bed. She sensed it in his every small but genuine smile, the casual affection, the endearments, in the time he asked to spend with her.

God, did it make her pathetic that she was another woman believing she could change a man?

Probably.

But the knowledge didn't dim her smile as she knocked on his door, then pushed it open.

"Josh," she greeted, entering his inner sanctum. "I know we were supposed to meet at…" She trailed off, taking in the guarded, aloof expression she hadn't seen in a week. "What's wrong? Did something happen?"

She rushed forward to his desk, but drew to an abrupt halt when he rose, that glacial stare not melting or wavering from her face. No, it hardened, and dread curdled in her stomach. What the hell was going on here?

"Josh?" she whispered.

"Joshua," he corrected in an arctic voice that matched his gaze.

Only her hands flattened on his desk kept her from crumbling to the floor. But it couldn't prevent her heart from cracking down the middle and screams wailing from every jagged break.

"What's going on?" she rasped. "Why—"

Without shifting his contemptuous regard from her face, he slowly spun the monitor on his desk around to face her. She dragged her eyes from the stark lines and sharp angles that she'd just traced with her lips the night before and shifted them to the computer screen.

A thread of emails. From an address named Anonymous.

She skimmed them, her horror growing, the slick, grimy strands twisting around the happiness that had filled her only moments earlier, strangling it until only sickness remained. Bile surged up from her stomach, past her chest and raced for her throat. Convulsively, she swallowed it down.

Not because of what the emails stated; she had no idea who had sent them or what they were implying by paying to make sure Joshua had received the DNA test. Because she hadn't received any money. But obviously, just one glance at the anger and disdain in his green-and-gold eyes, and she knew—*she knew*—he believed she had.

The nausea swelled again with a vengeance.

"I don't know what this is supposed to mean," she said, reaching for a calm that had abandoned her the moment she'd stepped into this office. "No one gave me money to give you the DNA results. But you don't believe me," she added, voice curiously flat.

"What, Sophie? I'm supposed to believe you over my lying eyes?" he drawled, eyes snapping fire. "I wondered why you would show me the test when you were so adamant about protecting your research and sources." He loosed a harsh, serrated bark of ugly laughter. "Now I have my answer."

"You really think I would do this? Accept a bribe to trick you into believing you had a daughter?" she demanded, her own rage kindling, burning away the pain. For now. "For what? Why would I do that?"

"You're a reporter, Sophie. I don't know. An editorial piece that could grace the front of your paper might be a very good reason." A terrible half smile curved the corner of his mouth. "How would your editor in chief feel if she knew her star reporter resorted to underhanded tactics just to get a story?"

So much for the anger. Pain, red-hot and consuming, blazed a path through her. She could barely draw in a breath that didn't hurt. But she wouldn't allow him to see it. She'd given him everything—her trust, her faith…her love. And he'd shit over all of it.

No, he'd get nothing else. Most definitely not her tears or her pride. Fuck him.

"I don't know why I'm so surprised," she said, jerking her chin higher. "This is what you wanted. What you were waiting on. And that email is just the convenient excuse."

"Should I know what you're referring to?" he asked, the man who'd made her laugh, made her cry out in the most unimaginable pleasure, gone. And in his place stood the man of ice she'd originally met those weeks ago.

"You're so transparent, Joshua," she murmured, shaking her head. "You've just been waiting for me to screw up. To disappoint you. To leave you. Just like everyone else. But the sad part of it is I wouldn't have. I would've stayed by your side for as long as you asked. Longer. But you can't trust that. You can't possibly believe someone would put you first, would love you enough to never abandon or hurt you."

"Sophie," he growled, but she cut him off with a slash of her hand.

"No. You would rather self-sabotage and destroy what we had, what we could've had if you'd just let me love you and let yourself love. Instead, you would accuse me of something so horrible, so cruel that it's beneath me and definitely beneath you. You're nothing but a coward, Joshua Lowell." She shoved off the desk, silently promising her legs they could crumble later once she was in her car and away from this place, this man. But not now. "You've been running scared for so long that you can't even recognize when someone is running toward you and with you, not from you."

Pivoting, she focused on putting one foot in front of the other and not stumbling. Concentrated on just getting away. Even as part of her hoped, prayed he would call her name. Apologize. Take back the ugliness that had breathed in this office.

But he didn't. And another part of her broke.

As she reached the door, she paused.

Without looking back over her shoulder, she grabbed the doorjamb and stared straight ahead into the dim outer office.

"I love you, Joshua. When I didn't believe in it anymore, you showed me it could exist again for me. I don't regret that. But I do regret that you would rather hold on to the past than my heart. And for that, I pity you."

She pulled the door closed behind her.

Closing it on him…and who they could've been.

Eleven

"Well, if it isn't Joshua Lowell. Slumming it." Joshua glanced up from his whiskey to see a tall, lean but muscular man with dark brown hair and blue eyes sink down onto the stool next to his. "To what do we owe this honor?"

Ignoring the man and his irritating smirk, Joshua returned to his drink and stared blindly at the flat-screen television overhead, where a basketball game he couldn't care less about played. But anything was better than his empty, lonely apartment. Everywhere he looked, memories of Sophie bombarded him. In his living room. On his rug. In his kitchen. In his bed. It'd been only four hours since she'd left his office, her words ringing in the air long after she'd left.

I love you, Joshua... I do regret that you would rather hold on to the past than my heart. And for that, I pity you.

She loved him. How could she? He'd warned her he didn't do relationships. Didn't do happily-ever-afters. She'd called him a coward, but he had his reasons. And they were good reasons. They were...

Damn. He rubbed the bridge of his nose, pinching it, before lifting the tumbler to his mouth for another sip.

Yeah, even boring games, the din of conversation and subpar alcohol was better than the memories as his only company. Still, he thought while he glanced at the guy next to him as he called the bartender by name and ordered a beer, that didn't mean he wanted to be chatted up by a stranger with a chip on his shoulder. That smart-ass greeting had clued Joshua in that this man with his hard eyes and harder smile wasn't a fan of his.

Fuck. He'd come to this bar in the neighboring town for some peace, not more judgment from a drunken asshole.

"I heard the rumor you were here drinking, but I didn't believe it. Daryl, get another round for Mr. Lowell," he called to the bartender. "He looks like he could use it."

"No, thank you," Joshua told Daryl. "I'm good with what I have here."

"What? My money isn't good enough for a Lowell?" he drawled, a steel edge to his question. No, not a question. A gauntlet thrown down on the bar top between them.

Too bad for him, Joshua didn't feel like picking it up. That required too much effort, and he was just too tired.

"Do I know you?" Joshua turned, facing the other man, who seemed vaguely familiar, but his mind couldn't place him. "Because if not, then can you just tell me what your problem is with me so I can go back to my drink?"

A faint snarl curled the corner of his mouth. "Why am I not surprised that you don't recognize me? Why would you? From that lofty tower you rule from, it would be difficult to distinguish between the peasants. Even the ones you had a hand in destroying." Before Joshua could reply, the guy stuck his hand out. "Zane Patterson. Maybe you know the last name, if not me."

Patterson. The whiskey turned to swill in his stomach, roiling. God, yes, he knew that name. It'd been the name of one of the families that had been his father's clients.

"Oh, so I see you do remember." Zane nodded. "I guess that makes you somewhat better than your father, who screwed us over and never looked back."

"Yes, I do, and yes, he did," Joshua agreed, earning an eyebrow arch from Zane. Had the other man expected him to deny the accusation? To defend Vernon. He silently snorted. Not in this lifetime. Or the next, if his father was indeed there instead of lying around some beach surrounded by younger women and mai tais.

"What are you doing here, Lowell?" Zane asked, picking up the beer the bartender set in front of him. Sipping from the mug, he studied Joshua over the rim. "Drowning your woes, maybe?"

"Listen, I understand why you of all people can't stand the sight of me. But I'm here, just trying to have a drink. You can hate me from across the room."

"Still so high and mighty," Zane murmured. "Even after finding out you're no better than the rest of us. Worse, I'd say. You wouldn't catch me abandoning a kid of mine. But like father, like son, I guess."

Shock slammed into him, nearly toppling him from the stool. "What the hell did you just say to me?" he rasped.

A sardonic smile darkened Zane's face. "You heard me. Don't tell me the reporter didn't give you the DNA test results? I specifically chose Sophie Armstrong to share that with."

The shock continued to resonate through him like the drone of a thousand bees, but anger started to rush in like a tide, swallowing it. "You paid Sophie to make sure I received it?" he ground out.

"Paid her? Hell no. It was free of charge. And my pleasure." He again smiled, but it nowhere near reached his icy blue eyes. No, that wasn't correct. They weren't icy. Something volatile and...bleak darkened those eyes. Pain. If Joshua wasn't mired in it, he might not have been able to identify it. "Someone anonymously emailed the results to me," Zane continued, his level voice not reflecting the turmoil he would probably deny existed in his gaze. "And I just passed them along. The test spoke for itself, so I really didn't give a damn who sent them. But whoever it was must've known I wouldn't mind paying it forward. Your father and family destroyed my world, my family." Gravel roughened his tone, and Zane jerked his head away from Joshua. A muscle ticked along his jaw as he visibly battled some emotion he no doubt hated that Joshua glimpsed. After several seconds, the other man returned his regard to Joshua, his expression carefully composed. Too blank. "I was only too happy to return the favor. Everyone believes you're this perfect guy when you have a child out there that you won't even take care of. I can't wait for people to find out just who you really are."

Oh God.

He'd fucked up.

Numb, Joshua turned back to face the bar, Zane's hurt scraping Joshua's skin, his bitter words buzzing in his ears. He'd sent the DNA tests. Free of charge. Sophie had been telling the truth. No one had paid her to show him the results. She hadn't lied to him.

But... He'd known that, hadn't he?

Deep down, where that terrified, lonely and angry twenty-two-year-old still existed, he'd known she wouldn't have been capable of betraying him. She'd been right about him; he was a coward. So scared she would leave him like everyone else he'd loved, he'd jumped on the first obstacle that had presented itself to push her out the door. Save himself the pain of her rejecting him and walking away from him.

Even though he'd known she could never do what he'd accused her of. Not sweet, honorable, honest, strong Sophie. She said that she knew him better than anyone else, but he also knew her. Fear had kept him from acknowledging it in his office, but the truth couldn't be denied. He did know her.

And he loved her.

He *loved* her.

She'd seen beyond his tainted past and who his father was and had accepted him, believed in him, when he hadn't even been able to do the same for himself. She'd seen him as blameless, as a hero for so many people, as an artist with a passion and a dream. Sophie had never given up on him.

Now it was time he didn't. Time he believed in himself. In them.

Setting the drink on the bar, Josh reached into his jacket and removed his wallet. He threw down several bills that covered his drinks and a healthy tip before turning back to Zane.

"I'm sorry my father caused you and your family so much pain. He was greedy and selfish and had no thought whatsoever for who he would hurt. But I was every bit as much of a victim as you were. I lost my family, too. But I refuse to apologize or take on his guilt and shame anymore, though. I've tried to make amends for his sins. But I'm tired of it. I'm done."

Without pausing or waiting to hear what Zane Patterson had to say to that, he pivoted and strode out of the bar.

For the first time in a decade and a half, feeling…free.

* * *

"Dammit," Sophie muttered, jerking the strap of her laptop bag from the car door where it'd snagged. Huffing out a breath, she let it slip to the ground and reached in the back seat for the cardboard box that contained some of her personal items from her desk.

Tears stung her eyes as she scanned the framed photo of her and her mom on vacation at Myrtle Beach a couple of years ago, her favorite "only the strongest women become writers" coffee mug and several other knickknacks. She'd waited until almost everyone on her floor had left for the evening before she packed up most of the items and carried them to her car. Fewer questions that way. Especially since she hadn't yet informed her boss that she was leaving her job with the *Falling Brook Chronicle*.

It'd been her decision, and not one she made lightly.

And not because she feared Joshua would follow through with his subtle threat about informing Althea of being paid to pass on the DNA test. And also not because she was afraid her editor in chief would fire her after finding out she and Joshua had slept together.

No, she was leaving the paper and Falling Brook for herself.

Start over fresh.

Free of memories of Joshua and her own foolishness.

Maybe she'd return to Chicago. Or even go somewhere totally new, like Seattle. She'd visited once in college and had loved the eclectic and vibrant energy of the city...

"Sophie."

No. It couldn't be. Her stubborn, starved brain had conjured up his voice. She squeezed her eyes close, trying to banish it. The last thing she needed was to start imagining him when she was trying to let him go.

"Sophie, please. Can I have just a minute?"

Okay, this was no dream. Even her mind couldn't envision Joshua Lowell saying "please."

She carefully set her box back onto the seat, then pivoted.

And she really should've taken several more minutes to prepare herself for coming face-to-face with him after yesterday. God, it was so unfair. He'd stomped all over her heart. That should wear on a man. He should at least have new wrinkles. Bags under his eyes. Gray hair.

Horns.

But no, he was as beautiful as ever.

Damn him.

"What are you doing here, Joshua?"

"What is that?" he asked instead of answering, his gaze focused on the cardboard box before jumping to her face. "Are you planning on going somewhere, Sophie?"

"That isn't any of your business." Not anymore. Sighing, she shut the rear door and picked up her laptop bag. She'd just come back for the rest of her stuff later. "Now, please answer my question. What are you doing here?"

"I came to see you," he said.

She shrugged a shoulder, moving past him toward her apartment building. "Well, you've achieved that objective, so if you'll excuse me…"

A firm but gentle grip encircled her elbow, and she briefly closed her eyes, thankful her back was to him. He couldn't witness the pain and longing that streaked through her at his touch. She vacillated between ordering him to never put his hands on her again and throwing herself into his arms, begging him to hold her…to love her.

Why, yes. She was pathetic.

Deliberately, she stepped back, out of his hold. Then shifted back even farther so even his scent couldn't tease her.

Pride notched her chin up high as she forced herself to

meet his gaze. A gaze that wasn't cold like the last time they'd been together. No, it was softer, even…tender.

She hardened her heart, made herself remember how he'd accused her of lying to him, betraying him. Made herself remember that he'd cracked her heart in so many fragments, she still hadn't been able to find all the pieces.

"Sophie, one minute. That's all I'm asking, and then if you want me to, I'll walk away and never bother you again."

"Thirty seconds," she shot back. That was what he'd given her the first time she'd bulldozed her way into his office.

As if he, too, recalled the significance, a small smile curved his mouth. "I'll take it." He rubbed a hand across the nape of his neck and moved forward, but at the last second, halted. Respecting the distance she'd placed between them. "Sophie, I'm sorry. I'm so sorry for not believing in you. For accusing you of selling me out. For jumping to conclusions and painting you as the villain. For looking at you through the lens of my past instead of seeing who you really are. You were right about me. I was so scared you would leave me so I used whatever excuse I could to push you away first. I would rather be alone than risk the chance of someone hurting me again, betraying me again. And I punished you for my fears, my shortcomings. I'll never forgive myself for letting you walk out that door believing that I thought you capable of that. I know words are inadequate, but, sweetheart, I'm so fucking sorry."

Her lungs hurt from her suspended breath. His apology reached beneath skin and bone to her bruised and wounded heart, cupped it. Soothed it.

But the words were a little too late. The damage had been done. And she couldn't undo the hurt, the humiliation. The rejection of her love.

Her rejection of herself.

"Joshua, a few years ago, I met a man. Fell in love with him," she whispered. "I didn't know it at the time, but he was using me for his own ends. Not that you've ever done that," she hurriedly added, because of all he'd done to her, Joshua was incapable of that kind of perfidy. It just wasn't in him. "But I almost lost my career—I almost lost myself—because I loved the wrong man. A man who didn't love me in return. I did lose my way, though. And I promised myself I would never give up my job, my independence, my integrity, my soul for another man. The cost was too high, and I wasn't—I'm not—willing to pay it. But standing in your office last night, I found myself on the precipice of doing just that. I may not have betrayed you, but I almost betrayed myself. I won't put myself in that position again. I refuse to." She shook her head, a heavy grief of what could've been for them an albatross around her shoulders. "Thank you for coming here, but I don't need your apology. I know who I am. I know what I deserve. A man who loves and trusts me. Who won't ask me to be less so he can be secure. A life where I can have it all and not feel guilty because I compromised myself to get it."

"You do deserve all of that, Sophie," he rasped, the fierceness in his voice widening her eyes, leaving her shaken. "All of it and more. I—" He took that step toward her that he'd hesitated over moments ago. "I am that man who loves and trusts you. I'd never ask you to be less so I can be secure, because the greater you are, the happier you are, the more successful you are, the better I am as a man. The man who loves and supports you. Compromise? If you compromised who you are, I would never know the joy of having all of you, just as you are. Brilliant, strong, determined, driven, beautiful. Sweetheart—" he tunneled a hand through his hair, disheveling the short, dark blond strands "—you've shown me that I don't have to bear my father's burdens any longer. You've taught me that I'm not forgotten, that I am so much more than I ever believed possible. I thought what happened with my father fifteen years ago was the worst thing that could ever happen to me. But if it hadn't occurred, you wouldn't have written an article on it. You wouldn't have come crashing into my life. And, sweetheart, all the pain, all the fear, all the loss—I'd go through it all again in a heartbeat if it meant meeting you, touching you…loving you." He closed the distance between them and cradled her cheek. "If that box means you're leaving your job, please don't do it. That's a compromise you should never make."

Tears stung her eyes, and she choked on the hope that insisted on rising in her chest. She'd called him a coward yesterday, but now it was her who was terrified. Of being crushed again. Because unlike Laurence, he could destroy her, and though she would find a way to cobble herself together again, she wouldn't be whole.

No, she couldn't.

Not again.

As much as she loved him, she just…couldn't.

"Joshua, I'm sorry. I can't. I love you—I probably always will—but I'm not that strong. I…can't."

She couldn't contain her sob as she cupped his hand and turned her face into it. Kissed it.

Then fled into her apartment building.

Twelve

Joshua stood near the bank of elevators, the animated and excited hum of chatter from Black Crescent's lobby reaching him. Beyond the wall he stood behind congregated reporters and cameramen from the tristate area. All hungry and anticipating the announcement that Joshua had promised to deliver. Anything concerning Black Crescent Hedge Fund would've stirred their interest, but on a Saturday morning, coming from Joshua himself, who never did press conferences, they would've jumped on this tidbit. Just as he'd hoped.

The media expected a business-related statement. And they would receive that.

But so much more.

Joshua's future rode on this press conference.

"Ready, Josh?" Haley asked, laying a hand on his upper arm. Concern and just a bit of sadness darkened her hazel eyes. "Are you sure about this?"

He nodded. "I've never been more certain about anything in my life." He covered her hand with his and clasped it. "And just in case I've never said so before, thank you for everything you've been to this company and to me. Those first few years, I don't know if I would've been able to make it without you."

Tears glistened in her eyes, but, Haley being Haley, she tipped her chin up and cleared her throat. "You're right. You wouldn't have," she drawled.

He chuckled and, giving her hand one last squeeze, moved forward into the throng of media.

At his appearance, the noise reached a fever pitch as questions were lobbed at him from overeager journalists. But he ignored them as he stepped to the podium and microphone, scanning the crowded lobby for one person...

There.

Sophie stood in the middle, lovely and composed.

Relief barreled into him. He'd been afraid she wouldn't show up—had even placed a call to Althea to request Sophie's presence. But that hadn't guaranteed she would've agreed. Seeing her here, though, the anxiety that he'd fought off all morning kicked in the door of his calm. This was the most important moment of his life. Hell, he was fighting for his life—his future.

I love you—I probably always will—but I'm not that strong.

Her words, so final but so weary, echoed in his head. The resolve in her voice had set his heart pounding, terrified he'd lost her. But hope, his love for her and, yes, desperation refused to let him give up. He would go to war for her. He just had to hold on to her declaration of love. And his belief that she was stronger than both of them put together.

"Thank you for coming here today on such short notice," he said into the mic. Immediately, the voices hushed, but the excitement and tension crackled in the air. "I'm going to share my announcement and will take only a few questions at the end."

He inhaled, his eyes once more finding and locking onto Sophie. Her silver gaze met his, and he found the strength to continue there.

"Fifteen years ago, I took the helm of Black Crescent Hedge Fund after my father embezzled money from the company, nearly bankrupting it and devastating his clients and their families. Since that time, I've rebuilt the business and have tried to make reparations for his crimes. But today, I will be stepping down as CEO of Black Crescent."

A roar of disbelief filled the lobby and camera flashes nearly blinded him. Still, he kept his attention on Sophie, spying the shock and confusion that widened her eyes and parted her lips. Questions bombarded him, and he held up his hands, warding them off. Again, silence descended.

"Over the next few months there will be a search for my successor. He or she will be carefully handpicked to replace me as CEO. I'm sure you're all wondering why I'm resigning. I plan to go back to my first love, my art. I gave it up to run Black Crescent, but I've decided to return to it. And possibly—if the woman I'm in love with will agree to marry me—to plan a wedding."

Again, the room erupted. But he cared only about Sophie's reaction, and his heart seized at the shock and tears and...and love. *Please, God, let that be love glistening in her gray eyes.*

"I let my pride and fear blind me and hold me hostage for far too long. And I'm praying that it doesn't cost me her love. I've spent too many years in my father's shadow, worrying what other people thought. If I was worthy enough. But she brought me out of the dark and into the light with her love. And because she loves me, I am worthy. And I want to spend the rest of my life proving that she didn't make a mistake by taking a chance on me. If she'll have me."

He stared at her, silently willing her to let him tell the world her identity. But more, silently asking her again for her forgiveness and her love. Her hand in marriage.

It seemed like an eternity passed as he stood behind that podium, reporters yelling at him, cameras flashing again and again. But still, he caught her nod. Caught that beautiful smile that lit up her face, her eyes and his heart.

"Sophie, will you come up here with me?"

She didn't hesitate, but wound a path through the throng, and like Moses with the Red Sea, they parted, letting her pass. He didn't pay attention to anyone but her. His heart swelling larger than his chest as she neared. And when his hand finally enfolded hers, something inside him that had been hollow, filled. That lost puzzle piece slotted into its place, and he was whole. Complete.

He drew her close, and closer still until she walked into his arms. Bending his head over hers, he pressed a kiss to her hair. A shiver worked through him and he didn't care who saw it. She was in his embrace again. Her scent enveloped him. She warmed him. And God, he'd been cold for so long.

Leaning back, he cupped her face, tipping her head back. The tears he'd glimpsed seconds ago tracked down her face, and he wiped them away with his thumbs, brushing his lips across her cheekbones, the bridge of her nose, her lips.

"Sophie Armstrong, I'm who I was meant to be with you. I was created to love you, and I not only cannot imagine a future without you, I don't want one without you in it. Would you do me the honor of being my wife?"

"Yes, Josh," she said without hesitation and with a certainty and confidence that erased the hurt, shame and pain that had dogged him for fifteen years. "I love you, and there's nothing I want more than to live by your side."

With reporters exploding into chaos around them, he claimed her mouth.

And his future.

* * * * *

HIDDEN AMBITION

JULES BENNETT

To my girls, Grace and Madelyn. Thanks for keeping things running while I was pressed for time with this deadline. You two are my world.

One

Haley Shaw bent over the gift boxes, searching around the obscene bouquets of flowers and cupcake boxes, just trying to find her damn yellow highlighter.

"That's quite a display."

The low, throaty voice was all too familiar...and all too arousing.

Haley straightened and turned to face a smirking, sexy Chase Hargrove. The persistent man was vying for the coveted position of CEO of Black Crescent Hedge Fund. The successful investment firm had been through hell and back, and Haley had stuck through it all—which made her the target of all the résumés and all of the bribes. Hence the gifts cluttering her normally pristine work space.

"I assume you were referring to the flowers and boxes and not the fact I was bent over with my backside facing you while looking for my highlighter," she stated, smoothing down her conservative dove-gray pencil dress.

His deep brown eyes held hers. "Of course."

Sure. That naughty grin gave him away and she had a feeling a powerful man like Chase always held his emotions and cards close to his chest. He wanted her unnerved, thrown off track. Well, it would take a hell of a lot more than charm and a little flirting to really get her attention.

Haley prided herself on her professionalism. She'd worked too hard, overcome too much, to land where she was. True, she was an executive assistant, but she had power here at Black Crescent and she never let her emotions, or a man, get in the way of her duties.

Not even this sexy man who was very qualified to take over the coveted CEO position and potentially become her boss.

"Do you have an appointment?" she asked, knowing full well he didn't.

Chase had been popping in and out over the past several weeks, ever since Josh Lowell had announced he was stepping down and the CEO position would be available. Chase had turned in a rather impressive résumé and had even landed an interview a few weeks ago. The position had been offered to Ryan Hathaway, but ultimately, Ryan turned down the coveted title. So the search continued as Chase moved closer to the top of the list. Hence Chase pursuing the job...and her.

Not that she minded a sexy distraction, but she really did need to get her work done and there was no chance of that as long as Chase stood at her desk with that panty-dropping stare.

Maybe he really was here for the job, but he spent an exorbitant amount of time charming her.

Haley was Josh's right-hand woman and everyone thought she was the gatekeeper in regards to the top position. Haley had to admit, she didn't hate all of this attention. Who could be mad when cupcakes, flowers and chocolates were delivered on the daily?

"I do have an appointment," he amended with a naughty, crooked grin. "With you."

Confused, she crossed her arms over her chest. "Me?"

"For lunch."

Oh, he was a smooth one. He thought he could waltz in here, pour on the charisma and she'd just take him up on a day date? Clearly he knew nothing about women...or at least this woman. She didn't let anything interrupt her work. Or at least, she never did before him.

"I'm not free for lunch." She lifted one vase, then another, on her desk, glancing for all the things she'd lost in this chaos. "But you go have a nice time."

"What are you looking for?" he asked, obviously in no hurry to go.

"My highlighter," she informed him. "I keep getting all of these gifts and I've run out of room for things I actually need. I normally have everything in a designated spot, but now…"

She tossed her hands up, frustrated with how quickly her space had become unorganized.

"When we go to lunch, we can stop and get you as many new highlighters as you need," he suggested. "My treat."

Haley glanced up and really wished her belly would stop doing those schoolgirl flops over a hot guy and his offer to buy her dollar markers.

So what if his shoulders perfectly filled out that black suit jacket? So what if his messy hair looked like he'd just rolled out of his lover's bed? He wouldn't be rolling out of her bed, so she really had no place fantasizing about such things.

She had important issues to tend to and getting distracted by a man who likely wasn't interested in her, but in how far she could get him in this field, was not one of them.

The phone on her desk rang and she sighed. "If you'll excuse me, I need to get back to work."

She took the call and moments later when she hung up, she was surprised to see he had actually left. But there wasn't a doubt in her mind that Chase Hargrove would be back. A man like that never gave up.

Chase clutched the surprise in his hand and headed into Black Crescent Hedge Fund for the second time that morning. Determination and revenge were a combination that no rejection could penetrate.

No matter how many times he had to show his face, flirt a little or buy silly bribes, he'd sure as hell do it. A little humility was nothing in comparison with what his family had gone through at the hands of Vernon Lowell.

The sneaky bastard had squandered millions and disappeared fifteen years ago, but Chase would never forget the struggle his family went through after his father was framed by Vernon to take some of the fall.

Chase's father had landed in prison for a few years, paying for his actions after Vernon had left a neat and tidy paper trail leading right to their door.

Now Chase had the opportunity to seek his own justice, since Vernon was never caught. His son Josh was now at the helm, and Chase didn't find him exempt from the damage.

He hadn't counted on the perks of the revenge plot, though. Getting an eyeful of Haley Shaw was certainly an added bonus. There was something about her unruffled attitude that made him want to just get his digs in where he could...which was why he didn't mind one bit that she'd caught him staring at her ass.

He wasn't a jerk or a guy who took advantage of women. He respected women, but if a male held the position that Haley did, Chase would certainly be going about this via a much different route.

As he stepped through the double glass doors, he nodded to the receptionist and headed toward the elevators. One day soon, this would all be his. Chase had the credentials and was more than qualified to settle perfectly into the CEO position. But if not, then he'd at least get the scoop he needed to help bring Black Crescent down for good. They deserved nothing less and Haley was inadvertently going to help him.

As for the top slot here, Chase didn't need it. He sure as hell wasn't hurting for money, but he wouldn't mind adding another investment firm to his portfolio.

Chase stepped out of the elevator and walked toward Haley's large circular desk, and once again the overwhelming scent of flowers assaulted him. He shouldn't be surprised at all the candidates vying for her attention, though they were being too predictable. Boxes of gourmet chocolates? Oversize floral arrangements? Cupcakes from the local bakery? Please. Those candidates were amateurs and utterly boring.

Haley had her back to him and was holding a stack of papers, muttering beneath her breath. A woman getting caught up in her work was damn sexy, but he wasn't here for seduction. Shame that. Having Haley under different circumstances wasn't something he'd turn down. Classy, smart, powerful… She was the entire package of sex appeal.

Chase pushed lustful thoughts from his head and tapped his knuckles on the edge of the desk. She startled and glanced over her shoulder, her wavy blond hair framing her face.

"Back so soon?" she asked, quirking a brow.

Damn if her sarcasm didn't up his attraction to her. He had to admit, this challenge wasn't proving to be boring. He actually looked forward to his interactions with Haley.

Chase held up the present. "I brought you something."

Her eyes darted to his hand and she turned fully to face him. "Seriously?" She laughed as she circled her desk. "Is that a bouquet of highlighters?"

He extended the gift. "You couldn't find yours and you had enough flowers and gourmet-cupcake boxes."

She stared at the bundle for a second before she took the variety of colors. The wide smile on her face was like a punch of lust to his gut. Not exactly what he'd come looking for, but something about her simple style and natural beauty appealed to a side he didn't want to be appealed to.

Lust and desire didn't follow guidelines, though. He couldn't help this attraction and he couldn't help but wonder if she was getting that kick of arousal, as well.

"Well done," she told him with a wide grin. "I admire someone who thinks outside the box."

Chase shoved his hands in his pockets. "Admire enough to go to lunch? You do get a lunch break, right?"

"I do," she confirmed. "But I'm not going to lunch with you. I have other plans."

"Cancel them."

She cocked her head. "Are you always demanding?"

"When I see something I want."

And there it was. A glimpse of desire he hadn't quite been sure about flashed through her eyes. Well, well, well. Maybe he could keep working this angle and come out with the job and a side fling. Win-win.

"Fine," she conceded. "We'll go to lunch, but we will not talk business."

Not talk business? No problem. He could gather information from her without her even realizing he was doing so. He hadn't gotten this far making billions by not being able to read people.

Besides, he'd already worn her down—by a bouquet of highlighters, no less. Chase was confident he would get damaging intel from her and she wouldn't have a clue she'd even let him in.

"Lead the way," he said, gesturing to her door.

Chase followed those swaying hips and reminded himself he was here for a purpose, a vendetta, not to see how quickly he could slide that zipper down and have her out of that body-hugging dress.

Only time would tell which one of them came out on top... But Chase didn't intend to lose.

Two

Haley nodded her thanks to the concierge as he opened the door for her and Chase. The posh, up-scale restaurant was a bit over-the-top for a lunch between virtual strangers, but this was where he'd chosen and she actually did love their Mediterranean salad.

"Welcome back, Mr. Hargrove," the hostess promptly greeted them with all smiles. "I have your usual table all set up."

Haley bit the inside of her cheek to keep quiet as she followed the hostess back to the corner of the restaurant. The intimate table for two offered a spectacular view of New York City, one she appreciated when she ate here at night.

Once they were seated and alone, Haley glanced

across the table. "So, how many women do you bring here, Mr. Hargrove?"

"Chase," he corrected with a crooked grin. "And not many."

"Yet you have a usual table and I can't imagine a man like you eating alone." She pulled in a breath and leveled her gaze. "Chase."

His eyes dropped to her lips the second she said his name and she seriously wished she would've kept the *Mr. Hargrove* in the conversation. It wasn't like her to get all tingly at the sight of a man, but no man had looked at her like he wanted to devour her...at least not in a long time.

Maybe she needed to date. Perhaps she'd been working too much. Once this new CEO position was filled, she would work on her social life. But not with a man like Chase Hargrove.

Chase was a man who no doubt liked nice things, always had a sexy woman on his arm and demanded people to bow to him. She'd seen enough of his type over the years in this business to know exactly what he required. She was most definitely not his type.

No, Chase flirted and was no doubt going to all this trouble to get into that top slot at Black Crescent. She wasn't stupid, but she'd let him play his little game if that made him feel better about himself.

And, hey, she got new highlighters and a lunch out of it, so this wasn't a total loss. Besides, the view across the table was rather appetizing.

"I'm confident enough to eat alone," he replied. "I

often meet acquaintances here or friends and, yes, I have brought a date here a time or two."

"And what category are you sliding me into?" she asked, smoothing the cloth napkin onto her lap.

Those dark eyes shielded by heavy lids could make a woman forget whom she was dealing with. But Haley wasn't a ditz, despite how she'd been treated for years by her family.

She'd fought damn hard to get where she was today, with no help from her parents. Being an executive assistant wasn't easy work and oftentimes could be overlooked considering the amount of behind-the-scenes tasks that were involved. That wasn't the case with working with Josh. They clashed every now and then, but they also had a mutual respect for each other.

And now they were working closely together to find the perfect replacement to take Black Crescent into a successful, prosperous future.

Haley prided herself on how loyal and dedicated she had been to a company that had floundered amid the biggest scandal this town had ever seen and had climbed back up out of the ashes.

True, she may have gone only to a community college, but that didn't make her degree any less important or inferior to her brother's Ivy League status.

"Which category do you want to be in?" he retorted.

Pulling herself back into the moment, Haley pursed her lips and weighed her answer, but thankfully the waiter came by. Of course Chase knew the man by name, asked about his work, made a joke and laughed. This must be a favorite hot spot for Chase... or the man owned the place.

Josh trusted her to see things he didn't. Allison Randall, the executive recruiter Black Crescent hired, did the professional vetting on his résumé. Everything was perfect.

Too perfect? Haley made a mental note to dig into Chase's past and find out just what he was up to. Of course, he'd had a remarkable résumé and all of his references had checked out, but she wanted to know more. She wanted to dive into that personal side of him that he hadn't revealed.

Haley didn't believe he'd go to all this trouble just to be the CEO of Black Crescent. And she certainly didn't believe he was trying to sway her into dating him—maybe bed her.

Haley and Chase both placed their drink orders and sent the waiter away. Before they could circle back to the conversation, her cell chimed and she slid the phone from her purse. One glance to the screen and she sent Chase an apologetic smile.

"I need to take this," she told him.

Chase nodded. "I understand. Business first."

But it wasn't the business he was thinking and she didn't necessarily need privacy, so she eased back in her seat and answered.

"Marcus," she greeted. "I was going to call you this afternoon."

"I just wanted to touch base with you regarding

the latest funding," her right-hand man told her. "The latest investor doubled their original donation."

Haley gasped. "You're serious?"

She didn't miss the way Chase stared at her, hanging on every word. This call had nothing to do with Black Crescent and everything to do with Haley's charity that was like her baby.

"Very," Marcus replied. "That means we can take on seven more high school seniors."

Haley closed her eyes and pulled in a deep breath, relieved they could take on more teens in need. This was the best news. She'd been struggling to get to the stack of applicants from area high schools.

Her nonprofit, Tomorrow's Leaders, aided teens who wouldn't be able to go to college without the funding of an outside source. Not every kid wanted a student loan they'd have to pay back before some even found a job. These underprivileged kids deserved the best opportunity for a solid foundation to jump-start their futures and Haley was all too happy to make it happen.

She had been that underprivileged kid. Her parents had put her older brother through Harvard, but that had sucked up their entire savings. They'd believed he would become some master surgeon or celebrity attorney... Hell, she didn't know what their plans had been. All Haley knew was they had low expectations for her and no money to expand her education beyond high school. So Haley had worked her ass off to pay for the community schooling and graduated top of her class without any outside help.

"I will take this evening and look through the files again," she told Marcus. "I can't tell you what a blessing this is to know we can take on more kids."

"I knew you'd be thrilled. That's why I wanted to call and not text. I hope I didn't interrupt anything."

Her eyes met Chase's again and he didn't even bother to hide the fact he was staring.

"Your timing was just fine," she stated. "I'll get back with you late tonight or early tomorrow about the applicants."

Haley disconnected the call and slid the phone back into her purse.

"Kids?" he asked, raising his brows.

She smiled. "Well, teenagers, but considering I'm thirty-four, they're kids to me."

"You work with teens?" he asked, clearly shocked, and if she was reading him right, maybe a little impressed.

"For several years now," she confirmed, proud of the work she'd done all on her own. "I run Tomorrow's Leaders. It's a nonprofit organization that assists college-aged students who wouldn't otherwise be able to go. Not everyone wants the black cloud of student loans looming over them when they graduate, and many kids can't afford to further their education and they aren't all eligible for scholarships."

Chase listened, his eyes never wavering from hers. Not everyone knew what she did in her spare time. Not that she wasn't extremely proud of the work she'd done, but she wasn't one to brag and she didn't really have the time to socialize between finding a new CEO and running her charity.

"Impressive," he stated as he leaned back in his chair. "You're one busy woman."

"Which is why I often eat lunch at my desk," she informed him.

"Then I'm doubly glad I got you out of there."

Chase smiled, which really shouldn't make her belly do flops, but the man was a little more potent than she'd first given him credit for. She had to remain on her toes where this one was concerned.

"How long have you been doing this nonprofit?" he asked.

Haley never tired of talking about her cause. She didn't talk to many outside of her office or those directly involved with Tomorrow's Leaders. Her family didn't even know what she did, but then again, she rarely saw or spoke to them.

But who knew, maybe Chase would want to become a donor.

"Twelve years," she informed him. "As soon as I finished school, I started campaigning for donors and working to get something up and running. The first year, I was only able to help one guy, but that was better than nothing. Even if I could only help one person a year, I would still fight just as hard for funding."

Chase stared across the table, then leaned forward, resting his forearms on the white cloth. "What makes you so vigilant about this subject? You went to college, right?"

"I did," she confirmed. "But my backstory is not up for discussion."

Discussing her whys for the whole nonprofit organization wasn't her favorite topic, and the last thing she ever wanted was for someone to believe she felt sorry for herself. She didn't pity her childhood or how she managed to make it through college. If she didn't have those hardships, she wouldn't be the strong career woman she was today and she wouldn't have founded Tomorrow's Leaders. Maybe her parents hadn't done her a disservice after all.

Added to all of that, Chase was still out for his own gains and she didn't want to give him any insight to her personal life. This was nothing more than a lunch between strangers. If he was trying to seduce her, well, that was a whole other level of consideration for her to think about.

"Maybe on our second date," he stated with a grin.

Haley laughed. "This isn't a date."

"No? Well, then we'll have to fix that." He curled his hand around his water glass and tipped his head. "Friday at eight. I'll send a car to pick you up."

Haley stared at him for a moment before she busted out laughing. "Does that usually work for you? Just to demand like that?"

He shrugged. "Do you have other plans?"

"My personal life really isn't your concern," she replied.

"And yet you shared your nonprofit with me and had such compassion in your tone," he retorted. "I'd say that's pretty personal."

"Maybe I was hoping you'd want to donate."

His lips twitched and she knew he was biting back a smile. Good. He needed to keep those sexy smiles to a minimum for her sanity.

"One hundred thousand dollars."

"Excuse me?" she asked.

"I'll give Tomorrow's Leaders one hundred thousand dollars if you go out with me on Friday."

Haley narrowed her eyes, disappointed he'd resorted to buying her. "I can't be bought, not even for my foundation."

Obviously he wasn't used to taking no for an answer, but he might as well get used to it because she was not giving in. Okay, the highlighters had won him a lunch, but no more.

They placed their orders and Haley really wished she would've stayed in her office for lunch like always. She had too much to do, too many things to oversee, and she honestly hated leaving in the middle of a workday.

Being so valuable within Black Crescent made her feel a sense of worth, one she hadn't found with anything else in her life. She'd come there as an intern straight out of college and had only grown with each passing year. There were secrets she knew that she would never reveal, and that was why Josh Lowell entrusted her with the daunting task of helping him find his replacement.

Because she was the longest-standing employee, résumés were sent to her and not to Josh, or even to Allison Randall, the executive recruiter.

Haley and Josh had both laughed about the fact people were wanting to deal with her, because she wasn't the final decision maker. Although, she rather enjoyed knowing how powerful some people thought she was.

Her cell chimed again and she didn't even apologize for taking this next call. After Chase had offered a ridiculous amount to take her on a real date, she didn't care what he thought or if her manners were lacking.

Josh's name lit up her screen and she slid her finger across to answer.

"Hey, Josh."

"Haley, sorry to interrupt your lunch. I just had a quick question."

"No problem at all."

The waiter came with their food and Chase made work of cutting up his chicken, but she knew he was hanging on every word.

"I can't find Matt's résumé," he began. "I had it before his first interview and I wanted to look at it again."

The names slid through her mind, but Matteo Velez stood out. Matt's résumé was impeccable and he'd aced the first interview.

"I still have it on my computer," she told her boss. "I'll get it to you as soon as I get back."

"I ran into him the other evening when I was out with Sophie," Josh told her. "He bought my dinner, actually."

Josh chuckled, but Haley rolled her eyes. Everyone thought they could get ahead by buying their way, but that didn't fly with her. She'd rather have actions, not money being tossed around.

A lesson Chase would do well to learn.

"Please remember, I'm going to need someone personable I can get along with once you're gone and I don't know Matt too well."

"I promise not to leave you with a bastard," Josh stated. "Get me his résumé when you can. With Ryan out of the running, I just want to look closer at Matt. He did seem like a nice guy, and that was before I found out he bought my dinner."

"I'll be back in thirty minutes and I'll get it right to you."

"I knew I could count on you," he stated before hanging up.

Haley really did dread the day when Josh would leave. He'd been an upstanding boss and she'd come to think of him as a friend. But he wanted to start a new chapter in his life and she really couldn't blame him.

After the scandal with his father disappearing and pilfering millions from clients, Josh had rebuilt Black Crescent Hedge Fund. His twin, Jake, had wanted nothing to do with the family business and had taken off for Europe. And their youngest brother, Oliver, had his own issues, namely being a recovering addict and professional partier. He had his own mess of a reputation to overcome, and stepping into the top role of a tarnished hedge-fund company was not a position he was ready for.

So, Josh stepped up and Haley had been right there by his side, helping him rebuild. People who went through hell together shared a special bond. It would take one very exceptional man or woman to replace someone as strong and resilient as Josh Lowell.

"Sounds like the hunt is still on," Chase casually mentioned as he pierced a baby potato with his fork. "I imagine you and Josh are having a difficult time narrowing down a potential replacement."

"No work talk," she reminded him with a smile. "But if you want to talk business, you can tell me what exactly you do. I want to know what's not on your résumé."

"Eager to learn more about me?" he asked with a mischievous grin. "I deal with investments, but I also travel and help other companies across the globe work on strengthening their own firms."

Which sounded like the perfect replacement for Josh. But Chase would have to have more than the perfect answer to get the position, and this certainly wasn't an interview.

"Are you from here?" she asked.

"Born and raised about twenty minutes away," he told her. "My father was also an investor and my mother was a stay-at-home mom. I'm an only child. Nothing much to tell, really. I went to college on a full-ride football scholarship. My parents struggled a bit, so I'm not sure we could've afforded it other-wise."

That would explain that broad frame and she

could easily see him in the role of a star athlete. She also wouldn't mind seeing him in those tight pants.

Focus, Haley. You don't even like football.

Haley was surprised at how similar they were in fighting for what they wanted and being so headstrong, but she wasn't going to admit any such thing. Chase was clearly looking for that edge up and she certainly wasn't going to just hand him the ammunition.

All of her attraction aside, Josh had the final say over the new CEO, and Haley wasn't so sure being sexually drawn to your new boss was the best position to be in.

"I have updated my résumé since my first interview," he went on. "You have a new copy in your inbox."

Shocked, she set her fork down and dabbed her mouth with her napkin. "And when did you resend?"

"Right before I came back with your gift," he explained. "I rebuilt a multibillion-dollar firm in Europe and I included those stats and references. They'll all give me a glowing recommendation, by the way."

Damn it. He was getting more qualified by the moment.

Haley instantly had a vision of working with him day in and day out. She'd been side by side with Josh for years now and never once had she been attracted to him, not in the intimate way. He was certainly a handsome man, but she'd never gotten those giddy feelings…nothing like with Chase, and she'd only been with him for an hour.

Giddy? No. Almost arousing, which was even more dangerous.

Yeah, working with Chase Hargrove for hours on end would be a mistake. No doubt he would continue to try to wear her down.

Good thing she was on to him.

Three

Chase felt confident about his lunch date with Haley. Flirting came easy and he'd actually found himself caught up in her beauty, and suddenly charming her didn't seem to be a chore.

He'd been stunned to learn of her charity work. That someone with a demanding career spent her spare time helping those less fortunate was a hell of a turn-on…and quite a juxtaposition to how the Lowells were.

Sure Joshua gave money here and there, probably guilt money, but the Lowells still held themselves up on another pedestal, towering above everybody else.

Chase stood in his living room and stared out the wall of one-way windows overlooking the river. The lights from Falling Brook sparkled against the darkened sky and calmed him. Though his mind continued to race, he at least felt peace about where he was heading.

Plotting and planning had gotten him to where he was today. Being a prominent international investor gave him an obvious edge up to slide into the CEO position at Black Crescent Hedge Fund. Not that he cared about that position. He wanted information to bring the company and the Lowell family down once and for all.

He'd seen his parents struggle after all of their savings were lost. His father had gone to prison for fraud thanks to Vernon's antics, and those attorney's fees hadn't come cheap. His mother had ultimately suffered a nervous breakdown and had needed medical attention. Nothing motivated Chase more than someone harming those he loved. His parents were doing so much better now, but that heaviness still hovered over them. They certainly weren't the same, but they were still a strong family and still pushing through each day to be their best.

Chase needed to continue to get closer to Haley. She'd thrown him off his game for a moment when she'd started discussing her charity. How did she find time to run such a thing when she was always at Black Crescent? Her job as executive assistant was demanding and he knew she put her entire heart and soul into that position. If the woman never even took a lunch break, that was loyalty and dedication on another level.

Did Josh demand that type of work or was that all Haley wanting to go above and beyond?

Clearly she didn't have much of a social life between the two full-time jobs vying for her attention. He made a mental note to check into Tomorrow's Leaders and find out all he could about what sounded like a brilliant charity. Whether she agreed to a date or not, he would make a sizable contribution because he loved the concept. He would do so anonymously so she didn't think he was literally trying to buy her affection. He wasn't that much of a bastard. That's something the Lowell family would do to get attention and make gains.

But Haley would agree to a date with him, with or without the monetary help. He wouldn't mention the donation again, because that had been a little shady. The words had slipped out before he could think better of it and he'd immediately regretted putting her in that position or making her feel like she was nothing more than a bribe.

Just because he'd charmed her into lunch didn't mean he would be able to go that route again. No. Someone like Haley needed to be kept on her toes and surprised. He didn't miss the way she smiled and was actually impressed with the ridiculous highlighter bouquet.

Chase pulled his cell from his pocket and sent off a quick text to his assistant, putting his next plan into motion. An immediate reply confirmed why Dave was the perfect right-hand man. He would get right on it and now Chase just had to do a little more charming with Miss Shaw. The highlighters were a nice touch, but that gesture had barely scratched the surface of his next tactic.

Chase smiled as he headed toward his in-home gym. He needed to hit the weights, maybe the punching bag, and burn off some energy. He had big plans to carry out and a woman to mentally seduce... though if she wound up in his bed, well, he wouldn't exactly turn her away.

Haley hadn't had time to do much digging on Chase. A whole new flood of résumés came through her inbox, not to mention more flowers she'd had to find room for.

The bouquets were getting ridiculous so she'd started passing them out to coworkers. Now every office in the building had an obscene display and she could at least see her desk again.

Those cupcakes, doughnuts and chocolates had made their way to the break room, too. If she ate everything that had come her way, she'd need a new, bigger wardrobe, and that wasn't something she had time for.

Haley settled back in at her desk and scooted closer to her computer. The bundle of highlighters on her desk caught her attention and she couldn't help but smile. She didn't want to smile at Chase's gift. That's what he wanted her to do. He wanted her to think about him...which was basically all she'd done since their impromptu lunch date.

No, it wasn't a date. It had been a meeting of sorts.

She didn't date, never had the time or found a man who interested her enough to pull her from her work.

Yet Chase had done exactly that for one hour. He'd gotten her to leave the office and he'd put very little effort into doing so.

But he'd smiled, he'd been adorable in that over-bearing sort of way and he'd offered to donate to Tomorrow's Leaders. Albeit, the donation came at a price. Well, she couldn't be bought. She would just continue to work on other contributions where her social life didn't have to come into play.

Damn that man for making her read too much into him. He wasn't after her, per se. He wanted a position that she could help him with…if she wanted to do such a thing. Which she did not.

Becoming CEO would be up to Josh. Her personal feelings weren't the deciding factor.

"Are you going home any time soon?"

Haley glanced up from her computer screen, which she'd been staring at blankly for the past ten minutes, and spotted Josh.

"In a bit," she told him with a smile.

Josh's dirty-blond hair looked as if he'd been raking his fingers through it over the course of the day. He'd already shed his suit jacket, which he had draped over one arm. He'd loosened his tie and she figured the stress of finding a replacement was getting to him. This was certainly not a decision to be taken lightly.

"I can't believe you're leaving," she added. "It's

not even six o'clock yet. You usually have a few more hours in you."

Josh's smile widened. "Sophie made me promise to take off early. She's surprising me with dinner and some other plans she's keeping to herself."

Haley loved that Josh and Sophie had found each other. The two were so in love and Josh had definitely turned into a totally different man because of her. Not so long ago, the stress and CEO position had really been getting to Josh, so much so he would bark orders at her or just be frustrated and act almost as if he didn't want her here.

During those times she cleverly did not point out the fact she'd been here even longer than he had, knew the inner workings as much as he did. When she'd been in college, Haley had actually worked for Vernon Lowell as an intern. Her loyalty to this company was the reason she stayed while almost every other employee bailed when Josh took over. She helped him rebuild Black Crescent.

Recently, Sophie had softened something in Josh, and now Haley almost hated to see him go. He was like the brother she never had. Well, she had a brother, but there was no solid relationship there. Haley was honestly closer with her work family than her actual biological family.

"I hope you have a good night," she told him. "Sounds like fun."

"Speaking of fun, what made you get out for lunch earlier?" he asked, a wry grin on his face as if he knew some dirty little secret.

"Sorry to disappoint." She turned in her chair to face him fully. "It was just a business lunch with an acquaintance."

A really over-the-top-sexy acquaintance who had charmed her into submission.

Not that Haley would tell Josh exactly whom she'd had lunch with, especially since Chase had already had an interview with Josh. Added to that, several weeks ago Sophie had caught Haley and Chase flirting.

Sophie had intervened, asking Haley if everything was okay. Thankfully, Josh knew nothing of this harmless encounter. Haley didn't want to be seen as flirting or dining with a potential prospect for the highest position at Black Crescent. Haley had never slept with a coworker or her boss and she sure as hell didn't intend to start now.

And she hadn't been lying when she'd told Sophie she could handle Chase. She could...until he'd shown up with that absurd gift that ultimately landed her in his car and at his personal table at one of her favorite restaurants.

She'd have to be more vigilant when it came to that sly mogul. She'd also have to get serious about that research so she could uncover more about the man who wanted to become her boss. She needed more hours in the day to get everything done, but this little bit of work couldn't be shared. She didn't want anyone to know her special project on the side. This was totally personal.

"Well, take the night off," Josh told her, pulling

her back to the moment. "You've been working too much."

Haley laughed. "Never thought I'd hear you say that. We're both such workaholics."

"I just have a different outlook on life now." Josh shrugged with a wide grin. "I need to get going. Have a good night," he told her before he headed down the hall.

Considering she and Josh were usually the last two to ever leave the building, she had to assume she was alone. Haley pulled up her favorite playlist on her computer and set the music to a higher volume to help distract her from the wayward thoughts regarding a certain billionaire competing for her attention.

As she searched through her emails and hummed along to the songs, Haley was pretty proud of herself for making her way through the bulk of the latest résumés before sending them on to Allison Randall, who would narrow the list even more. Josh wanted only the top three for interviews. With Ryan out, and Chase and Matt already interviewed, that meant they were getting close.

Her cell chimed and she did a quick glance, then stilled. She didn't recognize the number, but with having a charity, she couldn't ignore calls just assuming the other end was a telemarketer.

She paused her music and grabbed her phone.

"Hello?"

"Miss Shaw."

That low, familiar voice shouldn't send shivers through her, but here she was trying to tamp them down.

Haley eased back in her seat and pulled in a deep breath. "Mr. Hargrove. I won't insult you by asking how you got my personal number."

His rich laughter slid through the phone and did nothing to help those shivers she was trying to ignore. No man had ever had such an effect on her before. Dates were one thing, kisses were another. Those could lead to shivers… But a voice through the phone? Never.

"I assume you're still at work," he said.

"I am."

"Do you ever leave that office?" he asked.

Haley came to her feet and circled her desk. She crossed to her small refrigerator she kept in the corner and grabbed a bottle of water. She wasn't about to remind him that she did indeed leave the office when she was coerced by a sexy, charming lunch date.

No, not a date. She'd better be more careful where those thoughts wandered. Sexual fantasies were one thing, and something she couldn't avoid, but thinking in terms of dates and an actual relationship could get her into more trouble than she was ready for.

"I take quite a bit of pride in my work," she informed him. "Besides, I'm rather busy trying to fill some very big shoes."

"Yes, the CEO position. What evening do you think you could take some free time for yourself?"

"All to myself?" she countered, taking the bottle

back to her desk. "Or are you asking for my time to be spent with you?"

"Beautiful and smart. I like that."

Haley wasn't about to address the *beautiful* comment. Allure oozed off him and words were so easy to string together for someone like Chase. A man with power and money was likely used to getting what he wanted and just assumed all women found him irresistible.

Damn it, she couldn't deny she fell into that category. But what else could she do when sexy was his default mode?

"So what is it exactly that you're trying to ask, Mr. Hargrove?"

She took a seat and crossed her legs, leaning back in her chair and trying to maintain her composure.

"I have Broadway tickets for Wednesday night," he informed her. "I'd like you to join me."

Haley stilled. Broadway tickets? Like…a date? Hadn't she just finished her mental lecture on not dating this guy?

Lunch during business hours was one thing, but a play with a man trying to become her boss was an entirely different matter.

"I'm not sure that's a good idea."

"I assumed you'd say as much," he retorted with another low chuckle. "What would make you feel better? If we called this a date or if we called this a business meeting?"

She pursed her lips and considered her options.

"What would make me feel better is honesty. You called me, so what context did you call me in?"

"A date."

His swift, confident reply had her heart beating faster, her nerves kicking into high gear. Did he really want to ask her out? Could he really be chasing her as a woman and not for the part of her that was a stepping-stone to the most prominent position at Black Crescent?

"And I'm the only woman you could think of to ask?"

"You're the only woman I *wanted* to ask."

Oh, why did he have all the answers, and why was she allowing this fascination to pull her in more and more?

Because she was curious. She couldn't ignore her attraction any more than she could stop the sun from setting. Besides, it was just a play. They couldn't exactly get too carried away in a very public place… right?

"Fine."

"Fine?" he asked, then chuckled. "Well, don't get overly excited about it."

"Mr. Hargrove, if you want someone excited and falling all over herself at the idea of a date with you, then you've asked the wrong woman."

That rich laughter filled the phone and she gripped it tight. Her heart beat even faster and her stomach flopped at the prospect of being out with Chase.

"Oh, I've asked the right woman," he corrected.

"And you're going to need to call me Chase since we're dating."

"We're not dating," she corrected.

"Not until Wednesday. I'll see you then, Haley."

He hung up, leaving her speechless and wondering what the hell she'd just agreed to.

Four

"Are you sure this is what you want to do, sir?"

Chase watched through his window as the city streets went by. He paid his driver to drive, not to dole out unsolicited advice. Granted, Al had been Chase's driver for over ten years and he often gave advice...which Chase normally valued.

He didn't want to hear it now. Maybe Chase was making a mistake, but he wanted Haley and that had nothing to do with the revenge or the job and everything to do with the fact that she intrigued him. He couldn't explain why this woman was the one whom he wanted to spend time with, the one he ultimately wanted in his bed.

But he wouldn't ignore what he wanted...not the

job and not the woman. There was no reason he couldn't have both.

"I'm positive," Chase replied.

"I'm not sure getting cozy with Haley Shaw is the best move at this time. She's innocent in all of this."

Al knew everything. He knew the backstory of Chase's father going to prison due to the money trail left by Vernon Lowell, and Al was aware that Chase refused to rest until the Lowell family was brought down...even if that meant seeking justice via Vernon's children.

But he was right in the fact that Haley was an innocent. Granted, she'd stuck through the scandal and Vernon's skipping town and then the transition when Josh took over. She had to know everything that went down, but she was ever the loyal employee...and Chase's best option for finding any nugget of inside information he needed to plan his attack.

"She's the in that I have," Chase stated, turning to catch Al's judgmental reflection in the rearview mirror.

There was one secret Al didn't know. There was no way in hell Chase would ever mention that what started out as harmless flirting and using his charms had turned into a full-on attraction that Chase couldn't fight.

He hadn't expected to find her conservative, stuffy exterior so damn sexy. Those slim dresses that hit just past her knee combined with simple nude heels gave him fantasies that he was best to keep to himself.

"I can't talk you out of this, can I?" Al asked as he pulled in front of Haley's house.

Chase smiled. "Just wait here. We'll be back."

Al's sigh of disapproval didn't escape Chase, but he didn't need approval. While he respected Al as much more than a driver, Chase also had to live his own life and make his own decisions...and mistakes.

Taking Haley to a Broadway play wasn't a mistake, though. Bedding her? Well, that might be a mistake, but he wouldn't turn down the opportunity. He certainly hadn't gone into this thinking of seduction, but he also wasn't taking it off the table.

No man in his right mind could ignore the natural, simplistic beauty that Haley offered. The fact that she didn't fall all over herself and almost posed as an unexpected challenge was a hell of a turn-on. Combined with her loyalty to her job... He admired a woman who remained focused.

Still, he had no clue what made her remain so faithful to the Lowell family and Black Crescent. Haley had been with them since college, from everything he'd learned about her. Why the hell would she stay during the scandal when Vernon literally ruined people's lives? How did she justify such actions?

No matter what her reasoning was, that wasn't his problem. He needed to get some scoop from her, anything that would help him in getting ahead and solidifying his revenge.

His cell chimed in his pocket, but he ignored it. Nothing was more important than taking Haley out tonight. Maybe by getting outside the office, after business hours, she would relax and let loose. And perhaps she'd be easier to uncover.

Chase knocked on her door and within minutes Haley stepped out. It took every ounce of Chase's willpower to keep his mouth from dropping.

If he thought she was sexy in those little conventional dresses at the office, that was nothing compared with this sleeveless black jumpsuit with a plunging neckline. She wore a pair of strappy black sandals showing off her red polished toes... He hadn't expected the red.

With her blond hair curled and red glossy lips, Haley looked completely different from every other time he'd seen her.

And she'd just changed the dynamics of this little game. He didn't know she'd be bringing her arsenal of sex appeal into battle, but he was more than ready to tussle with her. Haley wasn't stupid or naive. She'd dressed like this on purpose with every intention of throwing him off his game.

Well, maybe it would be her who was thrown off. She agreed to this date, so he obviously had some hold over her if she couldn't turn him down. Chase had to make sure he kept the upper hand here or he'd wind up losing sight of everything he'd set out to gain.

Chase composed himself and took a step forward to greet her.

"You look sexy as hell," he murmured when he got closer.

Haley smiled. "It's not often I go on a date, so I wanted to be a little extra tonight."

"I appreciate it."

Haley's eyes leveled his as those red lips curved into a killer smile. "Oh, I did this for me. I love a feeling of empowerment... Don't you?"

She sashayed past him. Chase shook his head as he followed those swaying hips down the front steps.

What in the hell had he gotten himself into? The woman was purposely antagonizing him and clearly loving every second of the torture.

Chase might not know what he'd gotten himself into or how this would ultimately play out, but he knew this task of schmoozing Haley was not going to be boring.

The real question was...just who was seducing whom here?

Haley had no idea how Chase got tickets so last-minute to the most popular show on Broadway, but she didn't care. Their seats were the best, the show was spectacular and now they were walking down the busy city street in Manhattan.

Lights twinkled from each and every building, the warm late-summer air washed over her and people bustled about. She loved this city, especially in the summer. It wasn't often she got away from work to enjoy a social life out on the town. Once the new CEO was in position, she really should take more time for herself and get back into the swing of nightlife and a good time. She was still young, she still had memories to make.

"You up for a drink?" he asked.

"I have to be at work early in the morning," she told him.

He slid his hand into hers as if that were the most normal next step into this evening. Everything about this night felt like a real date. He hadn't brought up work, which was both surprising and refreshing.

"One drink," he promised. "I know the perfect place."

No doubt he knew the perfect place, a place where he took all his ladies. She didn't want to fall in that same line of the women he had a pattern with. She wasn't one of his usual dates and she didn't want to think of this as anything more than what it was...a game.

While she wasn't quite sure his angle or why he was going to such lengths to charm her, she had to keep her guard up. Having a bit of fun in the process wouldn't hurt anything. A little flirting, sexual banter, maybe even a fling... But anything that happened would be on her terms and because she wanted it to progress. Chase couldn't, and wouldn't, have a hold over her.

Yeah, right. Just keep telling yourself that.

"One drink," she replied. "But only because I'm out of Pinot at home."

And there went that rich laughter again. That pure male, all rough-and-low laughter she'd come to associate with him. The weeks of flirting and harmless banter had somehow led them to this night, and she wasn't sorry she'd said yes. Quite the opposite. Haley was well aware of what this was and what it wasn't.

Chase wasn't out for some exclusivity or a relationship. He wasn't out for even a fling. He wanted to get that top slot and he was really going all out to win her affection.

"I'll have to make a note to get you a box of Pinot," he told her. "I know a wonderful distributor. They can be at your door first thing in the morning."

Haley glanced his way as he assisted her toward the next block. "I think that's a bit of overkill, don't you? I mean, what would I do with an entire box?"

"Throw a dinner party," he suggested. "Or maybe go smaller and invite someone over to help you drink it. Glasses optional. I think other, more intimate ways could be the theme."

He threw her a glance that had her head spinning and visions forming. Late nights with a glass of wine on the balcony off her bedroom before moving into her oversize master and having the pale liquor poured all over her while Chase's tongue traveled the same path—

"How many students are you going to fund this fall?"

His question caught her off guard and had her mind spinning in another direction. "Excuse me?"

"With your charity," he added, guiding her across another busy intersection as if he hadn't just put a naughty thought in her head. "How many teens were you able to fund?"

"Oh, um, eighteen. I'm hoping we can squeeze a couple more out of the applicants that came through."

"Do you get much else done besides looking at résumés and applications?" he asked. "Between the charity and Black Crescent, I mean."

Haley hadn't thought about her work in that manner, but she actually didn't get much else done.

With a shrug, she smiled. "I love what I do. Both jobs. I wouldn't have it any other way."

"You're clearly giving your time to everyone around you. Is that why you don't date much?"

He gestured toward a doorway with a large black-and-gold awning. Thankfully, they were here and she didn't have to dive into the boring whys of her social life. Couldn't someone just enjoy her work? Why did she have to defend her lifestyle to someone who didn't even know her?

In no time, she and Chase were escorted up the stairs and into a private room with their own bartender. But of course they were. Why would he take a seat at the bar with common folk when money talked and he could have privacy?

Haley took a seat at an intimate, curved booth. Chase slid in beside her, but he didn't crowd her. They placed their drink orders and were left alone. Haley couldn't ignore the tingle of arousal that coursed through her. The way Chase had looked at her all night, the simple way he took her hand—she might be a helpless romantic, but those were the little things that got to her.

The sexy man in the suit didn't hurt, either. There

was something to be said about a well-dressed man who knew how to fill out a tailor-made jacket.

"We could have sat down in the bar," she told him.

Chase flashed her a smile and eased his arm along the back of the bench. "We could have, but then I wouldn't be able to hear you. If you want good music, though, downstairs is the place to be. I happen to know the owner."

"Are you the owner?" she asked.

Chase laughed. "No, but we went to college together."

"Harvard? Yale? I can't remember what Ivy League school you indicated on your résumé."

He shook his head and leveled that dark stare her way. "Hardly Ivy League. I went to Ithaca on a football scholarship and I studied business. I was smart in school, but nothing an Ivy League school would've looked twice at. My family couldn't have afforded for me to go anywhere without my scholarship, so I'm just thankful I was athletic."

Interesting. That was a whole side of him she didn't know. A man who came from meager beginnings to make a name for himself and become a billionaire mogul was quite impressive. Maybe he wasn't the egotistical man she'd first believed. There was nothing wrong with an ego, but now that she knew he warranted that sense of pride, she could appreciate him so much more.

The bartender delivered their drinks and promptly left them. Haley took a sip of her Pinot and toyed with the stem of her crystal glass.

"I went to community college," she found herself saying before she could stop herself. "I have zero athletic ability. My only hobbies are singing off-key in the shower or making spreadsheets in my sleep."

Chase's chuckle seemed so genuine, not like he was purposely trying to appease her or keep her attention solely on him.

"I'm sure you have talents," he stated. "You don't have to be athletic."

"I played softball once." She lifted her glass and took another sip. "It was a short-lived career. I was eight and I did cartwheels around the bases instead of running them during warm-ups."

Chase's lips twitched as if he was holding back his laugh. "And did you end up taking gymnastics?"

"No. My parents couldn't afford lessons." She glanced to her glass and slid her thumb up the delicate stem. "I didn't always see eye to eye with them about most things anyway."

"Are you close now?"

Haley shook her head. "We still don't have the same vision."

"They have to be proud of your work," he replied, shifting to face her better. "You've become quite successful."

Haley smiled and pulled in a breath. "To them, I'm a secretary. Nothing near as exciting as a doctor or lawyer like they wanted my brother to be."

"And is your brother a doctor or lawyer?"

Haley shook her head again. "No. They paid for him to go to a fancy college and he ended up flunking out. Too much partying, but that's none of my business."

"How can they not be proud of all the work you've done?" he asked. "You've been with Black Crescent for so long, you're irreplaceable."

Haley bit the inside of her cheek to keep from laughing. She always felt like she was invaluable, too, but that was just her battered ego. She liked to think that they couldn't live without her, but if she left, someone would replace her and the company would keep running.

"You really do know how to get on someone's good side," she informed him. "Flattery doesn't always get you to the top."

"No, but my impeccable résumé will." He flashed that killer grin once again and took a sip of his bourbon. "Everyone knows you're the backbone of that operation. Who knows what would've happened all those years ago during that scandal if you hadn't stayed on."

"I was just an intern back then."

"Who was far more knowledgeable than most," he retorted. "When Josh stepped into the role of CEO, I guarantee you were the one who had to get him going and made him look good to the general public."

Haley shrugged. She didn't need accolades or credit for her work. She truly enjoyed helping others, and just because Josh's father had been a liar and a cheat didn't mean Josh or his brothers were the same.

Many people in the town didn't feel that way,

though. Some still blamed Josh for Vernon's actions. The brothers had all been held under a microscope when their father split, but Josh was the one who had truly stuck, trying to salvage the family name and business.

"So what's your angle here?" she asked Chase, smiling when he quirked a brow. "You want the CEO position so bad that you're willing to fake date me? Or is there something else you're after?"

His eyes darkened as they dropped to her lips. She realized her open-ended question held too many possible answers the moment the words had slipped out.

"Oh, there are several things I want, Haley."

You can bet they center on that promised shipment of wine.

She'd put herself in this position. She'd wanted to know what it would be like to go out with someone like Chase, knowing she had the upper hand because he needed her.

But now? Well, she wasn't so sure her control hadn't slipped. If she wasn't careful, she'd wind up in bed with the man, and just her luck, he'd also become her boss.

Haley leaned in closer and murmured, "Sex isn't on the table."

"No?"

He kept that dark gaze on her. Part of her wanted to back away, come to the realization that Chase wasn't in all this for her. But the other part wanted to ignore those waving red flags and see what would happen if she just leaned in a little. Would he close that distance between them and put his lips where his eyes had been? Would she let him?

Yes, she would. She wanted to know what those lips would feel like. She wanted to feel his hands glide over her bare body. Would that fantasy ever become reality?

"I'm aware I'm not actually your type," she informed him, picking up her glass and draining it. "But I'm going to figure out your angle. I can't believe you're going through all of this just to land a position at Black Crescent."

He eased over in the bench, his arm sliding even farther behind her back as he leaned in closer to her face. Those eyes once again dropped to her lips and she couldn't stop that knee-jerk reaction of licking them.

Anticipation soared through her. Was this when he'd kiss her? Was this when she'd welcome that much-awaited touch?

"Maybe I'm trying to land you," he murmured against her lips.

Haley couldn't suppress the shivers and couldn't deny the flirting and fun and games had taken a new direction, and she wasn't sure which way she was supposed to go.

Five

"Are you with me?"

Haley blinked away the daydream and stared up at her boss. Josh stood in front of her desk, one hand in his pocket, the other holding a résumé.

"I'm sorry. What?"

His brows drew in. "Is everything okay? You seem off this morning."

Maybe that's because she was left hanging for that kiss last night on her date/nondate with Chase. Maybe because the man was driving her out of her ever-loving mind as she tried to anticipate his next move. Or maybe she should remove herself from this crazy ride she'd gotten on and save her own sanity.

"Yes, I'm fine," she assured him with a smile.

Haley came to her feet and straightened her pencil dress. "You were saying?"

Josh stared at her another minute before glancing down to the paper in his hand. "I was saying that I'd like to set up a second interview with Matt Velez. Remember I told you I talked to him outside of the office? I'd like to bring him in again."

Haley was well aware of Matt's résumé. Along with Allison, they'd vetted each and every one that had come through. Haley wasn't sure Matt was the perfect applicant for the job of CEO, but she was also slowly getting swayed by her hormones and not her common sense.

She had an obligation to the company to help secure a solid future, which also meant her job and many others. She couldn't let Chase and his methodical plans to woo her hinder her decisions.

"I'll get that interview set up right away," she assured Josh. "Do you prefer Monday morning after your conference call?"

"That's fine. I know it's short notice, but see if Allison can fly in for it. And like the other ones, I want you in there with me," he told her. "It's only fair that you have a say over who you'll be working closely with. After all, you're the one who will be with our new CEO the most."

Haley nodded, pleased that he was taking her feelings into consideration. But if she had to weigh in on whom she wanted to spend most of her days and evenings with here at the office, her answer certainly wasn't Matt.

A commanding man with dark brown eyes and light brown messy hair came into mind. The man with broad shoulders, perfectly tailored suits and heavy-lidded eyes who made her think only of rustled sheets and sleepless nights.

"Haley?"

"I'll get it scheduled," she told him, forcing herself back to the moment and her duties. "No problem."

"Is there anything you want to tell me?" he asked, brows drawn in.

Josh cared about each of his employees. Haley had come to think of him as a friend, someone she could trust and rely on. But there was no way she could confess what was truly going on. He wouldn't understand and he likely wouldn't like that she'd been technically dating one of the applicants.

Haley reached for the résumé and laid the paper on her desk. "I'm just a little distracted, but nothing that will affect my job."

Well, that was somewhat of a lie considering she spent a good portion of her time fantasizing when she should be focusing on the next phase of Black Crescent.

Josh sighed and slid his hands into his pockets. "You know you can talk to me," he told her.

"Just a date I had the other night," she confessed. "I'm trying to tell myself he's not the guy for me, but it's getting more difficult because I'm developing feelings I really shouldn't have."

Josh's intense stare quickly turned amused as a wide grin spread across his face. "I didn't think Sophie was for me, either, but look how that turned out. I didn't realize you were dating anyone."

Neither did she, and she wasn't quite sure what to call all of this she and Chase were doing. He was toying with her. He had to be. But she was human with very real feelings and she couldn't stop her attraction. She had to believe he was attracted; either that or he was a damn good actor.

Still, that didn't mean she could let her guard down. Chase wasn't gullible and he wasn't stupid. He was meticulous and no doubt had a well-laid plan. She just had to make sure she stayed one step ahead of him.

"Well, we only had one date," she explained to Josh. "I've just been so wrapped up in work and Tomorrow's Leaders, I haven't had much of a social life lately. I'm sure I'm making a big deal out of nothing."

"Don't discount your feelings," he warned. "You're allowed to have a social life and you're also allowed to leave before it gets dark outside, you know."

Haley laughed. "I'm aware, but I feel guilty when there's so much to be done to get ready for the transition of the CEO."

"You stood by this company when the shit hit the fan with my dad. I have no doubt whatsoever that you will make the next transition smooth, and anyone who takes my place will be thankful to have you."

She wasn't one who thrived on compliments; that's not why she did her job. But she wasn't going to ignore Josh's praise by blowing off his kind words.

"I appreciate that," she told him. "I'll get this interview set up for Monday."

"Great." He started to turn away but stopped and met her gaze once again. "Whoever this guy is, he's damn lucky to have you."

Haley smiled and simply nodded her silent appreciation.

How did she explain that she went on a date with an applicant? Or the fact that, while there was most definitely sexual tension, she wasn't fully convinced that he had the truest of intentions.

The next morning, Haley took a seat at her desk and opened a new tab on her computer. She didn't necessarily have the time to devote to extra work right now, but she needed to dig deeper into Chase Hargrove.

Instead of fantasizing about him, she had to find out who he really was. Haley wanted to know more behind the man, more about his motives for seeking out not only the CEO position, but also for being so aggressive in pursuing her.

She went to one site, then another, falling down the rabbit hole of this world-renowned investment mogul. He had a home in Cannes for which he'd paid over twenty million dollars, and Haley found herself basking in the view for just a moment before moving on.

She couldn't even imagine owning a home like that or even having the time to get away for a luxury vacation. Clearly Chase had made some damn good investments and took care of his clients or he wouldn't be able to afford such extravagance.

And knowing a sliver of his background and that he came from meager beginnings made this revelation all the more impressive.

The further back she went into his world, the more she realized he was much more than what was on his résumé.

He also hadn't been born Chase Hargrove. When the hell had he changed his name, and why? There had to be a story there because from what she could tell, his parents were still married, so the name change didn't make much sense.

Maybe digging into his parents was the way to go. Were they all estranged? He hadn't mentioned any such thing during their dinner the other night.

Yet more secrets she wanted to uncover.

When her cell chimed on her desk, Haley jumped. She glanced to see Chase's name lighting up the screen. She thought about letting him go to voice mail, but she couldn't deny the man and she wondered if that would ultimately be her downfall.

She liked to tell herself she wasn't saying no to him simply because she wanted to learn more... But in reality she wasn't saying no because she was selfish and wanted more. She just wished she knew where her curiosity would end up taking her and how far she'd let this game play out.

Pushing away from her computer, Haley turned to grab her phone.

"Good morning," she answered.

Chase's familiar chuckle slid through the line. "Nope, it's now noon."

She glanced to her computer screen and he was right. Obviously she'd fallen down the rabbit hole of Chase's life. Not that she would ever admit any such thing to him.

"You caught me," she replied. "It's been quite the morning."

Like finding out he wasn't exactly who he said he was. She wondered why, but that was something she'd definitely be finding out. If she flat out asked him, would he tell her the truth?

"Are you free tonight?" he asked.

"Depends on what you had in mind."

Another date? Did she want to keep getting tangled with a man who obviously had ulterior motives?

Yes, she did. She was intrigued, she was charmed... She was turned on. She simply couldn't turn off such strong emotions. Chase was a powerful man in more ways than one.

"I'll take that to mean you're free."

His low, gravelly voice did crazy things to her hormones. Things she hadn't felt in far too long, which made them impossible to ignore.

Why couldn't she get a grip with this guy? Why couldn't she just deny him and move on?

Because he'd left her wondering what those lips would feel like against hers. He'd left her wondering if he wanted her just as much as she wanted him. There was really only one way to find out.

"I can pick you up at your place at six if you're up for a surprise," he added.

She leaned back in her seat and stared at her screen, seeing the evidence in black-and-white that he wasn't on the up-and-up. But she never backed down from a challenge—hence why she was still at Black Crescent even after all of the scandal and their tarnished reputation. She'd stuck by Josh's side during the most difficult time when it would have been all too easy to pack up and leave like everyone else did.

So, Haley wasn't about to shy away from Chase. Didn't everyone have a few skeletons in their closet?

"I'll be ready," she told him. "But can I ask what I should be ready for? Are we skydiving or watching a movie? I need to dress accordingly."

Once again he laughed, and she hated how such a simple act could produce so many emotions. The arousal, the excitement, the thrill of the chase—though she still wasn't sure who was chasing whom.

"And what would you wear for skydiving?" he asked.

"Probably a blindfold because I'd be terrified," she joked.

"Bring that blindfold," he stated. "I'm sure we can find a better use for it."

The instant erotic image filled her mind and she knew without a doubt that he was crossing the line of flirting, and she didn't mind one bit. She was human, she was a woman with basic needs. Why should she deny having a little harmless fun?

Oh, right. Because he could end up being her boss at one point and she knew he was lying about something.

All of that still didn't squash her desires or turn off her attraction. The blindfold comment left her more than intrigued about what might or might not turn him on. She wouldn't mind digging into his fetishes.

"I'll be ready at six," she informed him. "Sans blindfold."

"Fine by me. I have a few you can borrow. See you then."

He hung up, leaving her wondering if he was serious or joking about that blindfold collection. Every part of her had a feeling he was quite serious, and that only aroused her even more.

How had they gone from harmless flirting to discussing veiled sexual games? Chase was a smooth one since she didn't have a clue how to answer that question. It was those smooth ones who could get a girl into trouble...but oh, the best kind.

Haley sighed and put her phone back on her desk, turning her focus back to the computer and back to the hunt to find the real Chase. She wondered why he changed his last name. What made him want to take on another? Surely he didn't have a falling-out with his parents. Or maybe he did. That was certainly something she could easily find.

She didn't have too much time to keep devoting to Chase today, but she wasn't done digging. Perhaps on their date he might divulge a little more and she could slowly uncover what type of man he truly was…other than sexy as hell and too charming for his own good.

He never did tell her exactly what they were doing or how she should dress. Still, surprises were fun. She didn't remember the last time someone surprised her with anything…save for the slew of flowers and pastries that came through from would-be applicants.

Pushing aside thoughts of Chase and any other distractions, Haley turned her attention to the latest résumés Allison had vetted. There was still a position to be filled and Haley wanted the absolute best possible candidate, considering she truly loved this company and she'd have to be working with that said individual day in and day out.

Part of her couldn't help but imagine Chase in that role. What would he be like as a boss? Could they even have a standard working relationship?

Granted, they hadn't actually crossed any lines physically, but mentally… Hell, she'd crossed them all several times. If they ended up in bed, how could they turn back and go to boss/assistant?

An instant image of him sweeping off his desk and laying her down filled her mind. She couldn't just ignore the need she had or the possibilities that rolled through her.

Chase Hargrove, or whatever his last name used to be, wasn't in the CEO position just yet, so that still made him free game. If he was going to come on to her like he wanted her, Haley was going to show him just how much she wanted him. There was no code of ethics that said she couldn't have a social life with an applicant.

If he was playing some sort of game with her, then she'd make him regret it. But what if there was no game? What if he actually wanted her and wanted to be CEO of Black Crescent Hedge Fund? There was no reason he couldn't want both, right?

And if that was the case, she had a feeling Chase Hargrove might just become a permanent fixture in her life…in one way or another.

Six

Haley sank deeper into the corner of her sectional sofa and curled her feet beneath her. Like most companies with summer hours, Black Crescent had short Fridays. After Chase's call, she finished a few things then packed up and headed home for the afternoon.

With the much-needed extra time, she planned to work on finalizing submissions for Tomorrow's Leaders, but she had already finished going through the list and she still had a few hours before Chase was due to pick her up for her date.

And she'd spent her time wisely, considering she uncovered more about him than she ever thought possible.

Haley stared at the computer screen, utterly stunned at the evidence she'd found. Her questions about Chase's motives were answered, but she didn't like what she'd uncovered and was almost sorry she'd been digging.

Chase's father, Dale Groveman, had done business years ago with Vernon Lowell. When everything with Vernon and Black Crescent exploded, apparently Dale took some of the fall and landed in prison.

According to everything Haley had found, that was about the time Chase's mother moved into a low-income apartment from their ritzy home out in the country. Then she was hospitalized shortly after at a mental health facility, but those records were sealed tight. Haley could only imagine the poor woman had a nervous breakdown considering there had been no prior medical issues.

They had lost everything and no doubt Chase was out for revenge. Her heart hurt for his family and so many others who had been affected by Vernon's actions. But was Chase using her? Was he interested in her on a personal level or only interested in using her as leverage in his plan to possibly destroy the company she'd loved for so long?

Haley closed her laptop, not wanting to see any more. She'd learned enough to have her mind shooting in all directions. There was a yawning ache deep in the pit of her stomach, one that she feared wouldn't be fixed anytime soon. She'd allowed herself to get swept up in this web. While she wanted to curse herself for being naive, she also had that sliver of hope that Chase wasn't only taking advantage of her. He seemed genuinely interested... Didn't he? Was he that focused on revenge that he'd turned into a hell of a good actor?

Had Chase targeted her specifically because he thought she would be easy access to get into Black Crescent? Did he like her as a woman at all or was everything an act?

Too many questions to try to decipher answers on her own. Only time would tell because she couldn't exactly go to him and flat out ask. She needed to play this smart and be cautious.

While the hurt continued to slide deep into her, this was nothing new to Haley. People had underestimated her for as long as she could remember. Her parents didn't think she was good enough or smart enough like her brother, which was why they'd invested all of their money into his schooling and not hers.

When she'd started as an intern at Black Crescent Hedge Fund, she'd been seen only as a young blonde with a curvy figure, so what could she possibly know?

Well, look at her now. She'd been around the longest and was the right-hand woman to the CEO. She was damn proud of herself for all she'd accomplished. True, she could go somewhere else with her credentials, but she loved this company and they had always given her the time she needed to work on her own charity.

Her mind circled back to Chase. She still didn't know why he'd changed his last name or what his plans were exactly, but she wasn't about to just let him do anything he wanted or try to harm this company in any way.

Turning the tables wouldn't be easy, but she was up for the challenge. First thing would be to get ready for this date and use every weapon in her arsenal. A killer outfit, sexy heels… She didn't mind making him suffer a little because she would maintain control of this situation now that she had a better handle on his motives.

If only she knew his exact plan…

Haley sat her computer on the coffee table and headed toward her en suite. A relaxing bubble bath would help calm her because she had a feeling she was getting ready to dive into a hell of a storm.

"That was the most amazing thing ever."

Haley's excitement seemed to radiate off her. Her smile widened, her eyes lit up and she seemed completely relaxed…just how he wanted her.

Of course, he was anything but relaxed since he'd picked her up and she'd come out wearing another sexy-as-hell jumpsuit. This one had a halter top, leaving her back exposed and taunting him with all that pale, creamy skin. The pants had slits that went high up onto her thigh, and the material had separated when she'd sat in the seat next to him in the theater. It had been all he could do not to toy with that high V over her leg and see just how far she was willing to let him go.

He'd started this charade months ago with harmless flirting, but he'd had no idea just how much being with Haley Shaw would affect him as a man.

When he'd first set out to destroy the Lowells, he honestly had no idea he'd come in contact with anyone as intriguing, as sexy or as challenging as Haley. Under other circumstances, he'd date her, seduce her the proper way and not have these damn guilty feelings getting in the way of his goals.

Damn it. He wanted Haley and it had nothing to do with the job or his revenge plot. She intrigued him, she aroused him and she flat out got under his skin in ways he'd never allowed another woman.

Chase slid his hand into hers as he led her back to his car. He'd given Al the night off, as he wanted total privacy with Haley.

"All I did was take you to see a movie," he told her.

She jerked her attention to his. "That wasn't just any movie," she reminded him. "That was an early premiere of the biggest blockbuster that will hit cinemas this year. I don't know how you managed the private showing, but that movie had been on my list since all the hype around it last year."

"I'm glad you enjoyed it. The producer is actually a friend of mine, so I had a strong connection."

As they reached his car, Chase maneuvered her toward it, expertly spinning her until her back was pressed against the door. He leaned in, one hand on either side of her shoulders.

Haley's eyes widened, then dropped to his mouth.

Arousal slammed into him, but he kept control over his emotions.

"Are you going to kiss me now?" she asked, her lips quirking into a slight grin as if she were daring him.

"It's time, don't you think?"

"Past time."

Chase leaned in closer, surprised and utterly turned on even more when her hands came up to frame his face as she pulled him down to meet her lips. She opened for him, threading her fingers through his hair, taking the kiss like she'd been starving for his touch.

He understood that all-consuming need. Since seeing her in her office on day one in her conservative dress up until now with her inner vixen coming out for their date, Chase was hanging on by a very thin thread.

Damn the job and his revenge. He wanted Haley with a fierceness that he'd never known. Why her? Why now? He was supposed to be focused on the plan he'd set into motion years ago. He'd waited for the perfect opening into Black Crescent and here it was…only this sexy distraction stood in his way and he had no clue where she fit in. Oh, wait. She didn't. There was no plan for a hot fling with the sexy assistant.

Chase trailed his fingertips over her bare arms, eliciting a shiver from her that racked into his own body. He'd thought he could control this kiss, but he wasn't so sure now.

How did one woman have so much power over him? How could she make him forget his goals, his well-thought-out plans of revenge and redemption?

Because she was sexy as hell, she was loyal to a fault—a trait he could understand and appreciate—and she challenged him in ways no woman ever had.

Haley laced her fingers through his hair and shifted, aligning their bodies in a way that left no doubt how turned on he was.

Chase reached down to her hips, gripping them in his hands, and held her still. He wanted her, but out here in a parking lot was certainly not the place. He'd planned on only a quick kiss, something to take the sexual edge off, but all he'd done was fan the proverbial flames.

Chase forced himself to ease away. Haley's lids slowly opened as she focused her attention on him.

"That was intense," she murmured. "And long overdue."

Chase agreed on both counts, but wasn't about to say anything. He needed to maintain his head about him, to focus, but Haley was charming, more so than he'd originally noticed. She had a heart of gold with her charity—one he'd looked up and thoroughly investigated.

He didn't want her getting caught up in the middle of his anger and retaliation. Chase wanted to go after Vernon himself, but since the old bastard was still MIA fifteen years later, Josh Lowell was next in line. There were other sons, but Josh was the one who had taken over Daddy's reins.

"Are you ready for the next phase of the date?" he asked.

Haley's brows rose. "Was that kiss a stepping-stone?"

Chase laughed, unable to ignore the way her brazen, bold attitude turned him on even more. At any other point in his life, he would love to see just where this fiery spirit led him, but he had to stay on track.

"Actually, we have reservations and we're going to be late if we don't get moving."

Haley slid her hands to his shoulders. "And would being late be such a bad thing?"

Honestly? He was ready to forget dinner and these reservations altogether. There was nothing he wanted more than to yank the silky tie around her neck and see that black material float down over her breasts. He wanted her alone, with no distractions, no outside forces giving him reasons they shouldn't be intimate.

If they'd met under different circumstances, he would've already had her in his bed. But he'd deceived her from the start and because he'd respected her as a woman, he'd taken this slower than he'd ever taken a seduction.

There was going to come a breaking point, though, and he had a feeling that moment would be sooner rather than later.

"Being late wouldn't be a bad thing," he finally replied. "But when I have you, it won't be quick and it won't be from making out in a parking lot."

He didn't miss the way her eyes widened at the term *when*. That's right. There was no more second-guessing where this was going because they both wanted it, and he wasn't going to ignore that sexual pull or deny either of them any longer.

"Awfully sure of yourself," she told him with a slight grin.

"Or maybe I'm sure of you," he countered as he slid his lips over hers before releasing her. "You're the type of woman who goes after what she wants. Am I right?"

Her eyes grazed over him, an emotion he couldn't quite identify coming over her.

"You have no idea how right you are," she replied.

As he helped her into the car, Chase couldn't help but wonder where he'd started to lose control. But if he didn't regain a hold over this situation, he was going to find himself lost and swept into Haley's world...where he had absolutely no business going.

Seven

"This view is ridiculously breathtaking."

Haley stared out at the skyline of Manhattan from their corner table on the third floor of The Pavilion. The setting sun cast a breathtaking orange and dark pink glow across the horizon. There was something so intimate about sharing a cozy dinner in a posh restaurant while the day came to an end.

Haley had been here only one other time for the wedding of a college friend, but that had been it and she'd always wanted to dine here with a romantic date.

She wasn't sure this fell into the romantic category, but her date fantasies were most definitely fulfilled—sexy man, sunset, dinner and wine.

"I couldn't agree more."

Haley turned her attention back to Chase and noted he wasn't looking at the skyline at all, but directly at her with a hunger in his eyes she recognized all too well.

She shouldn't fall for those perfect one-liners, but she couldn't help herself. He was damn good at this game. The kiss had left her wanting so much more, even though she knew she shouldn't.

Haley had no idea where he was going with his plans. She knew his motivation, but she had to keep on her toes or someone would end up getting hurt.

She pulled in a deep breath and leaned forward, resting her arms on the table. She had to know more about his motives, about the man who was even more mysterious than she'd first thought.

"Tell me why you want to be CEO of Black Crescent Hedge Fund."

To his credit, he didn't look surprised, but he did give a crooked smile and leveled her gaze. That lethal combo was what had landed her here to begin with. She couldn't turn down his charming words and his devilish looks.

So she was human. So what? She didn't know another woman who would turn down the advances of Chase Hargrove.

"Are we starting the second round of interviews already?" he asked.

Haley shrugged. "I'm just your date trying to get to know you better."

He kept his stare on hers as he leaned back in his seat. "Over the years, I've traveled and started up many investment companies. I know what it takes to make a successful company run smoothly, and Black Crescent is in my hometown. I love the people here and want to ultimately settle down."

Settle down? She hadn't expected that part. A man like Chase Hargrove seemed more the jet-setting, panty-dropping type than the wife, kids and minivan guy.

"So you're sliding into a family-man role, as well?"

He lifted a shoulder and grinned. "Someday. Family is very important to me and nobody would be happier about this than my mother, who reminds me often that she has no grandchildren."

So they weren't estranged. That helped her put another piece of the puzzle together. And he'd just handed her the perfect segue into her line of questioning, though her thoughts tumbled over one another because she had an instant visual of Chase in the role of a father and he just became even sexier.

"So, no siblings?" she asked, reaching for her glass of wine. "Were you terribly spoiled?"

She tried to remain calm, but her insides were a bundle of nerves. Between the growing attraction and tension and all of the unknowns surrounding Chase and his plot, Haley wasn't sure which emotion would overtake her first. This was all new territory for her, but she had to remain loyal to Black Crescent and Josh. They were like her family and she wanted to keep them protected at all costs—even if that meant sacrificing her own happiness.

But when Chase had kissed her, she'd gotten lost. Having his lips and hands on her had made her forget that she even needed to uncover his truths to begin with.

"Not much," he explained. "My mother had a large family, but she was unable to have any more children after me, and I definitely pulled my weight around the house. Maybe that's why I want a family. I want a houseful of children and a wife."

"Someday," she reminded him with a smile.

"Exactly. I'm in no rush."

And it was silly of her to instantly have thoughts pop into her head of being that said wife. She wasn't ready for marriage. She barely had time to do her laundry, let alone feed into a committed, long-term relationship. And children? She really loved her career, so she hadn't thought much about having a family.

Considering her background, she wouldn't even know what to do with a family of her own. Could she even be affectionate? Could she be supportive and loving? As much as she'd like to say yes, she honestly didn't know. There wasn't much to fall back on by way of role models in her past.

"So are you close to your parents?" she asked, toying with the stem of her wineglass.

Dinner had been served and removed long ago, yet they still remained chatting and drinking. Haley was in no hurry to see this night end. She rather enjoyed the company of a sexy, mysterious man.

"Very close," he replied. "My mother was ill for

a while years ago and my father wasn't able to care for her during that time. It was a difficult period for all of us, but I think we are stronger as a unit now than ever before."

Obviously that was the time she'd uncovered when they'd moved into a smaller place and his father went to prison. But she still wasn't 100 percent sure how his mother had been sick, though Haley had her suspicions.

"Is your mother okay now?" Haley asked, sincerely wanting to know.

Chase blew out a sigh and sat forward. "She's amazing. We all bounced back. Not much can keep us down."

"Determination is a big component of running a company," she told him.

He smiled and reached across the table to slide his hand over hers. "Determination is all I have these days."

The way he locked his eyes on hers and delivered such a statement with such conviction, Haley didn't know if they were talking business or not anymore.

"Care to carry this conversation back to my place?" he asked.

Those bold eyes continued to captivate her and she found herself nodding before she could fully think of why this was not a good idea.

"Why should I do that?" she asked. "You could end up being my boss if you have your way about this."

He leaned farther across the table, lifting her hand slightly and lacing his fingers with hers.

"I saw the sunset with you and now I want to see the sunrise."

Her heart tumbled and something clicked into place...something she hadn't known was missing. It wasn't just the sultry words; it was the fact she wanted this man. She wanted him from the moment he'd stopped into the office the very first time. She wanted him when he'd flirted with her over a bundle of silly highlighters. And she wanted him because she recognized determination and that was one very strong common thread they shared.

Maybe they wanted totally different things out of life and maybe he was trying to take down the company she loved so much. But this was just one night. Sex had nothing to do with the job and she was entitled to a social life, right?

For once she was putting her career aside for a night. Tomorrow, she would go back to being on the hunt for the secrets and motives Chase kept hidden. Who knows, maybe she would uncover something at his house. Maybe he'd slip and tell her a nugget of information that she could use to solve this mystery.

Haley wasn't giving up on finding out what he had planned, but she also wasn't giving up on this attraction. The sexual pull was too strong, too overwhelming.

She squeezed his hand and smiled. "I'd love to see that sunrise with you."

* * *

Chase hadn't planned on inviting Haley back to his place, but seeing her in that cast of the sunset, looking like she'd never seen anything more beautiful, had really given him a punch of lust to the gut.

Knowing she'd come from such a humble background and knowing how determined and loyal she was only made her that much more attractive. As crazy as it sounded, she was turning into someone he wanted to spend time with, someone he wanted to *be* with, and his newfound emotions had nothing to do with Black Crescent.

He knew he wanted her. That had never been a secret. But he also didn't want her hurt in the end. Nothing would make him give up his revenge against the Lowells. Absolutely nothing.

All he could do at this point in the game was make sure Haley was out of the direct line of fire. When he ultimately took down the company, he would make sure she had a very well-paid, well-positioned place within one of his own companies. He respected her, trusted her, and he couldn't blame her for anything that took place regarding the scandal that Vernon Lowell had orchestrated.

Chase pulled into the drive of his three-story home on the cliffs overlooking the river. He pushed aside all thoughts of Vernon. The old rogue man had been in the forefront of his mind and the main component of this revenge plot for years, but tonight, the only person Chase wanted occupying his mind, and his bed, was the beauty beside him.

Finally, he'd be able to peel her out of her clothes, just like he'd wanted to since he first saw her. He loved how she was conservative by day, but a little sultry, a little more of a vixen, at night.

The perfect woman…if he was looking for such a thing.

Chase pulled into the garage and closed the door behind him. He killed the engine, then turned to face Haley. Only the glow from the overhead garage light illuminated the car, but that was more than enough to see the desire in her eyes and the way her tongue darted out to moisten her bottom lip.

"You're sure about this?" he asked, not wanting to force her into anything she wasn't ready for.

Without a word, Haley leaned over the console and curled her hand around the back of his neck, pulling him toward her as she covered his mouth with hers.

Within the confined space, Chase didn't have the room to touch her like he wanted, like he'd been craving for weeks. He did maneuver one hand up to stroke the side of her face, then he trailed his fingertips down the column of her throat and into the deep V of her halter top.

She trembled beneath his touch and his arousal slammed into him. He wanted out of this car to where he had the freedom to do what he wanted to the woman he craved more than anything else.

At this moment, he craved her more than any revenge…and that was a hell of a dangerous game to play with himself.

Chase eased back and smoothed her hair from her face. Her warm breath washed over him. Her taste on his lips only urged him to hurry this process into the house.

He exited the car and went around to help her out, but by the time he circled the vehicle, she was out, staring at him like he was her every walking fantasy. The feeling was quite mutual, especially with her lips swollen from his. He couldn't wait to explore her passion further, to see her come undone at his touch.

Haley slid her hand into his and he led her into the house. The dim lights turned on as he made his way through to the sunken living area with an entire wall of windows. The sun had all but set and the twinkling lights across the river reflected off the blackened water.

"Your home is gorgeous," she stated, sounding almost surprised and impressed.

Chase didn't know why her approval made his chest puff with pride. Perhaps because his family had lost everything, including their pride, at the hands of the company Haley was so damn loyal to.

Refusing to ever be vulnerable like his parents, Chase clawed his way to the top. When his father had gone to prison and his mother had a nervous breakdown, their bank accounts had been wiped out and their home had been repossessed. Chase had vowed in that dire moment to never, ever be dependent on anyone ever again. He vowed to never let anyone have that much control over his life because everything could be taken away in a single second.

"This view is what sold me on the place," he told her as he gestured toward the impressive set of windows.

Haley stepped down into the living room and crossed to the glass wall. The reflection gave him the opportunity to see her both from the front and the back, offering him the best view of this remarkably sexy woman.

She stood there a moment, taking in the sights before she glanced over her shoulder.

"Do you bring many women here to seduce them?"

Chase couldn't help but smile at her bold question. "I'm not so sure I'm the one doing the seducing here."

Her brow quirked as her eyes gave him the once-over. "Nice dodge of the question, but I'll take your answer as a compliment."

She would. Haley liked retaining power just as much as he did. She was a dominant woman, likely underestimated in her position at Black Crescent. Did they realize what a dynamic powerhouse they had in their possession? Because Chase had been with her only a few times and he could see that she deserved to be in a higher position, definitely higher pay. He had no clue what her financial status was, but she deserved more. Having someone like Haley on his team would be invaluable.

And he fully intended to have her on his team... and in his bed.

Two totally different scenarios, yes, but he wanted her in any way he could have her. Now he just had to figure out how the hell to make sure she didn't hate him when all of this was over, but even more than that, he had to find a way to make sure she wasn't hurt. That was the last thing he wanted in the end.

"You're staring."

Her statement pulled him back and he realized she was still looking at him over her shoulder.

"Maybe I like having you here and I just wanted to mentally capture the moment."

Haley turned fully to face him, crossing her arms over her chest and pursing her lips. "Do you practice those charming lines in the mirror each morning or are you that smooth by default?"

Unable to keep the distance another minute, Chase moved forward and closed the gap between them.

"Nothing to practice," he countered, reaching up to stroke the back of his hand along her jawline. "I see you and something just pulls me. I can't explain it."

Something came over her eyes, something other than desire. Guilt? Worry? He had a heavy dose of both himself, but those emotions had no place here. Not tonight.

"I can't explain it, either," she replied. "But I know what I want and I don't care about the rest of the outside forces right now."

Another way they were so alike. They both shared a passion for each other and they hadn't even removed their clothing yet. He couldn't wait to get her in his bed, to bring out that fire in her and have his fantasies fulfilled.

"Nothing is more attractive than a woman who

knows what she wants." He reached around to toy with the ends of the tie on her jumpsuit. "Except maybe this outfit. Did you wear this to drive me crazy?"

"Perhaps. How did I do?"

He gave the tie a yank, sending the material floating down away from her breasts. Now, fully bare from the torso up, Haley merely stood before him with her eyes locked on his, clearly confident in her radiant beauty and sexuality.

"Damn good," he stated before he covered her mouth with his own.

Eight

Haley wrapped her arms around Chase's neck and arched her body into his. Was this really happening? Was she letting it?

Yes, and oh, hell yes.

Work didn't matter now. The CEO position didn't matter now. Those alarm bells going off in her head telling her why this was going to be a terrible idea in the long run didn't matter, either.

All that mattered was that she and Chase were both adults. Both very consenting adults who were going after what they wanted. She'd come here knowing full well what was going to happen. The promise of seeing that sunrise from his bed had been impossible to turn down.

But it was the anticipation of all the thrilling

things between now and that sunrise that had her more than ready and willing to come home with Chase.

"I've wanted you here for weeks," he muttered against her lips. "I want to take my time, but I need you too bad."

The feeling was quite mutual. She didn't care if he moved fast or slow, she just wanted to get this going before the ache inside her became too overwhelming.

Chase's hands roamed up her bare back as he eased away and stared into her eyes, then that heavy-lidded gaze traveled down to her exposed chest.

The way he looked at her made her feel sexy, like she was the most beautiful woman he'd ever seen.

With a boldness she felt only with him, Haley reached for the buttons on his shirt and slid each one through the slot…one by one. He kept his eyes on hers as she revealed tanned skin and a dark smattering of chest hair. She parted his shirt and yanked it from his pants.

In a flurry of hands and an occasional laugh when they fumbled, they had their clothes off and flung all around in a matter of moments.

Haley's heart beat so fast. She wasn't an innocent by any means, but there was something about Chase that made her want to remember this, that made her feel like something about this moment was special.

But it couldn't be. No. They were both playing a game of cat and mouse and she had no idea which position she was in…or maybe they kept trading off.

Either way, this night was only about physical because there could be nothing more between them.

"If you're scowling, then I'm doing something wrong."

His words brought her back and she smiled.

"You're doing everything right," she told him, looping her arms around her neck. "And I'm assuming these windows are one-way?"

Chase nipped at her lips, then her chin, and traveled down the column of her neck. "Privacy is imperative to me."

He released her for just a moment before grabbing his pants and pulling out protection. In no time, Chase had himself covered, and he turned back to her with a hunger in his eyes that had her entire body heating up even more.

When he hoisted her up and plastered her back against the glass, Haley shivered at the very idea that anyone could see them. Though she knew they couldn't, just the thrill of having Chase so out of control had her anticipation building even more.

"Tell me if you don't like anything," he murmured against her lips.

Haley locked her ankles behind his back and laced her fingers around his neck. "I won't like it if you keep talking."

He offered her a naughty grin as he joined their bodies. In an instant, everything around them vanished. Haley had been waiting for this moment, this man.

One hand gripped her hip and the other cleverly

traveled over her bare skin. He touched her, kissed her, consumed her. Every part of this was so perfect.

Haley arched her body against his as Chase's lips landed on the swell of her breast. Between the expert jerk of his hips and those hands and lips, Haley let out a moan she could no longer suppress. She was done hiding her feelings, done ignoring what she wanted. For tonight, she would be herself.

She might not trust Chase with his business motives, but she wholeheartedly trusted him intimately...because he wanted the same thing from this that she did. A good time and no strings.

His fingertips tightened on her hip as he pumped faster, his warm breath washing over her heated skin. Haley couldn't hold back her climax another second. The pleasure spiraled through her as her knees pressed into his sides. Chase captured her lips as his own body jerked and stilled.

She clung to him until her tremors ceased, and even then she wasn't ready to let go. She wasn't ready to face reality or harsh truths. She wanted to be selfish just a bit longer.

Chase eventually eased back, smoothing her hair away from her face as he stared down into her eyes. There was something she couldn't quite put her finger on, something almost remorseful in his gaze.

"Regrets already?" she asked, only half joking.

The muscle in Chase's jaw clenched as he shook his head. "I don't do regrets."

Well, that was good to know. She'd hate to think she was considered a mistake.

He slowly helped her get steady on her feet and Haley had a sudden sense of insecurity. She stood before him completely naked after having frenzied sex against a window.

What was the protocol now? Did she make a joke to take out some of the tension? Did she just get dressed like this was no big deal?

But this was a big deal. An extremely epic deal because she didn't do one-night stands. She didn't do flings. She sure as hell never slept with someone who could become her boss.

He wasn't her boss yet, though.

"Regrets?" he asked, mimicking her earlier question.

Haley threw him a glance as she went to gather her clothing. "No regrets, just trying to figure out what to say."

"You don't have to say anything," he told her, clearly comfortable with his state of undress...as he should be. "There are no rules here, Haley. We're adults."

Yes, but there should be rules. Shouldn't there?

"I should go."

Haley quickly dressed. She figured staying wasn't smart since this was just a fling.

As she adjusted the tie on her jumpsuit, Chase's hand settled on the small of her back. Stilling beneath his touch, Haley threw him a glance over her shoulder.

"Don't get lost in that head of yours," he told her with a smile. "Despite what you might think of me, I don't do this type of thing, either."

"And what thing is that?" she countered. "Flings? Sleeping with someone to get ahead in a job?"

As soon as the words were out of her mouth, she regretted them. She was being bitchy because she was confused and flustered. She still felt the tingling effects of their encounter and she was trying to sort all of this out, which was damn hard considering she still felt his touch.

"I'm sorry," she told him, turning to face him fully. "That was uncalled for."

Chase pushed her hair over her shoulders before framing her face and stepping to her. "Nothing to apologize for. But let's get one thing straight right now. When I land CEO, it won't be because we slept together. I wanted you. I want the job. The two have nothing to do with each other."

The confidence he exuded was so sexy. Everything about him was sexy, alluring, mesmerizing. Maybe that was why she was so confused about her feelings. Because she didn't do flings, she could easily see herself getting more wrapped up in this man, and that definitely would be a bad idea.

Chase slid his lips over hers. "Stay," he murmured. "No expectations. Just…stay."

As if she could refuse this man anything.

Haley wanted to stay, so she'd just have to figure out all the other stuff later.

After pouring Haley a glass of wine, Chase stepped out onto his balcony and crossed to the outdoor sitting area.

"This view never gets old," he said, handing her the glass. "It's always so peaceful and the perfect way to unwind after a long day."

She took the glass and curled her feet beneath her on the sofa. "I'd be tempted to sleep out here," she stated with a smile. "I'd definitely settle out here in my downtime with a good book."

Chase took a seat beside her, extending his arm along the back of the sofa as he shifted to face her.

"Downtime," he repeated with a chuckle. "Is that something you have?"

Haley sipped her wine and shrugged. "Lately? No. Josh pushes me to leave when he does or even take a day off, but there's just too much to be done."

Ah, yes. Josh. Let's talk about him.

"So your boss isn't demanding?" Chase asked. "All of this work is self-imposed?"

"Maybe a little of both," she corrected. "I demand enough of myself and take pride in my position. Josh and I used to really rub each other the wrong way when the transition was taking place and here and there over the years. He sees me as a little sister, and brothers and sisters argue."

Just like Chase thought…a bastard like his father. Haley was brilliant and anyone who couldn't identify that was a damn fool.

"It took a couple of years but he now sees me as an equal." Haley laughed and took another sip of her wine. "Actually, he's come to see that I'm invaluable in my position and he's been asking my opinion on the new hire. He's a great guy and I'm happy for him for going after his dreams instead of staying out of duty. That's a fine line to hold on to. Love or loyalty."

Love. Chase wouldn't know about that, but loyalty...hell, yes. He was going through all of this out of loyalty to his family. To seek justice and secure redemption.

"You will be invaluable to me when I take over," he told her.

Her smile widened. "You're so sure this is going to happen for you."

"Because it is," he assured her. "I wouldn't have started if I thought I would fail."

"Do you fail at anything?" she asked.

He thought to when he couldn't save his family, when his father went to prison and his mother had a nervous breakdown.

"Only one time. I vowed to never let myself get that vulnerable again."

Haley finished her wine and set the glass on the table before settling back into the sofa. Her head dropped back against his arm, her eyes meeting his.

"What makes you want this job so bad?" she asked. "You're successful already. You don't need the boost in your finances or ego...or maybe you do. I really don't know much about you."

Yet she'd slept with him and hadn't gone home. That just proved she was more invested in whatever was happening between them than he'd ever anticipated.

And maybe so was he. While he wasn't looking for any type of relationship, he couldn't ignore that he wanted her here, that he enjoyed her company even outside the bedroom. She challenged him, made him smile during a time when he'd been so hell-bent on revenge. She was refreshing at a time when he didn't know happiness or distractions were even possible.

"Finances aren't an issue," he agreed carefully. "I'm always looking for ways to grow and better myself. Black Crescent is the perfect next step in my life."

"Because of that whole family thing," she reminded him with a smile. "And what happens if you don't get the position?"

Chase couldn't help but laugh. "You're not a great motivational speaker, you know."

Haley's smile tugged at him… Everything about her seemed to pull him little by little closer to her world. It wasn't her world he'd set out to infiltrate, yet here he was spending more and more time with her and slowly being pulled away from his ultimate goal.

"Listen, I'm not the final decision-maker," she explained as she leaned closer. "I also shouldn't even be discussing this position outside of work. Not only is it unprofessional, it is disrespectful to Josh."

Yes, Josh. The golden boy. Well, Chase had been doing some digging on Josh. It was best to find out any hidden secrets and dirty details when taking down an opponent. Besides the whole replacement aspect he was working on, Chase also heard rumors that Josh had fathered another woman's baby…not his fiancée's.

Granted, Josh wasn't the one who had destroyed Chase's family, but the guy had swooped in and taken over his crooked father's company. There had to be some semblance of Vernon Lowell in the son who was so take-charge. Chase hadn't wasted his time digging into the other brothers' pasts, though it would be impossible to ignore the rumors that surrounded Oliver and his heavy addiction.

Chase leaned closer to Haley and rested his hand on her upper thigh. "You're invaluable to your company and I don't want you discussing anything you're not comfortable with."

Haley settled her hand over his and smiled. "It's not my company. If you ask my parents, I'm just an assistant. I'm pretty sure they think I sharpen pencils and make coffee all day."

More than once she'd mentioned her parents and their lack of respect for not only her, but also her critical role at Black Crescent.

"Have you ever told them your worth to the company?" he asked. Forget the fact she should be invaluable to her own parents as a remarkable daughter.

Haley let out a humorless laugh. "It's really not worth the fight. I struggled for good grades in school. I had to work my butt off for Bs and Cs. So they naturally dismissed me from growing up to be successful."

"Naturally?" he questioned, trying to tamp down his rage. "That's not natural parenting, Haley. Some kids work harder than others and some just have an easier time. That doesn't mean you can't be successful."

"Yes, well, I'm used to it and actually over it." She eased closer and slid her hand around his neck. "Let's not talk about them anymore."

That desire flashed back into her eyes, and if it was a distraction she needed, then so be it. He didn't mind being used by Haley to keep her mind off unpleasant things. Besides, he shouldn't want to get that personal with her anyway, right?

Yet he couldn't help himself.

Tonight he would take what he wanted, in return keeping Haley's thoughts solely on him. Tomorrow he would go back to trying to pry deeper into the company via her mind.

The end was in sight, and he was too close to having it all to turn back now.

Nine

"No, Mom. I'm fine."

Chase assured his mother once again. He couldn't be angry at her for consistently asking. The woman was worried about her son taking on the family that nearly destroyed them.

He clutched his cell and turned away from his desk to face the large picture window.

"I promise, I'm careful," he assured her as he glanced out onto the river.

The sun shone high in the sky and Haley had gone home after breakfast…which he'd served in bed. Last night had been a turning point, though he still wasn't quite sure which direction he was actually pointing to at the moment.

"I can't help but be concerned," she told him. "I hope you aren't making a mistake."

"Life doesn't come with guarantees, but I didn't set out to lose," he stated. "I know what I'm doing with Black Crescent."

With Haley, though, not so much. Oh, they'd had a hell of a good time last night, but he had no idea where this would go. If they'd gotten together under much different circumstances, Chase wouldn't mind seeing where this could lead. Considering he wasn't being completely honest with her, and that he wanted to bring down her beloved boss, Chase knew this fling could only be temporary at best.

"Promise that you'll check in so I don't worry."

Chase smiled. "I promise. There's nothing for you to worry about."

Once he finished the call, Chase held his cell at his side and pulled in a deep breath. While he always loved talking to his mother, he'd been waiting on his private detective to call this morning. He had been doing some deeper digging into Josh Lowell's past and Chase needed as much information as he could get if he was ultimately going to slide into that CEO position.

Haley was proving to continually be the ever-loyal employee and was not letting much slip. His plan had been to spend more time with her, to get her to somehow unknowingly let slide tidbits of information about the company, but she was still so close-lipped. If anything, she only sang Josh's praises and

the company's as a whole. She'd been there during
the fallout, so there was no way she wasn't fully
aware of every dirty deed that went down. Not everything was public and it was those insider details
he needed to uncover.

His cell vibrated in his hand. Chase glanced to the
screen and saw the call he'd been waiting on. Maybe
now he would get that ammunition he needed to secure his spot at Black Crescent and take down the
Lowells once and for all.

Matteo Velez sat across from her desk and waited
for his interview time. Haley watched as he went
from checking his phone to glancing around the
room. He seemed distracted, like something more
important occupied his thoughts.

More important than an interview for the CEO
position? That seemed quite off and extremely unprofessional.

Did he even want to be here?

The handsome businessman would certainly be
a sexy replacement for her current boss, but Haley
still had her sights set on another mogul.

While Matt may be a head-turner with that dark
suit and his intense stare, he wasn't the one who had
her questioning her sanity and getting lost in thought
during working hours.

No, that privilege belonged to the mysterious
Chase Hargrove.

Josh stepped from his office and caught Haley's

eyes, pulling her from her thoughts and back to the moment and the interview.

"Matt," Josh stated, turning his attention to the latest applicant. "I hope I didn't keep you waiting."

Coming to his feet, Matt shook his head and buttoned his suit jacket. "No problem at all. I'm thankful I managed a second interview."

"You deserve it," Josh corrected. "With a résumé like the one you have, you are already high up on the list."

Matt nodded. Haley found it odd that he didn't smile or seem thrilled at the prospect of being the next CEO. What was going on with this guy?

"My assistant, Haley, will again be sitting in on the interview," Josh said, gesturing to her. "She's been with Black Crescent the longest and she will be your greatest asset to the company."

Matt flashed her a grin. "The right-hand woman," he stated. "There's always one major player in any company who remains behind the scenes and works the long hours."

Haley laughed. "I'd say the long hours are a toss-up between Josh and me, but yes. I do love my job and whoever takes over this position will be working closely with me."

"Let's step into my office. Allison couldn't be here in person, but I have her on conference call."

Josh gestured to the open door behind him and let Haley step in first. She wasn't so sure that Matt had the truest of intentions. He didn't seem overly thrilled to be here, which could always be just nerves or anticipation. He could be a man who just held his emotions close to his chest.

He could also have ulterior motives like Chase. And if that was the case, then Haley had more work cut out for her. She'd never considered the applicants might have past issues with Josh's father or the family in general. It was fifteen years ago. Did people even hold grudges that long?

That was certainly something she needed to take into account. If she came up with too many red flags, she'd have to meet with Josh and express her concerns. Vernon had certainly destroyed quite a few families so it wasn't beyond the realm of possibility for those kids to now want revenge.

Haley settled into her seat and listened as Josh and Allison conducted the interview. Every now and then she interjected and asked her own questions, impressed by Matt's answers.

Maybe Matt should be in the running, but part of her wondered how she would feel if the position went to Chase…and how she would feel if it didn't.

The time was drawing near when a decision would be made and she would have to adjust no matter what the outcome.

All the more reason for her to follow up with that investigator she'd contacted Saturday afternoon about digging into Chase's past and the past of his parents.

There was more to the story than what she'd uncovered on her own and she wouldn't rest until she discovered the full truth of the man she was falling for.

* * *

"So you're telling me you finished your schooling in half the time?"

Just when he thought she couldn't get any more amazing, Haley threw out another fact from her past.

"I buckled down and wanted to be done," she told him as she propped her feet on his lap. "I still lived at home and working as an intern gave me enough to save so the second I graduated, I had enough to get my first apartment and a cheap car."

No wonder she was so loyal. Black Crescent and Vernon Lowell had given her a break and taken a chance. Likely they had been her haven when she wanted and needed to be appreciated and probably loved in a way she hadn't been before.

Ironic that's what she'd found in a company run by a scoundrel, but Vernon did different things for different people apparently. Or maybe Josh had taken on the new intern. Chase didn't know the dynamics there, and he'd be jealous if he wasn't sure Josh thought of Haley as a sister.

Chase slid his hand over Haley's delicate ankles. He'd coerced her into coming for dinner, where he'd prepared everything himself. He'd given his chef the night off again so he and Haley could have complete privacy.

Even Al had been given the night off from any duties. The less his well-meaning father figure/driver/shoulder to lean on knew the better.

"Where did you learn to cook like that?" she asked, resting her head against the back of the sofa and offering him a lazy smile. "I know they don't teach you how to whip potatoes on the football field."

"No. No, they don't," he laughed in agreement. "My mother is an amazing cook and she taught me a few things. Others I've learned on my own through trial and error. I do have a chef for various events and when I have company, but I wanted tonight to just be about us."

Her eyes held his, her smile slowly fading away. "Is there an *us*?"

"Whatever is happening here constitutes as an *us*." His hand slid higher on her leg, but he kept his eyes locked on hers. "Let's not look any further than this."

"*This* as in sex?"

Her bold question had him smiling as his thumb grazed over the curve of her knee. "We're both too married to our careers to worry about anything else right now."

Her legs shifted as she nestled deeper into the sofa, her eyes drawing heavier in that sexy, bedroom-glare type of way—the way that did absolutely nothing to hide the hunger and the desire she possessed.

The idea of her sharing that passion with another man set off a wave of jealousy he hadn't experienced with another woman. Part of him wondered if he'd just gotten in too deep with her, if their relatable backgrounds and drive for business made her seem like the perfect woman.

"People like us?" she repeated. "You told me you wanted a family."

"I do," he affirmed, his hand now splayed across her thigh. "But right now, I have other goals in mind."

Her gaze dropped to his mouth, then back up to his eyes. "We're not talking about the CEO position anymore."

"We're not talking anymore at all."

He inched up her body, his hands taking the hem of her little sundress higher, as well. He wasn't ready to talk, wasn't ready to look into all the messed-up emotions rolling through his mind.

Part of him wanted to know what would have happened had he met Haley under different circumstances. Part of him wanted to know what his mother would have thought of Haley. No doubt they would've gotten along...if Chase had let such a meeting take place.

But that was all a ridiculous line of thinking and a dangerous path to take at this stage in the game.

Haley arched against him, letting out a soft moan as her lids fluttered closed. That reaction was exactly what he wanted. Having her beneath him, ready to join together in the most primal, intimate way, was more than he'd ever thought when he'd first met her. He might not know what the hell he was doing in the long run with her, but he wasn't looking at anything beyond tonight. He couldn't even think about that or the guilt would overcome him.

Chase gripped her hips and jerked her beneath him even more as he settled between her legs. Her eyes shot up to his as a wicked smile spread across her face.

When she opened her mouth, Chase covered it with his own. He really didn't want to talk now and he was afraid of what she'd say. Communicating through their bodies seemed the safest way...at least for now.

Without words, Chase slid her panties down her legs, quickly rid himself of his pants, found protection and settled exactly where he wanted to be. And, if her moans and soft cries were any indicators, this was exactly where she wanted him to be.

Resting his elbows on either side of her head, Chase smoothed her hair from her face and made sure to keep his focus solely on her as he joined their bodies. Haley's ankles came around to lock behind his back, urging him deeper.

When her eyes connected with his, Chase stilled. There was some underlying emotion staring back at him, one he couldn't afford to dig into and one that would likely scare the hell out of him.

Closing his eyes might be the coward's way out, but there was no other option...not now.

Haley threaded her fingers through his hair, tugging ever so slightly. Chase rose up, gripping her hips as he went. Looking down at her with her hair a mess over his sofa, her dress bunched around her waist and her breathing coming out in short bursts had him quickening the pace.

There was something so addicting about this woman and until he found out how to break this cycle, he was damn well going to hang on for the ride.

"Chase."

The whispered word that slipped through her lips as her body tightened all around him had Chase reaching his own peak. Pleasure tore through him, his fingertips dug into her hips and Chase let himself go. Haley continued to whisper his name over and over. He found himself wrapped in her arms and legs, and he wondered how he'd been looming over her and was now being cradled by her warmth, her...

No. Not her love. Love didn't belong here and he sure as hell didn't want it.

As he lay half on, half off her heated body, Chase knew reality would hit sooner rather than later. At some point, he would have to complete his revenge and keep Haley out of the path of destruction in the process.

Ten

Haley stepped inside her front door and immediately slipped out of her heels. She'd been running around all day and had barely even sat at her desk. Between the ongoing interviews with Josh and CEO prospects and running to Tomorrow's Leaders to greet the newest recipients, Haley's feet were killing her.

She'd also missed lunch and the time had well passed any normal dinner schedule. Perhaps she should just pop open a bottle of Pinot and relax in a hot bubble bath. She definitely hadn't taken enough personal time lately with all the spare time she'd been spending with Chase.

Not that she was at all sorry. Her feelings for him were growing each time they were together. Granted, intimacy had a tendency to force people together at least in an emotional manner. Haley didn't do flings and she didn't take sex lightly. If she hadn't had some deeper pull toward Chase, she never would have slept with him.

She hadn't seen him since she'd left his house the other night after he'd blown her mind on his living room couch. They'd texted, but they'd both been busy with work… At least she assumed that's what he'd been busy with.

Haley bent to retrieve her shoes as she made her way toward her master suite. The next thing to go after the shoes was always the bra. She was so done with this day. While she'd accomplished quite a bit, she had run out of steam.

Her cell chimed in the purse she still had over her shoulder. With a groan, she stepped into her room and tossed her purse onto her bed before digging out her phone.

Marcus's name lit up her screen. With a sigh, she swiped the screen and made her way into her adjoining bath.

"I just left you," she said in lieu of a hello. "Is something wrong?"

"Not at all," Marcus replied. "In fact, everything is rather amazing. We had an anonymous donor just give enough to cover all of the textbooks for each of the new recipients starting college in the fall. The amount also covers anything else they may need as far as laptops, notebooks and individual class fees.

There's also a buffer amount for anything that may have been overlooked."

Stunned, Haley turned and sank down onto the edge of her bed. "Who paid for all of that?"

"The money came in electronically with a detailed note of what to purchase for the incoming students," Marcus explained. "There was also a message stating that there would be more donations at the beginning of each quarter for new classes. But honestly, that padded amount that's left would more than cover an entire year. I don't know who this guy is, but he's certainly invested in Tomorrow's Leaders. I mean, I'm glad, but I wish we knew who to thank properly."

Yeah, she did, too, but she also had a good idea who would suddenly be invested in her beloved charity. Not that she would divulge that information to anyone, not even her right-hand man.

"Well, let's just be thankful," she replied. "It's not like we haven't had anonymous donors before. We just typically don't have such specific notes."

"I know you would've seen the email, but I wanted to give you a heads-up," Marcus told her. "Go about your evening. I'm sure you were about ready to dive into a much-needed bottle of wine."

Haley laughed as she turned the knobs on her large soaker tub. She grabbed a bottle on the edge and dumped a hefty dose of lavender bubble bath in.

"You know me so well."

"I know you don't take enough time for yourself, so go enjoy. I'm sure I'll talk to you tomorrow."

"Thanks, Marcus. Good night."

She disconnected the call and stripped out of her clothes. After grabbing her kimono off the back of the bathroom door, she headed to the kitchen to get that glass of wine while her tub filled with hot, bubbly water.

Chase and his wily ways had her smiling. He thought he was sneaky—or perhaps he didn't. Maybe he'd fully intended for her to figure out who had deposited such a large sum.

Oh, sure, someone else could've left that deposit with a detailed email, but she didn't think so. He'd been impressed with her charity and had been eager to help.

Moments later, Haley padded back through her house and into her bathroom. The suds filled the white bathtub and the aroma instantly relaxed her. She set her stemless glass on the edge and slid the knot from her tie. The kimono landed on the floor as Haley stepped into the warm water.

She sank down, letting the bubbles consume her. Her glass and cell sat beside her, but she closed her eyes and dropped her head against her bath pillow. For just a moment, she wanted to lie here and do absolutely nothing.

Okay, maybe she wanted to think about Chase and those damn gestures that made her like him even more. Maybe she wanted to reach out to him and call him out on it. If nothing else, she did want to tell him thank you. She didn't have to make a big deal about thanking him and she didn't plan on embarrassing him, but she did want him to know how much she appreciated what he'd done.

Her cell vibrated again and she peeked out of one eye to the screen. Emails. Always emails.

Another vibration had her screen lighting up with a text from the PI she had digging a little deeper into Chase's parents.

Her curiosity got the best of her and she reached with her dry hand and swiped the screen. The text told her she might want to check her emails ASAP.

Urgency had her tapping on the email icon and opening the message. Haley wanted to take in the entire email at once, so her eyes scanned over all the bullet points before she went back and read each word at a slower pace. Her heart clenched at the information revealed, the ache in the pit of her stomach gnawing as she read very plausible motivations for Chase's urgent desire to take over Black Crescent Hedge Fund.

His father had been incarcerated after a paper trail from the company and Vernon forced the police to take action. She'd known Chase's father had also been part of the embezzling, but she hadn't been sure as to what extent. According to the email, he had been a minor player in the game, but Vernon's well-laid trail led straight to Dale's door.

She read on, finding that his mother was institutionalized after she'd had a nervous breakdown, just like Haley had originally thought. Their family home had been foreclosed after his father went to prison and then his mother had fallen ill. Once his mother was hospitalized, Chase was left alone. No wonder that football scholarship had been so important. That's all he'd had left—his sport and his education.

Is that why he wanted to help her organization so much? To give kids a chance when they wouldn't otherwise have one?

She also read where he'd changed his name right after his mother had been sent for psychiatric help. He'd legally done so and the patterns from then on showed a timeline in black-and-white of Chase working toward revenge on Black Crescent and the Lowell family.

Haley swallowed as a burning sensation pricked her eyes and the back of her throat. He'd been angry for years, so angry he'd changed his major from education to business and graduated in record time... something he'd failed to mention when they'd been discussing her accomplishments.

Setting her phone back on the edge of the bathtub, Haley grabbed her wine. Sipping was out. Gulping was necessary now.

Clearly he'd been planning on trying to infiltrate Black Crescent. Had he been waiting for the CEO position to open up? There was no way he would've known that Josh wanted out because initially Josh had planned to stay. Granted, being a business mogul hadn't been Josh's first choice. He did put his family first and had done everything to rebuild the family name.

Yet now that he'd fallen in love with Sophie and

the two were planning a life together, Josh decided to pursue art, his true passion. Haley couldn't blame him. After all, he'd put his life on hold when his brothers didn't want to step up...or in Oliver's case of addiction, he couldn't step up.

Haley knew Oliver was doing better, had put that hellish time behind him, but he still wasn't up to taking over a corporation the magnitude of Black Crescent.

Finishing off her wine, Haley settled back against the cushy pillow and let all of this information roll through her mind. As much as she wanted to confront Chase and find the answers to her questions— mainly wanting to know if she'd been part of the plan all along—Haley knew she had to be patient and take her time here. There was too much at stake... namely her heart, but also the integrity and future of the company.

If Chase ended up as CEO, what would he do to the place that Haley basically called home? What would happen to all the employees who were loyal to Josh? Not to mention the elite customers they dealt with. Wouldn't taking down Black Crescent just be déjà vu of what happened years ago with Vernon?

Haley didn't like lies, betrayal or deceit. She prided herself on honesty and transparency, but she also prided herself on her strength and ability to withstand the toughest of situations.

There was only one way to find out what Chase's true motives were, and she was going to have to go against everything she valued and held dear.

Haley was going to have to turn a blind eye to her honesty and set a trap for Chase…all the while pretending everything between them was perfectly fine. In truth, the dynamics had completely changed. Her emotional involvement had already surpassed anything she'd expected or even wanted.

While she had no clue what would happen next or how her plan would play out, Haley was certain of one thing… Someone was going to get hurt.

Eleven

Chase wasn't at all surprised that Haley reciprocated the dinner idea and invited him to her place. There was something stirring between them, something that had nothing to do with his revenge plot or his career.

He genuinely liked her, wanted to spend more time with her. That caring side of her had him wondering how she could ever have stayed loyal to a company run by such a bastard. For someone so loving and giving of herself to others, she'd started working at a young age for the exact opposite type of personality.

On the positive side of things, Vernon had left before he could corrupt Haley. Chase hated to think what that man would've done to someone as innocent and generous as Haley.

With a firm hold on the raspberry torte he'd made, Chase rang Haley's doorbell and stepped back to wait.

Seconds later, the door swung wide, revealing a stunning hostess. Her hair tumbled over her shoulders and the little red dress she wore left absolutely nothing to the imagination, stopping high on her thigh and with a deep V in the front. The woman was already driving him crazy...and from the naughty smile, she knew exactly what game she was playing.

Damn his hormones and her for making him live in a constant state of arousal and need.

"Perfect timing," she told him. "I just took the dishes out of the oven."

Her eyes darted to the dish in his hands, then back up to his face.

"Did you throw the box away and put your dessert in that fancy dish just for me?"

Chase scoffed. "A box? I'll have you know I made this with my own two hands. I didn't buy it and I didn't even have my chef make it."

Haley's brows rose as she stepped back and gestured for him to come inside. "Why don't you tell me how you know how to make such a decadent-looking dessert over dinner."

She turned from the door and sashayed back into her home. Chase's gaze instantly fell to those swaying hips as he followed her, closing the door at his back.

The spacious open concept offered him an even bigger glimpse into her life. Simplistic furniture in pale grays in contrast against dark flooring but pops of colors in greenery from plants and bright throw pillows really pulled in both sides of Haley. The career woman in Haley always had a polished, conservative look. But that inner vixen and good-time girl came out to play once business hours were over.

The more he uncovered about this woman, the more he wished like hell they could have met under very different circumstances.

Haley busied herself scooping dinner onto plates and then she poured two glasses of red wine. She hummed a soft tune he didn't recognize but that he instantly found relaxing.

"My mother always hummed." The thought hit him and just tumbled out before he could stop himself. Interestingly enough, he found that he wanted to share more about his past with her. "When I was younger, she would always hum 'You Are My Sunshine.' Cooking dinner, folding laundry, that was just her song."

Haley stared across the long kitchen island and offered one of her sweet smiles. "You don't talk much about your parents. That's a beautiful memory."

His parents meant everything to him and while they certainly had their difficult times—some had seemed so bleak and dire—they always had each other. He and his mom and dad never lacked love or loyalty.

That was the entire reason he was here today. That path he'd started years ago led him to Haley. Guilt grew more and more each day. What started out as rage and anger had turned to desire and passion.

"Everything okay?"

Haley's concerned question pulled Chase back to the moment. He nodded and grinned.

"Fine," he assured her. "What can I do to help?"

She continued to stare, her brows drawn in worry. Chase didn't want to get into the mess going on inside his mind, and even his heart. While he did a damn good job of keeping his heart protected, that didn't mean he was a complete bastard. He cared for Haley, there was no denying that, but he also still had a job to do...literally.

He hadn't come this far in his life, in his plans, to get sidelined by hormones and an innocent woman who had him questioning everything.

When she continued to stare, Chase came around the island and picked up the plates. "Where to?"

He waited, hoping she wouldn't pry any deeper into his past. There was nothing more he could reveal without giving away who he truly was and what he was doing centering himself into her life.

"Let's go out on the balcony," she finally stated. "It's such a nice night."

She led the way through the living room and out onto the spacious balcony overlooking a sloped backyard with a small pond and fountain. Such a simple space, but so perfect for Haley. She had a beautiful home in an upscale part of town and she didn't have to tell him that everything she had, she'd worked her ass off for. No one had helped her, least of all her family. All of her accomplishments were only because this woman had drive and determination and wouldn't let anyone stand in her way.

And that right there was so damn sexy, he couldn't even deny that she was quite possibly the most perfect woman he'd ever met.

Too bad she could never be his.

"Oh, do you care to go into the dining area and grab the napkin holder from the table?" she asked. "I'll go get the utensils."

"Sure."

Chase stepped back into her house and passed through the living area to the small dining room. Spread across the table were papers, which caught his attention with the Black Crescent Hedge Fund logo on several documents. The napkin holder was nowhere to be seen on the table, but the highlighters he'd brought her were lying in a bundle on the side.

As much as he wanted to glance through those papers, he couldn't. A month ago, if given this opportunity, he'd sure as hell have taken advantage, but now… Well, everything had changed.

"Damn it," he muttered as he turned to glance around the room.

The sideboard had a decorative napkin holder full of napkins. Chase grabbed it and started to head out, but not before one last longing glance at the papers. Josh's signature was scrawled across the bottom of a few documents, but Chase ignored his curiosity.

Now wasn't the time to betray Haley's trust. He vowed to himself not to let her get hurt. He would do everything he could to prevent Haley from getting caught in the middle of this twisted web.

Walking away from those papers was the most difficult thing he'd done in a while. Maybe they wouldn't have shed any light on his master plan, but there was a possibility they would have.

What should he have done, though? Stood there sorting through the piles, or perhaps pulled out his cell and started snapping pics so he could look over them in his private time? And do all of that while Haley waited for him on the balcony for a romantic dinner? Only a complete jerk would do such a thing.

When he stepped back out onto the balcony, he saw that Haley had lit two small candles and had arranged a colorful bundle of flowers in a simple glass vase between their plates. She held her arms out, gesturing toward the table.

"Ta-da."

Chase laughed. "Is that why you had me step away?"

She shrugged and pulled the chair out for him. "I just wanted to do something nice. I mean, it's no bouquet of highlighters or homemade raspberry torte, but…"

Chase couldn't remember the last time someone did something for him. Not something that didn't have to do with business or using him to get ahead. Haley had no reason to use him, no reason to play him. No, in all of this he was the one using, and that damn weight kept mounting on his shoulders… Soon the heaviness would become too much to bear.

This sweet gesture of dinner and a romantic ambiance put a vise around his heart and he'd done so well in keeping his heart out of this equation so far.

Chase set the napkins on the table and turned to face her. That punch of lust he always experienced when he looked at her now layered with something else…something deeper, more meaningful, but definitely something he couldn't label.

Honestly, he didn't want to put a label on any of this because that would hint dangerously close to a relationship.

But physical, that was something he could grasp and control. It was an emotion, a reaction he knew.

Reaching for her, Chase curled his fingers around that dip in her waist and pulled her closer.

"This is all amazing," he told her, leaning in. "The dinner, the atmosphere, sexy dress. You didn't have to do all of this for me."

Her smile widened as she looped her arms around his neck. "Maybe I did it for us. Maybe I like spending time with you and I wanted to look nice even though we're staying in."

Hell yes they were staying in. There was no way he was taking her out because he wasn't sure how long he'd be able to control himself. Peeling her out of that dress had just jumped to the top of his priority list…even above those papers in the other room.

"Staying in is the best idea I've heard all day." He nipped at her lips, holding her hips flush against his own. "Did you wear this dress to drive me out of my mind?"

She tipped back, laughter dancing in her eyes. "Is it working?"

"You're lucky we've made it this long with our clothes still intact."

Haley framed his face and laid a quick kiss on his lips. "Dinner first. Then we can discuss dessert options."

She stepped from his hold and gestured to the chair she'd pulled out for him. "Sit and eat before it gets cold."

Reluctantly, he took a seat. "If this is some sort of foreplay, you're winning."

She reached for a napkin and snapped it open, then laid it in her lap. "I never lose," she promised with a leveled gaze.

As if he needed another reason to find her even more irresistible. But he needed to focus. Those papers and her sweetness layered with a heavy dose of sex appeal had really thrown him. He wasn't about to mention the papers, though. Likely she'd brought work home, and that certainly didn't surprise him.

Haley picked up her fork and speared a piece of beef. "So, tell me all about how you came to make amazing-looking desserts."

"Oh, they don't just look amazing, they taste incredible."

"Just add humble to your list of attributes."

Chase took a bite of what tasted like homemade noodles. "Humble has no space in my life. Confidence and risks have taken me everywhere I need to be."

"Please, no work talk," she begged. "I already had to bring home some forms to sort out and I just want one evening of doing absolutely nothing."

Chase set his fork down and reached across the small round table. "I'm glad you're taking some time for yourself."

"With you."

Chase raised his brows. "Is there someone else?"

"Oh, yes," she laughed. "I've been seeing all of the CEO applicants on the side. You know, just so I can see who I'm most compatible with."

He couldn't help but smile. A snarky comeback was another quality he appreciated.

"I deserved that," he told her. "When was the last time you dated before me?"

"Are we dating?" she asked.

The idea didn't bother him. What bothered him was the fact all of this was temporary. There was no long term here, even if he had the time to start feeding into a serious relationship.

"I'm exclusively sleeping with you and we've been out," he countered. "What do you want to call that?"

Haley pursed her lips as she reached for her wine. Swirling the contents, she leaned back in her chair and kept her focus on him.

"I'm not sure," she finally answered. "I like seeing you, I like sleeping with you and I don't want to do that with anyone else right now."

Right now. Did that mean she also thought this was temporary? Because the only reason he wasn't pursuing more was because he knew she would never forgive him for going after her beloved company.

So what was her reasoning for thinking this wouldn't grow into more?

And why the hell was he offended?

"So, about that torte," she went on. "Care to tell me how you came to that and are there any more hidden secrets you want to share?"

Hidden secrets? She wasn't ready to hear those, though he knew they would come out eventually. With the position he currently was in, he just had to make sure she didn't hate him and understood his reasoning for his actions once this was all said and done.

Twelve

Haley rolled over, her hand reaching for Chase, only to find the spot not only empty but also cold.

Confused, she sat up in bed and glanced around the darkened room. A sliver from the hallway light filtered in.

After dinner, she and Chase had enjoyed more wine and a brief chat on the balcony. It didn't take long for them to move inside for some much needed privacy. They barely made it to the living room before their clothes were shed. Once that frenzied sex had taken place, Chase had carried her in the most romantic way possible to the bedroom, where they'd taken their time exploring each other.

So where was he now? She'd fallen asleep in his

arms, nestled right against all of his strength and warmth.

The papers. Damn it. She'd left those out as part of her initial trap or plan or whatever the hell game she was playing in an attempt to test Chase's loyalty. She'd actually forgotten all about them once they'd started dinner. Of course, she'd sent him into the dining room to find her scattered mess. She'd purposely left the napkins in there, needing to get his curiosity pumping.

The papers she'd left out were actually private, but nothing that would harm the company. They did hold information that only she knew; not even Josh was aware of some of the contents. So if anything was leaked, there would be only one source.

Guilt curled low in her belly as she pushed the sheet aside. Swinging her legs over the side of the bed, she sat for just a moment and wondered what she should do now. She didn't like playing games, but she had to know where Chase really stood. Did he indeed want the CEO position or did he just want to destroy the company from within?

Did he want to destroy her in the process? Had she been part of his plan all along?

Fear spiraled through her, layering with the guilt and the worry. If he wasn't playing her, then she hated how she'd tried to set a trap. But she had to protect not only herself, but also Black Crescent and everyone in their employ.

Haley came to her feet and grabbed her kimono from the antique trunk at the end of her bed. After sliding into it and securing the tie, she padded out into the hall. The decorative clock on the wall showed just after five in the morning. Considering this was a Sunday and not a typical workday, she'd like to have slept in a little longer in the arms of the man she was falling for.

Falling for and possibly being deceived by.

Mercy, this was starting to become a serious mess.

Haley stepped into the open living area where she saw Chase in the kitchen, standing over her coffeepot.

Wearing a dark suit certainly made Chase Hargrove drop-dead sexy, but having him in her kitchen wearing nothing but black boxer briefs and a mop of bedhead was a whole new side of sex appeal.

Haley couldn't examine too deeply just how having Chase in her home made her feel. Inviting a man into her personal space wasn't something she did, but she'd needed to set the trap.

Ugh. Even those words floating through her mind made her nauseated. But thinking he was using her, that he might have gone into her dining area and leaked information about Black Crescent, made her feel even worse.

She shuffled her feet across the wood floor, causing Chase to turn. He offered her a crooked grin and raked a hand down his chest.

"Did I wake you?" he asked.

Haley shook her head. "I rolled over and you were gone."

"I'm an early riser."

Or maybe he wanted to catch her while she was asleep and rifle through her things? How long had he been alone in her home? Had he taken photos of the documents and already called his assistant or his family? Were his parents backing him?

She had way too many questions about the man standing practically naked in her kitchen.

Chase turned back to her coffee maker and sighed. He tapped a button, tapped another and shrugged.

"I was trying to figure out how to make coffee in this damn pot of yours, but there's only so far my degrees can take me."

Haley laughed, making her way around the bar island separating the living area from the kitchen. She stepped in beside him and glanced to the water, then the mess of coffee grounds he'd made on her counter.

"Well, it certainly helps to get the grounds into the filter," she stated. "Why don't you go have a seat and I'll do the coffee?"

He threw a heavy-lidded glance over his shoulder. "Is it because I've made a mess? I was going to clean that up, you know."

Haley patted his cheek. "I'm sure you were, but I can't stand chaos and this is already making my eye twitch."

Chase nodded and took a step to the side. "At least show me how to use this damn thing for next time."

Haley stilled, her attention going from the messy counter to the messy relationship.

"Next time?" she asked. "How often do you plan on staying over?"

Chase reached out and gave a slight tug on the tie of her kimono. "As often as you'll let me."

In a perfect world and under much different circumstances, she'd want nothing more than to have this man in her bed each night. She could think of no other way she'd like to fall asleep.

Unfortunately, she was almost positive she couldn't trust him and she had convinced herself that he was playing her...which meant she needed to stay at least one step ahead of him until she uncovered the real truth.

An uncomfortable heaviness settled deep within her. She needed space. She couldn't stand here next to him, both of them wearing very little, with all of these emotions. There was too much to consider, too much to worry about and contemplate.

With a smile, Haley faced him. "Let me handle the coffee. Go back to bed and I'll meet you there."

He leaned in, covered her mouth with his and caught her so off guard she had to grip his bare shoulders to keep upright. He released her just as quickly and took a step back.

Haley reached for the edge of the counter to maintain her balance as Chase headed back toward the bedroom. She waited until he disappeared down the hallway and into the master suite.

Blowing out a breath she hadn't realized she'd been holding, Haley closed her eyes and gathered herself. After she cleaned up the coffee grounds and got the brew going, she glanced toward the hallway once more before going to the dining area.

The light from the kitchen illuminated into the space and onto the table. The papers were exactly how she'd had them. Not one had been moved, and even though they looked like a mess, she knew in what order they had been placed.

Was he not using her? He'd had the perfect opportunity to look over these documents and she was pretty positive he hadn't done a thing.

The sound of the coffeepot coming to the end of the cycle pulled her away from the table. Her plan worked, or didn't work, depending on how she wanted to look at things. He knew these pieces were here, so if he'd truly been out to sabotage her or the company, wouldn't he have moved them around to read them or snap pictures?

What if he was in this only for her?

But then if that was the case, what happened if he was hired and became her boss? Then what would people think? The staff knew Haley had sat in on the interviews. Would they think she'd chosen him because he slept with her?

Haley tried to push aside all the questions as she made her way back to the coffee. Chase waited on her in her room, and now that she knew his intentions might be real and honest, she couldn't wait to spend the morning with him and maybe see where all of this could lead.

"I have some more information."

Chase steered his SUV through the streets of

downtown and listened as his personal investigator gave the details Chase had been waiting on.

"The information wasn't easy to come by and it's certainly going to cost you."

Chase rolled his eyes. The guy was the best in the business, but his ego seriously grated on Chase's last nerve. He wasn't in the mood for games. He just wanted the scoop he was paying for.

"What did you find?" Chase demanded as he came to a stoplight.

"The doctor that delivered the love child that is rumored to belong to Josh might have been a bit shady and untrustworthy…as was the mother of the child."

"How shady are we talking?"

"The doctor or the mother?"

Chase gripped the wheel and prayed for patience. "I want to know everything you found."

"Well, the doctor had been known to falsify a few birth certificates in his day," the investigator replied. "Hundreds if not thousands, in fact. He also manually changed DNA results once they were processed for a nice sum from his desperate clients. He practiced for over thirty years before he was caught and he's now incarcerated."

Interesting. The shady doctor working for a shady family. How quaint.

"The results also mention that the father could be Josh or his twin brother, Jake."

Well, at least that was something.

"And the more I dug into Josh's past, the more I found he's actually an upstanding guy. Nothing at all like his father. The guy seems to just want out of the family business, and I can hardly blame him. It has to be hell having the black cloud of Vernon Lowell hanging over your head your entire life."

"Send me over everything you found," Chase told him. "I need to see a few things for myself. I've already sent your payment, plus an extra bonus since you worked so hard."

Stroking that overinflated ego kept his investigator loyal and quiet. Those were two main qualities Chase demanded.

He disconnected the call with a tap to the screen on his dashboard. Instantly, music filled the vehicle and he cranked the metal up. He needed to think and when things were silent was when he nearly went out of his mind.

The light changed and Chase turned to take the familiar route leading to his parents' home—though his mind was still back on spending the weekend with Haley and those damn papers.

There was no way all of that was coincidence. He firmly believed she'd left those there for him to find. For one thing, the woman was neat as a pin and everything had a place. No way in hell would she leave papers spread about like that and not in tidy little stacks.

For another thing, she wouldn't leave out confidential work knowing someone outside the company was coming over. She was much more professional and much smarter than that.

Which meant she knew he had a plan. She might

not know exactly what his plan was, seeing as how his path had changed a few times, but she knew he wasn't on the up-and-up.

So now what? Did he keep playing this game? Damn it, he hated calling any of this a game. His revenge wasn't a game. His feelings for Haley weren't a game.

But he was too far in to all of this to pull back now. There had to be a way to get the company and the woman. And if Joshua Lowell was truly a stand-up guy, then Chase had to rethink that angle, as well. Josh wanted out, so clearly he wasn't like his old man.

As Chase turned into his parents' subdivision, his mind was already formulating ideas on how, if at all, he could meet up with Josh outside the office. Maybe Chase could tell Josh what he'd found and that would gain Chase more leverage over the competition.

Maybe there was a way to salvage all of this… the revenge and the uncertain relationship he was in.

Thirteen

The warm embrace of his mother always settled his mood for at least that moment. That same familiar body lotion she so loved still took him back to when he was a child and she'd hug him and tell him everything would be alright.

Now he was the one making sure everything would be alright.

Chase eased back. "Is Dad here?"

His mother shook her head. "He's out golfing with some buddies today. I'm so glad you could come by."

She reached around him to close the door, then turned. "Let's go into the living room. Do you want a drink or anything? I just made some cranberry muffins."

"No, I'm fine."

Chase followed his mother into the living room. He'd purchased this place for his mother once she'd finished her care and while his father was still in prison. The neighborhood was nice and quiet and the spacious home was all on one floor because he wanted easy access to things for his mother.

She took a seat on the sofa and Chase sank into the leather wingback chair across from her. She looked nice today, refreshed with a yellow top and white jeans. She'd pulled her dark hair back into that signature twist she always did.

"You look nice, Mom."

She laughed and narrowed her gaze. "You always said that when you wanted something from me."

Chase shrugged. "That might be true, but there's nothing I need. Can't a son compliment his mother?"

"Hey, at my age, I'll take all the compliments I can get," she laughed.

"I hardly think fifty-eight is old."

She reached over and patted his cheek. "I'm fifty-nine, which you well know, but thanks for that extra boost of confidence."

Chase eased back in the seat and rested his arm on the side. "So, what did you need to see me about?"

"You know I love to visit with you," she told him. "And I hadn't seen you for a few days."

Maybe because he'd been a little preoccupied by the only woman who could ever distract him from his goals and reality.

"Now who's the one who wants something?" he

countered. "You texted me to come over and I don't think it was so you could sit and stare at me."

She crossed her legs and lifted one slender shoulder. "Fine. I did want to talk to you not over the phone or text. I want to know what's going on with this revenge you're hell-bent on seeking and I want to know who the woman is who has been keeping all of your time lately."

His once feeble, meek mother had blossomed into a bold woman since her treatment. While he was damn proud of her for overcoming her demons, part of him was terrified. She was still his mother, she still deserved respect and the truth… He just didn't know how much to reveal at this delicate stage.

"I have been seeing a woman named Haley Shaw," he told her.

"And how does she tie in to this whole thing?"

Chase wasn't about to play dumb or insult her intelligence, so he answered honestly.

"She's Josh Lowell's personal assistant."

His mother swore under her breath before letting out a deep sigh. "Don't pull an innocent into this mess, Chase. She couldn't possibly know what happened years ago."

"Actually, she was hired by Vernon while she was still in college," he informed her. "But, I will agree that she is innocent. I started out just flirting, hoping to gain some inside information from her."

"And how has that worked for you?"

That knowing stare she held him with had all of that guilt he'd tried to suppress coming to the surface. He'd never wanted Haley to get so involved in his plot, but he couldn't stop the roller coaster he'd put her on, either.

"Oh no."

Chase pulled his attention back to his mother at her statement.

"What?" he asked.

"You're falling for her."

Shaking his head, Chase shifted in his seat. "I'm not falling for her. We're spending time together, we've gone out. She's an amazing woman. Career oriented and loyal, so that's something I can appreciate."

"You're falling for her," she repeated. "Or maybe you're already in love."

"I have no time or room in my life for love right now," he scoffed.

"Most people aren't looking for it when it happens, son, but you're in deeper than you think. Or maybe you're lying to yourself, I don't know, but if you can't face the truth then someone is going to get hurt."

Like he hadn't already thought of that? Like he wasn't sick thinking of the prospect of Haley getting caught in the crossfire?

Or worse…that she'd hate him forever. Once all of this was over, would she understand where he'd been coming from? Would she believe his feelings for her were real?

Oh, hell. They were real. Now what? Oh, this might not be love like his mother suggested, but there was definitely something more than just sex.

When all of this was over, and he was the CEO of Black Crescent, was there even a chance Haley would listen to him?

"Looks like you have some decisions to make."

His mother's soft tone had Chase easing back in the chair and closing his eyes. These weren't the decisions he wanted to make. He hadn't lied when he'd said he had no time for this, but he was going to have to make time and dig deep to find out where Haley stood. Was she more important than this vendetta or would he have to push her aside to continue his decade-old plan?

"I'd say the interviewing process is about to come to an end. If Ryan Hathaway had taken the job offer, this would've been over weeks ago."

Haley glanced across the large metal and glass desk to Josh. He leaned back in his black leather office chair and seemed quite content this morning. Not typical behavior for a Monday morning, but she was having a great start to her own week. She and Chase had spent the past two days together. They'd made love—could she even use that word at this stage?—and they'd gone to the local coffee shop for mimosas and waffles yesterday morning. They'd watched old movies and shared more details about what made up their personalities. Who knew the man had a secret crazy sock collection?

"Have you decided who you want to take your place?" she asked, crossing her legs and trying not to show her hand or hold her breath.

"I've narrowed it down to three I'd like to talk to again." Josh laced his fingers together and rested his forearms on his desk as he leaned forward. "But I need to talk with you before we move forward with anything else."

She didn't like the tone of his voice or the way he was staring at her like he knew her dirty little secret. Did he know?

So what if he did. Chase wasn't her dirty secret. He was the man she was seriously falling for.

"I've heard a rumor about you and one of the applicants. Chase Hargrove."

Haley inwardly rolled her eyes. Rumor? More like gossip mill. While she truly loved Black Crescent, she also knew this place was like any other office building and one little spark of news always escalated quicker than anything else.

"And what exactly did you hear?"

Because she guaranteed it wasn't near as juicy as what was truly happening, but that was certainly something she'd keep to herself.

Josh glanced down to his hands and blew out a sigh. "Listen, you know you're more than my assistant," he started. "I'm definitely on your side here."

Irritated, she sat up straighter in her seat. "I wasn't aware there were sides."

"There aren't," he amended. "Just listen. I'm not talking to you as your boss, not yet. Right now I want to talk to you as a friend. I've heard you were out with Chase Hargrove. Actually, I heard you were quite cozy while out, which makes me believe there

was nothing involving Black Crescent going on between you two."

"I have been out with Chase a few times, yes. He's
not an employee."

"No, but he is being interviewed and some might
see that as a compromise on your part."

Haley relaxed her shoulders, settling deeper into
the seat. She knew Josh wasn't her enemy. Her enemy
was all of those negative thoughts inside her mind
telling her that she should never have let things go
this far, so long as Chase was a contender for the
CEO position.

"You should know that Chase is in the top three
to take my place," Josh went on. "Would you continue seeing him or do you think you should take a
step back?"

Haley wasn't sure what to do. This company literally meant everything to her and Josh was like
family. She would continue her loyalty to him and
to Black Crescent Hedge Fund...but did that mean
she had to put aside her emotions? Did that mean she
had to put aside the one personal relationship she'd
sought out in years?

"I would never tell you who you can and can't
see," Josh went on. "I'm not in any position to tell
you what to do. That's all on you. My concern comes
from the friend standpoint and I don't want you hurt."

Well, that made two of them. But if Chase hadn't
touched those papers, then surely he wasn't using
her...right?

"I want to make sure he isn't trying to get close

to you in order to land this position," Josh added. "You're one of the most intelligent people I know, so I'm well aware that you wouldn't purposely let yourself be used. If you tell me you're positive he's on the up-and-up, then I'll believe you."

Haley offered a smile that she hoped was convincing enough for Josh to drop this matter for now. "Chase and I enjoy each other's company. We rarely talk work. In fact, we tend to discuss Tomorrow's Leaders. He's made some generous contributions and..."

The contributions. Damn it. Was he using her? Had she been so foolish, so blindsided by charm and sex appeal that she'd completely fallen for the oldest trick?

"Be careful, Haley."

Josh's concerned tone pulled her from her thoughts. She wasn't about to voice her own opinions or worries here. That was something she needed to sort out on her own.

"I'm careful," she stated as she came to her feet and smoothed down her burgundy pencil dress. "Was there anything else?"

"Should I call him for another interview or would you rather I not?" Josh asked, also standing. "I mean it when I say I want you comfortable with the person who steps into this role."

Not every boss would take that stance. Most people would only choose the person who was most qualified to be in such a leadership position, and no doubt Josh kept all of that in mind, but he also worried about her, which made her sorry he was going to be leaving. She'd been with him so long, she wouldn't know how to come in each and every day and not see his face.

"Are you tearing up?"

Haley blinked, cursing at the burning sensation in the back of her throat. "Shut up."

Josh laughed as he came around his desk and pulled her into his embrace. "If it helps, I'm going to miss you, too. But I promise to stop in. You won't be completely rid of me."

Haley wrapped her arms around him and smiled against his chest. "I'll let you take me to lunch so I can tell you all about the new CEO and we can talk freely."

"I look forward to it." Josh leaned back and stared down at her. "Especially if that person is Chase Hargrove."

Haley didn't say anything. What could she say? Maybe falling so fast, so hard with Chase had been a mistake, considering their positions. Maybe taking a step back for the time being was the wise move to make. Then once the new CEO was decided, whether him or another, then she could revisit a relationship and see where they stood.

But for now, and for the short foreseeable future, she needed to focus on the job and help Black Crescent cross over into a new chapter.

Fourteen

Haley had texted Chase that she needed to speak with him and that she was leaving work around five. Considering that that time was early for her, he had to believe whatever she wanted to discuss was serious.

After their weekend together, he thought they were progressing into something more. But he also had to come to the very real conclusion that she knew that his intentions weren't completely honorable.

None of this should surprise him, though. Haley was a smart woman. She didn't get to where she was by being played for a fool.

Granted there were people, like her disrespecting parents, who saw her only as an assistant. Chase knew full well the value of a loyal, well-trained assistant. They were just as vital in the daily goings-on within the company as the CEO. Just because their faces were behind the scenes didn't make assistants any less esteemed.

Chase pulled into the drive of Haley's cottage home and killed the engine. He wished like hell he knew what he was walking into. How could he formulate a game plan when he didn't have a clue about his opponent?

He cringed at his initial thoughts. This whole ordeal wasn't a game and Haley wasn't an opponent. She'd turned into so much more. At first he'd definitely been using her, but that was just harmless office flirtation. It wasn't until he uncovered her kind heart, her giving nature, the passion within that he realized he was in over his head.

But by then everything had escalated and there was no way he could back out.

There was also no way he could remain in his car mulling over all the ways his detailed plan spiraled out of control. He had to face Haley, but he would say nothing until he knew why she'd called him here. He knew all of this would come out eventually, but he'd hoped his secrets would expose themselves as he took over the company that destroyed his family. Not just his family, but also the lives of several other families in Falling Brook.

Chase stepped from his SUV and readied himself for whatever lay ahead of him. No matter what, he wasn't about to lose everything he'd worked so damn hard for...and that included Haley.

Before he could knock, the door swung wide and she stood before him still wearing her work clothes. Another one of those little dresses that seemed conservative but that drove him absolutely out of his mind. Her hair was down and over one shoulder and her feet were bare.

But that smile was missing. That smile she always greeted him with, that smile that always made him want to scoop her up and escape somewhere, just the two of them, and ignore the rest of the world... that smile that always managed to kick his guilt up another notch.

"Thanks for coming by." She gestured for him to step inside. "I hope you weren't busy."

"Never too busy for you," he assured her.

She closed the door behind him and started toward the open living area. He'd just left here only yesterday, yet the atmosphere seemed so different now. What exactly did she know or did she *think* she knew?

When she didn't take a seat, he knew nothing good was about to happen.

"What's going on, Haley?"

She licked her lips but leveled his gaze. "I've been lying to you."

Well, that was a bold statement to just jump right into and not one he was expecting at all. She was lying to him? There was so much irony in that statement.

"And how have you been lying to me?" he asked.

Haley took a deep breath. "I thought you might

not have the purest of intentions when it came to Black Crescent or to me. When you first came in, there was the flirting that I dismissed, but then things progressed."

He waited, listening to her reveal her truth all while he held his darkness deep inside. The guilt gnawed at him, more than he'd ever felt before, but he had to let her continue. He had to let her get this out into the open and off her chest... Then he could see how to proceed and what, if anything, he should reveal.

"Because I'm so protective of Black Crescent and Josh, I did a little digging around on you," she went on. "The attraction and the job became two totally different things and I did struggle with the separation of the two."

That guilt he had suddenly became layered with anger. She had been investigating him? From the beginning?

He had no right to be angry... But damn it, he was.

"Then I uncovered that you had changed your last name," she told him. Her eyes held his as her brows drew in. "I'm not completely certain why you did that, but I have some ideas. There is also the fact that while other applicants sent me flowers and cupcakes, you sent me highlighters and took me out to expensive plays and dinners."

"And those are all strikes against me?" he asked, still irked that she'd had him investigated.

"I couldn't be sure if they were strikes or gold

stars," she told him. "I wanted to think someone like you could be attracted to someone like me."

What the hell did that mean? He didn't get a chance to ask before she went on.

"Once you really started showing more interest, I couldn't help but wonder if it was me you were after or the CEO title."

Chase gritted his teeth and crossed his arms over his chest as he continued to listen. She had been second-guessing everything from the start. She had wondered his intentions from the very beginning and yet she still went out with him... She still slept with him.

"I decided to lay a paper trail to see where your loyalties laid."

That got his attention more than anything.

"You what?" he demanded.

"I'm so sorry," she told him, taking a step closer. "I had to know if you wanted to be with me or if you were really just out for the job."

Fury filled him and he hated himself for so many reasons, but namely for being played from the beginning. He was the one who was supposed to gather all of the information. He was the one who was supposed to make sure his game plan was flawless. But he'd been too occupied with the end result to realize that he'd veered off course of his well-laid plan.

"I know now that you didn't try to deceive me and I just... I had to tell you." She pursed her lips, her gaze continuing to hold his. "I didn't want anything between us because I think there's more here than either of us wanted."

Chase said nothing. What could he say? He was still processing the bomb she'd just dropped. Here he thought he was coming over because she had uncovered his secret, but she had turned the tables and everything he'd known thus far had all been a lie.

She'd questioned him from the beginning, but she'd never outright just asked him. So much sneaking, so many hidden thoughts that were damning to their relationship.

And he was just as guilty, he totally understood that, but he never expected this behavior from Haley. She'd been the bright spot in all of this, she'd been the distraction he'd needed, she'd been the one comfort he'd had because she provided something positive and perfect.

"You deceived me," he accused as the hurt continued to roll through him.

"I did." Haley took another step toward him, then another. "In my defense, I didn't know you well and I had to put my job and the company before any feelings I was developing."

He should've realized that from the beginning. One of the main things that had turned him on about her was that steely businesswoman she seemed to be.

Damn it, he had no right to be angry, but he couldn't help himself. Maybe he was angrier with himself for not seeing what was going on and for letting this happen… Because he had started all of this.

No, Lowell had started this colossal mess when

he'd chosen to interfere with the lives of Black Crescent's clients and then dole out part of the blame before fleeing and leaving everyone else to take the fall.

As Haley stood within reaching distance, Chase realized he wasn't the only bad guy. Here he'd been having guilty feelings, wondering how he could protect her from the fallout when he should have just kept his focus straightforward on his goal and not gotten sidetracked by sex. He never should've tried to incorporate flirting into the mix; that was such a rookie business mistake.

"Say something," she pleaded. "I'm sorry I didn't believe you. I'm sorry I went behind your back, but I'm telling you now hoping we can move on."

But they couldn't move on. While all of this newfound information from Haley threw him for a complete loop, Chase still couldn't give up on his goal.

Which meant he had to give her up. She'd come clean on her actions so they could move forward, but she had no clue that he was still lying. His anger right now stemmed from shock. He never would have guessed she would be playing him right alongside his own game...which just proved how remarkable she truly was.

Damn it, he wished he would've met Haley under much different circumstances. They would have been a dynamic duo had they teamed up together.

Chase took a step back. Haley's eyes widened as a shroud of sorrow filled her stare.

"I understand your reasoning for what you did," he began, but held his hands out when she started to step forward. "I don't think we should move forward with a relationship."

Haley stared a brief moment before she visibly composed herself. Crossing her arms, widening her stance and tipping her chin up were all indicators she was ready for a fight. But he'd been emotionally knocked for a loop and didn't have the energy right now. He needed to get out of here, to regroup. If that made him a coward, then so be it.

"You're that quick to throw away your feelings?" she asked. "Because I kept secrets to protect my job and my boss? I didn't know you in the beginning, Chase. If the roles were reversed, you would've done the same exact thing."

The roles weren't reversed and he'd done more digging and scoping out the competition than she knew.

"I came clean when I realized I had feelings for you," she went on. "Maybe you don't feel the same, though. Maybe you don't need me anymore now that you had such a great interview and Josh is considering having you in again to talk."

Another shocking revelation, but at the same time, Chase wasn't surprised. He was damn qualified for the position…a position that he still wanted and was starting to realize was all he had left.

Circling around to his ultimate goal was where he needed to land. Even though there seemed to be a vise around his heart, he had to remember the reason he'd started all of this to begin with. To seek justice for his family and all of those who didn't have the means to fight back. He had to make this right, and getting wrapped up in an even bigger web of lies with Haley was not the way.

"We both knew this was risky," he told her. "You stated more than once that I could become your boss and then where would we be? It's better to end things now, Haley."

He thought for sure he saw her chin quiver, but her eyes were dry and narrow. She pulled in a deep breath and nodded.

"Fine. I won't beg you to listen to my side and I sure as hell won't ask you to give me another chance. I'm not sorry for the why of all of this, but I am sorry if I hurt you. I would have thought you of all people would understand my justified actions."

Oh, he understood. Which was why he was getting back on track with his plan and putting any unwanted emotions aside.

Haley took a step forward, but she walked around him and went to the front door. He heard the click, but other than that there was complete and utter silence.

Of all the scenarios he imagined of how this would come to blows, Haley opening up about her secrets was sure as hell not one of them. And to add another tally mark to his coward column, he simply couldn't tell her he'd been lying from the start.

That guilt he'd had layered in a messy, sloppy manner with a dose of wounded pride.

Chase turned to face her, but she merely stood there with the door open and stared straight ahead to the wall. He took in her stoic profile and honestly didn't blame her for being angry. Hell, he was plenty angry with himself right now.

At least she was out of the equation for the most part if he could keep her aside. And in keeping her out of the way, he could regain his momentum and control over this takeover and revenge.

Without a word, and without stopping to look at her one last time, Chase made his way to the door and left. He'd barely stepped over the threshold when the door closed ever so softly at his back, but it was that definite click of the lock that was like a slap of reality to the face.

And he had nobody to blame but himself. He also had some serious decisions to make.

Fifteen

Chase loosened his tie and crossed his study to the bar in the corner. Drinking was never the answer, but considering he didn't have the answers, he didn't see how a drink would hurt.

He'd attempted a few online conference calls, but he didn't even care about business today. He'd dodged calls from investors, letting them go to voice mail.

For the past twenty-four hours since he'd walked out of Haley's house, he'd been in a foul mood. Trying to be a professional at this point was beyond even his realm of possibility.

He was still trying to figure out what the hell happened and how he'd missed any clues that Haley didn't believe him.

Chase poured two fingers of scotch and tipped the tumbler back. Slamming the glass back down, he was just about to pour another round when his cell vibrated in his pocket.

He pulled the phone out and glanced at the screen, fully intending to see a work associate, but his father's name popped up.

He might shirk his work for right now, but he'd never purposely ignore his parents.

Chase swiped the screen and answered. "Hey, Dad."

"I hope this isn't a bad time."

Chase stared down into the empty glass. "Perfect timing. What's up?"

"I won't keep you," his father went on. "Your mother said you were here the other day and we've been talking. I need to tell you that it's time to move on."

Chase gripped his phone and stepped away from the bar. He paced the study and ended up at the window behind his desk. The sun had started to set, giving a warm, orange glow across the horizon. The view should be calming, and would be at any other given time, but not today.

"Move on from what?" he asked, knowing exactly what his father was about to lecture him on.

"You're not a fool, Chase. Let this vendetta go," his dad pleaded. "I did my time and Vernon Lowell's sons aren't to blame. They are nothing like their old man. I was guilty of assisting in various acts and you're not mad at me."

Oh, he'd been plenty angry with his father when all of this went down. Chase had been pissed at his dad for putting their entire family's future in jeopardy. But this was the man who had provided and worked hard for their family, so forgiving him was much easier to do for Chase.

"I want that company," Chase stated. "There's no better poetic justice than for me to take over the place that ruined my family."

His father's deep sigh resounded through the phone. "Son, we aren't ruined. We had setbacks, we had a curveball thrown at us, but look us now. Your mother is healthy, and I'm living my life and not dwelling on the past. Let it go. Let it all go."

Chase ground his teeth, listening as his father made sense with each and every word. That didn't mean Chase had to like it. He wanted to get revenge, he wanted to make things right for his family and complete this circle once and for all.

"You need to focus on something else," his father went on. "Or *someone* else."

Of course his parents had discussed Haley, and while Chase would love nothing more than to focus on Haley, she had deceived him...and he had deceived her. What future could they base a relationship off with that kind of start?

And when she found out, she would hate him anyway. Because his deceit was far worse than what she had done. Now that he'd had a little more time to process things, that was the crux of his anger. He couldn't be too upset with her for only looking out for the only type of family she'd truly had. Isn't that what he was doing? Just looking out for family?

He admired the hell out of her because she didn't have to tell him a damn thing...yet she had. She'd been honest and up-front, which was a far cry above where he stood. So if he was going to look down in judgment to anyone, it would have to be himself.

"I know you don't want to hear any of this because you've been determined for so long," his father went on. "But I thought you should at least understand my side. I've moved on and I swear, once you do, you'll find peace and happiness that no revenge could ever bring you. Seeking your own justice will not change the past. Don't let this eat at you any longer."

Chase dropped his head between his shoulders and closed his eyes. The thoughts swirled around in his mind. A raging storm that continued to pound him over and over.

Could he find peace if he let all of this drop? Could he move on with his life?

For the first time in years, a sprig of hope popped up that had nothing to do with Vernon Lowell or Black Crescent Hedge Fund.

"Haley?"

Blinking away from her computer screen, Haley looked up to see Josh standing at her desk. "Yes?"

"I've said your name three times."

"Really?" she asked. "I didn't hear you."

His dark brows drew in. "I was standing right

here and you've been staring at a blank screen for several minutes."

Busted. She'd never been one to daydream at work or get caught in a zombie state.

Haley pushed back and turned her chair to fully face Josh, who still stared down at her like a worried parent.

"Maybe I just need more coffee," she joked.

Unfortunately, Josh knew her too well and wasn't buying her lame attempt to dodge his concern.

"What's going on?" he asked. "You've not been yourself for two days now."

Two days. That was when Chase had walked out of her home after he'd broken things off with her. She'd told him only a portion of what she'd done, what she'd found. She wanted to give him the chance to come clean himself, to tell her anything he wanted to get off his chest.

But he'd ended their relationship using some ridiculous reasoning and he hadn't acted like he was even bothered by letting her go. Perhaps their relationship had been growing on only one side.

"There's no issue if you end up hiring Chase Hargrove. He and I won't be seeing each other in a personal capacity anymore."

Josh glanced over his shoulder to the bustling staff around them. He leaned forward and lowered his voice.

"Are you alright?" Josh asked. "Because I was coming out to tell you he's on his way in."

"Wait." She sat up straighter in her seat. "He's

coming here? I don't have him down for an appointment or another interview."

She immediately turned back to her computer and pulled up the schedule, knowing full well Chase's name was nowhere to be found.

"He contacted me directly," Josh stated.

Haley refocused her attention back on her boss.

"That's another reason I came out here," Josh went on. "I figured something was up with the way you've been acting and the fact that he called my direct line, bypassing you completely."

Bypassing her, yeah, that sounded about right with his attitude last she'd seen him.

She couldn't deny that knowing he was on his way sent an unhealthy dose of panic through her. She wasn't ready to face him just yet. She hadn't quite found her emotional footing since he'd ended things.

"Do you want to talk about it?" Josh asked.

Haley smiled. She truly appreciated the way he cared for her, the way he wanted to help that had nothing to do with their working relationship.

"That's sweet of you to offer, but I'm fine," she assured him. "I mean, I'm hurt and angry, but I'll be okay."

The words slid out easily, but she knew actually living up to the promising statement would be much more difficult. And as much as she wanted to get up and head to the break room or anyplace else in this office to avoid seeing Chase again, she would sit right here, hold her head high, and put on the biggest damn smile.

No way would she let him know that inside she had been completely crushed to pieces. How silly was that? How foolish and naive to fall for someone in such a short time? She shouldn't have let herself get so swept away by charming words and a sexy smile, not to mention the way he filled out those damn suits.

And without the suit? That was even more impressive.

"I won't call you a liar, but you're not okay," Josh told her. "Chase should be here in about ten minutes if you want to step away from your desk."

Haley laughed. "You know me better than that."

Josh leaned back and smiled. "Yeah, I do. You're one of the toughest people I know, and for what it's worth, he's a fool."

"Yes, he is," she agreed. "But don't let the personal issues affect what's best for Black Crescent."

"You want me to beat him up for you?" Josh joked.

"Maybe if we were in third grade on the playground I'd take you up on that, but no. I'm going to sit here with a smile and act like nothing happened."

"I expect nothing less."

Josh turned toward his office, but glanced back over his shoulder. "Feel free to make him wait when he gets here. I wouldn't blame you if you want to be a little petty and spiteful."

Haley laughed again. "We'll see how nice I'm feeling once I see how he treats me."

Josh nodded and headed back into his office. Haley turned back to her blank computer screen and blew out a breath. There was no way she could start a new project and get anything of worth done in the next ten minutes. All she could think of was the moment when Chase would step through the doorway.

Being strong was the only way she would get through this. Her life didn't revolve around Chase or their fling...though what they'd shared had been so much more. He'd cared for her, she knew he did.

But she wasn't going to beg. She had too much going on in her life and she deserved someone who would be there for her as her equal supporter, not someone who required her to ask for the love she desired.

Ugh. Love. Did she love him? After such a short time?

Yes. She did. She loved the guy who took such interest in her charity, who spoke of his own struggles with education and trying to make a better life. She loved how he was witty, charming, commanding and attentive.

Haley closed her eyes and took a deep breath. She was going to have to shove all of those thoughts aside to get through this impromptu meeting. She wondered what Chase needed to discuss with Josh that was of such urgency, but Josh would tell her after Chase left.

She just had to remain calm and plaster that smile on her face to remind him of what he could have had and what he let go.

Sixteen

"I'm withdrawing my name from the list for the CEO position."

Chase stood in front of Josh's desk, wanting to do this in person instead of over the phone or email. Or maybe he'd just wanted to be a masochist and see Haley because two days without her had been too damn long.

"You found something else?" Josh asked as he leaned back in his leather chair.

"No, but at this point in my life, I feel it's best I continue with my global travels and work with startup investors. Black Crescent is a wonderful company, you should take all of the credit for that, but someone else should take over."

Josh's brows dipped in for a split second. "Does

this have anything to do with Haley or are you strictly talking from a business standpoint?"

Of course Haley would talk to Josh. They were close, as most coworkers were. When people spent over forty hours a week together, they tended to share everything and lean on each other for some sort of support. Haley considered Josh like her family, so her confiding in him was no surprise. Chase just wondered exactly how much she'd shared.

"Both," Chase answered honestly. "This is the right decision for all of us, trust me."

Though he had to admit, especially to himself, Haley had changed everything in him. His personality, his hatred toward this family, his outlook on the future.

Coming in here and letting go of this vendetta wasn't something he ever would have considered had his father not told him it was time to move on. After all, if his dad could let go, then Chase figured he could, too.

And with Haley in mind, Chase knew it was time to move on with a more positive mindset.

"If this is what you want, then I respect your decision." Josh pushed back in his chair and came to his feet. "But I'm going to offer some unsolicited, extremely unprofessional advice."

Chase nodded. "I assumed you would."

"I don't know the dynamics of what is going on or not going on between you and Haley, but I will say this. You will never find anyone more loyal to have in your corner."

"I'm well aware of how loyal she is," Chase stated.

So loyal she'd gone behind his back and dug up who knew what. But then she'd confessed once her feelings grew deeper…which was more than he could say for himself. He was still stunned at her honesty, but at the same time he was impressed that she'd exposed her secrets.

Everything about Haley touched something deep inside him, something he'd always kept hidden. That little nugget of emotion he didn't want anyone to tap into because he didn't have time for such things… not while he was so hell-bent on revenge.

But his father had said to let it go, and there was one more thing he could do to take things a step further to let all of this hatred go.

Chase slid his hands into his pockets and pulled in a breath. "I need to give you some advice as well and I'm completely overstepping my boundaries here."

Josh jerked slightly. "What's that?"

"It's no secret, the rumors of you having a secret baby."

Josh's jaw clenched, but he said nothing. Yeah, Chase was definitely walking a fine line, but this was pertinent information for Josh to have.

"I have some connections," Chase went on. "The hows and whys aren't important here. What you need to know is the doctor involved in all of this is shady as hell. He's been known to change DNA results for a nice fee."

Josh's lips thinned. "Is that right?"

"There's also a chance your brother Jake is the father," Chase said. "I thought you should know. Do what you want with the information, but if you look deeper into the doctor, that's where you'll find your answers."

Josh blinked, not showing much emotion. "Why did you dig into my past? What's in this for you?"

Chase had resigned from the potential position and he had given up some valid information, but he had hoped to avoid this part. Moving on, though, would consist of coming clean and telling the truth.

"I'm Dale Groveman's son," Chase replied. "My father used to work for yours and ended up going to prison for fraud."

Josh's eyes widened as he circled his desk. "Are you serious? What the hell were you doing trying to get a job here?"

He stopped, his eyes narrowing as he clearly mentally answered his own question. "You wanted to take over this company for what? To run it into the ground? Destroy it?"

Chase shrugged. "Honestly, I wanted to just prove that I could take it over. I wanted some type of justice, knowing that I was now in charge of the company that nearly tore my family apart."

Josh crossed his arms over his chest, his dark eyes zeroing in on Chase. "What made you change your mind?"

Haley.

"Everything changed since I first sent my résumé," Chase said honestly. "I've learned there's more to life than revenge."

Josh nodded. "There is and it's amazing how a woman can change your entire outlook on life, isn't it?"

Chase wasn't discussing his personal relationship with Haley. He'd come for what he intended and now he was done. There were other places he needed to be, other projects he should be focusing on. Because moving on wasn't just something he was doing regarding Black Crescent. He had to move on from everything that held him here...including Haley.

He'd lied to her, deceived her in ways that were unforgivable. Now that he'd cleared his conscience, he could go.

Ignoring the question, Chase pulled in a deep breath.

"I have the doctor's name who worked on the DNA and the facility he used," Chase stated, circling back to the paternity issue. "I can forward you all of my findings to do with as you wish."

As he took a step back, then another, Chase said, "I can let myself out, and good luck with filling the position and everything else."

Chase had just turned to face the door when Josh's words stopped him.

"Don't be fooled by her smile and strength. She's not like any other woman you'll ever meet, and she's able to handle more than you think."

Chase didn't acknowledge the words, but he completely understood what Josh was saying. Haley would hurt deeply because she loved so deeply. She cared with her whole heart and poured herself into those around her.

Including him.

That guilt he'd been carrying around for weeks seemed to amplify even more since he'd walked out of Haley's home. Chase reached for the knob and opened the door, stepping into Haley's work space.

She didn't even look up from her computer. Her hands flew across the keyboard as she continued right on working. Of course, she knew he was beside her, so she either didn't care or she was purposely ignoring him because of everything. Likely both. He deserved nothing less.

He approached her desk, willing her to look at him, but she never did. Chase stopped beside her desk, noticing a small bouquet of daisies in a vase on the corner. This was a far cry from all of the arrangements she'd had only a few weeks ago.

"Take care of yourself, Haley."

Chase continued toward the elevator without looking back to see if she even glanced up from her screen. He wanted her to have a good life, a great career and a lucrative charity. He'd already contacted his assistant to have more money sent next month, as Chase would be long gone from Falling Brook.

She was rather impressed with herself for getting a good bit of her work done for the day. She was trying to compile an informative welcome package to the new CEO…whoever that turned out to be. She wanted them to have a nice, smooth, easy transition.

Having Chase here made her wonder what was going on, but he'd left hours ago and Josh still hadn't said a word about the meeting.

And it was driving her crazy.

She checked her emails for Tomorrow's Leaders and replied to the ones that couldn't wait. Haley was about to shut down her computer when a message came across the screen for her to come into Josh's office.

Oh, now he wanted to talk after keeping her waiting for so long?

Haley pushed her chair back and moved toward Josh's closed door. Without knocking, she let herself in and found him standing at the window.

"Close the door behind you."

Haley did as directed and slowly crossed the office. "Are you finally going to tell me what that closed door meeting was all about with Chase?"

Josh turned and laughed. "I can't believe you didn't barge in here the minute he was gone and demand answers."

"I'm practicing self-control. How did I do?"

"Remarkably well." Josh smiled and took a seat on his windowsill. "I wanted to wait until the end of the day to talk. I had a few things to get done."

Haley stopped at his desk and crossed her arms. "So what did he want?"

"To withdraw his name from the running for the position of CEO."

"What?" Haley gasped. "He doesn't want the job? But why?"

"He said everything for him had changed," Josh explained. "He said he also had been seeking revenge because his father used to work for mine and his father ended up taking some of the backlash and ended up in prison."

Haley merely nodded.

"You knew?"

"I had him investigated," she told Josh. "I wanted to know more about him for myself, but I also wanted to know why he seemed so persistent. I knew there was more to him than just another billionaire mogul."

Every part of her was shocked that Chase had told Josh everything. He hadn't told her all of his history, but he'd come and revealed himself to Josh.

A good part of her couldn't deny the hurt that hit her hard from that revelation, but another part of her was rather impressed with Chase for owning up to his sins and secrets.

"I don't need to know what went on with the two of you," Josh said, then held up his hands. "I don't want to know. But I think he's a good guy. Despite the past issues with our fathers, neither one of us is holding grudges anymore."

Haley wasn't sure what to think, what to feel. It had taken everything in her not to turn and look at Chase as he'd left the office earlier. When he'd told her to take care, she'd bitten the inside of her cheek to keep from responding.

"I'm not sure what you want me to do with this information," Haley finally replied. "I mean, he's not going to be working here and we broke things off. You're singing his praises like that's something I need to take with me."

Josh shrugged and shifted in the windowsill to rest easily on one hip. "What you do is up to you," he told her. "I'm just saying, it might be smart of you to reconsider just letting him go. The man obviously loves you."

"Loves me?" Haley asked, shaking her head. "No, he doesn't. He's never said that, never even hinted such a thing."

"Because men have no clue how to express their feelings," he defended. "We're a little dumb in that area, so cut us some slack."

Haley couldn't help but smile, knowing how hard Josh and Sophie had fought to get together. There was something about people falling in love and finding happiness that made them want to play Cupid with others. That was fine. She was thrilled Josh had found his happily-ever-after and, who knew, maybe one day she would, too.

But she truly didn't believe it would be with Chase. No matter that she couldn't just turn off her switch to these feelings for him, if he didn't want to be with her, then things just weren't meant to be.

"I can see thoughts swirling around in your head." Josh's words pulled her from those thoughts.

"My mind is always working," she told him. "You know that."

"I know that you're probably thinking more about a man and less about work."

"So what if I am?" she countered with a shrug.

"I'll be fine, though. My personal issues won't affect my job."

"I never thought they would, Haley." Josh came to his feet and crossed to her, placing his hands on her shoulders and staring down into her eyes. "Listen to me. If you want to be with Chase, then go. Don't just sit back and let life pass you by."

Haley took in his advice, wondering if she should go to Chase or just let him go. She didn't want to beg, but was going after what you wanted begging?

No. There was no reason she couldn't fight for what she wanted. She wanted to know what Josh saw that she missed.

Did Chase love her? Well, she didn't know, but she was about to go find out.

Seventeen

Chase laid the stack of dress shirts in the garment bag and hooked the hangers through the top opening. Once they were all in, he zipped up the bag and placed it aside on his bed with his other belongings from the closet.

Turning a full circle around his room, he figured he'd gotten almost everything packed from here and the adjoining bathroom. He didn't have many possessions he just had to take with him. The furniture was of no use and didn't hold sentimental value. So long as he got his personal items, he would be just fine. He could lease this place, rent it, sell it—hell, he really didn't care. His time was up and there was nothing holding him here now. His parents were used to him traveling for business, coming and going as he chose, and he visited them often enough or sometimes flew them to where he was if he knew he'd be gone for a lengthy time setting up new companies.

Once Chase left Falling Brook, he planned on going to his condo in Florida. A little sunshine and beach time would do him good. Maybe that would clear his mind, who knew. He doubted seeing bikini-clad women would wipe his mind of the one he let get away.

Now there was only one thing left to do.

Leaving the old life behind without the black cloud hanging over his head was the only way to push forward. He needed closure and he needed to clear the air with Haley.

The alarm on his front door sounded through the house and Chase pulled his cell from his pocket to access the camera from the front porch.

Haley. Her black-and-white image appeared and his heart instantly clenched at the sight. He wanted to run to the door at the same time as he wanted to ignore her presence. If he hadn't lied to her in such a severe way, he wouldn't be such a coward. All of this guilt and pain had been brought on by him and there was nobody else to blame.

When she'd told him what she'd done by investigating him, he'd been shocked, but all of his anger hadn't been toward her... She'd just been an easy target at the time. No, everything that had gone wrong between them was all on him, and someone so loving and caring and giving as Haley deserved so much better.

How could one person pull out so many emotions, such a mixture of feelings?

He glanced to the screen again, noting her appearance. She still had on her work clothes, her hair left down but tucked behind one ear. Haley glanced toward the camera as if she knew he was looking at her at that precise moment.

His stomach knotted with nerves as his heartbeat kicked up. He shouldn't be surprised she was here after the bomb he'd dropped on Josh. No doubt Josh told Haley everything that went on in the office. He'd planned to see her before he left. A final piece of closure. But he'd been putting it off as long as possible because he was a coward. Now she was here and this was his last chance to make things right.

Chase tapped the button to let her in and he heard the front door open, then close. She was in his home once again and he had to remain calm. As much as he wanted to go to her and beg for forgiveness, he wasn't about to do that. First, he wasn't sure what all she knew, and second, maybe she wasn't here about that. Maybe she wanted him back.

Chase cursed under his breath. Hell no she wouldn't want him back, not if Josh told her what Chase's initial intentions were with Black Crescent.

Maybe she'd come here to tell him off, to berate him for using her... He would deserve nothing less. There was nothing she could say to him that he hadn't already said to himself. He was a total bastard for the way he'd treated her, but damn it, he hadn't expected to get so involved... He hadn't expected his heart to get involved, either.

Realizing he couldn't hide in his master suite forever, Chase stepped from the room and headed down the hall. The moment he crossed into the living room, his eyes met Haley's.

She stood there gripping her handbag, and for the first time since he'd met her, she almost looked nervous. Interesting. If she was here to explode all over him about his actions, she certainly didn't look upset.

"I didn't expect to see you again," he told her honestly.

"I didn't expect to be here again."

As much as he wanted to close this distance between them, Chase remained still. She'd come here for a reason. He just needed to give her the time to process her thoughts and speak or come to him when she was ready.

"So what happened to bring you here?" Chase asked. "You talked to Josh, didn't you?"

Haley stared at him for another minute, then glanced around, her brows drawing in as she spotted one of his suitcases by the sofa.

"Traveling for business?" she asked.

"You could say that."

Her eyes shifted back to him. "You're leaving."

Chase nodded. "I'm done here."

"Because plans didn't go your way?" she asked, a little extra bite in her tone than what he was used to.

"Because I ruined one of the only relationships

I've ever cared about and there is no reason for me to stay."

She jerked, obviously surprised by his response. Silence settled heavy between them, but Chase remained still.

Haley took a step closer, then another. She sat her bag down on the sofa, then glanced around the room. Chase didn't know what was going through her mind, but he wished like hell she'd say the reason for her visit because he was going out of his mind with scenarios.

He was also going out of his mind staring at her and not touching her. That damn black dress hugged each of her curves and he knew full well what each one felt like beneath his touch.

"Your father went to prison for his part in Vernon's scams," she stated, clearly not in the form of a question. "Then your mother battled her own demons."

Haley turned to face him, her eyes holding him in place. "And that left you alone to work through your anger without the guidance and love of those who mattered most."

Chase didn't like how she'd summed up his past in one statement that was so damn accurate. Yes, he'd been hurt, but his revenge hadn't been about his own hatred for Vernon Lowell. Chase had wanted vengeance for tearing his family apart and making them put all the pieces back together.

"Josh told you."

Haley folded her arms over her chest. "I've known

for several days, actually. Before I told you that I'd had you investigated, I knew. When I came clean the other day about what I'd done, I was giving you a chance to do the same, but you chose not to. You either didn't trust me enough or you were just continuing to use me."

Wait… She'd known? She'd known about his parents, what had motivated him to start this charade, and she still hadn't told him?

Because she was giving him a chance to speak up in his defense and what had he done? He'd walked out on her. Could he be more of a jerk?

"But Josh didn't act like he already knew when I told him everything," Chase stated.

"That's because I never told him." Haley dropped her arms and sighed. "Don't you get anything? Of course I was going to protect my company had I thought for a minute you would seriously do some damage, but I didn't want to tell him. I'd developed feelings for you and didn't want to betray you."

Something clicked into place at her final statement. The woman who had always put Black Crescent above all else, who'd even stood by their side during the most scandalous time, had put him first. She'd chosen to be loyal to him, to keep his secrets, and he didn't trust her enough to tell her the truth.

Chase pulled in a breath and took a step toward her. "You covered for me."

"I wanted you to tell me the truth," she told him. "I'd hoped if I told you what I'd done, that you'd tell me. So, when you broke things off and said nothing else, I assumed you were only in this to use me for information."

"That's not how it went down."

He took another step, and another, until he'd closed the gap between them. He was close enough to touch her, but Chase clenched his fists at his sides.

"You surprised me when you told me what you'd done," he stated. "I never thought you would have done something like that, but now I realize you were protecting Black Crescent and yourself."

"We do what we can to protect those we love." She offered a sad smile, one that broke his heart. "Before I go, I want to know if you ever had feelings for me, or was all of this just a game to you? Were you only after—"

Chase gripped her face and covered her mouth with his. He couldn't stand not touching her another second. He also couldn't listen to her doubt what they had anymore. Everything they'd shared was real. Everything he felt for her was real.

Now he wanted to show her.

Haley gripped his wrists and opened for him, her passion pouring out of her, and Chase wanted nothing more than to strip her out of this dress and show her exactly how much he'd missed her...how much he needed her.

He eased back slightly, resting his forehead against hers.

"Everything we shared had nothing to do with my plan," he told her. "I started flirting with you thinking I'd get information to use later, but then I lost myself. The flirting turned into a need I couldn't explain and before I knew it, I'd fallen in love with you."

Haley jerked back, her eyes wide. "You love me?"

He hadn't meant to just let that slip out, but yes. He loved her and it felt damn good to have those words out in the open.

The punch to the shoulder was quite unexpected and shocking. She struck before he even saw her move.

"What was that for?" he asked, shrugging his shoulder.

"For putting me through hell, you jerk!" she fired back. "Not only did you deceive me from the beginning, you didn't come clean when I gave you the chance, and now you say you love me? So, what, you were just going to leave town and take those feelings with you?"

"What was I supposed to do?" he countered, staring into her fiery eyes. "I'd screwed up. You deserve someone who's going to be honest and open with you. Someone who's devoted to you, who puts you above all else."

She stepped away from him, propping her hands on her hips. "And you can't be that man? Here all this time I thought there was nothing you couldn't do."

So now she was getting back at him by attacking his pride. That was fine, he deserved her frustration and anger...maybe not the punch, but he'd let that slide. He'd been a complete jerk to her from day one, yet here she stood.

Which likely meant only one thing.

"You love me."

Her brows drew in. "What?"

"You love me," he repeated, reaching for her once again. "I know you do or you wouldn't be here. You wouldn't be so hurt over what I did if you didn't care."

He gripped her hips and pulled her flush against his body.

"And you wouldn't have kept my secret from Josh if you hated me."

Her lips thinned, but she said nothing.

"No denying the truth now?" he asked with a smile.

"I hate you for making me love you."

Chase laughed, knowing he'd won. "That makes no sense, but you're even sexier when you're angry."

Her hands flattened against his chest as her bright eyes held his. She was so damn pretty she stole his breath. And she was his. There was no way he was letting her go again. She'd come here to fight for them, which just proved she was the one for him. He wanted a woman who wouldn't back down. He wanted a woman who understood his mind, his heart. He'd found her.

"You're not moving," she told him. "You're staying in Falling Brook."

Chase smiled. "Yes, ma'am."

She slid her arms up over his shoulders and around to the back of his neck, her fingers threading through his hair. "You're also going to marry me. That family you wanted? I want one, too...with you."

The excitement and anticipation pumped through Chase. He gripped her backside and lifted her body against his.

"Did you just propose?" he asked.

"If that's what you want to call it." She slid her lips over his ever so slightly. "More like I just laid out your life plan."

Chase nipped at her lips as he turned to head toward his bedroom. "Go right ahead and plan my life, so long as you're in every aspect."

She slid her mouth over his, silently answering him. The moment Chase stepped back into his room, he eased Haley down to her feet and went to make quick work on that zipper going up her back.

He peeled that dress off her body, watching as it slid down and puddled at her feet. She kicked it aside, leaving her only in her matching lacy bra and thong and her black heels.

"You're going to be the death of me," he murmured as he reached for her once again.

She laughed as she skirted out of his touch. "Not so fast," she told him. "You have on too many clothes and I don't like the look of this bed with so many bags on it."

He turned, remembering he'd been in the midst of packing when she'd come by. Chase took about two seconds to clear the garment bags off, discarding them onto the floor without a care. There was only one thing he cared about right now and she was standing before him with a desire in her eyes that he wanted to dive into.

Chase kept his gaze on Haley's as he jerked the shirt from his pants and unbuttoned just enough to slide it up and over his head. The rest of his clothes and shoes flew off in quick succession, leaving him completely bare. And the way her heavy-lidded stare raked over his body, he wasn't sure how much longer he could hold back from tossing her onto that bed and showing her just how much he'd missed her over the past few days.

"Now who's wearing too many clothes?" he asked, reaching for her once more.

"Take them off of me," she commanded with a naughty grin.

A blond strand fell over her eye, giving her an even sexier look. How did he get so lucky to have her come back into his life?

Reaching around her back, Chase flicked the bra clasp. Haley watched him as he removed the straps from her shoulders and down her arms. He flung the garment over his shoulder before moving on to her panties.

He hooked his thumbs in the lacy straps over her hips and eased them down, dropping to his knees as he went. Her hands went to his shoulders and she balanced on one foot, then the other as he removed her thong.

Haley standing there in her heels, staring down at him, might have been the most striking, breath-taking view he'd ever seen.

He trailed his fingertips up her legs, over her knees, inside her thighs and straight to her core.

Haley took a wide step as she continued to hold on to his shoulders and watch.

The second he eased one finger inside her, Haley's lids fluttered down as a moan escaped her. Chase held on to her hip with one hand while pleasuring her with the other. In no time, her hips pumped against his hand and Chase couldn't tear his eyes away from the erotic sight.

Haley's nails bit into his bare shoulders as she tossed her head back and cried out her release. Chase waited until her body stopped trembling before easing away and coming to his feet. He wrapped his arms around her and lifted her to carry her over to the bed.

"Tell me again," she muttered as he laid her down. "Tell me you love me."

Chase came over her, resting his elbows beside her head as he grazed his lips across hers. "I love you, Haley. Forever."

Eighteen

"I'm not sure I'm ready for this," Haley stated. "This is quite a step in our relationship."

Chase laughed as he pulled in front of a small cottage and killed the engine. He turned to face her, taking her hands in his.

"It's just my parents, Haley. You're not going before a firing squad."

Nerves danced all through her belly. It had been over a week since she'd gone to Chase's house and told him how she felt. It had been the best eleven days of her life, staying with him, talking of plans for their future.

But parents? What did she know about parent relationships? Hers were nonexistent and Chase knew that. Yet here they were, ready for Sunday afternoon lunch.

"You proposed to me," Chase reminded her. "Did you think you wouldn't meet my parents at some point?"

She glanced down to their adjoining hands and shrugged. "I hadn't thought that far yet. I just knew I wanted to spend my life with you."

He smiled and squeezed her hands. "This is part of my life. My parents are going to love you just like I do."

Haley let out a sigh. Having him say he loved her never got old. She could face anything with him by her side...even parents.

"I'm not good with parents," she whispered. "I don't know how to act or who to be. Are they proper like using the right fork or do I just follow their lead?"

Chase leaned forward and kissed her before easing back. "Honey, this isn't an audition. They already love you because I do. Trust me on this. Just be yourself."

Haley pulled in a shaky breath and nodded. Chase stepped from the car and circled the hood to open her door. He extended his hand and Haley held it tight as they headed up the steps to the cozy front porch with a swaying swing.

Before they could knock, the front door flew open and his mother squealed with delight. His father came up behind her with a wide smile. Haley instantly felt some of the pressure ease off her shoulders.

His mom threw her arms around Chase's neck and kissed his cheek. "I'm so glad you guys are here."

Then she turned her attention to Haley and hugged

her, as well. Stunned, Haley returned the gesture and wrapped her arms around Chase's mother.

"You don't even know how excited I am to meet you," she stated, pulling back with a huge smile. "I hope you like chicken and potatoes. I also made a cheesecake with a raspberry glaze."

"Stop fussing," his father insisted. "You're worrying over everything."

Haley instantly found herself relating to this woman. Fussing and worrying over everything was pretty much her job. Haley already felt a kinship to Chase's mother and they hadn't even made it off the porch.

"Come on in," his father said and gestured. "Lunch is ready. I put everything out on the back patio. It's such a nice day."

Haley followed them through the home and outside to a darling eating area beneath a pergola draped with wisteria.

"Have a seat anywhere," his mother told them. "We aren't formal here."

That was good to know. Haley could tell this place was one of those homes where everyone felt welcome and invited. There was no pressure to be someone you weren't.

Such a far cry from how she'd grown up. No wonder Chase was so giving, so…perfect. He'd had a loving environment and loving support system behind him at all times. Even during the difficult days, he'd had his family.

"Chase tells me you run Tomorrow's Leaders," his

mom said as she took a seat across from Haley. "I've heard of that organization and I think it's absolutely wonderful how you're looking out for those kids."

Haley smiled. "I don't do much," she stated. "It's the donors who really make things happen."

"Don't sell yourself short," his mom replied. "If it weren't for you, the donors wouldn't know how to help. An education is so important and there are too many kids who can't afford schooling. Not everyone can get a scholarship."

"That's exactly right," Haley agreed.

The conversation flowed from the charity to Chase's next project, which he informed them was setting up a company in LA to start up their own investment firm. He'd already asked Haley to accompany him, but she wasn't sure if she should leave for vacation in the midst of the new CEO hunt.

Though she doubted Josh would care. Josh seemed to like Chase and Josh totally understood what being in love was like.

"So tell me what my son did to get the attention of someone as wonderful as you," his father said after they'd finished eating.

Haley set her glass of wine back on the table and laughed. "Honestly, it was a bundle of highlighters."

"Highlighters?" his dad asked. "Son, you can do better than that."

Chase laughed and came to his feet. "I completely agree."

He dug into his pocket and pulled out a box. Haley gasped as she stared up at him.

"I know you already asked me to marry you," Chase started. "But we haven't made things official."

He opened the box and went down on one knee. Haley stared at the classic emerald-cut diamond ring and tears filled her eyes.

"I wanted to get you something that suited you," he told her. "Something classy, elegant, flawless."

"It's beautiful," she murmured through her tears.

"I want to spend my life with you," he told her. "I want to help you with your charity, I want you to help me grow to be a better man. I want everything, but only with you."

He took the ring from the box and Haley held out her finger. He slid the diamond on and it fit absolutely perfectly. She didn't know how he knew her ring size, but she wasn't about to question it.

Chase came to his feet once again and pulled her up with him. He wrapped her in his arms and kissed her as his mother let out a squeal of delight once again.

"Welcome to the family," his father stated.

Haley turned to see his parents across the table. Both were beaming and Haley realized she was inheriting a family to call her own. Having a man by her side and a loving family was all she'd ever wanted.

Chase wrapped his arm around her waist and Haley realized that she could indeed have it all, and that some things in life were worth fighting for.

* * * * *

CONSEQUENCE OF HIS REVENGE

DANI COLLINS

To all the Dreamers among us,

I first conceived of this story when I heard the
Olympics had been awarded to Whistler, BC.
That was at least two houses and three computers ago.
At the time, becoming a published romance author
was a dream that I wouldn't see fulfilled for years.
Yet here is that story, in your hands.

Dreams don't always come true right away, but they
do come true. Chase yours. You'll get there. xo

CHAPTER ONE

"How could you fire me? I haven't even started work yet!"

Cameo Fagan tried to keep her voice to a hiss so it wouldn't echo across the hotel lobby, but she couldn't keep the panic out of her tone. She had already given up her job at the other hotel and, far worse, she had given up her *apartment*.

"Technically it's a withdrawal of the offer of employment," Karen hurried to say, holding out a splayed hand that begged for calm. She was the HR manager for the Tabor chain of boutique Canadian hotels. A mutual friend had put them in touch six months ago, when the renovations had been in full swing at this Whistler location. The Tabor was holding a soft opening on Monday with a gala for their official opening in two weeks.

Cami had thought she and Karen got on like a house on fire. She'd pretty much been hired on the spot.

"But…" She waved toward the narrow hall behind the front desk. It led to the offices and the very basic, but extremely affordable, staff quarters in the basement of the hotel. "I was going to move in this weekend."

Karen gave her a helpless look. She knew as well as Cami did that apartments in Whistler were impossible to find, especially on short notice. "It wasn't my decision. I'm really sorry."

"Whose was it? Because I don't understand." *Don't cry*, she willed herself. The universe did *not* have a plan to constantly pull the rug every time things started to go her way. She refused to think like that.

Even though it often felt exactly like that.

Karen glanced around the lobby where a handful of decorators were measuring and holding up swatches while workmen were putting the finishing touches on the fireplace mantel.

Lowering her voice even more, Karen said, "It hasn't been announced yet, but Tabor was bought out by an Italian firm. I guess the previous owners were in trouble after all of this." She lifted her gaze to the mural painted on the ceiling, one of many high-end touches included in the refurbishment.

That indication of deep pockets was why Cami had been willing to give up her very good job and take a chance here. Now her stomach clenched.

Italian? Or *Sicilian*?

"Are the new owners starting from scratch with the hiring? Because I'll interview again. I don't mind."

Karen's shoulders fell and she shifted uncomfortably. "It was, um, you he didn't want. Specifically."

"Me!" Cami's references were stellar, her work ethic highly praised. She went the extra mile every time. "He thinks I'm too young?" She'd run into that before, but when she explained how much experience she had, she was usually given a chance. It couldn't be sexism. Karen seemed to be keeping her management position.

"I'm really sorry." Karen looked and sounded sincere. "I don't understand it myself, but I submitted the list of hires and yours was the only name he scratched. He was quite adamant."

"*Who?*" Cami didn't want to believe she could still be

haunted by the Gallos, but her heart was plummeting into her shoes. The universe didn't have it in for her. Nor did the Italians. One Sicilian seemed to, though.

The elevator pinged, cutting off whatever Karen was about to say. Her gaze slid to the opening doors. "Him," Karen said. "Dante Gallo."

Cami didn't have to ask which man Karen meant. Everyone in the group wore smart business attire, but one wore his bespoke suit with more assertiveness and style on a frame that was tall and alpha-postured. His jaw had a shadow of sculpted stubble and his dark hair was close-cropped, but devilish. His stern brows and sharp gaze stole any hint of approachability from his otherwise beautiful features. He was both gorgeous and severe. The kind of man used to getting his way by any means necessary, powerful and confident enough to make life-altering decisions in a blink. The women trailing him were flushed and sparkly-eyed, the men awestruck and quick-stepping, anxious to please.

Cami was awestruck herself, even feeling a coil of something in her abdomen that was sensual and wicked and *wrong*, especially when his predatory attention swiveled to her the way a hawk's head turned when a hare caught its attention.

Her heartbeat picked up as his focus honed in.

The entire planet stopped spinning as their gazes clashed. Or, rather, she felt as though they were caught in some kind of time slip. Everything continued to whirl around them in a whistling blur while thick amber soaked in, filling her veins with a honeyed sweetness that held them suspended in a muted world. Her vision dimmed at the edges, glowing golden. She stopped breathing. Something ancient resonated in her, a vibration as old as life itself.

That internal quiver expanded. Sensual warmth suffused her in a way that had never happened. She told herself this acute awareness of self and him was the heat of surprised recognition and anticipation of a confrontation. Animosity, not attraction. She had stalked him a couple of times online and had imagined a face-to-face conversation a million times. This was shock at finally having her opportunity, not fascination.

Definitely not desire pinching a betraying sting between her thighs.

She clawed back from her lack of self-control and found her resolve. This time, she wouldn't be leveled without a whimper of protest. Maybe he had a right to be angry with her father, but this grudge had gone on long enough. Did he really think he could destroy her just because of her name?

As her pulse beat a war drum in her ears, she waited for recognition to dawn in his features.

It didn't come, which was insult to injury. Her confidence began to waver while tendrils of vulnerability crept in.

Then she realized his gaze was heating with interest. *Male* interest. His forbidding mouth relaxed the way a man's did when a woman invited him to approach because attraction was reciprocated.

The sizzle under her skin became a conflagration, heating her all over, teaching her by fire that she was part of the human race after all. She did a lot of people-watching from behind her hospitality counters and was always intrigued by the way people coupled up. It baffled her because she had never felt such a simple and immediate pull herself. A receptiveness that couldn't be hidden.

Today, it happened. Basic animal magnetism took hold of her, shocking in its power because it was completely against her will. Mortifying, since she was the one providing the entertainment for Karen and anyone else who wanted to notice. She was sending all the wrong signals with her dumbfounded, dazzled stare, but her gaze was glued to his.

A slither of defenselessness went through her. She didn't want to react this way! Trolling online hadn't prepared her for the force of masculinity that came off him, though. He made her ultra-aware of her femininity. Her body made tiny adjustments, standing taller, stomach tightening. Her fingers itched to touch her hair.

The reaction was as disarming as he was, causing a fresh shyness to burn her cheeks.

Nerves, she insisted to herself. Pique. Genuine frustration at losing the job she had thought would finally give her the chance to get ahead. All because of him, she reminded herself, and used her animosity to grapple past her overwhelmed senses. And yes, maybe she owned some of the responsibility for his grudge, but *no*. She had tried really hard to fix things. Enough was enough.

She forced herself to step one foot in front of the other, advancing on the lion whose tail was flicking in lazy concentration. He looked entirely too powerful and ferocious. Too *hungry*. Each step brought her into a light and heat that threatened to sear her to her soul, but she ignored the adrenaline and excitement coursing through her arteries.

While he wore a hint of a smug smile because she was approaching him and not making him work for it.

"Mr. Gallo." Her voice seemed to fade as she spoke. She had to clear her throat. "Might I have a word?"

No one had spoken to him in such an imperative tone since he was a child. Dante bristled, but the reflexive assertion of superiority that rose to his lips didn't emerge.

Like most men, he categorized women very quickly into yes, no, or off-limits. Wedding ring? No. Coworker? Off-limits—for now.

Neatly packaged brunette with skin like fresh cream, a figure that didn't stop, and rose petal lips that managed to hold a curve of innocence and sin at the same time? One who moved with a dancer's grace and possessed the strength of character to look him in the eye without flinching?

"Yes" wasn't a strong enough word. She was a new category. Have to have. *Mine.*

That lightning-quick bite of hunger was disturbing. He had a healthy sex drive—*very* healthy—but one he easily controlled, always relegating it to nonwork hours.

Yet with this woman his brain switched off, and his libido quickened in anticipation. Why? He searched for what made her different. Her clothes were low-end, but well-chosen to showcase her figure. Her breasts bounced a little, ample and firm, making him wonder about her bra. Lace? Demi-cup? Her round hips promised a nice plump ass atop those trim thighs, making the words, "Turn around," simmer in his throat.

The particular shade of plum of her blazer framed a thin, white line against her collarbone. A scar? A twist of protectiveness went through him. He had a strong impulse to brush back her rich, dark hair and kiss that spot. Make it better.

Embers of desire glowed hotter in his belly, thinking of the ways he would pet her and stroke her until neither of them knew anything but pleasure. Until they drowned in it. He liked the look of her wavy tresses. The spill of her hair moving as she walked. No hairspray. He could run his hands through that shiny fall, gather those silky strands in his fist as he held her still for a kiss that would appease and ignite...

Damn. He was going to tent his pants if he wasn't careful. She was only a woman. They weren't hard to come by. Never had been. He was here to work and indulge his grandmother, not take up with a local for after-hours fun. His entire world was one of responsibility and duty to his extended family. Selfishness was not an option. Hadn't been since his youthful foray into chasing a personal dream had exploded in his face, cracking the very foundation of his family's existence.

For the first time in a long time, however, he saw something he wanted strictly for himself. Not that he saw her as a thing—although he was barbarian enough to experience a certain titillation at the idea of owning a woman—but there was more. As she paused before him, potential hovered between them, too abstract to grasp, too real to ignore.

He forced his gaze to her face, trying to work out why her pretty, but not particularly striking features were impacting him so deeply. The women he usually went for were socialites. They wore layers of makeup that enhanced their features to the highest degree, and invited him with seductive smiles. They oozed sophistication and a desire to please.

This one was a natural beauty with lovely arched brows and a tipped-up nose. Her bare face made her look rather innocent while her eyes were a pedestrian hazel arranged in a starburst of brown within a circle of gray-green.

When had he ever looked so closely at anyone's eyes before?

When had he ever seen such a gamut of emotion? On her, they truly were windows to the soul. He read intimidation and bravery and something that made him think of butter and honey melting on his tongue.

He had an urge to laugh, not in dismissal, but enjoyment. So few people challenged or excited him these days.

"Let's go into my office." He waved at what would be the manager's office after he was satisfied this investment would turn a profit. His cousin, Arturo, was quite the vulture for deals like this, and usually handled the transition of a buyout. Once Arturo had heard their grandmother wished to tag along, however, his calendar had suffered a conflict.

Dante hadn't thought much of Arturo's priorities, but rather than scold him, he'd opted for taking the opportunity to spend a few days with the woman who had raised him—a woman he reluctantly acknowledged wasn't immortal.

She was supposed to be here soon, for a tour and lunch he recalled with distraction, glancing at the clock and feeling a pull of priorities. In this moment, this younger, nubile woman captured nearly all of his attention.

He closed the door. "I don't believe we've met." He held out his hand, palm itching for the feel of her in his grip. He might never let her go.

Her chin set and she took his hand in a firm, no-nonsense shake that was surprisingly powerful, sending a thrill rocketing through him. He wanted to tighten his grip and hang on. Pull her in and race to the inevitable.

When she spoke, he was too nearly lost in the clear, engaging tone of her voice to make sense of the words.

"I'm Cameo Fagan. Your new manager."

Her name ricocheted inside his skull, tearing holes in his psyche. All of his assumptions about her, where they might be going and how their association would progress, became a tattered mess. In the blink of an eye, ten years dissolved. He was watching his competitor announce a self-driving car that bore shocking resemblance to the one Dante was creating. All the money and time he had invested evaporated. The shock of the loss put the final stressor on his grandfather's heart, and it gave out.

Dante was left with an enormous hole in the family finances, extensive dependents looking to him to take up the charge and a bitterness of betrayal that sat on his tongue to this day.

He dropped his hand, so appalled with the way her soft heat left an imprint in his palm he brushed it against his thigh.

She flinched, and her erotic mouth trembled briefly before she firmed it, setting her chin a notch higher.

He waited for his sexual interest to fizzle. And waited. But the *No* that screamed through him was his inner animal, howling in protest at being denied. His libido *wanted* her. The rest of him recoiled in disgust. How could he be the least bit attracted to a *Fagan*?

"You're not to be on this property." He had made that clear after seeing her name on the list of new hires. One email to his office in Milan had confirmed she was related to *the* Stephen Fagan. That had been that. Her father had betrayed him. He wouldn't trust another one of them ever again.

He reached for the door latch, ready to expel her, distantly anticipating the physical struggle if it came to that.

She didn't move, only folded her arms, which plumped her breasts. "I don't know how they do things in Italy, but this is Canada. We have laws against wrongful dismissal."

He left the door closed, frustration morphing into fury. A desire to crush. He'd never met anyone who had lit his fuse as quickly or made it burn so hot. White and blistering. But he kept his tone icy cold.

"Italy has laws against theft. Most go to jail for it. Some, apparently, escape to Canada before they're convicted. Perhaps I should take *that* up with your government."

Her breath sucked in and her pulse throbbed rapidly in her throat. Her eyes were hot and bright. Tears? Ha.

"You're being paid back," she said through clenched teeth. "That can't happen if I don't have a job, can it?"

"Even if that were true, it wouldn't make sense for me to give you money so you could give it back to me, would it? No gain in that for me."

"What do you mean, 'even if it were true'?" She dropped her fists to her sides.

"Let's pretend such a thing as compensation is even possible, since the design of my self-driving car had potential to earn indefinitely, but I've never seen a red cent from anyone, so—"

"Where has it been going, then?"

The sharpness of her tone sent a narrow sliver of doubt through him, thin as a fiber of glass, but sharp enough to sting because he almost fell for her outrage. He very nearly *wanted* to believe her, his body was that primed for her on a physical level.

But that was a Fagan for you. They could make you believe anything.

He shook off his moment of hesitation with a snap of his head. Trust led to treachery. He couldn't, *wouldn't*, trust her.

"Don't pretend your father has made any effort to compensate me. He hasn't. He *can't*."

That took her aback. Her complexion faded to gray, sending a brief shadow of concern through him.

"Of course he can't." Her brows pulled into a distressed knot. "He's dead."

She looked from one of his eyes to the other, expression twisted in confusion, as if she thought he ought to know that.

He didn't keep tabs on a man who had cost him a fortune and set his family back, leaving him at his most vulnerable. Dante was so furious at her temerity, at her attempt to work another con on him, and with himself for being momentarily drawn by her, he let one vicious word escape.

"Good."

It was far below him. He knew it even before her lips went white. Her mouth pulled at the corners as she tried to hold on to her composure, but those wide, far from plain Jane eyes of hers grew so dark and wounded, he couldn't look into them.

"You've done me a favor," she said with a creak in her voice. "I'd rather starve than work for someone who could say something like that."

She moved to open the door, but his hand was still on the latch. Her body heat mingled with his own, charging the air. The scent of fresh mountain air and wildflowers filled his brain, making him drunk.

"Let me out."

He saw the words form on her pink lips more than heard them. They rang in his head in a fading echo. He didn't want to. The encounter had become so intense, so fast, he was reeling, not sure if he'd won or lost. Either way, it didn't feel over.

Cold fingertips touched the back of his hand. Her elbow caught him in the ribs before she pushed down and pulled the door open, head ducked. Her body almost touched his. He thought he heard a sniff, then he was staring at her ass—which was even more spectacular than he'd imagined.

She escaped.

He slammed the door closed behind her, trying to also slam the door on his impossible desire for her. On the entire scene.

There was no reason he should feel guilty. The wrong her father had done him had been malicious and far-reaching. Dante had foolishly dropped the charges in exchange for an admission of guilt and a promise of compensation, letting the man escape because, at the time, his life had been imploding. His grandfather's sudden death had meant Dante had to set aside his own pursuits and take over the complex family business. Its interests ran from vineyards to hotels to exports and shipping.

All of that had been put in jeopardy by the loss of the seed capital his grandfather had allowed him to risk on his self-driving car dream. The consequence of trusting wrongly had been a decade of struggle to find an even keel and come back to the top—yet another reason he wanted to give his grandmother some attention. He had neglected her while he worked to regain everything she and her husband had built.

Cami Fagan ought to be *grateful* all he had done was refuse to hire her.

Nevertheless, that broken expression of hers lingered in his mind's eye. Which annoyed him.

Someone knocked.

He snarled that he didn't want to be disturbed, then flicked the lock on the door.

Cami was shaking so hard, she could barely walk. She could barely *breathe*. Each pant came in as a hiss through her nose and released in a jagged choke.

Get away was the imperative screaming through her, but she could hardly see, she was so blinded by tears of grief and outrage. Good? *Good?* Had he really said that? What a bastard!

She was so wrapped up in her anguish, she almost missed the faint voice as she charged past an old woman sitting on a bench, half a block from the Tabor's entrance.

"Pi fauri."

Despite drowning in emotion, Cami stopped. She and her brother *always* stopped, whether it was a roadside accident or a panhandler needing a sandwich.

Swiping at her wet cheeks, she raked herself together. "Yes? What's wrong?"

"Ajutu, pi fauri."

Cami had a few words in a dozen languages, all the better to work with the sort of international clientele who visited destinations like Whistler. In her former life, she'd even spent time with Germans and Italians, picking up conversational words, not that she'd used much beyond the very basics in recent years.

Regardless, *help* was fairly universal, and the old woman's weakly raised hand was self-explanatory.

"I'm sorry, do you speak English? *Qu'est-ce que c'est?"* No, that was French and the woman sounded Italian, maybe? *"Che cos' è?"*

The woman rattled out some breathless mumbles, but Cami caught one word she thought she understood. *Malatu.* Sick. Ill.

She seated herself next to the woman, noting the senior was pressing a hand to her chest, struggling to speak.

"I'm calling an ambulance. We'll get you to the hospital," Cami told her, quickly pulling out her mobile. *"Ambulanza. Ospedale."* One didn't race with champions down the Alps without hearing those words a few times.

She could have gone back into the Tabor and asked Karen to call, but she had her first-aid certificate, and this was exactly the type of thing she'd been doing since her first housekeeping position at a motel. The woman was conscious, if frightened and very pale. Cami took her pulse and tried to keep her calm as she relayed as much information as she could to the dispatcher. With the woman's permission, she was able to check her purse and provide the woman's name along with some medication she was taking.

"Do you have family traveling with you? Can I leave a message at your hotel?"

Bernadetta Ferrante pointed toward the Tabor, which sent a little shiver of premonition through Cami, but what were the chances? Dante Gallo seemed to be traveling with an entourage. Bernadetta could be related to anyone in there.

She asked a passerby to run into the hotel to find Bernadetta's companion, then pointed into the sky as she heard the siren. *"Ambulanza,"* she said again. "It will be here soon."

Bernadetta nodded and smiled weakly, fragile fingers curling around Cami's.

"What the hell have you done?" The male voice was so hard and fierce, it made both of them jump.

Cami briefly closed her eyes. *Of course it was him.* What were the chances of two head-on collisions in a row?

Bernadetta put up a hand, expression anxious.

Dante said, *"Non tu, Noni,"* in a much gentler tone, before he returned to the gruff tone and said, "I'm speaking to her."

The ambulance arrived at that moment. Cami hovered long enough to ensure she wasn't needed to give a statement, then slipped away. Bernadetta was already looking better, eyes growing less distressed as she breathed more easily beneath an oxygen mask, while Dante left to fetch his car and follow to the hospital.

Cami trudged through the spitting spring rain to the next bus stop, only wanting distance from that infernal man. At least the crisis had pulled her out of her tailspin. Tears never fixed anything. She had learned that a long time ago. What she needed was a new plan. While she waited for the bus, she texted her brother.

My job fell through. Can I sleep on your couch?

CHAPTER TWO

MAKING COOKIES WAS the perfect antidote to a night of self-pity and a morning of moving boxes. Besides, she had a few staples to use up and a neighbor to thank.

When the knock sounded, she expected Sharma from down the hall. She opened her door with a friendly smile, cutting off her greeting at, "Hell—"

Because it wasn't Sharma. It was *him*.

Dante Gallo stood in her doorway like an avenging angel, his blue shirt dotted by the rain so it clung damply across his broad shoulders. He was all understated wealth and power, with what was probably real gold in his belt buckle. His tailored pants held a precision crease that broke over shiny shoes that had to be some custom-crafted Italian kind that were made from baby lambs or maybe actual babies.

Oh, she wanted to feel hatred and contempt toward him. Only that. She wanted to slam the door on him, but even as her simmering anger reignited, she faltered, caught in that magnetism he seemed to project. Prickling tension invaded her. Her nipples pinched, and that betraying heat rolled through her abdomen and spread through her inner thighs, tingling and racing.

Woman. Man. How did he make that visceral distinction so sharp and undeniable within her? Everything in her felt obvious and tight. Overwhelmed.

Claimed.

Hungry and needy and yearning.

She hated herself for it, was already suffering a kick of anguish even as his proprietary gaze skimmed down her, stripping what little she wore. The oven had heated up her tiny studio apartment to equatorial levels, so she had changed into a body-hugging tank and yoga shorts. Her abdomen tensed further under the lick of his gaze.

Stupidly, she looked for an answering thrust of need piercing his shell, but he seemed to feel nothing but contempt. It made that scan of his abrasive and painful, leaving her feeling obvious and callow. Defenseless and deeply disadvantaged.

Rejected, which left a burn of scorn from the back of her throat to the pit of her belly.

She should have slammed the door, but the timer went off, startling her. With emotion searing her veins, she made a flustered dive toward the oven and pulled out the last batch of cookies, leaving the tray on the stove top with a clatter.

Pulling off the mitt, she skimmed the heel of her hand across her brow. What was he even doing here? Yesterday's interaction had been painful enough. She didn't need him invading her private space, judging and disparaging.

She snapped the oven off and turned to see him shut the door as if she had invited him in. He stood behind the door, trapping her inside the horseshoe of her kitchenette.

Her heart began thudding even harder, not precisely in fear—which was frightening in itself. Excitement. How could part of her be thrilled to see him again? Forget the past. He was a cruel, callous person. *Good.* She hated him for that. Truly hated him.

She didn't ask how he'd got in the building. She wasn't the only one moving this weekend. The main door had been propped open the whole time she'd been loading boxes into Sharma's car and taking them to the small storage locker she'd rented.

This felt like an ambush nonetheless. What other awful thing had he said to her yesterday? She set aside her oven mitts and said, "You're not welcome on this property."

He dragged his gaze back from scanning her near empty apartment. His eyes looked deeply set and a little bruised, but she didn't imagine he'd lost sleep over *her*.

A weird tingle sizzled in her pelvis at the thought, though. She'd tossed and turned between fury and romantic fantasies, herself. He was ridiculously attractive, and this reaction of hers was so visceral. In her darkest hour, she hadn't been able to resist wondering, if they didn't hate each other, what would that look like?

Tangled sheets and damp skin, hot hands and fused mouths. Fused bodies? What would *that* feel like?

Not now. Definitely not *him.*

She folded her arms, hideously aware she only had a thin shelf bra in this top, and her breasts felt swollen and hard. Prickly. If she had had a bedroom, she would have shot into it and thrown on more clothes. Her chest was a little too well-endowed to get away with something so skimpy anywhere but alone in her apartment, especially when her nipples were standing up with arousal.

She became hyperaware of how little she wore. How close he stood and how small her space was. The studio apartment ought to feel bigger, stripped to its bare bones—a convertible sofa that had been here when she moved in, along with an oval coffee table, a standing lamp and a battered computer desk. All that remained of her own possessions was an open backpack and the sleeping bag she was taking to her brother's. The emptied space felt airless and hollow, yet bursting with tension. Like her.

"What are you doing here?" she asked when he didn't respond to her remark.

"My grandmother would like to thank you."

Could he say it with more disdain?

"Is she…" She took in the signs of a rough night, suddenly gripped by worry. "I called the hospital. They don't share much if you're not family, but said she'd been released. I thought that meant she was recovered."

"She's fine."

"Good." She relaxed slightly. "What happened?"

"Asthma. She hasn't had an attack in years so didn't bring her inhaler."

There was definitely something wrong with Cami because even though he took a tone that suggested speaking to her was beneath him, his accent and the subtle affection and concern in his tone made his talk of asthma and an inhaler sound ridiculously kind and endearing. Sexy.

The heat of the oven was cooking her brain.

"Well, I'm glad she's all right. I didn't realize she was your grandmother—"

"Didn't you?"

What now? Her brain screeched like a needle scraping vinyl. It struck her that a tiny part of her had wondered if he was here to apologize. Or thank her himself. Wow. How incredibly deluded of her.

It made her ridiculous reaction to him all the more unbearable. Of all the things she hated about him, the way he kept making her feel such self-contempt was the worst. She normally liked herself, but he made her mistrust herself at an integral level. He said these awful things to her and she still felt drawn. It was deeply unnerving. Painful.

"No," she pronounced in a voice jagged by her turmoil. "I didn't. And yes, before you ask." She held up a hand. "I would have helped her even if I'd known she was related to you. I don't assume people are guilty by association and treat them like garbage for it."

She had to avert her gaze as that came out of her mouth, never quite sure if she could truly claim her father was innocent. He had signed an admission of guilt, that much she knew, but had told her brother he was innocent. If he *was* guilty, was it *her* fault he'd stolen Dante's proprietary work and sold it to a competitor? She just didn't know. The not knowing tortured her every single day.

It made her uncertain right now, one bare foot folding over the other, when she wanted to sound confident as she stood her ground. Her culpability was reflected in her voice as she asked, "How could I know she was related to you? You don't even have the same last name."

"Sicilian women keep their names." He frowned as though that was something everyone should know, then shrugged off her question. "I'm not on social media much, but she is. It wouldn't take more than a single search of my name to pull up our connection."

"It would take a desire to do so, and why would I want to?"

"You tell me. Why did your father target me in the first place? Money? Jealousy? Opportunity? You knew who I was yesterday. You must have looked me up at some point."

Further guilt snaked through her belly. Had she been intrigued by him even then? Not that she had admitted to herself, but how could she not want to know more about a man who had such power over her and remained so out of reach?

"Maybe I did." She tried a shrug and a negligent shake of her head, but only managed to loosen her ponytail. She grabbed at it, dragging his gaze to her breasts, raking her composure down another notch. Challenging him was a mistake. It was an exercise in bashing herself against bulletproof glass with no hope of reaching whatever was inside. She knew that from the few times she had been desperate enough to try getting in touch, to plead her case, only to be shut out.

At least she was in a better place these days, even though it was still a precarious one. Her brother was looking after himself now, if barely scraping by under student loans. Her being jobless and homeless didn't mean he would be without food and shelter, as well. She actually had a place to go to now that her own life had imploded again.

That meant she didn't have anything left to lose in standing up to Dante. She dropped her arms and lifted her chin.

"Are you accusing me of somehow causing your grandmother's asthma so I could call for treatment?"

"No. But I think you recognized her and took advantage of an opportunity."

"To do what? Be kind? Yes. Guilty!"

"To get on my good side."

"You have one?"

He didn't move, but his granite stillness was its own threat, one that made a dangerous heat coil through her middle and sent her pulse racing.

"You haven't seen my bad one. Yet." Then, in a surprisingly devastating move, he added, "Cami."

She felt hammered to the floor then, all of her reverberating with the impact of his saying her name. A flash in his eyes told her he knew exactly how she was reacting, which made it all the more humiliating.

Sharma chose that moment to knock, forcing her to col-lect her bearings. Cami had to brush by him, which caused him to move farther into her apartment. Her whole body tingled with awareness, mind distracted by thoughts of his gaze touching her few things, casting aspersions over them. Why did she even care how little he thought of her?

"Hi," Sharma said with a big smile.

Cami had actually forgotten between one moment and the next who she was expecting. Her own baffled, "Hi," reflected how out of sorts she was, making Sharma give her a look of amused curiosity.

"Everything okay? Oh, you have company." Intrigue lit her gaze, and she waved at Dante. "Hi. Are you our new neighbor?"

Cami caught back a choke. The Dante Gallos of the world didn't live in places like this. He'd probably wipe his feet on the way *out*.

"He's just visiting." Flustered, she set a brown bag of cookies on a small box of dishes she wasn't keeping, but that Sharma's young family might find useful, and re-turned Sharma's keys at the same time. "Thanks for the car today."

"It was bad enough you were moving out of the build-ing. You can't leave *town*," Sharma said, making a sad face as she accepted the box. "What happened with the job?"

"I'll explain later." Cami waved a hand to gloss past the question, not willing to get into it with the demigod of wrath looming behind her, skewering her so hard with his bronze laser vision she felt it like a pin in her back. She was a butterfly, squirming under his concentrated study, caught and dying for nothing because her plain brown wings wouldn't even hold his attention for long.

Sharma's gaze slid over to him and back as if she knew Dante had something to do with it. "Okay, well, nice to meet you." She waved at Dante, then said to Cami, "Gotta run to get Milly, but say goodbye before you leave."

"I will."

As she closed the door, Cami ran through all the should-have-saids she'd conjured last night, as she had replayed her interchange with Dante in his office. Through it all, she had wished she could go back and change a decade's worth of history, all to no avail.

No matter what threats he was making, however, she knew this was a chance to salvage something. To appeal to whatever reasonable side he might possess. Maybe. Or not. Perhaps talking to him would make matters worse.

Still, she had to make him see she was trying to make amends and hopefully ease this grudge he had. It was killing her on every level; it really was.

As Dante waited out Cami Fagan's chat with her neighbor, his brain was still clattering with all the train cars that had derailed and piled up, one after another, starting with the news her father was dead—which had been strangely jarring.

Initially, before their association had gone so very wrong, he'd looked on Stephen Fagan as a sort of mentor. Dante's grandfather had been a devoted surrogate after Dante's father died, and an excellent businessman willing to bet on his grandson, but he hadn't had the passion for electronics that Dante possessed.

He'd found that in Stephen, which was why he had trusted him so implicitly and felt so betrayed by his crime. Maybe he'd even believed, in the back of his mind, that one day he would have an explanation from the man he'd thought of as a friend. Damaging as the financial loss had been, the real cost had been his faith in his own judgment. How had he been so blind? Something in him had always longed for a chance to hear Stephen's side of it, to understand why he would do something so cold when Dante had thought they were friends.

Hearing Stephen was dead had been... Well, it hadn't been good, despite his claim otherwise. It had been painful, stirring up the other more devastating loss he'd suffered back then. All the losses that had come at once.

As he'd been processing that he would never get answers from Stephen, someone had knocked insistently, informing him his grandmother was unwell. Rushing outside, what had he found?

Cami.

In the confusion, she'd slipped away, but she'd stayed on his mind all the while his grandmother was treated. The moment she had recovered, his grandmother became adamant that she thank the young woman who had helped her.

Back when she'd been grieving the loss of her husband, Dante hadn't dared make things worse by revealing how he'd put the family's security in jeopardy. It was one of the reasons he hadn't pressed charges against Stephen—to keep his grandmother and the rest of the family from knowing the extent of their financial woes. He hadn't wanted anyone worrying more than they already were.

Instead, with the help of his cousin, he'd worked like a slave to bring them back from the brink.

That silence meant Noni didn't understand why he was so skeptical of Cami's altruism. He didn't want to tell her he would rather wring Cami's neck than buy her a meal, but he wasn't about to let his grandmother go hunting all over town for her good Samaritan, possibly collapsing again. He also sure as hell wasn't going to give Cami a chance to be alone with his grandmother again. Who knew what damage would be done this time?

So, after a restless night and a day of putting it off, he'd looked up her address from her CV and had come here. He'd walked up the stairs in this very dated building, wondering what sort of debts her father had paid off since he clearly hadn't left much for his daughter, and knocked.

Then *Smash!* She had opened the door, plunging him into a blur of pale pink top that scooped low enough to reveal the upper swells of her breasts and thin enough her nipples pressed enticingly against it. Her red shorts were outright criminal, emphasizing her firm thighs and painting over her mound in a way that made his palm itch to cup there. The bright color stopped mere inches below that, covering the top end of a thin white scar that scored down past her knee.

He'd barely processed the old injury when she whirled away in response to a buzzer. The fabric of her shorts held a tight grip on her ass as she turned and bent to retrieve something from the oven, making his mouth water and his libido rush to readiness.

He had spent the night mentally flagellating himself for being attracted to her at all, let alone so intensely. Cami was beyond off-limits. She was a hard *No.* Whatever he thought he might have seen in the first seconds of their meeting had been calculated on her part. Had to have been.

She had known who he was.

And now he knew who she was, so how could he be physically attracted to someone who should repel him? It was untenable.

Yet the stir in his groin refused to abate.

She turned from closing the front door, and her wholesome prettiness was an affront. A lie. He curled his fist and tried not to react when she crossed her arms *again*, plumping that ample bosom of hers in a most alluring way. Deliberately?

"I don't know how to convince you that I had no ulterior motive yesterday, but I didn't." Her lips remained slightly parted, as though she wanted to say more but was waiting to see how he reacted first.

"You can't. She wants you to come to the hotel anyway. To thank you. Not the Tabor. The one where we're staying."

Surprise flickered across her face, then wariness. "And you're here to intimidate me all over again? Tell me not to go anywhere near her?"

"I'm here to drive you." Was she intimidated? She wasn't acting like it. "But it's true I don't want you near her. That's why I'll supervise."

"Ha. Fun as *that* sounds—" She cut herself off with a choked laugh. Her ironic smile invited him to join in the joke, then faded when he didn't.

Something like hurt might have moved behind her eyes, but she disguised it with a sweep of her lashes, leaving him frustrated that he couldn't read her as easily as he wanted to.

She moved into the kitchen to transfer the last batch of cookies onto the cooling rack. "Too bad you didn't put it off until Monday. I would have been gone. Tell her I've left town."

He moved to stand on the other side of the breakfast bar, watching her.

Such a domestic act, baking cookies. This didn't fit at all with the image he'd built in his mind of her family living high off his hard work and innovation. Nothing about her fit into the boxes he'd drawn for Fagans and women, potential hires or people who dined with his family. Nothing except...

"Unlike you, I don't lie, especially to people I care about."

"Boy, you love to get your little digs in, don't you? When did I lie to you?"

When she'd mentioned he was being paid back, for starters, but, "Forget it. I'm not here to rehash the past. I've moved on." Begrudgingly and with a dark rage still livid within him.

"Really," she scoffed in a voice that held a husk. Was it naturally there? An emotional reaction to his accusation? Or put there to entice him? "Is that why you fired me without even giving me a chance? Is that why you said it was 'good' that my father is dead? My mother died in the same crash. Do you want to tell me how happy you are to hear *that* news?" The same emotive crack as yesterday charged her tone now, and her eyes gleamed with old agony.

He wanted to write her off as melodramatic, make some kind of sharp comeback so she wouldn't think she could get away with dressing him down, but his chest tightened. Whatever else had happened, losing one's parents was a blow. He couldn't dismiss that so pitilessly.

"I shouldn't have said that," he allowed, finding his gaze dropping to the scar etched onto her collarbone. She had that longer one on her leg, too. Had she been in the accident? He tried to recall what he had known about Stephen Fagan's family, but came up with a vague recollection of a wife and a forgotten number of children.

Why did he find the idea of her being injured so disturbing? Everything about this woman put him on uneven ground. He hated it. There was already a large dose of humiliation attached to her father's betrayal. He'd been soaked in grief over losing his grandfather, but guilt, as well. The old man had loved him. Indulged him. And Dante had failed so very badly, even contributing to his grandfather's death with his mistake.

An acrid lump of self-blame still burned black and hot within him. He had had to take that smoldering coal in hand, shape and harden it with an implacable grip, and pull himself into the future upon it.

Since then, nothing happened without his will or permission. He was ruled by sound judgment, not his libido or his temper. Certainly not his personal desires. Yet anger had got the better of him yesterday. *She* had. And emotion was threatening to take him over again today, especially when she muttered, "No. You shouldn't have."

The utter gall of her was mind-blowing.

She clattered the cookie sheet and spatula into the sink. Her ponytail was coming loose, allowing strands of rich mink and subtle caramel with tiny streaks of ash to fall around her face. It gave her a delicate air that he had to consciously remind himself was a mirage. That vestige of grief in her expression might be real, but the flicker of helplessness was not. Fagans landed on their feet.

"Look," he said, more on edge than he liked. "Helping my grandmother was a nice gesture, but I'm not giving you back that job, if that's what you were after."

She lifted her head. "It was a coincidence!" She dropped some cookies into a brown paper bag and offered it to him. "Here. Tell her I'm glad she's feeling better." Her hand tremored.

He ignored the offering. "She wants you to come for dinner."

"I have plans." A blatant lie. She set the bag on the counter between them.

"I'm not letting you hold this over me. Or skirt around me. Put on a dress and let's get it over with."

"I've packed all my dresses."

"Is that your way of asking me to buy you a new one?" He had played that game a *lot* and couldn't decide if it grated that she was trying it. Under the right circumstances, he enjoyed spoiling a woman. Cami's heart-shaped ass in a narrow skirt with a slit that showed off her legs—

"No," she said flatly, yanking him back from a fantasy that shouldn't even be happening. A pang of something seemed to torture her brow. Insulted? Please.

"What do you want, then? Because clearly you're holding out for something." He *had* to remember that.

"And you're clearly paranoid. Actually, you know what I want?" Her hand slapped the edge of the sink. "I want you to admit you've been receiving my payments."

"What payments?"

"Are you that rich you don't even *notice*?" She shoved out of the kitchen and whisked by him to the rickety looking desk, then pulled up short as she started to open a drawer. She slammed it shut again. "I forgot. It's not here. His name is, like, Bernardo something. It's Italian."

"What is?"

"The letter! The one that proves I've been paying you back." She frowned with distraction, biting at her bottom lip in a way that drew his thoughts to doing the same. "My brother has the file, though. He took it last fall."

"Convenient."

"God, you're arrogant."

He shrugged, having heard that before. Recovering his belief in himself had been the hardest part of all. His ego had taken a direct hit after misjudging her father. He'd questioned himself, his instincts and his intelligence, which almost crippled him as he faced the Herculean task of recovery. In the end, he had no choice but to trust his gut above anyone else and get on with the work. He would have been dead in the water otherwise.

He refused to go back to self-doubts. He faced everything head-on and dealt with it as expediently as possible. "Let's get past the games. I know you have a hidden agenda. Speak frankly."

"I don't! I'm exactly what I look like. I applied for a job for which I am fully qualified. You came along with your sword of retaliation and cut me off at the knees. Then I was nice to a little old lady who happens to be your grandmother. Now I have to move and get back on my feet. *Again*."

Her hand flung out with exasperation as she spoke. She smelled like the cinnamon and vanilla she'd been baking with, sweet and homespun. All smoke and mirrors.

"How was I supposed to know you would buy the Tabor when I interviewed six months ago? I'm not trying to pull a fast one on you. You're the one out to get *me*." She managed to sound quite persecuted.

He shook his head, amazed. "You look like you're telling the truth, but so did your father. It's quite a family talent, I have to say." Then, because he was so damned tempted to reach out and touch her, he neutralized that secret weapon of hers. He gave her luscious figure a scathing once-over and said, "Of course, he didn't work the additional diversions you employ."

Her jaw dropped open with affront, but her gaze took a skitter around the room. She blushed, seeming disconcerted. Caught out, even. "I'm not— You showed up here unannounced! As if I'd throw myself at *you*."

"No?" He was needling her, determined to maintain the upper hand, but that tiny word seemed to flick a switch.

She flung back her hair to glare at him. "You're the last man on earth I'd want anything to do with!"

She faltered as she said it and tried to give him a scathing once-over, but her lashes quivered. He could tell by the way they moved that her gaze traversed his torso and down to the muscles in his abdomen. His stomach tightened with the rest of him. In those charged seconds, he grew so hot, his clothes should have incinerated off his body.

When she brought her gaze back in a flash of defiance, there was a glow of speculation in their depths. The light shifted, or, more accurately, the fog of animosity in her eyes dissolved into a mist of desire.

The air shimmered, hot and oppressive between them. All an act, he reminded himself, but, *What the hell.* He ought to get *something.*

"If you want to talk about compensation, I'm listening." He suddenly seemed really close. His voice was like whiskey-soaked velvet.

"What?" She took a step back, reeling from the way her body was betraying her. She was trying to rebuff him, but everything about him overwhelmed her senses.

She came up against the wall and he flattened his hands on either side of her head, not touching her, but caging her. She set her hands on his chest, alarmed then intrigued by the layers of heat and strength that pressed into her fingertips. He was pure vitality, enticing her hands to splay and move in a small stroke of curiosity that quickly edged toward greed.

How did he disarm her so quickly? How had they even wound up like this? She could feel his sharp nipples stabbing into the heels of her palms and it pleased her. Excited her. She wanted to run her hands over his chest and onto his lower back, exploring everywhere.

She had to quell a whimper of helplessness. This desire was terrifying and exhilarating at once. Deadly, yet impossible to ignore.

His pupils swallowed all the color in his eyes, drawing her into the darkest unknown.

"What are you offering?" His arousal was so tangible in

his voice, it felt like a caress from her shoulder down her chest. A sweep of bumps rose on her skin and her breasts grew heavy and swollen.

"Cold?" The corners of his mouth deepened and she couldn't read his eyes.

This was bizarre and damning, yet compelling. She felt as though a drug had been released in her system that made her languid and euphoric. She didn't move away. Couldn't. Her breaths moved unevenly, and she could swear she felt the brush of his erection against her.

His muscles were like iron. Rather than shoving him away, she dug her fingers into flesh that had no give, exploring against her own willpower. How could the inherent strength in him, that wasn't even being exerted against her, make her so weak?

He was doing something to her, though. It was a force that gripped her without effort. He wasn't even touching her. She was the one touching him, yet she couldn't escape. Couldn't make her body push him away. She stood there and watched his face draw closer, filling her vision. She waited, lips parting, mind blank, until his mouth touched hers. *Hot.*

Why she held still for his kiss, she didn't know. It was beyond stupid, yet she let it happen, wanting to know something she couldn't even define. She tensed, maybe expecting punishment. Cruelty, even. He wasn't a kind man. She already knew that.

He *was* cruel as he kissed her, but in a way she couldn't have anticipated. He used gentleness to tease her lips into opening wide, then slowly worked their mouths into a firmer fit, angling and sinking closer, waiting until she was moving her mouth against his before he settled in to fully plunder.

A deep quiver rang through her. Recognition. As

though she'd been waiting all her life for this. Her body gave a small shudder and sighed in relief. *This one.*

That should have scared the hell out of her, but she was so entranced by the sense of discovery, by the flood of heat and need, she let the kiss continue. She let it draw out, going on and on while she sank deeper and deeper into sweet pleasure.

She had never progressed much further than a kiss. Had never wanted to. Not like this. This kiss was beyond anything she'd ever known. It was *right*. It picked up all the pieces of herself she'd left scattered and broken and fit them together again, making her feel whole and alive. Omnipotent.

Worldly and womanly and exalted.

Her fingers moved, testing the firmness of his pecs, then slid in a blatant caress across the flex of his muscles, squeezing and shaping, tracing the ridges of his ribs and flowing to the hollow of his spine.

He growled and dropped his hands to her waist, stroked her hips in a sweeping circle of his big hands, then he cruised his palms up to cup her breasts, thumbs raking across her nipples. The twin sensation was so sharp and electric, she bucked.

He settled the weight of his hips against hers, pinning her to the wall, forcing her to take that continued gentle torture of her nipples. Heat plunged into her loins, and there was no denying what she felt there. She was screamingly aware of the stiffness of his arousal against her. His thighs were hard and hot, pressing hers to open so her mound was firmly in contact with that hard, hard shape. She throbbed under the pressure of him against her so intimately. When had she ever wanted something so earthy and base? Never. Not before this moment and this man who kissed her to the point she stopped thinking.

His thumbs circled and teased with an expertise that made her wriggle, the acute stimulation lifting her hips into his. *More.* That's all she could think as she kept kissing him, suffocating, but unwilling to stop. *Keep doing that. I want more.*

The way they were consuming each other was blatant and more primal than anything she'd ever known. Her arms lifted to circle behind his neck, arching her breasts into his relentless hands. He pinched her nipples and she whimpered at the pleasure-pain, legs growing weak and pliant under the pressure of his. She stroked her fingers through his hair, luxuriating in the feel of the short, crispy strands, before drawing his head down to increase the pressure of his kiss to the point of near pain. It wasn't enough. It could never be enough.

His tongue thrust in and her hips ground against his, seeking the most acute sensations she could find. Nothing had ever made her act so animalistic. That's why she'd never gone all the way. She'd never been compelled to by her own body, but oh, the way he was massaging her breasts was driving her crazy. She was so aroused, she actually mewled with loss when he lifted his head and dragged his hands down to her hips.

He watched her as he held her still for the blatant, deliberate thrust of his hard sex against hers. The flush on his face was barbaric, dark and satisfied as she gasped and met his erotic movement with a wanton, inviting rock of her own. A moan escaped her lips as she climbed ever higher on the steps of arousal toward the precipice of bliss.

Her hands clenched in his shirt and she pressed her head into the wall, giving up her lower half to his, inhibition gone. She had to bite her lip against groaning even louder as he rubbed against the bundle of nerves that was barely protected by the thin fabric of her yoga shorts. Her eyes fluttered closed and she held her breath, quivering with tension, so close—

With a hiss, his hands hardened on her hip bones before he thrust her back into the wall, releasing her to step away.

Stunned, she scrambled for purchase on the empty wall, panting as she fought to remain standing. Her body *screamed* for his, making this rejection the height of cruelty.

His cheek ticked, but he didn't look nearly as shattered as she felt. He was aroused, but held a cynical gleam in his eye that cut her to the bone.

"We'll finish talking about that later. Get dressed. Comb your hair. We're running late."

"What?" Her knees threatened to buckle.

If she thought he sounded strained, or as though he balanced on a razor's edge of his own, the impression evaporated as he smiled, merciless and self-assured. The peaks and valleys in his face stood out in sharp relief, light and dark. Beautiful and indifferent.

"Since the compensation you're offering comes with such a high rate of interest—" the corner of his mouth curled at his own pun "—I'll give you a chance to make your case. But my grandmother is expecting us." He glanced at the gold watch on his wrist, the face black and numberless, with only two needle arms. "We need to leave."

"I'm not going anywhere with you."

"You want to finish talking now?" His withering inflection told her they wouldn't be using their mouths for words.

CHAPTER THREE

"No!" CAMI SHOVED off the wall and stumbled toward the sofa, where her backpack sat open. She grabbed at the cowl-necked pullover that came to hand and hugged it to her front. "Get out."

She wanted him away from her so she could make sense of what had just happened.

His nostrils twitched and he gave her a long moment to absorb that by leaving, he was getting what he wanted. He wasn't obeying.

"I'll wait in my rental. If you're not out in ten minutes, I'm coming back."

Her heart pounded. She bit her lip against saying another word, gripped by incredulity, but having enough sense to know she needed him out of here so she could get herself back under control. As the door clicked, she sank onto the sofa and tried to decide if she wanted to cry or scream or swear. Maybe all of the above.

Why had she kissed him? Let alone so lustfully he thought she was offering to prostitute herself? It was humiliating!

It hadn't felt humiliating while they were doing it, though. He'd made her feel things she'd never felt with anyone.

Why *him*?

All her life she'd waited for the right man. Dating and relationships were distractions she couldn't afford, so avoiding going all the way hadn't been difficult. It wasn't as though she thought of her virginity as holy or golden, but she came with baggage and liabilities. She didn't feel like a catch. When she did have sex, she expected it to be with someone who had earned her trust, loved her for who she was and deserved this part of her life that was, as yet, unmarred by memories of anyone else.

Now Dante Gallo had barged in and set the bar on sexual encounters to unimaginable levels. She very much feared reaching it again would be unattainable. Where would she meet another man who made her feel like that?

"Oh!" She buried her face in her pullover, still restless and tingling. *Aroused*, damn him. She was sensitized and filled with yearning. She would have slept with him. Totally would have let it happen, which wasn't her *at all*. She'd never understood when other women behaved wildly, having sex with courier drivers in the back of a van or going home with a stranger, saying things like, *I was really into it. We got carried away.*

Cami had disparaged such stories. *She* never got carried away. She had secretly feared there was something wrong with her. Like she was a tiny bit frigid.

Nope. She just hadn't meant Dante Gallo.

But he was the *wrong* man. Totally, utterly and completely.

Yet she could still feel that deliberate way he had thrust against her. In that moment, she had felt as carried away and *with* someone as it was possible to feel. She had thought they were both in the moment, edging toward ecstasy together.

A fresh rush of excitement flooded her loins along with

a sting of fresh mortification. He hadn't been nearly as caught up, and she should have been thinking about—

She jerked her head up, ardor finally subsiding as she remembered what they'd been talking about before the kiss.

How did he not know about her payments? She was so faithful about making them. Had been for five hard years, no matter what other financial disaster had befallen her. There was always something. A rent increase or her brother's new shoes.

Despite making a decent salary and living very frugally, she was consistently flat broke because she made the equivalent of a generous mortgage payment to Dante Gallo every single month.

His playing dumb about that had her popping onto her feet and dragging on some proper clothes. She didn't care about dinner with his grandmother, but she wasn't about to face him in next to nothing again.

Or let him come barging in after her.

She put on the outfit she had left out for her travel to Vancouver tomorrow. It was a classic wool miniskirt in charcoal, black tights and the soft blue pullover she had squeezed a couple of tears into a minute ago. A pair of knee-high boots that were actually worth a fortune finished it off. The mother of a ski student had given them to her because they hadn't fit in her suitcase back to France. That was precisely the reason Cami had left them out to wear tomorrow.

She felt tough and feminine and confident every time she zipped the supple leather up her inner calf. They had just enough heel to give her some swagger and always earned her compliments, boosting her ego.

She had needed that kick of self-assurance as she prepared to leave for Vancouver and her brother's decrepit sofa in his shared basement suite in a dodgy part of the city.

With a glance at the clock, she saw she had two minutes to run a brush through her hair and lock her door. She tapped her bank code into her phone as she walked outside, searching her recent transactions until she found the one from last month.

She glanced up as she reached the parking lot and paused.

Dante was on his phone, too, leaning on a black SUV. The rain had stopped, but the clouds were low and heavy, bringing on early dusk, casting him in uneven light. He was shadows and power and had touched her as if she belonged to him. She still felt his hands on her, still felt under his spell.

No. She was a steady, levelheaded, smart woman who controlled her own life. She had grown up fast and shouldered responsibilities way beyond her years.

Yet he erased that by lifting his glance. A fair distance separated them, but she felt him take her in from eyelashes to boot tip.

She had never felt so anxious for approval. So green and uncertain in herself or her own autonomy. Her near climax at the touch of his body was right there, torturing her with her own weakness.

Yet, maybe there was a twisted piece of her that felt so guilty about her father, she wanted Dante's punishment and blame. Maybe that's why this attraction was blindsiding her this way.

"You look nice. *Grazij.*"

His words stung through her, mostly because she was so affected by the lukewarm compliment. "I didn't dress for *you*. Here." She strode forward, holding out her phone as if it was a shield that could deflect all his barbs and ability to undermine. "See?"

He didn't take the phone. He steadied her hand and glanced at the screen.

She held her breath, pulse tripping while she tried not to be affected by something so innocuous as his touch over the backs of her fingers. Everything they'd done in her apartment came rushing back to torment her. She wanted to pull back, but made herself stand there, heart hammering, watching for some kind of change in his expression. She thought she might have stopped breathing and begun to shake.

Dante didn't know what the hell he was looking at. He was still half-blind with lust. This woman had got him so hot, so fast, he'd nearly lost control from a randy bit of necking. She had gone from wary and surprised, to participating, to what appeared to be a surrender of the most exquisite kind.

Appeared.

Somehow, at the last second, he had remembered who she was and hadn't let her get the better of him. He'd had to stand out here in the spit of spring rain, counting down the minutes with a barely acknowledged hope that she would defy him. Speculating what he would do if she forced him to go back in there and finish what they'd started had *not* helped cool him off.

She had emerged on time, looking lovely in an elfin way, with her short skirt and sleeves falling past her wrist. Her hair was loose and lifted on the evening breeze while she closed in on him with purpose, her insanely sexy boots making soft splashes as she strode through shallow puddles in the pavement.

As she stood here with her hand trembling in his, he

wondered how he'd found the will to leave her without stripping them both naked and driving into her. Was this closeness of hers still part of her act? He couldn't afford to think her reaction to him was anything but a put-on, but damn did he want to.

"Well?" An underlying huskiness in her tone seemed to stroke over his skin, making his back prickle.

"Well what?" He let a finger steal beneath the edge of her soft sleeve.

She snatched her hand back. "Do you recognize the amount?"

"No."

"It's the same every month. Who does your bookkeeping?"

"My accountant." Why was she going on about this? "But I know where my money comes from and where it goes." He opened the door of the SUV.

"But—"

"Do you need help getting in? It's starting to rain again." The fat drops were falling in a more steady patter, soaking through his shirt.

She let out a huff of impatience and swung into the vehicle with surprising grace.

"Ask him," she demanded when Dante climbed behind the wheel. "Ask your accountant."

"She," he corrected, then rested his forearm on the steering wheel as he gave her a frustrated study. Was she really trying to prove something here? Or was it more of her shell game tactics? Either way, there was an easy fix. "Fine. Give me that." He held out a hand for her phone.

She tucked it into her chest. "What are you going to do?"

"Take a screen shot and send it to myself. I'll forward

it to my accountant." He glanced at his watch. "But it's two in the morning there. She'll be asleep."

With a disgruntled scowl, she warily handed over her phone.

He turned the scratched fossil this way and that, giving her a side-eyed frown. "Is this what they call a 'classic'?"

"Do you know what they want for a 'free'—" she hooked her fingers into air quotes "—upgrade? Do not get me started on the racket that is cell phone plans."

He smirked, bemused by her ire against something so inconsequential.

He clicked the screenshot and tapped in his details. The whoosh sounded and a ping emanated from his pocket. He handed back her phone and took out his own, sent the message, then tucked his phone back into his chest pocket to start the engine.

"Oh, I wasn't—"

Her hand went to the door latch, but he was already backing out of his spot. The seat belt reminder pinged and rain drummed harder against the roof. He flicked the wipers to their highest setting so they *slap, slap, slapped*.

She gave a dismayed sigh and put on her seat belt. "I wasn't going to go with you."

"Why not?"

"Because an inch turns into a mile with you."

He considered that as he turned onto the main road. He didn't take anything from a woman that she wasn't willing to give.

"You didn't call a halt," he reminded. "I did."

A loaded silence filled the interior. Everything else might be an act, but she'd looked as close to finding fulfillment as he had. It made her too damned tempting.

"You'll be nice to my grandmother."

"I *am* nice, not that you would even know what that looks like. For instance, when I come across someone who needs help, *I help them.*"

"I'll withhold judgment on that." Fagans were self-interested, greedy, faithless and deceptive.

She waited until they were almost at his hotel to respond shakily, "You realize that my father stole your schematics and research. *I* didn't."

He slowed to turn into the entrance of the hotel, then braked beneath the colonnade and jammed the vehicle into park before he swiveled to confront her.

"You still benefited."

What might have been a wince of guilt dented her features, but the hotel's valet opened her door and she turned away to step out of the vehicle.

Dante slammed out of his side and strode around to hand over his keys, then led her through the lobby to the elevators.

"Where—?"

He waved her through the doors that opened, waiting until they closed to explain, "Some of my employees are staying here. I can't be seen dining with you."

"Oh, but you can be seen taking me to your room? Employees here know me. Maybe I don't want them thinking I'm some kind of escort. Did you think of that?"

"No," he replied without apology, and was now distracted by the idea of hiring her for an evening. Of having the power to order her to do *exactly* as he pleased.

As if she was imagining it herself, and had her own erotic images painting through her mind, a delicious pink blush rose along her cheekbones. Her lips parted to allow a sip of air, leaving her mouth looking incredibly inviting.

The elevator stopped, throwing her off balance.

He caught her elbow to steady her. "Really," he said, hearing how she affected him in the way his voice deepened to a graveled tone. "Your acting belongs on the screen."

Cami jerked out of his hold and escaped through the opening doors, then halted to glare back at him. It was really hard to stalk away in a huff when she didn't know where she was going.

He smirked. "Noni's room is this way."

He didn't take her arm again, but her skin tingled. All of her felt as if it floated, yet the anchor of his mistrust dragged at her. She didn't know how to prove herself to him, and was growing increasingly frustrated by the effort. If she didn't have this lack of defense around him, it wouldn't hurt so much, but it did.

"You won't bring up your father. She doesn't know anything about that." The sudden grimness in his tone sent a shiver through her.

As if she enjoyed talking about that. Her throat ached, but she didn't know what to say. She couldn't believe she was even here, going through with this dinner, but she *was* nice and didn't want to be rude to his grandmother just because Dante was clawing up her insides.

He paused to knock on a pair of double doors. A female butler let them in, mentioning that their hostess was taking a call and would join them in a moment. She offered to pour drinks.

Hovering with tension, Cami glanced around the suite. The drapes were closed, but she could tell it was one of the hotel's best, with a mountain view from the picture window. If she recalled correctly, there was a Juliet balcony outside the French doors. The gas fireplace was glowing, and a small dining table was set with china, silver, crystal and fresh flowers.

She had only ever been on the service side of places like this. She had to fight the urge to strike up friendly conversation with the butler, whom she regarded as her equal, rather than try to find common ground with Mr. Tall, Dark and Daunting.

He was watching her as though he expected a misstep any second.

Just as she thought she would incinerate from the eye contact, Bernadetta appeared, coming through from the bedroom with a warm smile. She was small and plump, gray hair smoothly gathered in a round bun. Her color was much better, the lines in her face softened. She immediately apologized for not using her English yesterday.

"You were distraught. I'm so glad you've recovered," Cami said, accepting the woman's gentle touch on her shoulders and soft kisses on each of her cheeks. She smelled like rosewater and motherly love, melting Cami's heart if not her tension.

Bernadetta greeted Dante with similar affection.

"Thank you for fetching her. You're a good boy." She patted his cheek, which seemed a ridiculously tender thing to do to a man who was so obviously a *man*.

Bernadetta took the armchair, forcing Cami to lower onto the love seat next to Dante, thighs almost touching.

"I'm blessed with a doting family," Bernadetta said. "That's why I was delayed greeting you. I've been taking calls all day. That was Arturo, Dante's cousin. He's in Australia, looking at a property, but he saw my post in the family group and wanted to reassure himself I was feeling better. He seemed to think your name sounded familiar," she said, taking Cami by surprise. "Do you know him?"

Startled, she shook her head. "I don't know any Arturos, no."

The wrinkles in Bernadetta's forehead deepened with puzzlement. "He asked me if Cami was short for Cameo."

"It is, but I don't believe we've met. Unless… I did live in Italy briefly, ten years ago. I was only fourteen and it was Northern Italy. The Alps. Not Sicily."

Dante's expression had hardened.

She licked her lips. She wasn't the one steering this conversation into dangerous waters! "If I met him in passing, I don't recall," she mumbled in a rush.

Bernadetta leaned forward with interest. "What brought you to Italy?"

"Skiing." Her conscience pressed like a bed of nails on either side of her as she said it, now a victim of her own censure, not just Dante's. "My parents moved us there so I could train under a world-class coach." One who had cost a fortune.

She looked to the hands she had folded in her lap.

Was her dream the reason her father had stolen from Dante? She would never know. But she would always feel it was a factor, one that made her responsible for all that had happened to Dante, her parents and her brother. If her father hadn't wanted to give her that training, he wouldn't have stolen the money. They wouldn't have had to leave Italy and come back to Canada. They wouldn't have been on that icy road outside Calgary that had cost her parents their lives.

"Downhill? You were racing for Canada?"

"And slalom. I was hoping to make the team, but—" She cleared her throat. It took all her effort to smile through the excruciating pain of losing so much. Her chance, her coach, then her parents. For a while, she'd even lost her brother. She had learned how to slap a glossy prevarication on harsh realities, though. "I was injured and couldn't continue."

"You don't ski at all anymore? That's a shame."

"Oh, I do," Cami said ruefully. "It's a bit of an addiction, but I can't do it full-time, otherwise I'd give lessons for a living. I offer private lessons to children when I can. It works out well for tourist families. Parents can enjoy the more challenging runs knowing their children aren't getting lost or winding up on a run beyond their level."

"What a lovely thing to do. There, Dante. Let me send you skiing with Cami, as a thank you to both of you for looking after me so well on this trip."

Her pulse spiked. *Oh, heck, no.* "Dinner is more than enough," she hurried to protest. "Honestly."

"Pssh. Dante works too hard. You'll be doing me another favor. I was going to ask him to take me up the gondola tomorrow, to force him to take a break, but after my mishap, I'm just as happy to stay indoors."

"I wouldn't want to impose on your family time." She glanced at Dante, unable to read his stony expression. "I'll be leaving for Vancouver soon, anyway." *Help me out here.*

"Oh, when is that? My niece and her husband will be coming to fetch me Monday, to drive me into the city. I'm staying with them until I fly back to Sicily. We have more than enough room to take you with us."

Dear Lord. Could she dig herself any deeper? Cami silently begged Dante to conjure an excuse on her behalf.

He only sipped his drink and said, "Thank you, Noni. I didn't think I'd have the chance to ski, but I'd like that." The cool, half-lidded look he sent Cami warned against rejecting the old woman's offer.

Spend the day with him? What sort of sadist was he? And what sort of masochist was she that she held out a shred of hope for…something if she did. Softening? Understanding? A chance to redeem herself in his eyes?

"That's very generous of you," she mumbled into her own glass, confused by her reaction. "Thank you."

The first course arrived, and the butler invited them to the table. Cami was able to keep the conversation with Bernadetta to neutral topics from there on, but it was a difficult evening. An oppressive yearning made her hyperaware of Dante and her own body language. Of the fact she was supposed to ski with him tomorrow.

Mix her one true love with a man she hated? She *had* to get out of it.

"That was weird that your cousin thought he knew my name."

Dante had worried the whole thing was coming out of the bag and grudgingly appreciated the way Cami had changed the subject.

"He does." Dante glanced at the phone that had been pulsing regularly through dinner. Arturo wanted to hear from him. "Our mothers were the eldest of seven sisters. We ran wild on the estate all summer, especially after I lost my parents and lived with my grandparents permanently. He didn't share my passion for cars or electronics, but he always encouraged me to follow my aspirations."

For a time, Dante had wondered if it was an attempt to push him from being their grandfather's successor, but Arturo had never enjoyed taking responsibility. He'd matured enough to be an asset on the acquisitions side of the family business, identifying opportunities like the Tabor, but back in their youth he'd been a playboy, partying and gambling in the stock market. He'd done surprisingly well at it, fortunately.

"When our grandfather died, Arturo was with me

through every step, especially helpful with the way I'd been compromised by your father. He offered more than moral support. Financing. I needed it." It was a lowering thing to admit, one that made his teeth clench to this day. "We're like brothers. Naturally, he wants to know why I'm consorting with the family that betrayed me."

Color rose in her cheeks.

The elevator stopped and the doors opened.

"I can find my own way home," Cami told him as she crossed the lobby in a brisk clip.

He paced her easily, not even bothering to acknowledge the remark, only handing his ticket to the valet as they reached the entrance.

"We'll wait in here where it's warm." Cami hadn't brought a coat, and the spring weather was looking closer to winter now that night had fallen.

"What if you're seen with me?" Cami challenged in a scathing whisper, giving him a wide-eyed look that was equal parts impending doom and disdain.

Dante's thoughts on fraternization were evolving, given their kiss, but he would address that after he'd had time to work through it more thoroughly.

That's why he hadn't yet returned his cousin's texts. He should be pushing Cami out the door and out of his life, but he couldn't forget—literally couldn't stop thinking about—the way she had felt in his arms. All through dinner, while she'd been advising his grandmother on which shops carried the best local art, he'd been thinking about taking her to his room. Spending the night with her, finishing what they'd started in her apartment.

Sleeping with his enemy would be the height of insanity, but there could be something very satisfying in it. As long as he maintained the upper hand. Carnal hunger gnawed at him, warring with his good sense.

The valet arrived, and they walked outside where the chill on the damp air made their breath fog. She waited until Dante had pulled away from the hotel to say, "I can't go tomorrow. I sold my skis, and I'm not letting your grandmother rent any for me."

His grandmother wasn't exactly on a fixed income, but, "I intend to pay."

"Then I am definitely not going."

"She'll want to see photos proving how much fun we're having." He enjoyed making that facetious statement, especially when it provoked a tiny noise of frustration in her throat. He smiled in the dark. "Why did you sell your skis?"

"Is that a real question? I don't have a job or a place to live." She spoke like she was explaining it to a child. "I needed cash to rent a storage locker."

He made the turn toward her neighborhood, which was in the most modest part of a very affluent resort town. "What did your father do with all the money?"

"You tell me," she said tightly. "You said earlier that I benefited from his crime, but I didn't. Not in any way that I can tell."

"No?"

She moved restlessly in her seat, muttering reluctantly, "Maybe I was supposed to. Maybe he was trying to pay for my training. I don't know. I was fourteen, totally in my own world, barely aware what a mechanical engineer *was*, let alone who he worked for or what you were making together. I was close to getting a sponsorship, not a huge one, but enough to help. It fell through. Maybe he got desperate."

Her tone of self-recrimination sounded real enough to niggle at him when he wanted to think of her as remorseless. "Did he have other debts?"

"Not that I know of. Living in Italy was expensive, I know that. We sold everything to go and had nothing when we came back. Both of my parents worked professional jobs, but we could only afford a tiny apartment in Calgary. They had a lot of hushed conversations, not saying much about any of it directly, but money issues were obvious. The only way I was able to train again was by getting my own job and saving up. After they were gone, and I knew more about what had happened, I assumed Dad had made a settlement of some kind. Gave the money back. That's why I was surprised so much was still owed."

"He promised to repay me every euro."

"I know." She clipped and unclipped the clasp on her handbag. "I've seen the statement he signed."

Any time over the years that Dante had looked at that document, he became so sick with himself, he walked away. Now he was finally confronting the past with a woman who beguiled even as she threatened a second betrayal. He ought to be running far and fast. Instead, he was thinking the unthinkable.

"The only thing Mom ever said about any of it was that he admitted to something he didn't do so he could come with us back to Canada and avoid a long legal battle."

What else would the wife of a criminal say to their children? "What about your brother? Older? Younger? Does he have money?"

"No." She snorted. "He's at university in Vancouver, trying to get into the medical program."

"He wants to be a doctor?"

"Yes."

"That's expensive. Postsecondary isn't covered in Canada, is it?"

"He has a couple of scholarships, but yes. He'll be up

to his eyeballs in student loans for years by the time he's done, so there's been no benefit for him, either."

"I can check that, you know."

"Don't you dare even think of interfering with his plans," she warned with a tremble in her voice. "That's a red line for me. It really is."

And she would do what? He parked outside her building, finding her threats laughable. Useful. Clearly her brother was a pressure point.

She left the vehicle at the same time he did, and colored when she saw him come around to her side.

"You're supposed to wait for me to open it for you," he chided.

"This isn't a date. Why on earth would you walk me in?" On the heels of that, she made a noise of realization, turning her head to the side, profile flinching. The streetlamp above her showed the light rain condensing on her hair in tiny sparkles, highlighting skin that was alabaster smooth. Her expression showed a brief struggle. He heard her swallow before she spoke in a voice that held a pang. "I'm not going to kiss you again."

"No?" His chest tightened, and he made himself hold the distance that his libido was screaming at him to close. "Run inside, then."

She turned only her head to look at him, face shadowed. Angry? Maddened, certainly.

So was he. This shouldn't be happening. He ought to hate her. He did resent her. He resented this. But when she only stood there, blinking rapidly, he stepped forward and wove his fingers into her hair, clasping her head in his hands.

A helpless noise broke from her throat. More surrender than protest. She tilted her head back and parted her lips, offering her mouth to his. A gratified groan rumbled in his chest as he took the kiss she offered. Took and took and took, rubbing his lips across and against, parting and seeking and ravaging.

If he was being too rough, she didn't let on that she didn't like it. Her hands bunched into his shirt beneath his jacket, scratching lightly at his rib cage then clinging, pulling him in while her mouth moved under his and she moaned with pleasure that echoed his. When he swept his tongue into her mouth, she swirled her own against it, sucking delicately, making his hands tighten in her hair, driving him insane.

He was going to ache all damned night from this. Everything in him wanted to take her inside and *take* her. But he remained standing there in the growing fall of rain, plundering the sweetness of her mouth until she finally pulled away to gasp for breath.

His own chest rose and fell like he'd been running a four-minute mile.

She dropped her hands and backed away another step, forcing him to let his own hands drop.

"Why is this happening?" Her whispered question sounded disturbingly vulnerable, like they were victims of the same tragedy, aligning them when he needed to remember she was only trying to coax him into forgiving her father's crime.

He was damned close to doing it, if she would only, "Ask me to come in." His voice wasn't anything he recognized, ragged with sexual hunger and hard with the imperative gripping him.

She shook her head. "No."

Toying with him?

She had the back of her hand pressed to her mouth. If her lips felt anything like his, they were hot and stinging.

There was only one way to soothe that. His gut tightened in anticipation while he gritted his teeth in frustration.

He could accept that a trick of hormones had him reacting to a woman who was his mortal enemy. What he would not allow was for her to use his desire to manipulate him.

"Be ready early, then." He managed to speak as if his interest had already waned.

Her gaze came up, shiny in the silvery light. Wounded?

"I'm not skiing with you! The only thing I want to hear from you tomorrow is that your accountant has confirmed I've been paying you back all this time. Feel free to text an apology at that point."

"You just never quit, do you?"

"It's the *truth*."

"Be ready," he warned. "Or I'll make inquiries about your brother."

Her head jerked like it was a blow she hadn't expected. Like she didn't understand he would find every advantage and use it without mercy.

"My father called you a visionary, you know." She sounded disillusioned. "I remember because I was jealous that he talked about you with so much admiration. He was just as proud of me, but it still made me work harder, wanting to measure up to someone he regarded so highly. I thought you were someone worthy of his respect. I guess I was mistaken."

"As was I, thinking he was worthy of mine."

She sucked in a breath, proving he'd landed a jab as sharp as hers had been. He smiled despite experiencing no satisfaction.

"Good night, Cami."

"Good*bye*, Dante." She hurried away, sexy boots leaping over puddles, graceful as a gazelle.

As he watched her retreat, skin so tight he could barely

breathe, he acknowledged that he was rooting for her. He wanted, by some miracle, to hear that she had been trying to make some sort of restitution to him. It would make this lust so much more palatable.

Which was why he was so disappointed when the email came through in the morning, proving yet again that Fagans were liars.

CHAPTER FOUR

"I DON'T UNDERSTAND." It was the understatement of the year. Of the decade. She couldn't even comprehend what she was seeing. Her stomach had plummeted into her shoes along with her heart, her blood and her brain. Even her breaths felt like she had to draw them with great effort from the center of the earth.

She looked from Dante's phone, to his remote expression, back to his phone. It still didn't make sense.

"How can there be no record?"

He released a very quiet sigh. "You've taken this as far as it can go, Cami. It's time to abandon this pretense of yours." His gaze was flinty with warning. Dislike?

Her insides grew sharp and jagged. A sick feeling churned in the pit of her belly.

"It's not a pretense!" It was a terrifying disaster.

Her heart picked itself up and began to run. Her mind whirled, trying to grasp at a course of action, but it was like trying to catch a snowflake, each one melting and disappearing on contact. This simply couldn't be true. He was wrong. His accountant hadn't looked hard enough.

"I need to talk to my bank," she managed weakly, touching her temple and finding it clammy. Surely they would have a sensible explanation. Please, God.

"It's Sunday."

"I can't wait to sort this out. It's thousands of dollars missing!"

"Is that right?"

"Don't be sarcastic!" It came out sharpened by the tears she was suppressing.

She had actually gone to sleep with a certain peace of mind, thinking she would finally be vindicated in his eyes. He would realize she wasn't the lowest form of life, and maybe they could move forward from there, toward… she didn't know what. Something she refused to imagine until it was possible, but it was beyond out of reach now. He still reviled her and, she suspected, thought even less of her for "lying" to him.

How could the money not be showing up in his account?

She had to tell Reeve. He had taken all the files last summer, when he'd been trying to get his student financing in place, to demonstrate need. They'd had a spat about it, actually. She hated anyone to know about their situation, feeling ashamed of it. He was incredibly bitter they were in this position at all—that *she* was. He couldn't help her pay it down. He needed every spare cent for tuition and food. He kept saying they had paid enough, but she saw no other option.

She texted him with shaky hands, keeping it vague, just asking him to scan the most important documents, not saying anything about Dante's accountant.

She wasn't surprised when there was no response. Reeve often spent Sunday at the library or some other quiet location, catching up on assignments or reading.

When she lowered her phone, Dante lifted his brows in expectation.

"What? Oh, for heaven's sake! You can't expect me to go skiing." She was having a crisis over here. And he *hated* her. He couldn't possibly want to spend the day with her. She certainly couldn't withstand hours of his derision.

"I don't want to disappoint my grandmother."

She opened her mouth, wanting to claim a need to visit the bank but then remembering it wasn't open. She considered phoning the hotline, but doubted the after-hours customer service would be able to do anything. This felt like an in-person problem that would require an official ordering a proper investigation into her own records and the bank's.

"I'm catching a bus in a couple of hours."

"My grandmother invited you to travel with her to Vancouver tomorrow."

"And where do you suggest I spend the night? I'm turning in my keys on my way out of here." Her backpack was buttoned up, and she was wearing the same clothes she'd worn last night.

Dante lifted one corner of his mouth, as sexy as he was arrogant.

"With you?" Wicked temptation coiled through her, much to her chagrin. He knew it, too, which made it worse. "Please," she dismissed in a scoff she wasn't able to pull off. "I was not fishing for an invitation."

His brows twitched in a silent, *Sure you weren't.* "How much do you want?"

"To spend the night with you?" she nearly screeched.

"To play tour guide on the mountain," he drawled, not bothering to hide the amusement crinkling his eyes. Those tiny lines were annoyingly attractive, making her wish she could prompt a smile that attractive without the mockery at her expense.

Awful man, twisting her up like this. "A thousand dollars," she blurted.

"Done."

"I was joking!"

"I wasn't. Let's go." He jerked his head at the door.

"No."

"You want to negotiate spending the night, as well?" His tone lowered to a velvety, lusty tenor that wrapped her in erotic bonds.

"Stop treating me like I can be bought." Her voice was barely audible, not nearly as belligerent as she was going for. She was damned near pleading for him to show some mercy—which was futile.

His gaze dropped to the boots she was wearing.

She shifted her weight, unable to hide them. "These were a gift."

"Ah." *So supercilious.* "What sort of gift would you expect from me, then?"

"Respect?" she suggested sweetly.

He held his eyelids at a cool half-mast. "That's something you earn."

"And I would earn buckets by taking your money, wouldn't I? As I told your grandmother last night, I teach kids to ski. One of their mothers gave me these. They weren't from some random man I slept with. I don't do that."

His expression didn't change. He said nothing, not even a skeptical, *No?*

She blushed, all too aware of how off the scale her reaction to him was and how it sent all the wrong messages. Maybe he had a reason to wonder about her, considering the way she'd behaved with him, but— Oh, damn him anyway.

"Can you get out of my life, please?" She swept the hair off her brow, aware she was trembling. Teary.

How could he not be getting her money?

He pushed his keys into his pocket with a quiet jangle,

gaze so intense it just made her feel all the more fragile. It was a struggle to keep her lips steady.

"I want to believe you, Cami, I really do," he said quietly. "But you can understand why I don't. Can't you?"

Her eyes grew hotter. "Can *you* understand that I'm freaking out, right now? I thought I was paying you back!" Her phone ought to be snapping in two. It was certainly going to leave a bruise across her palm where she was clutching it with all her strength.

His jaw hardened, and she heard a subtle exhale of tested patience.

Her phone rang. She glanced at the screen, saw it was Reeve. "Hi," she answered.

"What do you need those papers for? I thought you were on your way here."

"I haven't left yet." She flicked a glance at Dante, certain he could hear her brother as clearly as she could.

"Good, because Seth's brother just got here. I said you were coming, but if he could use the couch tonight—"

"That's fine." Cami tried not to wince. The suite belonged to Seth, so she couldn't really take the sofa from his brother. "I can stay with Sharma." Probably. "But can you send the scans? I don't want to wait."

"I'm at the library. It'll be a few hours before I'm home. Why? What's up?"

"I want to check something at the bank in the morning," she prevaricated, then hurried to forestall more questions. "I'll text when I'm on my way. Happy studying. Eat a vegetable. Coffee beans don't count."

"If you were a science major, like me, you'd know different. Over 'n' out."

She ended the call and texted Sharma, then faced Dante again. Why was he even still giving her the time of day?

Oh, she had such a burning desire to prove herself to

him. If she could just get him to believe this one thing...
But what would it change? Her father's betrayal still existed. Nothing could erase that, and it left her so exhausted inside, she wanted to cry.

"*Now* are you ready?" He moved to shoulder her backpack.

"You really insist on skiing?"

"I do."

Was she rationalizing? Finding a reason to spend the day with him?

She was filling her day with the one thing guaranteed to work out her stress. That's what she told herself as she closed her apartment for the last time and followed him out.

Cami certainly knew her way around the village, the hill and, most important, skis. He bought some, since he would be in town a few weeks.

She quizzed him thoroughly about his preferences and experience before recommending a pair, shrugging off her extensive knowledge of edges and bounce, wax and seasonal conditions in the area. "I'm a geek for this, what can I say?"

She disappeared while he was picking out ski pants and a pullover, leaving him mulling that she had nothing to gain from what she had just done except personal enjoyment. There was no attempt to earn a commission or his favor. It seemed an act of selflessness, which aligned with her acting so kindly toward his grandmother, but still went against his preconceived assumptions.

The way she had seemed genuinely alarmed over the missing money transfer was another puzzle piece that didn't fit. He was trying to work out what she thought she could gain from such an outrageous lie when he met up with her at the lift line.

She wore rented skis and clothes he'd seen her pull out of her backpack, which she'd stored in the back of his SUV—a thin black turtleneck, skintight yoga pants and a lightweight red windbreaker. Sexy as hell.

His brain blanked, unable to think of anything else.

It didn't help that in that moment the sun broke through the thin film of clouds, making her that much more incandescent with silvery streaks in her hair. She perched a pair of sunglasses on her nose and smiled with an excitement that was contagious and utterly entrancing.

"You said you like powder?"

It was why he'd wanted an early start. All that rain in the village last night was reputed to produce a foot of talcum-like snow at the top. Left to his own devices, he might have found a pocket or two, but Cami knew all the bowls and untracked slopes and the shortest distance between them.

He let her lead, and they roared down one untouched run after another. By the time the snow was growing heavy under the warmth of afternoon sun, he was pleasantly tired.

"Lunch?" It was closer to happy hour.

"I should take a break," she agreed. "I haven't skied that hard in ages."

He frowned, realizing fine trembles were quivering through her. "You should have said you were getting tired."

"Your grandmother wanted us to have fun," she reminded. "I'll take the beginner run to the lodge. You can take the diamond, if you like."

"I'll stay with you, but there's a chalet midway, isn't there? Let's eat there."

She nodded, and he followed at a distance so he could make sure she didn't fall.

He'd watched her more than once today, convinced that at least her family's reasons for going to Italy had been genuine. She wasn't afraid of speed, and her turns were a thing of beauty, precise even now, when she was being lazy, playfully kicking up a spray of snow as she criss-crossed the slope.

She moved gingerly once they removed their skis and were shown to an outdoor table on the overlook, though.

Dante ordered white wine and shareable appetizers, then asked, "Have you pulled something?"

"Just an old break that wants to be babied." She buried the response in her glass of water, gaze hidden behind her sunglasses. Then her nose turned to the stark white peaks jabbing at the intense blue sky. "That would make a nice backdrop for a selfie if you want one for your grandmother."

He took out his phone and they moved to the rail. The view of rolling peaks gave a sense of being on top of the world.

They turned their backs to it and he flicked to his camera setting, looping his free arm around her. She stiffened and flashed a startled glance up at him, flushing with instant awareness.

The simmer of lust hadn't abated in him. Her slender figure was undeniably feminine, yet strong and resilient. She smelled like wilderness and woman. The weight of her resting against him had his skin feeling too small to contain him.

As they held eye contact, and the pink in her cheeks deepened, the smolder inside him grew to an inferno, but there was more beneath the physical response. He was oddly pleased by this perfect day. Something like gratitude welled in him that she'd made it so enjoyable. He leaned in to kiss her, unable to resist.

She gasped and her mouth parted under his, receptive and delicious, clinging and encouraging, her hunger as depthless and instant as his own. As with the other two times, the match caught immediately. Passion flared so high and quick, it singed his brows.

With a tiny sob, she abruptly pulled her head back, lashes wet and blinking. "Please don't."

His blood drummed in his ears as he hovered inches from kissing her again, taking in the pang of her voice, nearly fearful, and the anguish in her wet lashes.

"I don't know how to handle this," she whispered. "Please don't embarrass me in front of people just to prove you can."

She wasn't playing coy. Her distress was real and worked like a burr into his heart, prickly and uncomfortable. He did like knowing he provoked such an unfettered response in her, but he wasn't trying to degrade her with it. He wanted to drown in it. *With* her.

She tried to slip away and he tightened his arm, snapping back to the business at hand. "Smile," he said gruffly, hand not quite steady as he held up his phone.

She swallowed, lifted her sunglasses into her hair and swept a fingertip under each eye, then tilted her face up to the screen. "Turn it to video."

He did and she smiled, fresh-faced and beaming with natural beauty, yet so unguarded, it caused an unsteadiness in his chest.

"Thank you, Bernadetta. We've had a wonderful day." Her voice was husky, and she blew a kiss with a hand that trembled.

"*Grazij*, Noni," he said, arm tightening around Cami

in an impulse to protect and reassure. He wanted to insist he would never hurt her, but he already had.

The fist clenched with righteousness inside him gave a twist of guilt. He kept his turmoil from his expression as he scanned to capture the view behind them before ending the recording.

"*Grazij*, Cami," he said as he released her to send the clip.

"I enjoyed it." She flashed him a look of lingering vulnerability, then moved to their table, seeming to deliberately look for a more neutral conversation as she commented, "It's nice that you're so close to her. My grandparents were gone before I was old enough to remember them."

Their wine had been delivered. They sat, clinked, sipped and sighed.

"It's too bad she isn't seeing more of the area." Her sunglasses were still on her hair, leaving her serene, sun-kissed expression wide open for his admiration. She looked across the view the way he looked across the vineyard at home. Like it brought her peace. Restored her.

For one second, he wondered if he could blame Stephen for indulging her, if mountaintops were where she belonged. He shook off the damaging thought, saying, "She was here with my grandfather years ago. Nostalgia brought her. I think she's disappointed by the signs of progress. She prefers to stay in her hotel room where she can pretend he just popped out for ice."

The signs of age in her were eating at him.

"They traveled extensively when my grandfather was building their fortune. When she heard we'd bought property here and said she'd like to see it, I thought it was a resurgence of her old travel bug, but it's more about revisiting a place she enjoyed with my grandfather. That's why she walked to the Tabor the other day. I arranged a car, but she preferred memory lane. Last night at dinner was the first time she's talked about anything but being here with him. I don't mind. She's telling me stories I've never heard, but it's made me realize how much she misses him."

It made him realize how much he'd been in his own world, concentrating on work at the expense of spending time with her.

"How long were they married?"

"Almost fifty years."

"Amazing." Her gaze eased into wistfulness that faded to melancholy. "It must have been so hard for her to lose him."

"It was."

"You must have been very close to him, too. You said you lived with them after your parents died? How old were you?"

"Eight." He scratched his cheek, becoming aware he was sharing far more than he meant to. He took a sip of wine.

"So young." She frowned, introspective. "But there's no good age, is there?" The empathy in her gaze dropped the bottom out of his heart. How had they come to get so personal? "Do you have brothers and sisters?"

"No." He had to clear his throat. The abandonment instilled by his parents' death had been unbearable, making him wish for siblings at the time, but it was a very long time ago. His grandfather's loss had hit him hard, though, stirring up his sense of being adrift. Losing his grandmother would be the same grief all over again, which was why he couldn't bear to contemplate it.

"But I have, quite literally, hundreds of cousins. Aunts and uncles galore." All of whom he was responsible for. If the weight of that was heavy at times, well, that didn't matter. They were all the family he had.

"I always thought being part of a big Italian family would be fabulous." Her mouth tilted. "Is it?"

"Sicilian," he was compelled to correct, then shrugged, impatient to move on from talking about himself. "I have no complaints. You have just the one brother?"

"Reeve, yes."

"Older?"

"Four years younger."

Their food came, a sampler of local specialties including elk tartar, seared scallops on nasturtium leaves and smoked salmon with sunchoke chips.

"Thank you." She smiled shyly, wariness still hovering around her edges. "I ran down my groceries and only had a yogurt cup for breakfast."

Before he could remark on her being so active on very few calories, she asked, "If you're into self-driving cars, how did you come to buy out the Tabor?"

"I took over the family corporation, Gallo Proprietà, when my grandfather died. We have holdings in other interests, but it's mostly hotels, restaurants, some shipping and other import-exports."

"I know what Gallo does, but that's what I mean. Self-driving cars aren't really in the company's repertoire. Why are you running a resort conglomerate if your passion lies in something completely different?"

"I was always intended to be my grandfather's successor. I took a double major in business and computer engineering because it interested me. When I left school, self-driving was still a sci-fi story, but I believed in it. My grandfather believed in me, and we all expected him to be around longer than he was. It seemed a safe bet to explore my hobby for a few years, but we lost him unexpectedly. I had to put it aside and take up the leadership at Gallo."

"Do you like running it?"

"I don't dislike it. It doesn't matter either way. I did what needed to be done." Did she realize how closely she was skating onto thin ice?

"Have you pursued anything to do with cars since then?"

Not that he admitted to anyone, having learned the hard way to keep his cards against his chest. "Why? Are you looking for another bite of technology to profit from?"

The pretty inquisitiveness that had grown in her eyes dimmed to hurt. "And here we are again," she murmured in a tone that cooled several degrees. "I can't blame you for being cynical, but I'm not my father. I'm just making conversation."

So much for a pleasant day.

"When did Stephen—?" he started to ask, since he had been wondering.

"Eight years ago." She had stopped eating to dig into the pocket of her jacket, pulling out a credit card.

"Put that away," he growled.

She set it on her phone and looked for their server.

"Put it away or I'll take it."

She scooped both phone and card into her lap, glaring at him. "I'm not going to sit here and be accused of things I haven't done."

"I liked him," he bit out, furious all over again, just like that. Hurt. Betrayed. "That's why I couldn't believe he did that to me." He picked up his wine, but it tasted sour. He'd lost his appetite, too. "How did the crash happen? Drunk driver?"

"Icy roads." Her voice held a crack, and the words gave the knot around his heart a hard, abraded yank. "I got a job at a ski hill in Banff and was moving there for the winter, so I could train in my off-hours."

"How old were you?" She couldn't be more than twenty-five now.

"Sixteen."

"Is that when you broke your leg?"

"Yes." She didn't have to tell him she felt guilty for being the reason they were on the road. He could hear it in the heaviness of her voice. Could read it in the anguish tightening her profile. That also caused a weird pang in his chest.

"It wasn't just a broken leg, though, was it?" He looked at the white line next to the hollow at the base of her neck.

"Collarbone and a punctured lung. I had six surgeries over two months, then rehab for a year. Lucky to be alive, so I can't complain."

Reeling under the idea that she might have died, he asked, "Was your whole family in the car?" He already knew they had been.

Her mouth tightened. She nodded. "Mom died instantly. I was unconscious. Dad talked to Reeve for a few minutes, tried to tell him what to do, how to stop the bleeding. Reeve was twelve and had a broken arm. He managed to climb up the embankment to flag down help. It took a while for a car to come along, but they stopped, which is why I'm still here. That's why we always stop."

The hairs on the back of his neck lifted, thinking he might never have met her if not for those strangers.

"That's why I helped your grandmother. That's why Reeve wants to be a doctor. He felt so helpless. Don't interfere in his plans, Dante." She looked him dead in the eye, hers glossy and bright. "It's not about my father or what he might have cost you. It's about helping people you and I don't even know and never will."

Dante hadn't consciously thought her brother was becoming a plastic surgeon or some other high-paying specialist, but to hear he had such a personal, karmic reason to pursue a medical degree took him by surprise. Unsettled him.

Careful, he reminded himself. Fagans were liars.

But this was too brutally real. He'd seen the scars. He could hear the agony in her voice.

"What happened after the accident? Where did you go?"

"A group home." She pulled her lightweight jacket around her. "Reeve was able to stay with a school friend. I was glad about that. They were good people. But taking him was a hardship, not that they would say so. They couldn't take me, as well. I was fine."

It struck him that he'd known her barely forty-eight hours, and he couldn't count the number of times she had assured him she was "fine."

"It was hard to see him, though. I was in Edmonton and he was in Calgary. Once I turned eighteen, I moved to Calgary, found work and an apartment. Got custody of him. We figured it out from there."

Her phone pinged and she flicked at the screen. "Reeve is home. I'm sending you the documents he scanned."

Dante's phone pinged, but he didn't look at it.

"What?" she prompted, frowning at his hesitation.

"He's had all day to concoct something," he admitted, trying to be dismissive, but he was affected by all she'd just said. Surgeries. Family broken and sent to a group home, yet she was quick to smile and offer help.

Her jaw dropped open, astonishment hollowing her cheeks. Then her eyes grew sharp and bright, brow spasming once before she looked away.

"I'm wasting my time." She stood and walked out.

If he called out to her, she didn't hear. She was too busy trying not to let on that lactic acid had set her leg on fire.

She clung to the rail down the outer stairs to the ski rack, gritting her teeth.

Do. Not. Cry. He wasn't worth it. But she was dangerously close to tears, and it wasn't all physical. He kept breaking down her defenses, giving her a day fashioned straight from her most cherished dreams, then kissing her so tenderly she damned near cried at the sweetness of it.

She had put a stop to that kiss, which had taken monumental effort, but she had been feeling so fragile under the press of his mouth. He could have had her making love in public, she was that susceptible to him.

She couldn't understand why or how he stripped her down so easily. She had poured her heart out about her parents, reliving the pain, trying to earn some tiny shift in his regard by conveying there had been a cost. He didn't need to punish her. She lived in torment every day. At the same time, she felt enormous empathy for him that he had lost his own parents.

Yet he couldn't even be bothered clicking his phone to glance at the albatross he had placed around her neck after she had already lost everything.

They had absolutely nothing left to say to one another. And it gutted her.

She took the more gradual green run down to the bottom, skiing cautiously and mostly on her good leg. She was shaking with exertion when she turned in her skis. Maybe some of her tremble was rage, but she was too tired to pick it apart. She just wanted to get to the bus station—

Oh, *damn*. Her backpack was in the back of Dante's SUV. Dear God, would this man never stop torturing her in one way or another?

Gathering her things from her locker, she limped outside, wondering if he had already left. She would have to wait on a bus and go to his hotel, wait there for him.

"Cami."

Her nemesis was right there, skis off, changed and everything, looking dark and glowering as a god of wrath.

"How—?"

"I took the black run."

Of course he had. "Rub it in, why don't you?" She limped around him. "I need my backpack." She was furious and hurt, most especially because he had ruined her favorite thing in the world—skiing. Today had been perfect. For a while.

She sniffed.

Don't cry!

She suddenly found herself swooping toward the sky, horizontal, as if she'd slipped on ice and was flying up, but she landed in the cradle of his arms.

"What the *hell* are you doing?" Her oversize handbag swung off her shoulder, and she thought she was going to tumble as she grappled to secure it.

He was so strong, he held her firmly until she stilled again. It felt amazing to be carried with such confidence. Strange and wonderful and terrifyingly good. She hated him, wanted to bash him, but her nose clogged with emotion and her throat stung. His virility made her weak. She felt safe, held like this. Coddled. It took everything in her to resist curling into his embrace and sobbing against his neck.

Then he spoke and his voice was so grim, he chilled her blood.

"How the hell do you know the name Benito Castiglione?"

"You read it?" She let him carry her while she searched his expression, desperate for a sign that what he had seen had changed his mind about her.

He looked worse than skeptical or remote. Hostile. Furious.

Chest going hollow, she said weakly, "I don't know him. He's just the guy who told us where to send the money and how much. Why? Who is he?"

"He *was* my patent lawyer. But he's dead. He died a few days after your family left Italy."

CHAPTER FIVE

CAMI BLINKED, TRYING to comprehend.

A tiny spark of hope danced in her periphery, wanting to believe this news meant the money was sitting in a dormant account somewhere and would be returned to her like lotto winnings. But deep down she knew that wouldn't happen. No, she knew she had lost that money as surely as she'd lost the Tabor job and her parents and any chance at a gold medal. That's how her life *worked*.

She stopped trying to think at that point.

Her life had fallen apart that many times, she simply couldn't face another level of disaster. That's why she'd gone skiing. The world looked different from the top of a mountain. Up there, she was a tiny organism on a timeless planet. For a little while, she had skied fast enough to outrun reality.

But like a deadly game of snakes and ladders, she had landed at the bottom yet again. Her emotions slithered and coiled into all the dark places she had visited over the years, which was a miasma of fear and depression. She tried to think what her next steps should be, but only found a void. Her brain was paralyzed.

She swiped at a tickle on her cheek, realizing she was crying. Dante had put her into the passenger seat of his rental, and she was leaking silent tears like a giant, pathetic baby. Searching her bag, she came up with a tissue and blew her nose, trying to scrape her composure together.

Dante pulled to a stop and she squeezed her eyes closed and open, blinking hard to see through her matted lashes. They were at his hotel.

Well, what did she expect? That he would drive her back to her apartment building? They weren't friends. She had not—despite heroic efforts—paid him back a dime of the money her father had stolen. He owed her nothing.

Her breaths grew tighter as it sank in that she had lost her chance to prove she wasn't a liar. There was no earning his good opinion now. She would only sound like more of a raving lunatic. He had a right to feel contempt toward her, but it hurt like hell that he still did.

The valet opened her door and she slid out, gingerly putting weight on her sore leg as she limped to the back of the vehicle for her backpack.

"Dante."

He turned back from walking toward the entrance. His dark glower cut her in two.

What remained of her fragile self-worth shrank further into a hard ball inside her chest. Her voice sounded fraught when she spoke, waving at the back of his SUV. "I need my backpack." She'd sleep on the floor at Reeve's. It wouldn't be the first time.

What would her brother say about all of this? She was supposed to be older and wiser, but she had messed up *again*.

This was so unfair. Everyone had things go wrong in their life, but no one's life went *this* wrong, did it? When she was trying so hard to be good and do the right thing?

"We need to talk. Come inside."

"I can't." Her emotions were barely held in check. Once she had processed all of this and figured out a course of action, she would be fine, but right now it all seemed so big and overwhelming. Impossible. Where had the money gone?

Don't be pathetic. No more tears. She bit her lip, fighting the pressure in her chest and behind her eyes.

"You need me to carry you?" His voice was gruff as he came toward her. "Do you need a doctor?"

"No. I mean I can't talk to you. It hurts too much," she said baldly, hand trembling as she swept her fingertips beneath her eyes.

A muscle pulsed in his jaw. "I want to know exactly what is going on." He put his arm around her, not really giving her a choice as he took most of her weight and drew her into the hotel.

She went because she was tired and had nowhere else to go. She needed to sit down and think, maybe get a few answers of her own. She went because, just for a minute, she needed to lean on someone stronger. Even if he hated her.

He didn't release her in the elevator. He smelled really good, like snow and pine and spicy man. She stood there dumbly against him, absorbing his body heat, barely resisting tilting her head against his powerful chest, grateful for human contact when she was feeling so hideously small and persecuted.

A moment later, they entered what had to be the platinum penthouse. It was a beautiful space with a main floor lounge in soft earth tones and buttery leather furniture, cozy accent pillows and a gas fireplace throwing off heat. There was a discreet kitchenette around the corner with a powder room beyond. Stairs led to what she presumed was a master bedroom in a loft while a wall of windows rose up both stories, overlooking the mountains. On a summer's day, four doors would fold back on themselves, opening to a terrace and letting nature inside.

"This is really nice," she murmured as she moved to look at the view turning golden with the last of the day's sun.

"Noni doesn't like stairs or she would have had it." He turned away and began making coffee, asking if she took cream and sugar while the machine gurgled.

She dug into her handbag, coming up with a blister pack of pain pills with two left. She popped them out and limped over to pour herself a glass of water, quivering under his watchful eye as she swallowed.

"Why did you ski so hard when it's not good for you?"

She had wanted to spend time with him. That was the uncomfortable truth. Her heart squeezed. Too much about this man affected her. Pulled at her so strongly, she was now just a frayed mess of loose threads.

"I won't get another chance for a while. Make hay while the sun shines, right?"

Cami's wan smile and the way she avoided his gaze didn't strike him as completely honest, but Dante didn't know what to believe anymore. He shook his head and carried their coffee to the table in the lounge.

She followed and sank onto the sofa, then picked up her mug, wrapping her hands around it. Her nail beds were white, and the tip of her nose red. He probably should have sent her into the bath, but he needed answers. He was still in shock after seeing Benito's name attached to a letter dated a mere two years ago.

"So." He hitched his pant leg as he sat down across from her. "Explain."

"I—" The anxiety around her eyes increased. "I don't

know how. I thought I'd been paying you back all this time. Not from when we left Italy. I didn't know what was going on then. Only what I told you before, that my parents kept us in the dark about a lot of it. I only knew we had to sell everything. My *skis*." She tried to throw away the remark like it didn't matter, but her voice thinned. The way her brow crinkled in a small flinch revealed how hard that had been for her.

Judging by her passion for the sport, he could imagine what a stab in the heart it had been. Almost as lethal as when he'd realized his precious design work had been copied from his computer and given to his competitor.

"I assumed later that Dad had made a lump sum payment to you, but I have no proof of that. Apparently, I don't have proof of anything." Her empty hand came up.

If she'd been in a witness box and he in the jury, he couldn't have picked apart her visage more thoroughly. The slant of her lashes, the color returning to her cheeks, the tension in her brow and the pull at the corners of her mouth.

He searched meticulously for clues as to whether she was lying or telling the truth, half thinking he should have gone with his first instinct and let her ski away and out of his life once and for all. As she had walked out on their late lunch, he had told himself she wasn't worth the head games. He was better than this. Smarter.

But he hadn't been able to resist glancing at the attachments she'd sent. The second he'd seen Benito's name and the date, his brain had exploded. He'd gone after Cami only to see her skiing away on one leg. He hadn't realized she'd cut down the beginner run until he was on the steepest one and couldn't see her. He'd caught up to her at the bottom, but he'd been worried—sickly worried—when she took so long to show up.

The effect she was having on him was as disturbing as all the rest. Part of him still wanted to walk away from all she was stirring up, but he couldn't. Not just because of this new twist with Benito, either. He resented feeling this compelled by her. *Ensnared.* How was she even doing it?

He let his fist land on the arm of his chair as he made himself focus on the external facts, rather than trying to unravel the internal.

"Are these all the letters you've received from Benito?"

"Just the most recent. Did you see the one where I asked for a phone call with you a year ago?"

"Why? What did you want to say to me?"

"That—" She struggled a moment. "I know you don't care, but this has been difficult. Finding the money." Her tone grew raw enough to scrape at his conscience. "I was trying to help Reeve with school. I wanted to work out a different payment scheme. He said you wouldn't negotiate. That I had to stick to what was agreed or go to court."

"Agreed by whom? Your father?"

"I don't know." She looked conflicted. *Afflicted.* "I didn't know anything concrete about what Dad had done until I was out of the system and moved to Calgary. Some government-appointed something-or-other handled the probate on my parents' estate while I was still in hospital. The only records I ever saw were the papers that Benito forwarded. All I knew was that my parents had been broke. There was nothing to come to us, but the will stipulated that once I turned legal age, I could be Reeve's guardian, so I made that happen. He'd been with me a few months when the letters started arriving."

"From Benito."

"Yes." She nodded. "I was really scared. I couldn't afford a lawyer, especially for an international crime. He sent Dad's confession and that said it all. Dad was guilty and had promised to pay you back a ridiculous sum." She looked to the ceiling, as if trying to keep the moisture in her eyes contained. "I'm not *you*. I don't have a family corporation behind me with properties all over the world. I have a used anchor of a laptop and my mother's wedding band. There was nowhere for me to even begin finding that money. But I know I'm on the hook for it, since I'm pretty sure Dad took it to pay for my training. I'm not trying to dodge it, Dante. I'm just saying, you can't get blood from a stone. I've been doing the best I can."

He thought of the tiny apartment with the well-used furniture. The relic of a mobile phone and the fact she had taken over-the-counter medication, not prescription opiates.

But she was also very protective of her brother's aspirations.

"What happened after you started sending the payments?"

"I wound up overextended and got us evicted because I missed rent." Her voice was heavy with culpability. "I lost Reeve for a couple of months until I got on my feet again. He's never forgiven me for that." She sighed heavily. "Life lessons, right? The social worker was actually really helpful. Got me a grant so I could take the hospitality program and that led to my jobs with hotels and the transfer here when Reeve started going to school in Vancouver. Rent in this town is killing me, though. That's why I thought the job at the Tabor was a good move. I would finally have some breathing space, but…"

He had pressed the detonator on that.

He set the side of his finger along his lips, trying to work out whether she was the victim of a con or trying to make *him* into one. Again.

"What happened to Benito?" she asked.

"He was murdered over gambling debts, if the rumors are true."

"Oh, my God!"

"Yes, it was quite a shock. Especially as he hadn't yet filed my patents. I turned to one of his colleagues, but there wasn't much they could do except offer advice. The evidence against your father was circumstantial. They advised me I could spend years and a fortune trying to prove his guilt, and probably never get restitution, or I could settle for a confession and a promise of a settlement. Which is what I did, keeping the whole thing as confidential as possible, so as not to damage the viability of Gallo Proprietà. We were in rough shape. I had to be careful."

"I'll go to the bank tomorrow and stop my auto withdrawals, ask them to dig up what they can about who owns the account where the payments have been going and switch them to you." She touched two fingers between her brows. "I just feel like such an idiot. It never once occurred to me to check he was a legitimate lawyer. Or that he was *alive*."

Dante belatedly picked up his phone and forwarded the attachments from her brother to his own lawyer, requesting an investigation.

"Stopping payment should flush out another communication from the fake Benito, right?" she asked.

He tilted his head, agreeing with her logic, even if he still had reservations about whether the fake Benito had been created in Italy or on her brother's laptop.

A shadow passed behind her eyes. "You're still suspicious of me. I guess I can't blame you, but… I don't know how to convince you. I don't know how to fix this. This theft has been an awful cloud that has hovered over me for years. I look back and feel so selfish. So single-minded and stubborn. So *responsible*."

She swallowed, looking ill.

He ought to revel in her self-recrimination, but he couldn't help thinking her drive was the quality a champion needed. Her lack of fear and love of speed would have taken her only so far. True achievement took grit. In fact, she probably wouldn't have recovered from her injuries if she hadn't had that blind will to overcome obstacles.

A strange regret hit him that he hadn't paid more attention when her father had spoken about her. He vaguely recalled an invitation to visit their chalet and watch a race. Dante had been caught up in his own goals and self-interest, but wished now he'd seen her when she'd been coming into her own as an athlete. They'd been well-matched today. He could only imagine how much better she would have been if she hadn't been injured. She would have been on podiums; he had no doubt.

"You were eighteen when the letters started coming?"

She nodded mutely.

A gullible age. She'd been in a vulnerable position, playing parent to her brother. He could see how easy it would have been for someone to take advantage of her. But who would know enough of the circumstances to do it? Only the main players, most of whom were dead. One of Benito's colleagues, perhaps? The criminals to whom he'd owed debts?

Was this a confession of youthful ignorance? Or a well-honed ability to manipulate?

That face of hers was the problem. She projected innocence with those earnest eyes and delicate features. Skin he already knew was soft as down. Lips like flower petals. He only had to look at her and he ceased to care what she may or may not have done. He only wanted to devour her.

Heat began to pool in his lap. He shifted restlessly.

"I really do want to compensate you, Dante. I'd do anything to have this paid off and pushed into the past."

"Would you?" He couldn't help it. The haze of sexual need was coming over him, thickening his voice.

She flashed him a stunned look, then her hands went into her lap. She stared out the windows a moment, lips pressed into a flat line, eyes holding a sheen. "Why do you keep treating me like that? I've never slept with anyone for money or clothes or jewelry. I've never slept with *anyone*. Period."

"Ha!" Now he knew she was lying, and there was something terribly disappointing in that.

She glared at him. "Why is that so impossible to believe?"

"You're twenty-*four*."

"Don't judge me by *your* standards."

"You honestly expect me to believe you're a virgin?"

"When have I had time to date? What man wants to sleep with a woman with the kind of baggage I cart around?" She flung her hand through the air. "I don't care if you believe me or not! It's really none of your business, is it? Oh, wait. That's what you keep accusing me of, isn't it? Trying to make a business transaction of trading my body for the debt my father owes you. First of all, wow. Wish I'd thought of that sooner. So much easier than working three minimum wage jobs. Second, exactly what is a woman's virginity worth these days, anyway? Maybe I *am* interested."

Cami spat out the words, hot with insult, adding bitterly, "Times have changed, by the way. It's not the woman selling herself who is reviled. It's the man who takes advantage of her."

His cheeks went hollow before he stood abruptly. She threw herself into the sofa back. He barely leaned toward her, but intimidated all the same. She held her breath.

"I don't think either of us is vile. *That* is the problem." He shoved his hands into his pockets. "I keep thinking I want to sleep with you regardless of what your father did. That makes me a stupid man. I cannot let you take advantage of me the way your father did."

"I'm not trying to! I don't—" Were they really talking this baldly? It felt as if she was stripped naked. "I don't know why I keep kissing you. I don't act like that. I swear I don't."

"If your father hadn't damned near destroyed me, I would call it what it seems to be. Chemistry. Sexual compatibility."

How romantic.

She looked out the window again, toward her first love—snowy slopes. Had it only been a few hours ago that they'd traced through powder, crossing paths to braid a scrolling line into the mountainside? It had felt divine. Like they were made for each other.

"I always thought that when I felt like this about someone it would be…" She swallowed, embarrassed. "You know," she mumbled.

"A husband? That is not going to happen." His voice turned so cold and hard it left bruises in her ears.

"Someone I knew well enough to care about them," she corrected in a voice that frayed around the edges. "You honestly think I'd want to marry you? Yeah, that would work out, with this hanging over me. Talk about selling myself into sexual slavery."

He didn't like that. His expression grew even more stony. "Be careful, Cami. I'm trying to be patient, to hear you out."

She bit back a snide, *You started it.*

"I don't want to be attracted to you, either," she admitted, feeling naked as she openly acknowledged this wild compulsion inside her. "You have been squeezing my life in an iron fist for years. You have wiped out what little I have managed to build here, in the first place that felt like home. I have no future, not unless you grant me one. *You* have all the power, Dante. All I have is a thread of self-respect, earned by trying to do the right thing all these years. But you're taking even that, acting like my... my very natural reaction toward you is some kind of commercial product." She stood and looked for her handbag. "I can't keep doing this."

"You're not leaving."

Her racing heart thudded to a halt in her chest. "Excuse me?"

His expression was remote. "I'm going to the bank with you tomorrow."

"Fine. I'll meet you there."

"I'm not risking you taking off before morning."

"You don't even trust me to show up to one of the most important meetings of my life?"

"I do not."

Her heart stumbled all over again. "So you'll what? Lock me in here?" The thought of spending more time with him was terrifying. She had just admitted to attraction, and if she knew one thing about this man, it was that he didn't let an opportunity to get the better of her slide.

"So melodramatic," he drawled. "I'm extending my hospitality." Folding his arms, he added dryly, "Which includes the private jet tub upstairs."

Her muscles were so stiff, she very nearly whimpered at the lash of temptation that went through her. "That's just mean."

He moved to the house phone and said to a concierge, "I need a bag brought up."

CHAPTER SIX

DANTE DISAPPEARED TO talk with his grandmother, so Cami felt safe enough in the moment to use the tub. She needed time to think all this through and might as well work out her kinks while she did.

He turned up as she was about to enter the tub, making her heart dip and roll.

The room was humid with the scent of cedar off the paneled walls. The darkness outside disappeared behind the gather of steam against the window and the jets hummed beneath the burble of the churning water.

"I didn't realize you were joining me." She self-consciously kept her loosened robe over the ridiculously functional one-piece bathing suit she wore. It was bargain store brand in a flat blue, not sexy in the least.

Which was a good thing. He was only keeping her here because he didn't trust her, not because they had chemistry. *Sexual compatibility.*

She wished he hadn't named it. She dearly wished that was all it was for her, but her reaction to him was as emotional as it was physical. He was arrogant, yes, but he also showed great love for his grandmother. He had an admirable sense of duty to family, and his odd moments of protectiveness were positively swoon-worthy.

Her wobbly defenses disintegrated further as she took

in his broad shoulders and naked chest, flat abs and tiny red racer's suit. Something sharp and hot struck deep in her intimate places. The scrap barely covered his bits, revealing more than it concealed of the bulge at the top of his muscled thighs, making her curious as to whether he'd stay contained if he became aroused.

She yanked her gaze to the water, hot all over. With a flustered move, she threw off her robe, leaving it on the hook as she slipped into the water as quickly as her protesting muscles allowed.

He lowered into the other side of the round tub, mouth quirked in amusement as he spread his arms along the edge.

"What?" she asked crossly, suspecting he was laughing at her.

"Maybe you are a virgin."

She wasn't about to have *that* argument again. It hurt too much to hear him sound so cynical about it.

"Thank you for this," she made herself say, trying to steer toward a less intimate topic. She crooked her knee so the jet was aimed directly at her thigh. "A warm shower wouldn't have been enough."

"How did you start skiing?" His tone was lazily curious. He was relaxed, which should have put her at ease, but she was too sharply aware of him. Of herself and the swirling sensations in her middle and deeper that had nothing to do with the water.

"Mom raced." She tried to gather her scattered thoughts. "But she started late and didn't qualify for more than a few provincial games. She put my brother and me on skis from an early age, though."

"She supported your aspirations."

"A million percent."

"It wasn't you who drove the move to Italy, then. She wanted it for you."

"They both did, but once my coach said I should go, I pressed them until they made it happen." That was why the weight of guilt sat on her so indelibly. "What happened to your parents?"

"Boating accident. There was a storm."

"I'm sorry." Their gazes connected, and she felt that brief click that was more than sexual. Their stories were different, but they shared the same pain.

He broke the contact, slouching so he could rest his head back and look to the ceiling. As he sank down, something grazed her hip, making her start with a gasp. She realized belatedly it was his foot and glanced up in time to see his head come up. His mouth twitched.

His expression didn't change, but she felt the side of his foot nudge her hip. He was trying to get another reaction out of her while keeping that innocent look on his face.

She stared right back at him, deadpan, ultraconscious that things were happening below the surface they were refusing to acknowledge.

"Are you Catholic?" she asked abruptly, talking so she wouldn't think of the way a narrow line of hair had arrowed from his navel to the snug band of red drawn low on his hips. Damn. Now she was thinking about it.

"Not a very good one."

"Because you believe in birth control? Sex before marriage?" Why had she gone *there*? *Shut up, Cami.*

"Those are sins I confess to," he drawled. "Not something I 'believe' in."

"What do you believe in?"

He grew more serious. "Taking care of family. Loyalty. Responsibility."

She nodded agreement.

"Carpe diem, because you might not live to do the things you otherwise put off. Paying debts."

"Of course." She stiffened and lifted her leg out of the jet, setting her foot on the bench and massaging her thigh where her muscle felt itchy from the vibration of the forced water.

"Are you angry that you can't ski the way you want to?"

"Yes." She heard the rigidity in her voice. The resentment. "Are you angry you can't design cars?"

"Yes." For a long second, they shared another look of understanding, reflecting each other's frustration, connected at a soul level.

"But you could pursue cars in the future. You have the resources. Even if you wait until your retirement, it's always something you could go back to. I can't even try for senior games. My best hope is the occasional day like today."

He skimmed across to her, making her gasp at his sudden closeness.

His strong hands took possession of her thigh, so unabashed she instinctively tried to pull away, but he held on and dug his fingers into her tense muscles. "I didn't expect it to cost you so much. You should have said."

"Oh." She almost cried at the intensity of his touch, but the relief that came behind the pain had her shuddering and melting.

A very long time ago, she had had professional massages. His firm thumbs dug into her aching muscle with just the right amount of pressure. His hands kneaded their way up her thigh and down to her knee, then began working upward again.

"That feels really good."

She gave herself up to it, fingers gripping the edge of her seat, letting him find the tension and release it. Press and ease back, circle and stroke. Swirls of desire fluttered into her belly as his attentions went on. She tried not to reveal her reaction, even as secretive parts of her pulsed in yearning and her mind turned to thoughts she could no longer suppress.

His hands climbed her thigh again and she held her breath, imagination dancing toward "what if." What if he touched her *there*?

"Cami."

She barely heard him, his voice was so low. She dragged her eyes open and realized she had let her legs drift open. His hands were at the very top of her thigh, his thumbs tracing the leg of her bathing suit.

"I don't want you to be embarrassed by the way you react to me."

"Look at who we are. It's so wrong." It was true, yet she was turned inside out by the stillness of his hands, aching with longing because he was so near and yet so far.

"It's not smart." His arms gathered her to sit across his lap. She was so weak, she floated into place, entranced by the glow of desire in his eyes. "But it's not wrong."

She didn't see a difference, but she stopped caring. She lifted her mouth and he covered her lips in a hot, unhurried kiss, one that made her feel as though she was drowning, but delirious at being swept away.

Her butt cheek pressed into— He was hard. Really hard.

On the rare occasions she had made out with a man, this was always what made her alarm bells go off. She always ended things before her date started thinking she wanted to go further than she did.

She and Dante had barely got started, though. Her one arm crooked alongside his rib cage, and the other hooked around his neck so she could twist her torso into facing him while they kissed. And kissed and kissed.

Oh, he knew how to kiss! Five o'clock shadow abraded her chin, but she couldn't get enough of his lips. They were smooth and full, like an exotic fruit that was an aphrodisiac. The more she gorged on him, the more she wanted. She sought his tongue with her own, wanting that earthy contrast of textures, the deepening of intimacy.

She loved how he shaped her body, rocking her chest against his. She wiggled, encouraging the play of his fingers over her like he was a sculptor learning the shape of her spine, the curve of her backside, pausing to gently squeeze, then moving on, leaving a trail of inflamed desire in his wake. Her own hands splayed to stroke the supple skin across the cage of his ribs, the balls of his shoulders and the flex of his pecs.

Then, somehow—and she didn't understand why she did it or where she got the courage—she found his shape through the thin fabric in his lap. Drawing back, she looked into his face as she delved beneath the tight elastic waistband and closed her fist over what felt like smooth, wet satin stretched over a column of hot marble.

His breaths grew ragged as she explored him.

With his lashes so low, she could barely read the avid hunger in his gaze. He skimmed his hand between her thighs and eased her bathing suit aside, baring her to the hot water and the sweeping stroke of the backs of his fingers.

It was delicate, a taste, not a meal. Need sensitized her and a sob of pleading left her.

He kissed her as he fondled with more purpose, parting and exploring, making her twitch under the onslaught of sharp sensations, wet and dangerous, intimate and sure.

"Move your hand," he whispered against her lips, then covered her mouth in a deeper kiss.

She moaned a protest, wanting to keep touching him, but curled her arms around his neck, pressing her breasts to his chest.

He lifted his head enough to release a breath of laughter against her panting mouth. "I meant move your hand *on* me. Stroke me."

Oh. What an idiot! She ducked her head into his neck, aware by the shake that went through him he was laughing at her.

He was also removing her bathing suit! All the skin that had been covered turned silky and alive. It was a rebirth of sorts, making her feel new. He left her suit on the edge of the tub as she slid her hand under the water again, finding him, feeling him pulse in her touch as she gripped him. Caressed and explored.

He did the same to her and she quickly lost the plot.

With a helpless groan, she threw back her head, offering her mouth. He smothered her with his kiss. Ravaged her. Slid a long finger inside her and rolled his thumb, causing her to fill the room with cries of acute pleasure as he took her over the edge.

Had she given him any pleasure at all? She made a belated effort to squeeze him, but he stopped her, arms going hard around her as he stood in a sluice of water.

She was hot and lethargic and so incredibly aroused. Naked as he skimmed his gaze over her, inventorying her pale skin and white scars, the pink nipples that stood up even in the sultry heat of the spa.

As he looked her over, insecurity edged in. All she could think was that the ache he'd left in her hadn't been enough. She wanted a sharper stretch, a harder possession. She wanted him to make love to her. This man, the one who made her tremble. If he decided she didn't measure up...

"Are you really a virgin?"

"Yes." Was he going to call her a liar again? Reject her? She would die.

His nostrils flared. "Do you want to stay one?"

Stop? "No."

"Good." He carried her to his bed.

"We'll get the blankets wet." She started to sit up as he set her on the mattress.

He made a growling noise. "It doesn't matter." He stripped his microscopic suit and left it on the floor as he crawled over her, pressing her onto her back.

She tensed with nerves, hands going to his shoulders, not in protest, but caution. He was very intimidating, so big and muscled and *hard*. Like tensile steel beneath the press of her fingertips, but hot, so incredibly hot as he covered her wet, chilled skin with his own. They were both damp enough there was tack as he settled on her, sealing them together.

She had never been under the weight of another human, a *man*. Naked and trembling. She considered herself a strong woman, physically fit, but she was suddenly very aware of herself as small and slight. Vulnerable.

He could crush her. Hurt her. Break her in two.

He shifted his weight onto one elbow, heavy thigh pinning hers.

"When I saw this that first time, I wanted to kiss it," he said with a light trace of his fingertip against her collarbone, where the healed skin was sensitive and the bone still tender to the touch. He touched his lips to her scar, and her eyes fluttered closed under a swell of deep emotion, chest expanding so she could hardly breath.

How was this even happening? He was like a sorcerer. Brute force wasn't necessary. He cast a spell and overwhelmed her with her own sensuality. She was weak and conquered and she liked it. He didn't trust her and she probably shouldn't trust him, but as he nibbled his way up her neck, sending tingles through her nape, into her scalp and down to her nipples, she entrusted herself to him. Maybe the aggressive feel of his erection against her hip made her anxious, but it was the nervous excitement she had once experienced before a race. Anticipation of being wild and free.

Stroking her fingers through his damp hair, she brought his head up so they could kiss. She couldn't get enough of his mouth, and he seemed to like hers. Hunger met hunger and she found herself arching into him, naked breasts swollen and hard, all of her wanting to convey her surrender. It was instinctual. Elemental. *Mate with me.*

His big hand cruised up her waist and gathered her breast, then he lifted his head to watch his thumb play across her taut nipple, keeping up the teasing even when she gasped and writhed at the intensity of the sensation. Streak after streak of wired sensations sent pulses into her loins. Then he dipped his head and drew on her so strongly she gave a keening cry. Sexual heat flooded through her, piercing her sex. Any droplets of water left on their bodies evaporated in a sizzle that was nearly audible.

She stroked him with her whole body, loving the feel of his skin against her palms and belly and inner thighs. As her legs opened, he settled into the space, slid down and pushed her legs farther apart. *Claimed* her with his mouth.

Waves of pleasure worked their way through her as he stroked her with his tongue, the onslaught making her quiver with tension. With agonized need. She lost all inhibition. Gave herself up to whatever he wanted to do to her. She *belonged* to him.

Just as her peak neared, he rose over her, making her gasp in agonized denial. A plea hovered on her lips, tightened her chest, but she couldn't speak. His fierce eyes met hers, and she knew that *he* knew she was his. Utterly and completely. It was in the flare of his nostrils and the hard curl of satisfaction across his mouth.

But there was something else there. A glimmer of cynicism. He didn't quite believe she was a virgin. It was this infernal response of hers, clouding his view of her.

Reservation should have struck. Maybe resentment or refusal, but perverse anger hit instead. Let him take her and *see*. That would show him. Then he would know, once and for all, that she wasn't a liar.

Wouldn't he?

Either way, he was doing it. Reaching a long arm to the night table to retrieve a condom. As she watched him roll it on, a very feminine hesitation rose in her. Was it going to hurt?

She was about to find out. He settled so he was poised to enter her. She studied his face, tense and flushed and severe. He pressed and she instinctively stiffened, tightening all over, fingers splaying on the searing plane of his chest.

"No?" His gaze flashed to hers, white-hot as lightning.

"I'm sorry," she murmured, agitated. "I'm nervous." She made herself relax. Moved her hands to his sides, still wary.

He said something in Sicilian. His frown eased. He pressed a soft kiss on her lips and caressed where he was trying to invade. As a wash of pleasure returned in a sensual rush, she moaned and relaxed. He pressed into her.

It did hurt, but not a lot. A strong pinch and a determined stretch. A tremendous *fullness*. Incredible and incredibly intimate. He seemed to have a lot to offer. He
propped himself on his elbows, fingers in her hair as he
withdrew a fraction, then pressed in again. Each time
she thought that was it, he did it again, sinking deeper
each time.

She was shaking, thinking this wasn't the dreamy romantic act she had always imagined, but very, very real.
Everyone in the world did this, but it was the first time
she was doing it, and it was more physical than she had
expected. Carnal. Intense.

There was no hiding anything from him when connected to him this way. Her eyes might be closed, but she
couldn't hold back her small gasps. He had to know she
was trembling, even though he shook, too, shoulder blades
flexing under her hands.

She opened her eyes and saw his lips pulled back with
strain. A muscle pulsed in his jaw, and his breath hissed
through his teeth. Just as she thought she couldn't take any
more, he settled on her, belly to belly, fully seated inside
her, and opened his eyes to look into hers.

"Bedduzza," he breathed, thumb touching her temple.
"Hurt?"

A tear had leaked out the corner of her eye.

"It's just really… I didn't expect it to be this—" Intimate? Important? "It's overwhelming." She was different now. He was her first lover, and she would remember
forever that he looked so remote as he possessed her this
way. Fierce to the point of frightening. Yet tender enough
to kiss away her tear, leaving her feeling strangely divine.

"You're killing me." He eased her legs around his waist
and sank a fraction deeper, then he cupped her jaw. She
could feel the tension in his grip. The restraint. He said

something else in Sicilian before he covered her mouth in a kiss. Sweet and lavish, but with a purpose. He wanted to incite her passion and did.

Soon she was responding, moaning into his mouth, thinking a kiss was so much more significant when bodies were joined. She could feel him pulsing inside her. It made her needy and frustrated. She sank back into that world of sensation he seemed custom made to deliver to her.

He began to move.

It hurt, but assuaged at the same time. She didn't know what to do, but her body did. She undulated with him, finding the rhythm that fed the fire. They seemed as completely attuned to one another as they had been on the hill, meeting and parting, returning again and again to each other. Creatures of the earth doing earthly things.

As his tempo increased, so did her greed. Her arousal level. Somehow she was there again, ready to peak, clinging to him with every fiber of her being. Making agonized noises of acute pleasure while he moved faster and bit out something that could have been an order or a plea.

She couldn't hang on any longer. She let go and plummeted into the abyss, falling apart even as he pulled her in with him. His hips thrust deep and his cries underscored hers as they clung through the paroxysm that exploded, then melted them into a heap of boneless flesh.

Dante lay on his back, forearm flung across his brow, distantly aware of noises in the bathroom, but his brain was barely functioning. He didn't bother trying to discern what she was doing. He had managed to roll away long enough to remove the condom, noticed blood and handed her a tissue. She'd released a mortified gasp and retreated to the bathroom where she had left her things when she had undressed for the hot tub.

He stayed on the bed, sorry he'd hurt her, but wrung out by the best sex he'd ever had. His organ was still tingling. All of him was. His entire body was damned near singing like a choir.

He hadn't even meant to kiss her. When he had ordered her to stay, he really had been thinking he only wanted to keep an eye on her. Go to the bank with her tomorrow. Unravel the Benito mystery.

Okay, maybe sex had been hovering in the back of his mind because they'd acknowledged the elephant. *I don't want to be attracted to you, either.* Wanting her was a betrayal of himself, but fighting this attraction had proved to be beyond him. They were consenting adults, and he had thought she was as experienced as any millennial. He hadn't believed her about being a virgin. Not really. Not when she responded like she'd made love a thousand times.

He'd been as gentle as he could, once he discovered how tight she was, only really believing she was new to the act when the deed was done. When she'd had him in a vice of pleasure so acute it bordered on painful and a tear was trickling from her eye.

That fragility of hers had been the only thing that kept him this side of savage while a storm of possessiveness engulfed him. Maybe the imposition of restraint had made the build that much greater, he didn't know, but definitely he was affected by the knowledge he was the only man who'd ever enjoyed that passion of hers. Something truly base and barbaric wanted to be the only man who ever would. Their mutual release had been cataclysmic. Beyond his experience.

So good he already wanted to make love with her again.

So self-destructive. She was a lying, thieving Fagan.

Except she hadn't lied about being a virgin. That meant

he had to give a little more credence to her other claims. He absorbed that, disturbed. Suppose she *had* been paying him back in good faith. That meant there was a criminal making victims out of both of them.

She came out of the bathroom, footsteps heading toward the stairs.

He dropped his arm and saw she was wearing her miniskirt and droopy pullover. Did she have nothing else? He was sick of seeing her in that. He should take her shopping, as he would with any lover.

Is that what she was?

"Where are you going?"

She paused with her hand on the ball of the newel. Her teeth released her bottom lip into a small pout. Her brow crinkled with uncertainty. "To Sharma's."

An uncomfortable skip of alarm went through him along with his newfound possessiveness. His muscles tensed, ready to spring from the bed and drag her back there. "You're staying here, with me."

If he had any remaining doubts that she'd been a virgin, they were snuffed by her tortured profile as she looked away. He'd never witnessed such discomfort with post-lovemaking rituals. He always tried to keep things very friendly with his lovers, if casual. This wasn't casual, though. He and Cami were inextricably linked by their past and now by a unique experience. Her first time.

An edgy uncertainty wound through him. How would she remember this? How would he?

He would never forget her; that much he knew. The profoundness of this encounter was still hitting him, breaking down and rebuilding things inside him.

She kept her face averted, but he read her defensiveness. Underlying insecurity. Should he soothe and reassure? What message would that send?

As the silence protracted, she flinched and started down the stairs.

"Cami." He came up on an elbow.

She paused. Her shoulders fell. "I can't keep doing this, Dante."

"Neither can I," he lied, deliberately misunderstanding her. "You have done the impossible. Exhausted my libido."

"I'm sure you say that to all the girls," she shot back.

Ah. Now he understood. "You knew *I* wasn't a virgin." He curled his arm beneath his head and relaxed once more. "Frankly, you want your first experience to be with someone who knows the ropes."

"But I didn't expect it to be with a stranger. I barely know you! And I didn't expect to feel so..." Her jaw firmed as she faced him with a hint of cynicism. "Well, I guess I'm not supposed to feel anything, am I? That's how these things are supposed to work, aren't they?"

Why that stung, he didn't know. He came up on his elbow again.

"Come here." He patted the edge of the mattress. When she hesitated, he said, "Do you need me to come get you?"

She tightened her mouth and warily came across to perch on the side of the bed.

"Did I hurt you?" That question was burning a hole in his brain.

"No." She brushed at a fleck on her skirt. "I mean, a little. The normal amount, I suppose." She shrugged, blushing. "I'm fine."

He liked women, liked flirty ones who were sweetly perfumed, soft and indulgent of his needs. He liked to indulge them. Spoil them and pet them and enjoy the warmth of their bodies against his own.

This one was prickly and wary and someone he should

not trust. Nevertheless, she invoked a rueful remorse in him with her tart, "normal amount." He wished it was none.

He gathered her up and rolled so she was beside him on the bed, all elbows and resistant stiffness. She made a face and lifted her head off the pillow. "It's wet."

He threw it away and dragged a dry one into its place. Then he watched her try to avoid his gaze, expression grumpy. She wasn't trying to get away, but she didn't relax.

"I didn't believe you," he admitted, suspecting that was the real source of her desire to flee. "You're very sensual. That wasn't your first orgasm in the tub."

"Oh, please. I know how my own body works." She rolled her eyes.

"And now *I* do." He let that sink in, watching the pink that deepened in her cheeks beneath the fan of her lashes. "Does that bother you?"

"Yes. I get the feeling you've made a study of how to get that sort of reaction from women, and I'm just the latest specimen you've collected."

Nice. "So you regret giving me your virginity."

"A little." She reached to touch a button on the headboard. Sighed as she dropped her arm back to her side. "You already have all the advantages. Now you have this to lord over me, too."

"Why give it to me, then?" It was the other question sizzling in his brain.

Her mouth twisted. "I wanted to. I've never had much personal choice, so I take it where I find it."

He caressed her jaw, gently taking hold of it, feeling her tense, but he wanted to see into her eyes. They were brimming with anxiety. Defenselessness.

He stroked the backs of his knuckles into the warm

flesh beneath her jaw and below, down her throat, enjoying the way she shivered and softened. The *response* of this woman. She made him feel like a god. He wanted to strip her naked and bury himself inside her all over again, just to reach that level of supreme euphoria.

But she was so new to this, she didn't see how much power she had over him, which was a good thing.

He kissed her. Just long enough to find her response. To reassure himself it was there and, yes, maybe to reinforce his power over her. His hand was still on her neck, and he felt the throb of her pulse and the vibration of her helpless sob as it emanated.

He lifted his head and she ducked her chin. "What about you? Regret?"

"Yes."

Her breath rushed out and her eyes filled, stunned with injury. He touched her swollen mouth with his thumb, and she drew her lips in so the pad of his thumb rested on a flat line.

"I don't sleep with employees or anyone else with whom I have other types of relationships," he explained. "I prefer to compartmentalize. Keep lines drawn so feelings don't color facts."

She withdrew from his touch completely, sliding backward across the mattress. "And what you feel for me is hatred, isn't it? It bothers me that I made love with someone who hates me."

His chest tightened. Hatred was a damned slippery fish to hang on to right now.

Her lashes dropped and the corners of her mouth were heavy. "Maybe I deserve it, since it's my fault my father stole from you, but it still hurts." Her subdued voice held a lot of pain. "I said I'd do anything to get rid of that cloud over me, but I don't think this did anything except scrape away what little respect you might have had for me. So now I'm embarrassed and would prefer to leave."

"That option is not on the table."

"*Why*? I said I was a virgin and I was. Doesn't that earn a shred of trust?"

He couldn't let her go. That was the bald truth.

"Until I unravel this Benito mystery, I can't let my guard down with you." He knew that much, but he also knew he already had. "It will take some time for the bank to investigate, so you'll stay with me until we have some answers."

"*With* you. Here. In your bed." Her voice thinned to something that might have been resentment, but held an echo of longing, too. "Doing what? Paying off Dad's debt? How much did my virginity knock off the total, anyway? I'm such a terrible negotiator. I should have asked *before*."

She was throwing darts because she was hurt that he still mistrusted her. Her words still managed to get under his skin. "Do you want to put the past behind us or not?"

He meant that her snippy attitude wasn't helping, but she only railed on in the same vein.

"Let me guess. You'll also leave my brother alone if I sleep with you?"

"Sure." He had no intention of going after her brother. It was easy to agree.

Her eyes narrowed. "Exactly how many payments are you expecting?"

"We'll make love 'the normal amount,'" he quoted her pithily, through a smile that was more clenched teeth and growing ire. "But I won't make demands right now, if you're feeling delicate. Or salty."

"Oh, no," she said with a hot crackle in her tone. "If I'm going to get this debt off my back *on* my back, let's make sure I get it done."

"You really think you can shame me, you hellion?" He tangled his fingers in her hair, holding her pinned for gentle, gentle kisses. He teased and tantalized both of them until she was clinging to his lips with her own, moaning in frustration because his hand in her hair wouldn't allow her to lift her head and increase the pressure.

Her hands moved with agitation across his back, one snaking to try to take hold of his reviving shaft, but he caught both her wrists in one hand above her head. He used his free hand to caress her breast, taking his time to really appreciate the shape of her, the heat he could discern even through the knit of her pullover, the dainty circle of her areola and the exquisitely sensitive peak that jabbed beneath his thumb pad, making her breaths grow ragged.

She wriggled and made another noise of growing ardor, lifting her mound into the weight of his thigh where he pinned her hips to the bed.

"Dante," she gasped.

"I'm not a monster, *bedduzza*." He moved his hand to skim back and forth across her waist, stealing inch by inch beneath her pullover, feeling her tense stomach quiver and jump beneath his tickling caress. "Tell me you don't want this and I'll stop."

She made a tortured noise. "You'll make me want it anyway. Won't you?"

He found her braless breast and cupped the underside. She arched, trying to fill his palm. Her nipple stood like a shard of glass beneath the fabric of her top. They both ached for him to bare and lick and suck that taut tip, but he held off, nearly blind with desire. "If you really want to earn my trust, Cami, you have to be honest about what you want right now."

Her breath exhaled on a trembling hiss. "You," she confessed.

He gave her what she asked for.

CHAPTER SEVEN

CAMI WOKE ALONE. As she sat up, she breathed out a low, wincing breath. She was *so* sore. The jet tub might have forestalled some of the stiffness from skiing, but just as she hadn't let a few aches and pains hold her back from enjoying the slopes, she hadn't let it slow her down with Dante, either.

She buried her face in her hands, appalled. The man really did have an extraordinary libido, and apparently so did she.

Now she was paying for that physical activity. With a little whimper, she made her way into the shower, feeling only marginally better when she dried herself with aching arms. Her nipples were incredibly sensitive and even brushing her teeth was a tender exercise, making her look for bruising around her mouth. Her lips were chapped, but what had that man done to the rest of her? At no point had he been brutal, but he had been thorough.

And she'd loved it.

She was a sex fiend!

It was embarrassing, but as she thought of the way they'd come together again and again, the way his hands had felt on her body—his *mouth*… She was aroused all over again. Yearning and wanting another clash of flesh to flesh.

She clenched her eyes against her reflection, aghast by

the longing that overcame her, fresh and sharp. Glancing at the closed door of the bathroom, she wondered if he was still in the suite.

Be honest about what you want.

What *did* she want? Romantic love was not something she had been able to afford, quite literally. After losing their parents, her brother had been her world. Mentally, she'd felt miles ahead of men her age, and the few who had bought her coffee or a plate of pasta had been quickly scared off by her financial situation and depth of responsibility.

She had tucked away dreams of finding her soul mate like a pressed flower in a book, rarely remembered and even more seldom examined.

Dante was *not* her soul mate. He was her instrument of sexual awakening, but all she could expect from this relationship was maybe some sort of closure between them on her father's debt, one way or another.

That stupid debt! She glanced at the time and realized the bank would be open soon. She dried her hair, then dressed in jeans and a snug, waffle-knit shirt.

"Dante?" she called from the top of the stairs.

Silence.

She limped down to the main floor and had a very cursory look for a note—and painkillers—but found neither. He hadn't texted either, but he'd left a key card. At least she wouldn't be locked out if she ran to the lobby. Her leg throbbed like it was newly broken. She really needed something.

Ugh. She didn't want to be the first to text. What should she say? *I'm up? Where are you?* Far too needy.

She was in the elevator before she settled on her message.

Do you want to meet me at the bank?

He responded promptly.

We'll go together. Wait for me.

The reply pinged into her phone as she made her way across the lobby toward the gift shop. How long would that be? she wondered.

In the same moment, she felt a prickle of awareness, like the sun came out and found every inch of her naked skin.

A soft, aged voice said, "Cami!"

With her head bent over her phone, she had nearly walked right past Dante, Bernadetta and another couple, all sitting in the casual dining lounge where the buffet breakfast was served, finishing their coffee. She was separated from them by a row of ferns.

As Cami took a startled inventory, her gaze tangled with Dante's. All the wicked things they'd done to each other cascaded through her mind's eye, turning the middle of her chest into a furnace that radiated heat through the rest of her.

He looked like their intimacy was the furthest thing from his own mind, staring at her with a flat, hostile stare that silently conveyed, *I told you to wait for me.*

The sweet excitement of seeing him again drained away before it had fully formed, leaving her hollowed out by his disapproval.

"Dante said you decided to stay in Whistler and wouldn't be coming to Vancouver with us. He didn't say you were staying at our hotel." Bernadetta looked questioningly to her grandson.

He took a sip of his coffee, which struck her as buying time.

Cami's blush turned to one of indignation, then scorn,

as it impacted her that he was having breakfast with his relatives and not only hadn't invited her, he didn't want them knowing she'd spent the night with him.

"I'm staying with a friend," she provided, turning her attention to Bernadetta, even though she suspected Dante would consider her words a lie. They weren't "friends."

The old woman introduced her niece and husband. "Cami is the young woman who was so kind to me the other day."

Cami brushed that aside, saying, "I'm glad I could help, and it's very nice to meet you. Thank you again for the day of skiing, but I'm sorry. I'm on an errand. Safe travels." She leaned to return Bernadetta's light embrace and got the hell out of Dodge, so humiliated she could hardly bear it.

Dante caught up to Cami at the gift shop cash register, about to pay for a bottle of extra-strength headache caplets. She looked spectacular in curve-hugging jeans. The legs were tucked into her tall boots, accentuating the slender thighs that had hugged his hips last night while she gasped and moaned beneath him.

Her hair, that cloud of silk that had erotically grazed his skin and imprinted the scent of almonds and crushed flowers in his psyche, fell in shiny waves down her spine, drawing his eye to how narrow and delicate her shoulders were.

Leaving her this morning had been a struggle. It took everything in him now not to set possessive hands on her hips and draw her into his front, so he could shape her breasts as he molded her back into his frame.

He was obsessed, which was exactly why he'd made himself sit with his cousin and grandmother when his mind had been several floors up, making love to Cami all over again.

Yanking his libido to heel, he took over her purchase, signing it to his room.

"What are you doing?" she asked stiffly.

"What are *you* doing? You could have asked the concierge to deliver these."

"Hardly." She pried open the cap as they walked out of the shop.

"What do you mean?"

"Hotel staff are run off their feet. I'm not going to play prima donna and ask for something I can get for myself." She glanced toward the dining lounge. "Where's Bernadetta?"

"They've left."

She detoured into the buffet and helped herself to a glass of water, washing down two tablets, before dropping the medicine into her handbag.

"Would you like breakfast?"

"Bit late for that invitation, isn't it? No, thanks," she pronounced with disdain. "I'm going to the bank."

"The phone didn't wake you," he pointed out. "You seemed to need the sleep." He could have used another two or three hours himself. They'd bordered on debauchery. Every single minute had been fantastic.

"You didn't ask me to join you once you knew I was up. In fact, you were horrified that I happened by. Sorry to be such an embarrassment." Her heels clipped loudly across the tiles.

"Quit being so dramatic." He paced alongside her. "It was the opposite. Noni is so smitten with you, she didn't stop talking you up over breakfast. She *wants* me to continue seeing you."

"So then why—? Oh." She halted as they exited to the covered portico.

He handed his ticket to the valet, then pushed his hands into his pockets. Judging by the way Cami paled and stared stiffly ahead, she was connecting the dots.

"You don't want her to think we have a future," she summed up after several long, fuming minutes. "Because we don't."

"She's very anxious to see me married," he confirmed. "But I have no desire to tie myself down. It's not personal."

"I'm sure," she muttered, stepping forward as his vehicle came to the curb.

He didn't owe her explanations, but spoke once he was behind the wheel, pulling away. "I've never met a woman I trust enough to even consider marrying her. I can't bring myself to risk the family fortune again."

"It's one bludgeon after another with you, isn't it? Now it's my fault you can't fall in love and marry? My father's betrayal means you can't make your grandmother happy and produce an heir for everything her husband built? I'm sorry, all right? I'm sorry I ever wanted something as useless as a gold medal. Turn left at the next light."

He signaled and changed lanes. "I didn't say it was your fault."

"You *implied* it." She stared out her side window, but swung her head around a moment later. "And somehow, I'm supposed to be so good in bed that you get over that? Exactly how many orgasms will it take to open your heart enough that your one true love can walk in?"

"I don't know, Cami. How many until you quit acting like a martyr? Is this your bank?" He recognized the logo from the bank transfer she had shown him that first night.

"Yes. And what is that supposed to mean? I'm not being a martyr!"

"People are allowed to want things for themselves." He swung into a parking space. "I wanted to be on the cutting edge of a new technology. That doesn't make me a bad person who deserved to have his work stolen. You keep acting like wanting to ski competitively is a crime. No. It's just a dream, and people are entitled to go after their dreams. You think I don't respect you, but I'll tell you something. The way you skied yesterday was badass. It takes guts to send yourself down the side of a mountain at those speeds. Quit apologizing for being good at it. For liking it and wanting to prove how good you were."

She flinched at the word *were*.

"You do blame me, though." Her fingers picked at the stitching on her handbag. "You fired me."

"I did. But how I let the past affect me is my choice." Not that he'd consciously faced that before it came out of his mouth. He'd let Stephen's betrayal eat away at him, only becoming aware of how destructive it was since meeting her. "Your desire to ski didn't make me the way I am. You're not that powerful," he concluded dryly.

She was powerful enough to have him reassessing his reaction to her father's theft, though. He absorbed that while watching her thumb work against the stitching of her bag.

"I just really miss them," she said in a very small voice. "I know it's backward logic, but if I believe that making a wrong decision can cause someone's death, then making the right choices will keep others alive. Like Reeve. I don't want to believe death is just random bad luck. If that's how things work, how could I stop it from happening again? I don't want to be that powerless."

He sighed and reached to cover her hand, stilling her

twitching fingers and weaving his between them. "It is a terrifying fact that life is nothing but shaken dice." He hated that particular reality himself.

"Thanks," she muttered, extricating her fingers and reaching for her door.

He felt the loss, the sense of having disappointed her, acutely. His reaching out in comfort, offering a hand-holding, had been the least sexual, yet most intimate act he'd ever shared with a woman.

And she'd rejected it.

The bank meeting was even less fruitful than Cami had expected, and she had prepared herself for heart-wrenchingly low results.

The manager was nice enough. She sat with them for about ten minutes, took Cami's information, but told her the file would have to be referred to the bank's fraud department. Someone would be in touch.

She stopped future payments and very helpfully printed out the history of Cami's transfers to the Benito account, which subtotaled to a sickening amount. Cami could have financed her brother's bachelor degree by now.

She didn't know if she was supposed to feel foolish or vindicated as Dante glanced at it, but mostly she felt disregarded. He'd spent half the meeting texting.

Was she playing the martyr? Not consciously, but in case he had forgotten, he had taken her apart and put her back together last night. Several times. A tiny bit of regard this morning didn't seem like a big ask. He was flaying her to bits.

"Are you serious about my staying in Whistler?" she asked as they exited the bank. "Because there's clearly no point."

His head came up from his phone, distracted frown sharpening. "What do you mean?"

"You couldn't care less what the bank is doing and don't want to be seen with me, so—"

"I'm talking to the bank right now. Not this one, but the head office of Benito's bank in Milan. I know one of their VPs. I sent him an email this morning and didn't expect to hear from him because of the time change, but he's visiting his wife's family in America, so he's already started checking into it. He does not look kindly on the family bank being used as a laundry by criminals. He's established that the account is owned by a numbered company and says these transactions are often hidden by bouncing them through a few channels, trying to dodge detection. He'll keep digging."

"Oh." Her feet glued themselves to the sidewalk.

"Oh, indeed. As for not wanting to be seen with you, I explained why that's awkward with my grandmother. I was going to ask you if you would like to go to a club tonight, though. I bumped into an acquaintance over breakfast. He owns Afterglow. Said he'd put me on the list." He quirked his brow as though suggesting his acquaintance was being pretentious.

Afterglow was *terribly* pretentious. It was where all the celebrities went when they came to Whistler. She had secretly always wanted to see inside, but clubbing was one of those luxuries she'd always wondered about, but couldn't afford. Like everything about this man, his invitation tempted her simply for the chance to spend more time in his company, but she was so disconcerted, she could only shrug self-consciously.

"Do *you* want to go?"

"We can't make love nonstop," he said with a smirk of untold arrogance.

"Evidence to the contrary," she muttered.

He let out a bark of laughter, something that made standing on this sidewalk with him the most amazing place to be in that moment, contentious relationship or not. It made her yearn for something more with him. Something truly meaningful.

His phone pinged and he glanced at it. "I have to drop by the Tabor. Can you amuse yourself until lunch?"

He didn't threaten to tie her to the bed in his suite, she noted, but simply assumed she would stay with him.

She folded the printout she still held, thinking of the restitution she had failed to make, despite her best efforts. She really did want to put the past to bed, but wasn't sure if his bed was the place to do it. Walking away wouldn't allow for any sort of peace between them, though.

"I'm going to look for a job. See if I can scare up a place to live so I can stay here instead of moving to Vancouver."

A shadow of something moved behind his eyes, dissolving the humor that was lingering there.

He nodded. "Good luck. See you at lunch, then." He planted a kiss on her that left her heart pounding and walked away.

When they returned to his suite at the end of the day, a rack of dresses and accompanying accessories filled the lounge.

"What—?"

"You need something to wear to the club."

A dress. Not a wardrobe!

"I bought a new top to wear with my miniskirt." She'd found a steal on a sequined halter at the consignment store and showed it to him.

He made a face that said *meh*, and opened a bottle of wine.

"What's wrong with it?" She'd done a lot of hand-wringing today, wondering if she was making the right choice, but kept coming back to wanting him not to hate her. To see that she was doing the best she could.

"Indulge me," he said, jerking his chin at the dresses while pouring glasses. He seated himself on the sofa as though settling in to watch a sports final.

"You want me to model for you? That's rather objectifying, isn't it?" She tried to be indignant, but a secretive part of her was titillated.

"I call it foreplay, but if you'd rather not..." He shrugged, but the slant of his mouth suggested genuine disappointment. Enough to make her want to laugh.

"Is this your thing?" she asked, casting him a curious look as she fingered through the dresses. "Your kink? Do you go to strip clubs?" There was so much about him she didn't know.

"No. But I like to see beautiful women in beautiful clothing. I think that makes me one hundred percent normal heterosexual male. Vanilla, even."

"I'm not beautiful," she said absently, holding a dress of gold fringe against her front, glancing at him for his reaction.

He nodded approval, saying, "You are."

She glowed under the compliment, even as she denied it. "Prettyish, at best."

She slipped behind the rack and unzipped one boot, then the other.

"That's not me fishing for reassurance. Just honest self-assessment." She was pear-shaped, not hourglass. Her lashes needed about a pound of mascara to thicken them up to "average." Her face was on the roundish, girlish side, not elegant or aristocratic. "I have decent skin and nice hair, but I'm no supermodel."

"Women are idiotic, setting ridiculous standards for

themselves," he said as she skimmed away her jeans and top.

"As foreplay goes, yours sucks."

She heard his choke of laughter, then a growled "Yours is excellent. You're making me insane, hiding back there. Get out here."

She bit back a smile, suddenly taking great enjoyment in this flirt and play. This lighthearted teasing made her happy. Optimistic. She hugged the dress to her bare front for a moment, deciding to stop trying to figure out where they were going and embrace what they had. She slowed her movements, giving him a show beneath the rack of clothing by stepping one naked foot through the dress she was trying on, then the other, then very, very slowly shimmied it up her bare legs.

"You'll pay for that," he warned.

"I'm starting to worry we'll need a spreadsheet for all the debits and credits." Holding the front of the loose dress, she came around, growing nervous as she showed herself. She padded toward him and turned so he could zip her.

He set aside his wine and sat forward. "Lift your hair."

She did, felt the dress draw close around her, then his heavy hands settled on her hips. Every single fringe seemed to tickle across her cheeks. Her entire backside began to tingle. Little teases of arousal fluttered through her loins and upward to her breasts.

"Heels, *pi fauri*," he said absently and sat back.

Her whole body warmed as she moved away and chose a pair of gold sandals with an ankle strap and a four-inch spike.

"I'll help you," he said before she could sit to put them on.

His voice was very low and intent. He opened his thighs

so she could set her foot on the cushion between his knees. He took his time, caressing her arch and ankle before putting the shoe in place, then taking care with closing the buckle. He motioned for the other.

She had trouble balancing, knees nearly unhinged so she had to grasp at his shoulder.

"Walk to the window," he commanded softly.

She did, slowly, feeling his gaze on her like a million suns. Maybe she didn't consider herself beautiful, but in that moment, she felt glamorous and exotic. Prized.

It was strangely empowering. She struck a provocative pose as she looked over her shoulder at him, back arched, hip cocked.

"I don't like this one," she said haughtily. "I want to try another."

He sat arrested with his drink halfway to his mouth. His voice was velvet and leather, thick and smoky and sensual. "By all means."

She tried on one in a rich burgundy in a fabric light as air. The spaghetti straps barely held up the cups over a deep cleavage. The skirt was a handkerchief cut with high slits.

"What do you think?" She fluttered the skirt to reveal and conceal her legs nearly to her hips, deliberately teasing, though she wasn't sure which one of them was more affected. Her body was warm and her muscles growing lethargic with sensuality. "Too high school prom?"

"The black shoes, I think." His voice was a silken ribbon sweeping over her and coiling tight, squeezing her breath.

"No," she defied with a shake of her hair. "I want to try something else." She checked in with him and liked the way his mouth was deep at the corners, his eyes narrowed with absolute focus on her.

"The blue, then." It was a strapless mini with silver embossing, tight as a second skin.

"*Now* the black shoes," she stated, sauntering to collect them.

"Bring me that bag." He nodded to a pink bag with silk handles and a logo for designer lingerie that Cami hadn't noticed.

The wicked flutters in her abdomen grew as she brought the items across to him.

He plucked the tissue from the bag and spilled jewel-colored silk and lace across the cushion beside him, fingering through the items for long moments before taking up a miniscule scrap in midnight-blue with an edging of black lace.

She reached for it.

"I'll help. Hold still."

She was paralyzed, barely breathing as he hitched forward, legs opening so his knees bracketed hers. He grazed his flat hands up her thighs, beneath her skirt. The tightness of the knit in the skirt ironed his palms to her skin. His fingers slid across her hips, then hooked into the edge of her very boring, white cotton underwear. He eased them down until they fell in a bunch at her ankles.

"Step." He held the new ones for her.

She was losing track of which one of them was in charge. She obeyed, bones so weak she had to brace on his shoulder again. She quivered under the erotic scrape of lace up her thighs, at the way she thought she could feel the abrasion of his fingerprints against her skin.

He smoothed the thong into place, running thorough fingertips along her hips to ensure there were no twists. His thumbs followed the triangle across the front, causing a pulse of anticipation that was nothing but molten heat, so intense she nearly sobbed.

"I'm going to ruin them," she whispered.

"I expect I'll be ripping them off you very soon, *bedduzza*," he said, very slowly drawing his hands from beneath her skirt and gently tugging her hem into place. "Would you like to walk for me? Or shall we change your shoes first?"

"What do you want?" She could barely stand while he sounded quite composed.

"I would like to change your shoes."

She swallowed and set her foot on the cushion, skirt riding up and no doubt affording him quite a view as he first removed the gold ones, then eased the black velvet heels into place, tightening the ankle strap of first one, then the other.

As she started to draw her foot back to the floor, he tightened his hold on her ankle, urging her to stay exactly as she was.

Her hair fell in curtains around her face as she looked down at him. The helplessness she felt in that moment was terrifying, making her worry this was a huge mistake, yet she couldn't deny herself or him.

"I don't think you're ruining them," he said, watching her as he lazily caressed up her inner thigh to the damp silk. "I find your reaction incredibly exciting." He drew the fabric away from her folds. The backs of his knuckles swept her damp flesh once, twice, then he gently parted and explored more thoroughly.

"I don't…think." Couldn't think. Not at all. She swallowed and swayed. "I can't stand."

"No? How are you feeling otherwise? Tender?" He did wizardly things that made her bite her lip and moan. "All day I've been thinking about last night. How incredible it was. How delightful you are."

She didn't expect him to say such things. Her eyes

teared up. She teetered and he caught her, pulling her down so her knees straddled his thighs. They kissed, hot and urgent. She fairly attacked his mouth and only lifted her head because she felt him searching for her zipper and wanted to get her hair out of the way.

As her dress loosened, he brushed down the bodice. In virtually the same motion, he slid his hands under her bottom, shoving her skirt to her waist as he urged her to stand on her knees so he could suck her nipples.

They were ultrasensitive, and she had to set a hand on his jaw, urging him to be gentle.

He threw his head back and his expression was full of rapacious hunger and barely contained restraint. He slid down enough to dig in his pocket, then clutched the condom packet in his teeth while opening his fly.

He very easily dispatched her brand-new, worn-for-a-minute underpants with a twist of his wrist. A second later, she followed his guiding hand to take him in.

The ferocity in his eyes was her whole world as he filled her, inch by inch of granite thickness, heavy hands on her hips urging her to take up the rhythm they both craved.

Clutching at the back of the sofa, she rode him, lost to sensation. To pleasure. To a climax that had her arching and releasing helpless cries as she shuddered and quaked.

"Beautiful," he said through clenched teeth. "Do it again."

Dante had had mistresses before, but none like Cami. She was proving to be a delightfully quick study on the physical side of their arrangement, but remained a reluctant virgin to the rest, which was an exciting yet frustrating combo.

As his new manager for the Tabor prattled in his ear,

trying to impress him, he watched Cami talking to his HR manager for the chain. The Tabor's dining lounge was decorated for its gala opening with a sea and sky theme. Clear balloons stood in bubble strands under sparkling star lights set off by drapes in evening blue. Cami should have blended in, but she was stealing all the attention in an ethereal gown that made her look like a water sprite. It spilled down her figure in shades of green, backless and draping her ass to perfection. Short sleeves stood up on her shoulders, made of a netted fabric that stood up like delicate wings, increasing the impression Cami was a magical creature sent to enchant him.

Her hand lifted briefly, touching an earring again. She was terrified of losing them, which was part of that adorable, aggravating lack of assumption she exhibited with their relationship.

"I didn't see they'd included accessories," she had said when he presented the green sapphires with a matching oval-cut pendant. "They chose well, didn't they? Suits the gown."

She had just finished curling her hair into big, lazy scrolls of dark coffee and rich auburn shot with threads of gold. They had fallen in ribbons around the shoulders of her hotel robe, making his fingers itch to muss them.

"It's from me," he had informed her dryly, astonished that she was still taken aback by his attentive touches. "Lift your hair."

"When did you have time to shop? Is this from the boutique in the lobby?" She had turned to the mirror as he clasped the necklace.

"There's a shop near the Tabor." He'd mentioned the name of the local jeweler.

"These are *real*?" She'd spun, clutching at the pendant

like it was going to combust. "But just on loan, right? As advertising or something? Did they tell you what I should say?"

"They're a gift." A modest one by his standards, but the best the place had. Yet she had reacted as if he'd poured his mother's wedding necklace into her hands.

A darkness had passed behind her eyes before she'd shielded them with her thickened lashes. Her eyeliner tailing to a point at the corner of her eye, framing lids shaded with green and gold.

"You've given me too much already."

A handful of off-the-rack dresses and some underthings that were more for his pleasure than hers were hardly going to break the bank. Neither was the pretty bauble, yet her reluctance to accept it had niggled.

"You don't like them? They can be exchanged."

"I'm worried something will happen. I've never worn anything so expensive."

"Except skis?" Elite equipment cost a small fortune.

She conceded that point with a hitch of her shoulder, but then added in a mutter, "This isn't how this is supposed to work. I'm already in your debt enough."

He *hated* talk like that from her. It cheapened every press of her mouth to his body, every cry of ecstasy he wrought from her, making him think she was only here because of her father's theft, not because she wanted to be.

"I'm quite happy with the return I'm getting," he'd drawled, not quite disguising his aggravation. "Let me see."

Her gaze flashed once to meet his in the mirror, then she'd set aside her palette of rouge and turned, knuckles white where she clutched the edge of the vanity. Each time the past rose between them, the same flare-up happened between them, pushing them apart. He grew defensive, despite being the one who'd been wronged. She took on a haunted look that turned knife blades in his middle. He'd begun wondering what the hell he was doing, keeping her here with him like this, and had the unpleasant feeling she was wondering the same.

The bank had yet to supply any answers, so they had no way to resolve this impasse. His solution was to burn away misgivings with the white-hot passion they stoked in each other. Not the best coping strategy, but it was the one he'd reached for in that moment as he'd slowly, deliberately, tugged her belt loose so her robe fell open.

He'd drawn in a long breath as he drank in buttermilk skin framed in snow-white silk, pouted nipples hardening under his gaze to tight strawberries that made his mouth water.

He'd carefully centered the platinum-set stone on her breastbone, then lightly grazed his fingertips along the edges of the robe, spreading it farther, watching a flush burn down her stomach and thighs to the fine hairs of her thatch. He could practically smell her body readying for him. He'd dipped his head to taste one nipple, then the other.

"Dante," she'd whispered, pique dissolving into the tone that prickled his scalp.

He was ready in an instant, thick and hard inside his boxers. It took one casual twist of his wrist to free himself. Then he had hitched her onto the vanity top, dipping his knees to enter her.

"Condom," she'd gasped.

"I'll pull out." He couldn't wait. Thrusting into her was a dive from an arctic wasteland into the heat of a simmering hot spring, so intense it made his back sting.

But good, fiercely good. He'd cupped his hands under

her butt, cushioning her cheeks from the unforgiving edge of the vanity. She'd wrapped her legs around him and kissed him as he thrust.

He had never gone bareback before. The sensation was *too* good, sending shivers racing up and down his spine. She'd braced her hands behind her so she could arch, offering her throat, meeting his thrusts. Her breasts bounced with each impact. He'd lifted his gaze to his reflection in the mirror behind her, saw something approaching desperation in his expression that was too disturbing to confront and looked to the way her face contorted with the agony of sexual need instead. Need for *him*.

He'd increased his rhythm, trying to give her as much pleasure as he could. He felt the vise-like grip of her start to twinge and ripple. Her moans of enjoyment became sobs of abandoned delight. A growl of torment built in his throat as he'd held back his own release while he continued thrusting, hard and fast, into the powerful clench and shudder and pulse of her sheath. She was so exquisite he was quite sure he would die. She was going to kill him, head thrown back in surrender, bare heels against his ass finally easing as her panting breaths slowed into helpless bliss.

He pulled out and exploded across her stomach, straining under the force of it, completely taken apart and never likely to be the same.

His wet forehead hung against her damp shoulder, both of them shaking at the cataclysm. He lifted his head and they looked at each other as they came back to themselves, strangers who'd nearly been mowed down by the same train and were now indelibly linked by the experience.

With muscles that trembled, he had helped her find her feet and reached for a hand towel, drying her himself.

The pendant had swung across the tops of her breasts, reminding him why they'd come together in such a frantic, unrestrained coupling.

"You're my date," he had muttered, hearing the gruffness of postorgasmic gravel in his tone. "I have to look as wealthy as I am or rumors will persist that the Tabor is struggling. Say, 'thank you,' Cami."

"Thank you, Cami," she had repeated with an acrid pang in her voice. She immediately grew abashed as she touched the pendant, saying with more sincerity, "Thank you, Dante. It's beautiful."

But she hadn't met his gaze.

Now they were on that date, and he was still reeling from the encounter. Perhaps she was, as well. An introspective frown had persisted in her expression all the way here.

It bothered him. When had he ever concerned himself so deeply with what a woman might be thinking about a necklace he'd given her? If she didn't like it, she could return it. Sell it.

But he wanted her to like it. He wanted her to think of him when she wore it. Of the way they made each other feel. Every. Single. Time.

Damn, this evening was interminable. He glanced at his watch, still needing to give his speech and shake a few hands before he could have her alone again.

He knew what was really bothering him. He only had two more nights with her. That dwindling sand in the hourglass grated. His agile brain had already rearranged his schedule a dozen ways, looking to fit in an extension of his time here. What he'd really like was to bring her back to Sicily.

"Dante." The male voice, familiar as his own, had him turning in surprise.

"Arturo." He embraced his cousin with warmth. "What are you doing here?"

"Saving you. Again. What the hell are you doing?"

Cami could hear what Karen was thinking as she skimmed her speculative gaze down the dress that had cost more than either of them made in two paychecks put together, then took in the stones dangling from her ears and neck.

It's not like that, Cami wanted to say, but she was growing more and more sickened with herself because it was *exactly* like that.

Somehow, she had convinced herself that she and Dante were a normal couple. Dating. Lovers. It wasn't costing him anything to let her stay in the room with him. She had cooked for him twice in the kitchenette. They were getting to know one another and putting the past behind them.

But while her infatuation was growing into something more genuine, something she didn't even want to name because it was so vast yet elusive, he seemed quite comfortable withholding himself from all but their intensely passionate encounters. She was offering her heart. He was offering pillow-cut stones. Sharing showers and meals was not true sharing.

When he had given her this jewelry, relegating her firmly to "mistress," she had thought she might as well be sleeping with him to pay off her father's debt. Clearly he viewed sex with her as a commodity of one kind or another. It was more than lowering. It was a scorn of the heart she was leaving wide open in humble offering.

"I'm glad things are working out and you've found another position," Karen said, drawing Cami back to their awkward conversation where Cami had been trying to explain how she was on the arm of the man who had fired her so ruthlessly.

She had come over to thank Karen for helping her land the job she was starting next week. It was a night manager position with lousy hours, but beggars couldn't be choosers. Karen had kindly provided a statement that pulling the job offer to run the Tabor had been an internal decision, not a reflection of Cami's qualifications.

"Were you able to keep your apartment?" Karen asked.

"No, but I have some good leads."

"Where are you staying, then?"

"With a friend."

Karen's gaze flicked toward the bar where Dante had gone, promising to send over champagne.

Cami felt the shame that had been sitting like a knot in her chest climb her throat, reaching toward her cheeks.

"I should get back to my date," she murmured. "Good to see you. Thanks again."

All she was thinking was that she wanted to escape Karen's speculation, only noticing as she approached that Dante was talking to a man who looked like he could be his brother. He was equally handsome and well-dressed in a bespoke suit, with a five o'clock shadow and a similarly smoky tone in his voice.

He was speaking Sicilian, but as she approached Dante from behind, he looked at her over Dante's shoulder with the kind of lurid male assessment that made any woman's skin crawl.

She faltered.

Dante turned to spear her with a hard gaze.

The man switched to English.

"I don't care how good the sex is. You're underwriting a Fagan. Again. Please tell me you haven't forgiven her father's debt."

Cami felt the color drain from her face while her jaw practically landed on the floor. "Who *is* this?"

"My cousin. Arturo." Dante had spoken of him with affection more than once, but aside from being easy on the eye, she saw nothing to like, especially when he spoke again.

"I'm the man who put up his own money when your father stole Dante's. Perhaps you'd like to compensate *me* in kind?" His vile gaze skimmed down to her breasts and lingered.

"Arturo," Dante ground out, but as admonishments went it was damned thin. Meanwhile, he was looking at her like he had that first day in the lobby of this very hotel, like he couldn't believe she had the gall to exist.

"This was your idea," she reminded him. He had *made* her stay with him.

"I'm sure revenge has been very sweet, given that figure," his cousin continued, making her want to punch him in the face, but she couldn't stop staring into Dante's dark expression. "You can be forgiven for thinking with your belt buckle."

"Is that what it was?" she demanded in a voice that shrank. All of her was feeling small in that moment, so belittled she began to well up. She had been trying so hard to earn his trust, she hadn't thought to question his motivations. Her throat hurt like it was being squeezed. "You just wanted revenge?"

"What else is he getting beyond a good time?"

"Shut *up!*" she told that horrible man.

"That's enough," Dante said at the same time, but she couldn't tell if it was directed at her or his cousin. His jaw pulsed, and he reached for her arm. "Let's talk."

She evaded, backing away. "Let's not."

People were staring. Some might even have overheard

and the entire room now thought she was exactly what she had argued from the beginning she was not—a woman who could be bought.

And why shouldn't they see her that way? She stood here in a gown and jewels Dante had paid for. She was staying in his hotel room, eating food he provided for her.

She shook her head, hating herself so much in that moment she wanted to claw out of her own skin. Every single time she went after what her heart wanted—

Dear God, *no.* She couldn't feel anything toward him. Refused to allow it. No. It would kill her to be in love with him when this was only—

Biting her lip so hard she tasted blood, she gathered up her skirt and hurried out.

Cami swept out with her head high, but Dante could still see the sickly shade she'd turned. It matched the gown he had purchased in a week of what was starting to look like foolishly besotted behavior. He couldn't even defend it, unable to explain how he had let it escalate to a public parade of his own poor judgment.

"We all have our weaknesses," Arturo said as Dante fought an urge to go after her. "Yours is a desire to believe the best in people."

"She wasn't asking for any of this," Dante growled, accepting the neat whiskey his cousin handed him and knocking back half of it. "How did you even know I was seeing her?" It was a juvenile reaction, as if his cousin's interference was the problem, not the fact he was sleeping with the enemy.

Arturo seemed startled by the question. He sipped his own drink.

"I saw the post on Noni's timeline showing the two of you had gone skiing. The family grapevine is abuzz with her praises of Cameo Fagan." He ran his tongue across his teeth as though the name left a bitter taste. "I thought I should check in. That's all." He slid a sly look Dante's way. "Was she worth it?"

His cousin had a base sense of humor at the best of times, but it came across as particularly misplaced today. Especially when he snorted under the look Dante cast him.

"You are well and truly hooked, aren't you?"

He almost told his cousin that Cami had been a virgin. That her honesty about that had allowed him to begin to believe in her. He rubbed his thumb along the curve of his glass, thinking of the exquisite pleasure she had given him again and again.

But no more.

His world turned so bleak in that moment, he barely restrained himself from shattering the glass with his bare hand.

"She's been trying to pay me back, sending money to an account supposedly owned by Benito Castiglione."

Arturo's brows went up. "There's a name I haven't heard in a long time. He died, didn't he? Years ago?"

"Yes, but that's why—" Dante felt like a gullible idiot, trying to defend her. "Where would she even get that name to throw it at me?"

"Old paperwork of her father's?" Arturo guessed. "They're a resourceful bunch. I'm just glad I was able to stop you losing more than a few grand in trinkets this time."

"Sir?" The event planner who had organized this evening's festivities approached with trepidation. "Would you like to give your speech now?"

Not even one little bit. Dante felt as though noxious fumes filled his lungs, but he made himself go through the motions of finishing his evening, ignoring the avid looks from the staff and honored guests, smoothing over whatever ripples his small scene with Cami had created.

All the while, he was mentally combing through the moments when Cami had challenged his view of her, searching for the point where he turned from man into mark. The very beginning? When she helped his grandmother? Kissed him? Fell apart under his touch in the hot tub?

He grew more and more furious with himself, more ramped for the inevitable confrontation when he arrived back in his suite.

"She'll have cut and run with the goods," Arturo said. "Which is good. You don't want her hanging around, trying to convince you of her innocence."

He *had been* convinced. That was the problem.

"Do you want me to come with you?" Arturo shadowed him all the way to the door of his suite. Dante dismissed him with a snarl of impatience.

What had transpired between him and Cami was many things, but it was above all private. He pushed in and knew before the door had shut that the suite was empty.

What he didn't expect was to find her gown on the floor of the lounge, as though she'd shed it the second she'd entered, heels kicked off beside it. The jewelry he'd given her was on the coffee table. The only shoes missing by the door were her knee-high boots.

As he climbed the stairs, he discovered there was little satisfaction in finding all the lingerie he'd given her still in the drawers and all her new dresses, some still unworn, hanging in the closet. Even the pretty scarf with her name painted in calligraphy, which he'd bought while they enjoyed the town's street fair of local artists, was still here.

Her well-worn backpack, her battered laptop and her

toothbrush were gone, but the hotel shampoo was still here. She'd taken only what was undeniably hers.

He ran his hand down his face, wondering whether he'd given her too much credit or not enough.

His phone pinged and an email notification came through, advising him Cami had just sent a transfer—in the amount she'd been sending to Benito.

CHAPTER EIGHT

One month later...

DANTE SAW THE email notification and knew without opening it that it was another payment from Cami. Her third.

He rejected it exactly as he had the other two. Damn
her! Every time he almost managed to push her from his
thoughts—

Who was he kidding? She was there *all the time*, acting as a bar of comparison that made every other woman
who crossed his path too short or too tall, too polished or
too loud, too quick to make assumptions, too slow to get
to the point. Too insincere and not able to laugh. Not pos-
sessing a laugh he could stand to hear.

Those were the days. At night, he woke so hard he hurt,
dreams of making love to Cami dissolving into the harsh
reality that he was alone in his bed and would never feel
her beneath him again.

Leaning his knuckles on his desk, he gritted his teeth
and told himself it was over. *Let her go.*

His PA buzzed through. "Signor Donatelli has arrived."

"Send him in." Dante clicked off his phone and moved
around his desk to greet his guest.

They were distantly related through the marriage of
Vito's sister, but often crossed paths in business. Gallo

had worked with the Donatelli investment bank several times, so he and Vito were well acquainted and enjoyed a comfortable friendship.

"Are you holidaying? This is a long way to come for a house call," Dante said as they sat down with fresh espresso.

"It's a delicate matter." Vito steepled his fingertips. "One I thought best handled in person. It's taken a lot of digging and once I had an answer, I asked Paolo to confirm it. I wanted to be absolutely sure before speaking to you."

Vito's cousin was the president of the bank, which attested to the seriousness of the matter. Dante frowned.

"This is about the Benito account?" Dante sat back, trying to relax, but it was impossible. "I don't think I want the answer any longer."

Let sleeping dogs lie, he had thought each time he recalled that Vito had not been in touch. Dante didn't want to know that Cami had followed in her father's footsteps with skimming whatever she could from him by stringing him along as his reluctant mistress.

What *had* she gained, though? That was the part that drove him craziest.

"I am quite sure you do not," Vito said, tight smile revealing the ruthless man well disguised behind a picture-book family that included a stunning American wife and two young children. "But Paolo and I cannot, and will not, allow our bank to be used for crimes."

Vito's wife had been implicated in one herself. That's how the pair had met. She'd been exonerated, but it was the type of smudge that had only made the Donatellis that much more vigilant with their bank's reputation.

"Paolo is speaking with the authorities today. This is a

courtesy call, since you were the one who made us aware of the situation."

An image of Cami behind bars flashed in his mind. "What will it cost me to quash it?"

The words left Dante's lips before he could stop them, but the idea of Cami going to prison was beyond anything he could stomach. He shot to his feet as though he could physically reach her through the email in the phone he'd left on his desktop, somehow shielding her.

"We can't, Dante." Vito's tone was both quietly regretful, in deference to their friendship, yet impassively hard. "This sort of thing could take down our bank. He has to be stopped."

"*He?*" Dante spun. "We're talking about Cami Fagan. Aren't we?"

"She's the victim, yes." Vito nodded. "But Arturo is the criminal who has been representing himself as Benito and taking her money."

How the hockey playoffs were still on when summer tourists were invading the city, Cami didn't know, but she didn't complain. She needed the tips, and this working-class pub, with its big screens and loyal regulars, was brimming with generous fans.

She was tending bar and still run off her feet. At least they mostly drank beer, which meant about a million draft pours, but not a lot of time-consuming mixed drinks. Wings and margaritas night was a nightmare.

Either way, dropping a full tray of clean glasses was *not* helpful.

She did it anyway, when she turned from the pass-through and saw Dante at the end of the bar, looking right at her. He wore a leather jacket, sunglasses and a five o'clock shadow. His mouth was a grim line that sent a numbing sear of adrenaline shooting to her fingertips and toes.

I'm not ready, was her only thought before the tray hit the floor in front of her toes. The smash crescendoed above the din, and shards of glass peppered her pant legs.

The crowd roared as if she had scored a goal.

Her shift partner in the narrow space, Mark, said, "Nice job, kid," and reached past her for the second tray, then continued filling orders, double-time.

Cami did what many a server had done in such battle conditions. She swept the glass into the space behind the garbage bin, silently promised a proper clean up later, put the broom away, washed her hands and got back to work.

She was shaking like she'd been through a war, though. Or was still on the battlefield. *What was he doing here?*

Trying to ignore Dante was impossible, but she gave it a go, continuing to work, but taking a moment to get Mark's attention. "See that guy at my end of the bar? Can you serve him?"

"You got it, kid." Mark was a student friend of her brother's, which was how she got the job. "He wants to know what time you're off work," Mark said after providing Dante a beer.

"Half past get out of my life," she muttered, but didn't expect Dante, or even Mark, heard her. The music wasn't audible over the din of voices and sportscaster calls, and the servers were yelling to be heard across the narrow, scarred wooden top of the bar.

She would have to talk to Dante at some point, though. She had faced that two days ago, when she had used an over-the-counter test and learned her life would be intertwined with his forever.

Or not. It was still early days. Things happened, not that she wished for a miscarriage, but that was pretty much how her life always seemed to go, especially if something good had come along.

Was an unplanned pregnancy "good"? She hadn't had time to process it, just knew that either way, it was a disaster of some proportion. She had expected to have time to put a plan in place before she had to face him. Never in her wildest dreams had she expected him to come looking for her. Why was he even here? She so wasn't ready to talk to him yet!

She threw herself into work, feeling the loss acutely when Dante disappeared. Had it been an accident, his coming upon her? Maybe he didn't want to see her, which now made her perversely anxious to speak with him.

Minutes later, she spotted him where he'd found a seat and nearly dropped another glass. For the rest of her shift, each time she glanced over, he was looking in her direction.

When the game finished and patrons filed out, leaving free seats at the bar, he took one, saying, "Cami."

That voice. That *accent*. How was this man her complete undoing in every way?

"Mind walking me home?" she asked Mark as the servers came up with their last call requests. "Or should I text Reeve?"

"I'll walk you home," Dante said in a low growl. "My car is parked outside your house."

"Stalker," she started to say, then did a double take as she realized how truly awful he looked. When he wore stubble, he usually cleaned it up around the edges, but this looked like two days without shaving. Or sleep. His eyes were sunken pits, his hair disheveled, his face lined with weariness.

Not Bernadetta. She had been running a damp cloth over the marble top of the bar, but stopped. "What happened? Is your grandmother—"

"She's fine. But I have to talk to you."

She flinched at the granite in his tone and went back to her closing rituals. "You need to accept my transfers."

"It's about that, Cami."

Of course it was. She had stupidly pined for him all this time while he was here to talk bank balances. *Again*.

She shook her head, but when the lights came up, she said good-night to Mark and the rest of the staff, collected her purse and the fleece she'd stolen from her brother, and let Dante hold the door for her.

"What?" she prompted as they started down the sidewalk. Her guilty secret quivered deep in the pit of her belly.

"This is a terrible neighborhood," he said tightly, glancing into a dark alley as they passed.

"I didn't ask you to come here."

Grim silence was his reply.

She tried not to feel anything, but words, so many words, crowded her throat. She had had enough time to reflect on their affair and realize how badly she had been fooling herself, thinking they were friends. Or something. Maybe being a virgin had made her susceptible to seeing more than was there, but even before the blow up with Arturo, she had begun to realize she was nothing more to him than a paid companion. It had hurt *so badly*. His resurgence of suspicion had been a final nail in the coffin.

What would he think about her pregnancy? She didn't know how to tell him. Didn't think she could face his reaction. There was zero chance it would bear any resemblance to happiness.

She brushed a wisp of hair from her cheek with a shaky hand. "Where's your cousin?"

He drew a long, deep, pained breath.

"Never mind," she muttered. "I don't even care. He did

me a favor. You were treating me like— The whole thing was toxic and never should have happened."

I don't mean you, baby. She had to fight placing a protective hand over her stomach.

Dante swore and ran a hand down his face, not disagreeing.

She swallowed, focusing on putting one foot in front of the other when his next words had her stumbling.

"Arturo is negotiating a plea deal while investigations are underway into his bank fraud, industrial espionage and ties to organized crime. He's the one who did it, Cami. Not your father."

"What?"

Dante caught her elbow to steady her.

That tiny touch sent yearning shooting through her, blanking her mind for a millisecond.

"I don't understand."

"Neither do I." She heard the rage in his voice and the pain that underscored it.

His touch tightened briefly, then he nudged her into motion. She walked on in stunned silence, afraid to believe. She couldn't even try to comprehend what it meant for her, him, or them.

All of them.

"My father is innocent? That's what you're saying?" she finally had to ask. To hear it aloud.

"Yes."

"But he signed a confession."

"Desperate people do desperate things." He wasn't just talking about her father.

Would he think that's what this baby was? An act of desperation on her part?

They arrived at the dilapidated house that had been converted to four separate apartments a generation ago.

The landlord was decent enough. Leaks were fixed and there was always heat, but he didn't put a penny into it that he didn't have to.

A lot of students lived in this area, along with some struggling single parents and yes, some drug users and ne'er-do-wells. Cami had made do in places like this before without shame.

But Dante's rented town car stood out like a gleaming, manicured thumb from a weathered work glove, making her embarrassed of her circumstances. She was at an utter loss as to how to react to any of this.

"Is your brother up? I want to talk to him, too." He reached to open the gate and hold it for her. The chivalry disconcerted her. She dumbly led him around the cluttered side of the house to the stairwell of their entrance.

She tried the door and found it unlocked, which Reeve often did when she was due home. He was in his room and called, "That you?"

"Yes. Can you come out?"

"Lemme finish this."

She hung her brother's fleece on a chair back as Dante came in behind her.

He closed the door and pushed his hands into his pockets, taking in the shabby furnishings and the corner shelf she'd claimed as a makeshift closet. Her backpack stood beside it. Her bedding was folded and stacked on the end of the sofa.

"That's where you sleep?" he asked, glancing from the lumpy cushions back to her with an accusatory glance.

She ought to be feeling superior. Vindicated. Instead, she felt less than ever. She folded her arms, muttering, "Don't judge, Dante. You're in no position."

"I'm aware," he stated flatly, and took in the clean dishes by the sink, the cupboards long past needing painting, the mismatched furniture. "This is how you live? How you've been living all these years?" He met her gaze for one second before looking away, deep emotion contorting his face. "It makes me sick."

Her heart tilted on its edge and she wanted to say, *Whose fault is that?* But she could see he was in the throes of disbelief and betrayal as much as she was. She didn't want to feel compassion. He didn't deserve it. But she still suffered for him. A desire to reach out, emotionally and physically gripped her.

"I can't imagine how difficult this is for you," she murmured. He'd always spoken about his cousin with such warmth.

"I think you can," he said with weighty perception. "Having worn these shoes all these years. Wrongly." His voice dropped into his chest.

Her own chest ached, unable to stand seeing such a strong man humbled.

"What happened?" She tucked her cold hands beneath her arms, still unable to believe he was even here, let alone with such a message.

"Arturo has gambling debts. Big ones. It's been a problem from his twenties, not that I or anyone saw it. If he hadn't colluded with Benito and taken my design and emptied the account, framing your father for it, he might have been killed at that time. As it was, the windfall put him back in good graces with his bookie. He burned through it, though, and fell into trouble again. That's when he started badgering you to pay your father's so-called debt."

Reeve came out of his room. His scowl of confusion at having a visitor so late deepened as Cami introduced them.

"We're not talking to you. Just take the payments and stay out of our lives," Reeve growled.

Cami hadn't told him all that had transpired in Whistler, only that Dante had refused to hire her and that the payments had been going to a fake account. He was beside himself over the whole thing. They'd stopped talking about it to keep the peace.

"Dad didn't do it," she said numbly, but stating it with her own mouth didn't make it any less surreal. She explained, and Reeve swung his attention to Dante.

"When did you find this out?"

"A few days ago." Dante rubbed his stubbled jaw. "A lot has happened very quickly, but I needed to inform you and…" He drew a heavy breath. "Express my deepest regret that your father was implicated. I will be compensating you as best I can."

He reached into his jacket pocket for a narrow envelope and set it on the battered kitchen table.

"That's a reimbursement of the amount you deposited to the Benito account. There are things to unravel in terms of the settlement your father paid before leaving Italy. It's at least three times that, and you're entitled to interest and damages. You'll see in the letter from my lawyer that this is merely a deposit as a sign of good faith. More will be forthcoming. Hire your own lawyer and have them contact ours. Legal costs will be covered on my end."

"You can't be serious!" Cami exclaimed, thinking of Dante's struggle to recoup his losses the first time. "Won't that break you? I mean financially?"

Reeve made a choking noise. "Who cares? I'd like to break his face."

"Reeve!"

Dante only looked at him as if to say, *Go ahead*.

Reeve looked tempted but shook his head. "I'm going to be a surgeon. I'm not going to shatter my hand no matter how much you deserve it."

"It wasn't him, Reeve. He's as much a victim as we are."

"He took *ten years* to look at anyone but Dad. He *fired* you without even blinking."

Cami pressed her clasped hands against her navel, thinking that wasn't all he'd done.

"I want you to come back to Sicily with me," Dante said to her. A pang of fearful hope soared through her, abruptly falling when he added, "To make a statement."

"Like hell," Reeve muttered. "We'll communicate through lawyers. Stay the hell away from both of us."

"Reeve." Her brother didn't know there was another party in this who had some rights. Someone for whom she had to get things right to the best of her ability. *How?* She felt as though she was plummeting from an airplane without a chute, unable to grasp at anything solid.

"When are you leaving?" she asked Dante.

"As soon as you're packed."

"You don't owe him a damned thing, Cam."

"I have to give notice at my job. We owe rent in four days." She dug in her purse for the tips she'd brought home, intending to put it in the jar, but Dante halted her by speaking to Reeve as he pointed at the envelope he'd brought.

"There's enough to cover your tuition for the next few years along with significantly better housing. You sleep wherever you want, but she's either coming with me, or going to a hotel. I won't have her living like this one more night."

"We've already started looking for something else," Reeve said defensively.

It was true. He'd been pushing through exams and she'd been saving up for the damage deposit. His standards for himself were considerably lower than what he wanted for Cami, but now they were together and combining resources, they could afford something slightly better.

She hadn't told him yet that they would need room for one more. It struck her that all of her plans, once again, were being shaken apart.

"My grandmother would like to see you," Dante said. "She has never known anything about this until I had to tell her that Arturo was being arrested and why. She's extremely upset that you were hurt and would like to apologize. I want to put her mind at rest sooner than later."

"That's emotional blackmail," Reeve interjected.

"Look." Cami held up staying hands. "This is too much to take in. I can't think when I smell like spilled beer and nachos. I'm getting in the shower, then going to bed. You go to your hotel or wherever you're staying. I'll text you in the morning."

Dante was still there when she emerged fifteen minutes later. She hadn't come up with anything fresh while she'd been under the weak stream of hot water. In fact, she'd only realized how exhausted she was. How worried and ill-prepared she was for a baby. How terrified she was of Dante's reaction.

He and Reeve sat at the kitchen table, each with a cup of fresh coffee steaming before them. They had the paperwork open. The tension was so electric it crackled.

"You should have told me," Reeve said as she searched out her hairbrush.

"What?" She rarely kept anything from him so couldn't imagine—

"That you two were involved in Whistler."

Her heart took a plummet into her bare feet. She glared at Dante. "Why on earth would you tell him that?"

"He asked."

"What made you—?" She shot a look to her brother, the budding doctor.

He glared at her, and she realized he was remembering this morning, when he had asked with concern, *Did you throw up again?* It was the second time he'd caught her, but probably the tenth time it had happened.

He looked ready to spit nails. "He wasn't accepting your transfers. I couldn't figure out why."

Lovely. Now he knew the sordid depths she'd sunk to.

"I'm entitled to a private life," she muttered, digging through her bag for moisturizer, wanting to cool her hot face.

"Cami." Reeve waited until she looked at him. "We don't need this." He flicked a finger at the papers before him. "Whatever you think you have to do, you don't. With this debt off our backs, we have options. I'll take a couple years off school if necessary. We'll figure it out. We always do."

She had never loved him so much as she did in that moment. With a lump in her throat, she nodded. "Thank you. But... I should go. For Dad."

She hadn't consciously thought that through until the words left her, but she did want their father's name properly cleared.

Reeve's mouth tightened. "I'll go, then."

She shook her head. "No, I will." She also had to think about what her child might need. *Dante's* child.

She couldn't look at him. Her hands shook as she began to pack.

CHAPTER NINE

ADRENALINE HAD KEPT Dante going until he'd seen Cami. When he finally had his eyes on her, his world shattered along with the glasses she had dropped. The cold fog he'd barely acknowledged, the one that had encased him in the last month, since finding her gown on the floor, had finally lifted—only to be replaced by a more poignant, misty one. She was every bit as beautiful as he remembered, radiating light and warmth, looking soft and natural and sweet.

Until she'd seen him.

She'd closed up like a flower, a trampled one, turning away and refusing to speak to him. He had hated Arturo, then, genuinely hated his cousin for costing him this. Her.

Much as he'd loathed watching her sling beer past midnight, he had ignored his own ale in favor of drinking in the sight of her.

Until Vito had thrust her into the forefront of his mind again, he had refused to let himself reflect on his time with her. Not consciously. He had had flashes of concern, though. Was she okay? Eating? How was her leg? Every time he received a notice of a money transfer, he wondered where she was working. Where she was living.

She had seemed to favor her leg as she spent the next several hours on her feet, looking brittle and pale. Her hair had been piled in a messy knot so her neck was a fragile stem, her face closed and intent as she worked.

She smiled at her coworkers, but any sort of humor quickly died the moment her attention was forced to turn his way. Gone was the woman who had tilted cheeky grins at him and let him see inside her when they were alone.

God, he had missed her.

Now she sat beside him, but a silence had grown between them, impenetrable and thick.

He had expected more of a fight to get her on the plane, but of course she wanted to clear her father's name. Dante was anxious to do so himself.

Speaking with Reeve had been the strangest experience. Stephen's voice had come out of a face that looked so much like the man it was uncanny. Dante's throat had been thick with apology, as he saw his old friend in Reeve's demeanor. When Reeve had asked him point-blank if anything had happened between him and Cami in Whistler, pinning him with a sharp gaze, Dante had been so surprised, his face had told the truth before he could dissemble.

He'd felt stung under Reeve's disapproval like a callow youth, aware that any attempt to claim honorable intentions at this point would be met with disdain. Suspicion even.

Cami sure as hell didn't want to rekindle things. She'd made it clear she wasn't interested even before he'd told her about Arturo. She thought they were *toxic*.

Yet here she was. Quiet and compliant beside him. Subdued almost. If not for the hint of steel in her as she'd spoken to her brother and agreed to come with him, Dante would have thought she was on the defensive. Wary. Feeling as though he held all the power again when he had definitely lost the high ground.

She was probably tired. He was. Sick and tired. From

the moment Vito had told him Arturo was behind the theft, Dante had been nauseous. Absolutely gutted at the cost to Cami and her brother. Seeing how they lived had made it worse. He'd been completely sincere in saying he wouldn't let her live like that for one more night.

Along with fresh betrayal, fresh grief had hit. Stephen's loss was that much more unjust and difficult to bear. All the things Dante had seen in the man a decade ago, the belief in his ideas, the encouragement and desire for him to succeed, the fatherly pride, had been real.

He swallowed a lump, trying to feel lucky that he'd had three excellent father figures in his life, but a sense of being cheated remained.

"I won't forgive myself for cutting your father out of my life," he told Cami as the plane leveled off and the flight attendant left to bring the chamomile tea Cami had requested. "He was a good friend. I shouldn't have left his children to fend for themselves."

Cami turned from watching the lights fade at the edge of the black blanket that was the Pacific.

"I can't do this yet." Her voice was as wispy as the smoke of a snuffed flame. "I'm too tired to make sense of it. I just want to drink my tea and fall asleep and unpack all this when we get to Sicily. Do you mind?"

"No." He wanted to take her hand, console her. Say all the things that were weighing on his chest. "Use the stateroom." He nodded at the door behind them.

"Your private jet has bedrooms?" She snorted. "How many? Is there an indoor pool? A bowling alley?"

He couldn't tell if that was a dig or merely her dry wit rallying. "Just the one stateroom. And the theater." He nodded at the screen that showed their flight path.

"I'm fine here." Her elbows tucked into her waist, and she looked out the window at the void of charcoal.

He pinched the bridge of his nose.

"I wasn't presuming to join you. I won't come in unless I have to wake you because of turbulence. Then you'll have to come back to your seat."

She looked into the watery gold of her tea, but her mouth quivered. "I'm fine."

Tiny, tiny words that made his lungs fill with concrete.

She nursed her tea for the next half hour, then watched out the window again. Eventually, she fell asleep. He unbuckled her himself and carried her into the bed, so very tempted to lie down and hold her. There was a gaping wound from the base of his throat to the pit of his belly. He needed the compress of her warmth to stem the loss.

Instead, he draped a light blanket over her and went back to his seat where he dozed fitfully and snapped awake from dreams that she had disappeared from the plane.

She must have been as exhausted as he was. When he finally did wake from a deep sleep, his neck held a dull ache and his eyes were like sandpaper. Most of their flight had gone by.

"No, I'm totally fine," Cami was saying in a low voice to the attendant. "I just don't travel well. Toast would be great. Thanks."

"Air sick?" he asked as she came to her seat.

She was pale, her hair was finger-combed and she smelled faintly of toothpaste. "It happens," she murmured, not meeting his eyes in favor of making a thorough study out the window.

"Another few hours." He pointed at the progress map, which showed them halfway over the Mediterranean.

Despite the circumstance, he was looking forward to showing her his homeland, hoping for some reason that she would love it as much as he did.

"Dante…" She wore a tortured expression as she turned her face to meet his gaze.

The gravity in her tone was so ominous his lungs seized. His ears rang as he strained to hear her. "What's wrong?"

"I'm pregnant."

"Don't you dare ask me if it's yours," she whispered, glancing toward where the flight attendant would appear at any second.

She risked a glance at him, trembling as she had been since rising in a rush of morning sickness. She couldn't read his expression. He was a master at hiding his thoughts.

The flight attendant came to draw the table down from the wall and serve their breakfast. It was a meal of loaded silence and impossible entanglements.

When they were alone again, Cami said, "I need to know if it really was just revenge. Clearly I'm very gullible, and I know how angry you were—"

"Cami." His hand closed over her wrist, gentle, but heavy as a manacle. "I'm going to need some time."

The pressure of his touch over her pulse was so profound, her blood throbbed into his fingers like an open wound. Emotion pressed into the backs of her eyes. She couldn't swallow.

After a long minute, he released her to sip his coffee, then asked, "When did you find out?"

"A few days ago. I didn't do it on purpose."

"We." Was it her imagination, or was there a euphoric quality beneath his even, fact-finding tone? "Were you going to tell me?"

She realized she was wringing her hands and made them settle into her lap. "I hadn't worked out what to do. When you showed up last night… How are we like this? One catastrophe after another?"

He might have flinched, but the attendant brought fresh coffee.

They finished their meal in a quiet that was almost companionable, harking back to their comfortable mornings in Whistler. The ones that had given her hope they had something more than revenge and debts, blame and rancor.

"You're keeping it." She couldn't tell if that was an order or a request.

"Hopefully," she murmured. "One never knows. That's why you're not supposed to tell anyone in the first trimester."

He burned a hole through her with his gaze.

She lifted her shoulders defensively. "I've been sideswiped by life a lot. I'm not going to assume this will go as I hope it will."

He closed his eyes. "The honesty of you. I was better off when I thought it was all lies."

He didn't say he also hoped she had a successful pregnancy, and she was too unprepared to face his answer by asking if he did. They didn't talk much after that. He took several calls, speaking Sicilian, and she tried to read a book on her phone until they were preparing to land.

As her ears popped, she looked out and bonked her head into the window, trying to keep the gleaming peak in her sight. "Is that Mount Etna?"

His mouth quirked, the first softening she'd seen in him. "Yes. Why?"

Heart wobbling in thrill, she said, "I'm a mountain geek. It's so beautiful."

"I thought you only went nerd over skis."

"It's related." She leaned as far as she could, but lost sight of the peak as the plane banked. "When I first came to Italy, I spoke to a retiree who was ticking off every ski slope in Europe as a sort of bucket list thing. I didn't even know Mount Etna had a resort, but he said it was one of his favorites, that the views of the Mediterranean were spectacular. I made my own list and read up on all of the mountains, but this one seemed like such a long shot even before we had to go back to Canada."

"You can't ski," he reminded. "Not for a while."

Because she was pregnant. Taken unawares by the first big adjustment she would make in her life for the sake of the one growing inside her, she murmured a stunned "No," of agreement.

She wasn't upset by the need to take care, but the fact she once again faced a period of dark unknown distressed her. She would get through it, she knew she would, but the not knowing *how* brought a tightness to her chest. Just like that, the air grew heavy and oppressive.

Maybe it was because they were landing. She was suddenly quite homesick.

But she felt strangely at peace when she left the jet and walked across the tarmac to Dante's cobalt-blue sports car. There was something in his calm confidence that reassured her. He put the top down so the verdant afternoon air blew across her skin as he started away from the private airfield and she sighed, relaxing.

He pointed out the odd landmark as he drove, but mostly they let the breeze snap around them, blowing away travel weariness.

Cami couldn't stop craning her neck, utterly entranced. The stamp of centuries was everywhere, providing a sense of permanence and endurance.

Eventually he drove the car up a winding single lane through a vineyard, climbing to a hillock and cutting through a break in hedges to circle a fountain in front of a huge stone building. She dragged her gaze from a view that went for miles, expansive and breathtaking, and took in the worn stones of the courtyard and the vines climbing the front of what looked like a medieval castle.

"Is this a hotel?"

"It's my home." She heard the laughter in his voice and scowled at his back as he left the car.

How was she supposed to know that? She had known he was rich, but hadn't realized he was *this* rich. She was still taking that in from the passenger seat when he opened her door and offered a hand to help her out.

"It's beautiful," she murmured. *Intimidating.*

"It's a bit of a relic. My grandfather modernized with electricity and new plumbing, but aside from overhauling the kitchen a few years ago, I've only been keeping up on the necessary repairs. Noni's very comfortable. I don't like to displace her for anything that isn't absolutely necessary."

"Bernadetta's here?"

"Of course."

"But what will she think—" She realized he held her hand and carefully lifted hers away. "I don't want her to know I'm…"

It was hard, very hard, to look into his eyes, especially when his expression turned so grave. "Nothing is going to happen to it, Cami."

He couldn't *know* that.

"We're already dealing with enough. Me and her," she decided firmly. "Let's put off adding to it."

A muscle pulsed in his jaw, but he eventually said, "If you insist."

"I'm actually getting my way with you for a change?" she said as he retrieved her backpack from the trunk.

"You've had your way with me many times," he drawled.

Her breath left her in a sensual punch as she recalled

teasing him while trying on dresses. He'd let her take the lead more than once in their lovemaking, but she knew there was an element of *allowing* her. Dante was always the one in control. Wasn't he?

He was certainly tightly leashed right now, all vestiges of sexual memory gone as he showed her to a guest suite. "These rooms are yours, and you should already be connected to our Wi-Fi." He held up a phone and pointed to a tablet. "Call your brother. He'll want to know you've arrived safely. Please dress for dinner at seven. Your clothes are in the wardrobe."

He left her to explore her room, and she was grateful for the time to collect herself. She left a message for Reeve, dozed in the bath, then glanced in the closet, recognizing the dresses as the ones Dante had bought for her in Whistler.

She didn't know what to make of that, but as she glanced across the vineyard from her personal balcony and took in the abundance and sheer *richness* of her surroundings, she couldn't bring herself to greet his grandmother in her worn jeans and thinning T-shirt. She found the cache of makeup she'd also left in his suite that last night and painted some confidence onto her anxious face, then wriggled herself into a dress that still had a tag on it.

When he knocked, he was freshly showered and shaved, smelling deliciously of soap and spice and something she instinctively recognized as Sicilian. It was the scent of his home. The source of all that he was. Oh, he filled her up with yearning.

He took in her simple blue dress with its sweetheart neckline and rib-hugging bodice over an A-line skirt without comment. It was the most modest in the bunch. She was trying to show some decorum in front of his grandmother, but found herself shifting her feet, aching for a sign he liked what he saw. That he still found her attractive.

That he wanted to play a silly game of modeling with her. *Foreplay.*

She blushed and looked at his polished shoes.

"This way." He waved a hand, crushing her fragile ego with his absence of response.

She made herself hold her chin high and her shoulders back as they followed a corridor of rich red carpet. It was painful, though. She suspected the paintings were originals by men whose names were revered. She felt hideously unsophisticated that she didn't have the background to know or recognize their value.

Bernadetta rose to meet her when Cami and Dante entered the lounge.

"Oh, my dear." She looked older, which made Cami sad. The poor woman had to be devastated, first at having been kept in the dark, then on learning her grandson had not only committed crimes, but was facing the consequences.

Cami warmed the trembling hands that the old woman extended. "You have enough to worry about. Please don't be upset for me. I'm fine."

Dante made a noise, and Cami caught a flash of impatience on his face. She was stung by it, but focused on Bernadetta, sitting with her on the sofa to reassure her.

"You were so kind to me that day. You *are* so kind. And our family has treated you so terribly." Bernadetta's voice creaked.

"It's not your fault."

"Isn't it? Perhaps I was too lenient with Arturo's mother. She was my wild child. We should have brought Arturo to live with us after she divorced. He might have turned out differently." She lifted her rosary beads and pressed her lips to them.

Cami gently squeezed Bernadetta's free hand.

"Please don't dwell on things that can't be changed. Dante and I will make it right. You don't have to worry about me. Why don't you tell me about your visit with your niece in Vancouver? Did you see everything you were hoping to?"

"*Grazij*, for taking her mind off things," Dante said a few hours later, when his Noni had gone to bed and he was alone with Cami.

"She's so sweet. But I'm insanely curious about your home theater now." She moved to the rail on the south terrace that overlooked the lower slopes. "How could I have guessed it's an ancient *amphitheater*?"

The music had started while they were finishing dinner, catching Cami's attention and prompting his grandmother to describe the site built by the Greeks and restored with great care—and expense—by his grandfather, at Noni's behest. One of her greatest pleasures was listening to the pitches by theater companies and choosing the season's starlight production.

"We could walk down if you like. It sounds like they're still rehearsing. Unless you're tired?"

"My body thinks it's the middle of the day. I'd love to." She fetched a wrap, and they started down the path. After a moment, she drew a deep breath and let it out. "It smells fantastic out here. Is that orange blossom?"

"We have a grove, yes. How is your leg?"

"I'm fine." She halted abruptly to demand, "Did you just *tsk* me?"

"You say it *all the time*. You're not fine." More than jet lag was putting the strain around her eyes, and he had noted the subtle way she was favoring one leg. Then there was the pregnancy. He was still reeling under that news.

"I'm totally fine." She hugged her wrap closer and continued walking. "You don't know me."

"Untrue," he said under his breath, but she halted again.

It was dark, turning her eyes into dark pools with a pinprick of light as she stared up at him.

"Everything you've thought about me has been a wrong impression." She turned away, saying with anguish, "Everything I thought about you was misinterpretation."

Toxic. He kept hearing her say that, and it scored his soul every single time.

Yet, she carried his child. Wanted it.

The news of his impending fatherhood burned like a fuse, wanting to explode out of him, but who could he tell? His grandmother would love to hear it, but she would be devastated if something happened and *damn* Cami for putting that grain of doubt in his mind. He was already that attached to the idea of sharing a child with her, he would be devastated if it failed to happen.

"Dante!"

They came into the clearing of lights, and people stopped packing up water bottles and notebooks to greet him. He introduced Cami to the director and his cast. They were kind enough to move back onto the stage and perform part of a scene for her, much to her astonishment and delight.

"I'm sorry I won't see the actual performance," she said as they were walking back up the hill toward the villa. "That was amazing."

"Why won't you?"

"They said it opens in a month. I can't imagine I'll be here more than a couple of weeks."

He snorted at her naïveté. "You'll be able to see as many performances as you like. You live here now."

She halted in the middle of the darkened vineyard and flung around to face him.

"We're getting married, Cami. You had to know that."

Maybe she had given up the fantasy of being swept off her feet long ago, but seriously? That was his proposal? All her girlhood dreams went down the toilet in a single flush.

"Be still my heart," she muttered.

"Neither of us has a choice," he added, making her want to bark out a laugh at how brutal he was being.

"You're out of your mind." She started toward the villa again, but he caught her arm.

"Stay here. The windows are open. She might wake up and hear us if we get any closer."

"Are you listening to yourself?"

"Are you? Duty to family is everything to me." His grip firmed as he impressed the words through her. "*You* are family now." He drew her forward a step and set his free hand on her stomach, splaying his fingers and drawing a deep breath, as if he was overcome by the magnitude of her pregnancy.

The world stilled, and she imagined she could feel their baby's heartbeat rocking through both of them, hammering them together in indelible little pulses.

"Our baby might be, but I'm not." She said it to remind herself as much as him. "What are you going to do about the rest of your family? Abandon the cousin who is like a brother to you?"

Dante's breath hissed through his teeth. He dropped his hands from her, bunching them into fists. "He could have destroyed all of this." He jerked his head at their surroundings. "He abandoned me first. All of us."

"Has he confessed?"

"No."

"So things could still change. I want to believe Arturo is behind the theft. You have no idea how badly I need that to be the truth, but this nightmare never lets me wake up. And quite frankly—" she looked to the house, throat tight "—I can't help thinking you might wish my father *was* the real culprit. That way you wouldn't have to dredge this up again. If you don't already resent me for not being to blame, you soon will. Everyone in your family will."

"That's not true. My grandmother doesn't."

"This is going to drag on for years, Dante. It will be awful and expensive and draining. *I know how awful it will be.* You're going to want to point fingers. I don't want to be married to you when you decide you hate me—more than you already do."

She had to quit talking then. Her throat became too small.

"And now we come to the truth of the matter. I'm not the one filled with hate, am I?"

A ferocious ball of heat rose in her. "Okay, fine, yes. I hate you." She spat in a hiss, trying to keep her voice down. "Whether it was Arturo or Benito didn't matter. The person pressing like a heel onto my life all this time was *you*. I am brimming with resentment toward you, and I hate myself for being so weak as to sleep with you and get *pregnant*. There is no way on this earth that I want to be chained to you for a lifetime."

"Yet here we are," he bit out with a similar crack of frustration in his tone as he took her by the upper arms and pulled her close. "Bound by the child we conceived. But if you think that's all that chains us, you weren't paying attention when we made that baby." He covered her mouth with his own, kissing her with such ferocity, he burned away everything except the searing passion that had existed between them from the moment they'd met.

It was exactly as it had been so many times between them, running quickly beyond their control. She twined her arms around his neck and dug her fingers into his hair, pressing him down to deepen the pressure of the kiss, opening her mouth wide beneath his and meeting his tongue with her own.

It was struggle and reunion. Anger and anguish. Clash and fury and a clawing desperate heartache that made her pull at him, rather than push him away.

His natural need to dominate had him trying to take control, but she wouldn't have it. Not this time. She was too furious. He had used her, and this time she used him. She scraped his bottom lip with her teeth and arched herself to wriggle against him.

Excitement expanded his chest in a hissing breath. He skimmed the dress from her shoulders in one abrupt move that had her pulling back, eyes widening with shock as the air touched her naked torso. They were outside, in the vineyard.

"You're right," he growled. "Not here."

As he seemed to grapple himself back under control, something defiant and angry and incredibly hurt moved in her. She needed his passion to heal it. She needed to know she was stronger than him in this moment. That her will could prevail. She needed him to be as overcome as she was.

He started to turn her toward the house, and she flung herself into him.

"Yes, here." She leaped, opening her legs and forcing him to catch her with a grunt, then twined her legs around his waist.

They kissed again, but he swore against her lips as he took her to the ground beneath him. Cool grass tickled her shoulder blades and her sandal fell off.

His hot mouth slid down her neck, and she opened

her eyes to the stars. "I can't bear how easily you do this to me, Dante. Even when I win, you win. You own me."

He set his forehead against her jawbone. "It's the same for me, damn you. How do you not know that? You're all I can see right now. All that exists in my world. Do you think I'm proud of this reaction?"

The weight of his hips sat heavily between her thighs, pressing his hardness where she was aching with anticipation. That, coupled with his words, were all she needed to sink back into the throes. Her thighs shifted to better hug him, and her fingers began pulling at the top button on his shirt.

Even as she warned herself to cling to some sense, Dante was dipping his head to steal a taste of her nipple. Every other thought died then, lost beyond how good he made her feel.

She knew she ought to feel used by him. Manipulated even. But the care he took, and the way he seemed to shudder with restraint as he tasted her with such a sense of worship, was badly needed reassurance of his desire for her. Of this mad connection that shouldn't exist, but did.

She pressed his shoulder so she could get at the rest of his buttons, then didn't bother with opening them. She pulled his shirt apart so the buttons gave way until finally the heat of his chest settled over hers. They both groaned. His mouth climbed and paused as it often did on her collarbone, where the tiny raised white line always seemed to need a lick of his attention. Then his teeth scraped her nape and finally he kissed her again.

A moment later, he dispatched her panties into the weeds. She lay beneath him in the soil while he lifted on an elbow enough to open his pants. She guided him with her own hand, taking his damp crest into her core with a sob of relief.

He entered with a fierce thrust and a carnal groan. They were barely human in that moment. All civilization gone as they mated.

She scraped her hands down his back beneath his shirt, encouraging his hard thrusts as she raced toward the crisis. Her climax was so quick and shattering, she cried out with loss. He smothered her muted scream with his mouth and didn't stop moving. The rhythms of his thrusts kept her in that glittering plane of orgasm, not allowing her to descend. Within moments, she was overcome and sobbing out her ecstasy again, but still he didn't relent.

Over and over the waves of pleasure ground through her, until she was unable to tell where she ended and he began. All she knew was that he was the instrument of her ecstasy and she would never let him go.

Only then, as she accepted that he was a part of her, did she feel the muscles of his back tighten. He lifted his head and tilted it back, howling at the sky as he finally joined her in supreme joy.

She was softness and light, her hair silken against his nose, her scent clean and familiar and now carrying the aromas of his home. Latent orange blossoms and fertile volcanic ash.

The civilized man in him wanted to apologize for having her in the dirt like this, but there was no room in him for groveling. Possessiveness engulfed him. She was his. If he had to prove it again, he would. Every remaining hour of their lives, if necessary.

He couldn't drink in enough of her. Her throat, her still racing pulse beneath his lips, her sweet cry of surrender still ringing in his ears. The warm roundness of her perspiration-dampened breast hot in his palm.

As afterglow went, this was more like survival of a shipwreck. They were washed ashore, lucky to be alive.

"I didn't use a condom." He hadn't even thought of it.

"The damage has been done."

True, but he still should have at least thought about it. Conscious decision-making had abandoned him, however.

"Here I was afraid that you didn't want me anymore. Or wouldn't," she murmured.

"I don't see this wearing off."

"But it doesn't solve anything, Dante." She pressed his shoulder, urging him to gently extricate and roll away, allowing her to sit up. "It changes nothing."

Bits of grass stuck to her ivory skin. He brushed at her back and shoulders. She was like a goddess in the moonlight, casting a spell with her iridescent beauty. Her narrow spine broke something inside him that had hardened over the years and threatened to solidify again, every time he thought of his cousin's betrayal.

"In fact, if anything proves how disastrous our marriage would be, this is it. We're each other's downfall."

"Did you feel belittled by our affair?" He feared it was too late to ask that, having taken her on the hard-packed soil of the vineyard. "Because it was always just this for me. Madness, yes. A compulsion, but not something I was using to hurt you."

He heard her swallow, then she said, "I feel small. Made to feel small, because your feelings weren't involved."

"Were *yours*?"

Cami couldn't bear how vulnerable that question made her feel. She was peeled right down to the core by their lovemaking and had to dig deep for a deflection. "I was a virgin. Of course I built it into something bigger than it was."

"It was big, Cami. It meant something to me, too."

She couldn't look at him for fear he would somehow trick her into giving up her autonomy all over again. "That doesn't mean we should continue doing this. Or make it worse by getting married."

"'Worse?' What kind of a husband do you think I would be?"

"You don't want to marry anyone," she reminded him. "Certainly not me."

"That was true when I said it." His hot hand returned to splay across her lower back. "But I want to be married to the mother of my child. Maybe I didn't see myself marrying you when we were having our affair, but I've since seen enough passion, and enough compatibility in other areas, that I think we could build something."

"You said this was a compulsion. I don't want to be your drug addiction."

"You called us toxic. Let's both find a kinder vocabulary."

He sounded short, and she felt as though she hovered on a tightrope, carefully inching along into an abyss, in danger of falling at any moment, not even able to look up to the other side for fear it wasn't even there.

"You've been living in squalor, Cami." He sat up beside her, and his profile was jagged shadows and brutal angles. "I can't expect you to forgive me for that. Marriage is the best compensation I can offer. You'll be entitled to half my wealth, and our child inherits all of it."

"I don't want your money, Dante." She sighed with a pang.

"What do you want? To live alone in Canada, denying me access to my child and denying our child all of this? You're right. I won't let you have that."

She wanted his *heart*, but she never got what she wanted anyway. She threaded her arms into her dress and found her feet. "Can we just get through the investigation and figure out the next steps after that?"

He hitched his pants into place as he stood, then brushed his knees and looked to button his shirt before shaking his head at finding all of them gone.

"The effect you have on me," he muttered. "If you need time to get used to the idea, fine."

She snorted and walked away.

After breakfast the next morning, Bernadetta showed Cami around the gallery of family photos with great pride, offering up dozens of names and relationships. Cami would never remember all of them, but she was particularly taken by Bernadette's wedding photo. The young Bernadetta looked overwhelmed, but her husband was so handsome and powerful looking, Cami knew exactly how she'd been drawn into marrying him.

"Dante really takes after him. You must have loved him very much."

Bernadetta hesitated, which made Cami snap a startled look at her.

"Oh, I did. Very deeply." Bernadetta smiled at Cami's reaction, then a wistfulness passed over her expression as she looked back at the photo. "But it took some time. Ours was a marriage of convenience. It was a work-around for some red tape he was trying to avoid. I wanted out from under my father's thumb—he was a lovely man, but very strict. I somehow thought I'd have better chances with Leo. Dante takes after him in temperament, too."

"Oh. Poor you," she teased.

"Yes. They're a dominant force, the Gallo men." She looked at Cami as though she could see right through her. "And they don't love easily, but when they do give their heart, it is forever."

Cami was trying really hard not to wish for something so impossible. Nevertheless, yearning colored her voice when she asked, "What about you? Did it take a long time?"

"I resisted as long as I could. I wasn't even planning to sleep with him, expecting to save myself for my 'real' husband. That didn't last a day." Bernadetta gave her a wink. "He was very persuasive."

Cami couldn't help laughing. It was too astonishing for this old woman to be making jokes about sex.

"If I hadn't had a stubborn streak of my own, those first years might have been easier, but I needed some backbone to stand up to him. We found our way, though. So will you and Dante."

Cami's pulse skipped. Her first thought was that somehow Bernadetta had heard them in the vineyard last night, which was deathly mortifying.

"You didn't drink any of our excellent wine last night," the old woman said, her gaze sliding from her young husband to offer a soft look up at Cami. "If you think photos of you with Dante at the Tabor gala failed to catch my attention, you underestimate my desire to follow the antics of my very active family. My boys may have a few secrets from me, but I don't make it easy for them to keep them."

"I…" Cami's voice dwindled to a congestion she had to clear from her throat. "I don't want you to think I planned any of this." She *liked* Bernadetta. A lot. She didn't know how she would handle it if what seemed like her only ally turned her back on her. "It's… I'm still in shock." She wrung her hands.

"Oh, my dear, no one takes advantage of Dante. The only reason Arturo was able to was because he was that close to him all his life." Grief washed over her face as she mentioned her other grandson. "In fact, I fear Dante could be destroyed by what has occurred between them. The only thing that could save him is your forgiveness."

"Please don't put that on me, Bernadetta."

"If you reject him, if you deny him a place in his child's life, he will blame himself and sink into even more cynicism than he already possesses. I understand these last years better now, that it was more than Leo's passing and Dante's having to take up the mantle that made him so hard. But that's also how I know he's in danger of letting bitterness destroy him. It could close him off to me and everyone else who cares about him. The only thing that could counter that is love."

"No pressure," Cami muttered, tucking her hair off her face with a slide of her finger. "He doesn't love me." It was so painful, it came out as a whisper.

"Not yet, but there is only one way to keep a man that strong, strong. By giving him a weakness who is equally strong. I'm speaking from experience."

"I'm not you, Bernadetta."

"No, you're far braver than I ever was. Do you think I tried to break land speed records down an icy slope? Pshhh."

"Here you are," Dante said, coming into the lounge. "We should leave soon." He was taking her to the first meeting with investigators today.

Bernadetta grasped Cami's hand and beamed a smile at him. "You've made me the happiest woman, Dante. I don't know how I could get through all that we face without something as wonderful as a wedding and grandchildren to look forward to."

Cami choked.

Dante shot her a look, but it was the flinty one he'd sent her when Bernadetta offered to send them skiing. *Let her have this.*

He leaned to kiss his grandmother's cheek, saying, "I'm glad you're pleased."

"She guessed and I didn't know what to say," Cami grumbled when they were in the car a few minutes later. "I'm sorry."

"Why?" he said dryly. "Now we can sleep together."

"You—" She rolled her eyes. "You're really not angry?"

"I told you last night I wanted to marry you. You came around a lot sooner than I expected. *Grazij*, Noni."

"I still think it's a terrible idea."

And yet, as the days passed, he made it easy for her to think otherwise. Despite how difficult their meetings were, or how short his temper became in some of them, he was extremely protective and solicitous toward her. Between the appointments, he showed her his island home, spoiled her with impulsive purchases and pestered her to eat properly and mind her leg and wear sunscreen. They were back to their camaraderie in Whistler, but without the clock ticking down. It was poignantly sweet, building up her hopes.

At night—oh, the nights. Could she spend the rest of her life joining her naked body to his every single night? There, at least, she had no doubts.

In fact, as the days wore into high summer, and her new doctor confirmed her pregnancy was coming along with textbook perfection, and her brother's flight was booked so he could give her away at her wedding, she almost began to believe they had a chance.

She almost believed that someday, somehow, Dante might come to love her as she had come to love him.

Was she fooling herself all over again? Doubts crept in when she was alone like this, flicking through wedding dress images on the terrace. She lifted her gaze from the tablet to the idyllic view toward Mount Etna, astonished to find herself in the middle of a fairy tale.

She had learned the hard way not to believe in them,

so how was she here, living one? How long could it really last?

Desperate for reassurance, she went looking for her intended. He had a lot of pressures on him right now, but no matter how busy he was with work or anything else, he always looked pleased to see her. Sometimes he took a break for coffee with her, occasionally a flirty kiss turned into a sexy tussle on top of his desk. If nothing else, his physical infatuation with her kept her heartened for their future.

Today, however, he had someone with him. She paused beyond the cracked door, not wanting to interrupt, then freezing to the floor when she heard her name.

If one of his more passionate relatives had confronted him, Dante might have taken it less seriously, but his uncle Giorgio was a tax auditor, one of the steadiest, most analytical and logical men Dante knew. He was also a neutral party, being married to Noni's fourth daughter and never having shown favorites among his many nieces and nephews. He'd always been the ultimate egalitarian mediator, in fact.

"Arturo's behavior aside, her pregnancy is awfully convenient."

"You're a bit late for 'the talk,' *zu*."

"Have you had a paternity test? This wedding is very rushed. It's not like you to be so impulsive, Dante."

He was aware. When he had gone to Canada, he'd been driven by a need to provide restitution for Arturo's crime against Cami and her family. Yes, he could admit that deep down he had longed to see her again, but given the circumstances, he hadn't expected her to get on a plane with him, let alone into his bed. Her pregnancy had been a convenience for *him*, allowing him to pull her back into the intimate relationship he wanted.

Needed.

Damn, that scared him.

"You don't even know for certain that the baby is yours. We already have a lot to lose. Insist on a paternity test before you marry her and wait until Arturo's guilt is proved in court. You aren't responsible for his actions or anyone else's, but you are responsible for your own. Do your due diligence. Be certain this time that you're not just seeing what you want to see."

That stung because it was true. He had never once suspected Arturo's involvement because it was too great a betrayal to consider. He had let himself see Stephen as the thief instead.

"Keep your eyes open," Giorgio continued. "Even if the baby is yours, you have to question her motives. She was in a tight spot with you. It's not as if this is a love child."

Dante burned under that remark, trying to shutter himself to such a possibility because the idea of being in love meant being even more vulnerable to her than he already was.

"Point taken," he acknowledged, only wanting his uncle to leave before he betrayed himself further. "I'll give it more thought."

Once he was gone, Dante stood at the window, only realizing as her lounger stayed empty that he was waiting to see Cami come back to it. He was entirely too susceptible to her. Too dependent.

But the piece of the puzzle that his uncle didn't have, Dante realized, was that Cami had never lied to him. He had begun their association with condemnation of her and her family, yet she had proved herself again and again as truthful and trustworthy.

Sweat popped onto his brow as a disturbingly vivid memory came over him of that first time she'd proved it.

Her first time. She had trusted him with herself. Then, when she had had a chance to walk away from him with perhaps not riches, but certainly a bonanza by the standards she'd been forced to live under, she had left it on the floor of his hotel suite.

She had tried to pay her father's debt in good faith and, even more shocking, when she had learned her father was innocent, she hadn't taken a stake to Dante's heart. She hadn't hidden his child from him. She had agreed to marry him, despite all the ways he'd damaged her life.

At no time had she betrayed him. She was the most steadfast, loyal, *lovable*—

A flash of blue caught his eye. His chauffeur was carrying her battered, *full* backpack to the car.

Oh, hell, no.

What could she possibly say to Bernadetta except, *I'm sorry*?

Hovering the pen over the paper, Cami almost wrote, *I'm not brave like you*, but that just made her feel ashamed of herself for running away. What was she supposed to do, though? Put up with having an ax over her head forever? She couldn't. If today wasn't the end, then something else would come up.

Something *always* happened. She would far rather be the one to choose how she and Dante parted than invest more of herself and feel the break that much more deeply in the future. It already hurt so badly she could hardly breathe.

"What the hell do you think you're doing?" Dante asked, coming into the library and shutting the door with a firmness that was very close to a slam.

The sharp noise cut into her, making the agony she had been holding off flood through her in a wave. She tried sitting straighter in his grandfather's antique rolling chair, but when Dante came to lean on the desk and glare at her over it, she wanted to wither. She pushed to her feet, chest tight.

"My Sicilian isn't great," she told him, hearing the strain in her voice "But I got the gist. You want a paternity test. Fine." She threw down the pen. "But I'm not going to marry a man who won't take my word on something so basic."

"You're going to let one ugly accusation destroy the life we're trying to make? Which one of us is having trouble trusting?"

"Oh, come on, Dante. One accusation is all it took the first time. My entire *life* is still being destroyed by one ugly accusation."

Through the moisture gathering in her eyes, she saw his head snap back as though he took her words as a blow on the chin. His face contorted with emotion. Something that might have been despair shadowed his eyes.

"And you can't forgive me for believing my cousin instead of your father."

How was it that she could withstand her own pain, but not his?

"It's not about forgiveness. I wanted to believe my father was innocent despite the evidence." She tapped her chest. "I completely understand why you didn't imagine your cousin could have done it. We want to believe in the people we love."

"That tells me how *you* feel, then, doesn't it?" His face was sharp and tight, his lips white.

How could she admit to her own love when, "*You* don't love *me*!"

That was the excruciating heartbreak she was trying to escape, unable to face it when her own heart was so completely his.

"You will never believe in me, despite how much I've tried to prove..." She had to bite her lips to steady them. Swallowed past the tightness in her throat. "I can't live my life like that. If you don't trust me, I can't trust this." She waved between them. "I won't build castles on clouds." She started to walk around the desk and out of the room.

"I love you," he ground out.

The words went into her as an arrow, making her suck in a deep breath. "Don't. At least keep truth between us."

"You dare to suggest I would lie about *that*?" He grasped her by the shoulders, swinging her to face him. "I should have—" His hands tightened briefly on her, revealing the deep emotions gripping him. "I should have said it when we were still in Whistler, but do you think I knew what it was when I've never felt *this* kind of love before? Passionate and intense and so quick to rip me apart I still can't take it in?"

"Dante." She pleaded for him not to make this harder. "I don't get happily-ever-after. My life never works out. It always falls apart, and I can't bear that I'll start to believe the things you're saying only to have it all disappear. I have to go now, before it's more than I can survive."

"It's already too late. Leaving would kill us both."

She teared up and he smoothed his hand over her hair, soothing her as he drew her stiff body into his chest and pressed his mouth to her temple.

"This is my fault. I've destroyed your ability to believe in the future, but you have to give me a chance to fix that. To prove we have one."

"We're always going to be who we are." She set her hands on his waist, not sure if she wanted to embrace him or push him away. "The past is always going to have the power to rear up and destroy us. I can't live like that, waiting for it to happen. I can't build something that means everything to me, then lose it."

"So you want to throw it away now? No. Listen to me." His arms tightened and his breath stirred the hair near her ear, sending tingles down her nape. "We *are* who we are, but not who you think. We aren't enemies. We were meant for one another, Cami. If you leave today, we'll only come back together later. It's inevitable. Your father invited me to come see you ski, did you know that?" He drew back to look her in the eye. "I made an excuse, but if things hadn't gone to hell, I would have come one day and watched you and fallen for you then, because you're that amazing and wonderful."

"I was fourteen," she scoffed, closing her eyes against the alternate reality where she crushed on the young man who so impressed her father and he loved her back. She won medals while he designed futuristic cars. They married and had children who grew up knowing their grandparents.

"I would have waited for you. I did wait." He growled. "You didn't find anyone else, either. It took far too long, but we came together again under yes, difficult circumstances, but we *came together*. What are the chances of that? Hmm? And that we would fall for each other even with this mess between us?"

He combed her hair back from her face, tilting up her chin and letting his gaze wander the delicate line of her jaw, grazing gentle fingertips against her cheek and the sensitive hollow beneath her ear.

"We scare the hell out of each other, our feelings are so strong. So yes, our trust needs time to grow deeper roots. It's been rocky, but even if you aren't ready to believe in me, you have to believe in *us*."

Her chin crinkled. She searched his eyes for some evidence he was being fanciful, but he wasn't a man to make up nonsense.

"Can you really look past…everything?"

"I already did, when I kissed you the first time in Whistler. Can you?"

"I want to."

The tension in his hand, where it had slid to the side of her neck, eased into a gentle caress. "Because you love me?"

She could hardly take in that he was using that word. With her. Her chest felt too full, like it would split from the pressure swelling her heart. "I do," she admitted with a scrape in her throat. "I love you a lot."

He grew very somber. "You humble me with your capacity to forgive. Your generous heart. I will never take you for granted. You *can* believe in me. I *will* prove it to you."

He started to kiss her, but her hand went to the middle of his chest, holding him off. "But what about the paternity test?"

His expression softened. "Of course you're carrying my baby," he chided. "I could hardly tell my uncle I remember exactly when we conceived, in vivid detail, could I? My only regret is that you were angry with me that day. Unsure of us. But we were already in love, Cami. Damn right that's my child you're carrying."

He placed his hand over the very slight bump that was really only visible to him because he knew her shape so well. She blushed, but teared up, too.

"It was a very small chance we took that day, yet look how it's binding us together," he said, lifting his gaze to hers.

Perhaps they *were* fated.

As the light in his eyes continued to pour through her,

she began to believe it. With a shaky smile, she lifted onto tiptoes and let the love on his lips absorb into her soul. She didn't imagine she could taste it. She knew it as a tangible thing that filled her with growing joy and a euphoric certainty that was so sweet and precious, her tears sprinkled past her lashes onto her cheeks.

Three weeks later, she took her brother's arm. He was terrifically handsome in a morning suit. Her dress had an empire waist to hide her small bump.

"I don't want to give you away," Reeve said with a rueful smile. "You're all I have. But you look so happy..."

"I am, Reeve. I really am," she said, still stunned by it herself. The fragile trust between her and Dante had been growing exponentially, concentrating into something that centered both of them on a foundation that brought her peace for the first time in her adult life.

She spoke her vows a short time later, basking in the light of her husband's gaze. She looked to their future without trepidation and told him as much in their candlelit honeymoon suite.

"I don't know what our life will look like in ten years, but I can't wait to find out." He drew her into his arms.

Their kiss began sweet and unhurried, so tender she grew choked with emotion. He was every bit as thorough as he usually was, ringing pleasure through her again and again, but with a new quality to each touch, each kiss, each caress.

It was commitment and worship and love. So much love.

EPILOGUE

SOME MIGHT CALL it spoiling, but Dante held their son until he fell asleep.

Leo was tall for two, all arms and legs as he dangled against Dante's shoulder. His chubby limbs dropped to the mattress as Dante gently put the boy into his toddler bed.

Cami hadn't said a thing as her husband had spent the evening doting on their son, bathing him and getting him into his pj's, then reading and finally holding him and rubbing his back until the boy's head had been heavy on his shoulder.

Leo wasn't upset or ill. No, Dante was the one who had had a very difficult day. Arturo had been sentenced and taken to prison.

When Dante had come home drained and withdrawn, seeking comfort by coddling their son, Cami had done her best not to intrude. She knew how healing a child's love was, so innocent and unconditional and pure. Anytime her own ghosts reared their head, she looked at her son and fell in love with her husband all over again for giving her their child.

Children.

This entire week had been busy and difficult, so she had kept the news to herself. They weren't consciously trying for another one, and she wasn't entirely sure how he would react. With his mind in turmoil along with his heart, she hadn't wanted to put something else on him. Maybe it was even a bit selfish of her. She didn't want something that brought her so much joy to be linked in his mind with something that was nothing but pain.

He turned and saw her watching him from the doorway to Leo's room. He checked briefly, then hitched his shoulder in a rueful shrug.

She smiled her understanding. It was the sort of telepathic communication that came between parents who didn't dare risk waking an infant by speaking aloud.

As he carried the baby monitor from their son's room and closed the door, he caught her hand and drew her toward their own room.

Her heart took the skip and jump it always did when he touched her. A warmer, more tender emotion flowed through her. It was her turn. He needed *her* now.

They didn't speak when they entered their room. He only closed the door and drew her into his arms. The baby monitor clattered onto the dresser top so he could use both hands to remove her clothing.

His urgency sent a surge of need through her. She needed this, too, she realized as their mouths met in a clashing kiss. She hadn't felt threatened by these latest events exactly, but it had been a test, taking up Dante's time and attention. She needed this conflagration to fuse them back together again.

It was frantic and quick against the wall. He exploded with a muffled cry at the same time that she did, which wasn't like him.

As he stood panting and damp against her, he said, "That was a lot more intense than I meant it to be."

With a lurch that seemed almost drunken, he straightened, pulling her with him so she clung with her thighs to his waist, keeping them joined as he took them to the bed.

"I don't mind," she told him, kissing his jaw and neck. "I like knowing you can't resist me. That I can still undermine your control."

"But you're pregnant. I should be more careful." He lowered her to the bed and came down on top of her, hardening afresh within her.

"You know?"

He frowned. "You think I don't know your body as well as you do?"

"I wasn't sure how you'd feel," she admitted, revealing the tiny wrinkle of doubt on her heart. "If you were ready for another."

"Past ready. Elated. Aren't you? Is that why you haven't said anything?"

"I'm thrilled, but I was worried it was, I don't know, more than you wanted to hear when you were dealing with so much this week."

"Are you kidding? Having good news was the only thing that kept me going. If anything, I needed to know that you and I were stronger than ever." He cupped her head in two hands, touching his lips to hers. "I needed to know you were tied even more tightly to me, so you wouldn't let the past cause you to give up on us."

"I would *never* do that," she vowed.

He smiled. "No, you won't. And neither will I. I love you."

"I love you, too. Now let's have a do-over. See if you can last a little longer this time."

"I will take that challenge, *bedduzza*," he chuckled, then set about proving his staying power.

* * * * *

afterglow BOOKS

Introducing our newest series, Afterglow.

From showing up to glowing up, Afterglow characters are on the path to leading their best lives and finding romance along the way – with a dash of sizzling spice!

Follow characters from all walks of life as they chase their dreams and find that true love is only the beginning...

OUT NOW

millsandboon.co.uk

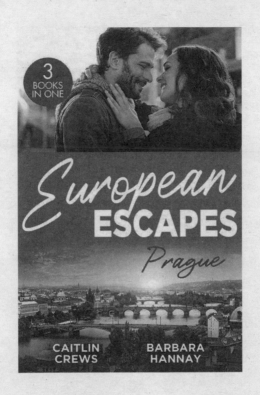

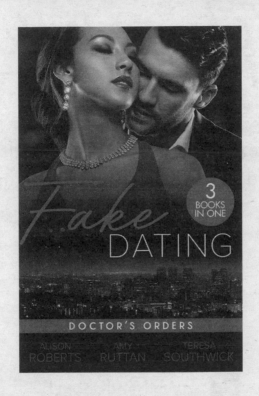

LET'S TALK
Romance

For exclusive extracts, competitions and special offers, find us online:

f MillsandBoon

X @MillsandBoon

⊙ @MillsandBoonUK

♪ @MillsandBoonUK

Get in touch on 01413 063 232

MILLS & BOON

THE HEART OF ROMANCE

A ROMANCE FOR EVERY READER

MODERN

Prepare to be swept off your feet by sophisticated, sexy and seductive heroes, in some of the world's most glamourous and romantic locations, where power and passion collide.

HISTORICAL

Escape with historical heroes from time gone by. Whether your passion is for wicked Regency Rakes, muscled Vikings or rugged Highlanders, awaken the romance of the past.

MEDICAL

Set your pulse racing with dedicated, delectable doctors in the high-pressure world of medicine, where emotions run high and passion, comfort and love are the best medicine.

True Love

Celebrate true love with tender stories of heartfelt romance, from the rush of falling in love to the joy a new baby can bring, and a focus on the emotional heart of a relationship.

HEROES

The excitement of a gripping thriller, with intense romance at its heart. Resourceful, true-to-life women and strong, fearless men face danger and desire - a killer combination!

From showing up to glowing up, these characters are on the path to leading their best lives and finding romance along the way – with plenty of sizzling spice!

To see which titles are coming soon, please visit

millsandboon.co.uk/nextmonth